An Antic Disposition

Also by Alan Gordon

The Widow of Jerusalem
A Death in the Venetian Quarter
Jester Leaps In
Thirteenth Night

An Antic
Disposition

Alan Gordon

ST. MARTIN'S MINOTAUR ✖ NEW YORK

www.minotaurbooks.com

Library of Congress Cataloging-in-Publication Data

Gordon, Alan (Alan R.)
   An antic disposition : a medieval mystery / by Alan Gordon.—1st ed.
      p.   cm.
   ISBN 0-312-30096-4
   1. Hamlet (Legendary character)—Fiction.   2. Kings and rulers—
Succession—Fiction.   3. Denmark—History—To 1241—Fiction.   4. Murder
victims' families—Fiction.   5. Fools and jesters—Fiction.   6. Fathers—
Death—Fiction.   7. Princes—Fiction.   8. Revenge—Fiction.   I. Title.

PS3557.O649A58 2004
813'.54—dc22

                                                                2003060368

First Edition: January 2004

10   9   8   7   6   5   4   3   2   1

In memory of Susan Snyder,
Professor of English Literature, Swarthmore College,
in whose living room I spent many happy hours discussing Shakespeare,
and who also loved *Gaudy Night*.

"Well, God give them wisdom that have it, and those that are fools,
let them use their talents."
—*Twelfth Night*, Act I, Scene V

This fool humbly thanks you for sharing your wisdom.

"As I perchance hereafter shall think meet
To put an antic disposition on . . ."

—Hamlet, Act, I, Scene V

An Antic
Disposition

ONE

Wild-eyed men in caves. Nuns in black. Monks who do not speak. We are left to believe. Fools, children. Those who have abandoned belief must still believe in us. They are sure that they are right not to believe but they know belief must not fade completely. Hell is when no one believes. There must always be believers. Fools, idiots, those who hear voices, those who speak in tongues. We are your lunatics. We surrender our lives to make your nonbelief possible. You are sure that you are right but you don't want everyone to think as you do. There is no truth without fools.
— Don DeLillo, WHITE NOISE

Swabia—1204 A.D.

The Black Forest, despite its foreboding name, is a pleasant enough place to spend one's summer. There are roads that penetrate it sufficiently to allow passage to the occasional pilgrim or peddler, and paths branching off from these roads for the braver hunters seeking the more elusive and dangerous prey. If you truly know what you are looking for, you might come across a stand of brush that is actually movable, if you took the time and trouble to move it. But there being no point to moving a stand of brush in the middle of a forest, you would go your own way, hoping to find shelter before sundown.

If you had taken the time and trouble to move it, and I recommend having at least one other person helping in this endeavor unless you enjoy being scratched or having branches whip back into your face, which at least has the benefit of amusing your companions who stood and watched you rather than helping, no doubt expecting that very result, then you would find, to your surprise, a path wide enough to accommodate a wagon drawn by a pair of horses. You might even find evidence that several such wagons had traveled this path fairly recently, although we usually are quite careful about erasing our tracks for a good distance after replacing the concealing greenery. If you then follow the path, and are not taken by our sentries, who are very well hidden, by the way, so that even I have trouble spotting them, you will emerge upon a small valley deep within the forest, unknown even to those who think they know these woods well. There is a stream, and a farm with several fields of crops as well as pastures for sheep and cattle. The very ordinariness of the scene is jarring set as it is in the middle of nowhere.

Yet, on closer inspection, the activity you would see on this farm is far from ordinary. An unusually large number of children would be running about doing the chores. Some of them will be herding the cattle while walking on stilts; some will be juggling the scythes used for harvesting, or standing with ease on the backs of trotting horses. You will hear songs from every corner, in every language, and you will think that you have stumbled upon some magical fairyland.

Unless you are a fool, in which case you have come to the right place. For this is the new location of the Fools' Guild.

We had to pack up and run from the old Guildhall, our crazy tumble of stones and beams in the Dolomites. Pope Innocent III had decided that enough was enough. Our usefulness to the Church was outweighed by our subversion of its hypocrisy. Rome saw our mockery as a greater threat to its power than any Saracen army lurking on its borders, and sent papal troops to put an end to our mischief.

But we saw it coming long before they did, and the troops arrived to find an empty hall and a village ignorant of our whereabouts, while we toiled on our new haven to provide enough shelter for the Guildmasters, the novitiates, and any visiting fools and troubadours staying through the winter.

We felt safe from the locals here. Swabia has an old habit of respecting fools. The historians of the Guild have often speculated that we originated in Swabia, where the *Narrenzunft* tradition predates Christianity. Even now, amidst all the saints' days, the villagers don masks and costumes in February and have a fools' festival to drive away the winter. And the winter always goes away.

There is a competing theory that we were derived from the old Dionysian festivals. My personal opinion is that we came from everywhere, and at some point the Guild just sprang into being centuries ago. It's difficult to know for sure when all you have are stories passed down from generation to generation. But those are one of our specialties, so they are as reliable as anything written down. I think writing is overrated as a means of preserving the past. Why should it be considered any more authoritative, just because some opinionated person with a little schooling had access to quill, ink, and paper?

The farm had only been partly prepared for our arrival. It had served as an asylum for old or incapacitated fools without any other means of survival, and the family running it did not have enough provisions stored to take care of the sudden onslaught of children. So, we jugglers, tumblers, tale-tellers, and musicians were pressed into strange and unfamiliar physical labors. Those proficient with bow and arrow, such as my wife and fellow jester, Claudia, turned huntsmen, bringing back deer that were roasted in pit fires for the evening meals. Able-bodied men such as myself were handed axes much larger than the ones we used for juggling and sent to make war against the surrounding trees. A new Guildhall was constructed next to the barn, with space enough for four different classes to be held simultaneously as a new generation learned the foolish arts.

In the afternoons, after the children returned from the fields and the adults from the forests, when everyone was spent, the real training began. Languages, music, dancing, repertoire, disguises, juggling, tumbling, fighting, passwords, and poisoning. The arts needed to entertain, the skills needed to accomplish our hidden goals, the wits needed to survive.

Every other day I taught tumbling and pratfalls in the barn, using the bales of hay as both seating and padding. On Saturdays I taught knives, both for throwing and fighting. Today, however, I was between classes, and back to hewing innocent trees, my tunic off and the leggings of my motley drenched in sweat. I was in the middle of chopping a newly fallen spruce into firewood when I looked up to see my wife watching me, idly tossing and catching three balls with one hand, her bow in the other.

"You're getting too muscular for your motley," she observed. "We have to be careful that you don't lose your flexibility. You're supposed to be a jester, not a strong man."

"You could always put me at the base of the pyramid for acrobatics," I said, twirling the ax over my head.

She looked at it with interest.

"I wonder if there are any tricks we could do with an ax that big," she said. "It's too large to juggle. Have you tried anything with it?"

"Just this," I said, and I spun and flung it with a two-handed grip. It turned end over end in the air and split a sapling about twenty feet away.

"Not bad," she said. "That should get us the price of a drink in most taverns, as long as we don't have to pay for the damage."

She fetched it and hefted it experimentally.

"Too big for me," she pronounced.

"It's a prop," I said. "Play it for laughs."

She plunged it into the fallen spruce, spat into each hand, grabbed the handle, and lifted. It didn't budge. She grimaced, spat twice into each hand, and heaved with all her might. The blade came up abruptly over her head, flying end over end and embedding itself in a tree trunk behind her as she fell onto her rump.

"Very nice," I said, helping her back to her feet.

She glanced behind her at the ax, its handle still quivering.

"That wasn't the tree I was aiming for," she said. "I had better practice before we try it on a live audience. We want them to leave as a live audience."

"We'll have plenty of time to practice," I said. "Father Gerald doesn't want to send any of us out until next spring when the fury has abated a little."

"Next spring!" she said in dismay. "We are going to be cooped up on this farm until then?"

"I'm afraid so," I said. "But we won't be cooped up, exactly. There are woods to explore, and songs to learn, and stories from all over Europe to hear. It's a rare opportunity, in a way."

I loaded the cut wood onto a sledge and pulled the harness over my shoulders.

"I just worry that we could be trapped here," she said.

"No one can find us," I assured her. "And it will give Portia a little more time to grow before we have to travel with her again. This is as safe a place for a baby as any."

"Speaking of which, where is she?" asked my wife.

"She's with Brother Dennis," I said.

"She's with Brother Dennis," she repeated. "You left her with an ostler who cares more about horses than about people. You left her in the stables with a blacksmith's fire and several large and irritable animals for her to play with. Where in your feeble mind did you come up with the notion that this constituted safety?"

"Dennis is very good with children," I said. "It's the adults he has trouble with. And Zeus will keep the other horses away from her. He adores Portia, maybe the only human he's ever taken to. Besides, she's in her cradle and can't crawl yet, so . . ."

There was a sudden commotion from the direction of the stables— a man shouting from inside and other fools dashing to help. Claudia gave me a look that said, "I told you so," another that said, "And I'll tell you again and even more later," and sprinted toward the barn. It took me a few seconds to untangle myself from the harness and follow her.

The cradle was empty, and fools were ransacking the piled hay, searching for our daughter.

"I swear, I just took my eye off her for a moment," protested Brother Dennis as Claudia grimly went from stall to stall. "I thought she didn't know how to crawl yet. She's only seven months old."

"They say that at seven months I was already telling the servants what I wanted," said Claudia. "The women in my family run to the precocious. Ah, there you are, my little scamp."

Portia had found Zeus's stall and had crawled under the gate to see her friend. She had both arms wrapped around his right foreleg, and the terror of the equine kingdom was nuzzling her gently.

"He's your horse," said Claudia. "You do the honors."

"Toss me a carrot, Dennis," I asked. I caught the vegetable and carefully entered the stall. "What say, old friend? Shall I trade you a snack for my daughter?"

Zeus looked up from Portia at the proffered bribe, then back at the baby. An instant later, the carrot was but a sticky stump. I reached down to pry Portia's arms away. She started sobbing, reaching for Zeus's muzzle as I lifted her up.

"Give her here," commanded my wife, and she took our daughter and started nursing her. She looked at the stable entrance, where several of the younger novitiates were watching with interest.

"I don't have enough for the rest of you," barked my wife, and they scattered, giggling. She grabbed one girl by the scruff of her blouse and hauled her back. She was about ten, with a plump face and hair that might have been blond if washed.

"What's your name?" asked Claudia.

"Helga," said the girl.

"I have a proposition for you, Helga," said Claudia. "Be Portia's nanny while I'm hunting, and I'll teach you how to use a bow properly."

Helga looked up at her, considering.

"Will you teach me a language, too?" she asked.

Claudia grinned. "Which one?" she asked.

"They say you speak the Arab tongue like a native," said the girl. "I would dearly love to know it."

"Done," said Claudia. "But be careful what you bargain for. If you learn enough Arabic, the Guild may send you to Beyond-the-Sea for your mission, and that's dangerous territory."

"I'm not afraid," Helga declared, and she held her arms out for the baby to prove it. Portia, having nursed and burped, nestled into the new nanny complacently.

"I like her," said Claudia as I retrieved my sledge and hauled the firewood into the Guildhall. "Maybe we should keep her."

"She's learning to become a jester, not a nanny," I said. "You'll be lucky if Father Gerald lets her do this much."

"Forgive me, Father," she muttered. "A question, husband."

"Yes?"

"With so much raillery against the Church, why does the Guild rely upon so many religious to run everything? Father Gerald, Brother Dennis, Brother Timothy, Sister Agatha . . ."

"They're a special order," I said. "They don't upset us."

"Are they fools who took vows, or religious who became fools?"

"Some of each, over the years," I said. "Sometimes a fool wearies of jesting, and seeks a simpler existence within the Guild. Sometimes we hear of a young monk or novice who cannot take ecclesiastical authority seriously, and we recruit them. Carefully."

"But don't they submit to Rome?"

"Rome thinks so," I said. "But this order was founded by a fool, they say, and instructs its members to ignore Rome when they feel it has lost its way."

"Has the Guild ever been banned before?"

"Oh, yes," I said. "There's an old burial yard around here somewhere from the last time the Guild fled the mountains. Sometime in the ninth century, they say, but that's before my time. Father Gerald might remember it."

"Oh, I might, might I?" came the irritable Irish rasp of our leader behind us.

"Why, Father Gerald," I exclaimed. "I had no idea that you were in earshot."

"Save it for the paying customers, Theophilos," said Father Gerald. "I know you too well."

He was an ancient man, with a face as cracked as a cobbled street after an earthquake. He had gone blind three years back, and relied on a simple oaken staff that became an extension of his body. And his will—he was known to dodder about, tapping the staff's end uncertainly, then suddenly whip around, pointing it unerringly at whoever it was who gave him cause for ire. Having seen him in my youth wield that same staff to more deadly effect, I kept my eyes on it whenever it was anywhere near me.

"I understand, Theo, that your daughter nearly escaped today," said Father Gerald.

"Yes, but..." I stopped. The staff's end was suddenly an inch from my nose.

"But nothing," he said. "You knew better than to leave her with Brother Dennis. The man's too distractible to be a nanny."

"We're making arrangements with one of the novitiates," I said.

"Which one?" he asked.

"Helga."

"Helga, Helga," he said. "Ah, yes, I remember her. A local girl, did you know that?"

"No, I didn't," I said. "She speaks Tuscan with no accent. Very impressive."

"Aye, she'll do for now," said the priest begrudgingly. "But she has to keep up with her studies. I'll have no nannying as an excuse to miss class."

"She won't," promised Claudia. "And I am going to be tutoring her in Arabic and archery as part of the bargain."

"Good," approved Father Gerald. "Theophilos, you will be doing what for her?"

"I hadn't thought about it," I said.

"Teach her some ballads," suggested Father Gerald. "You know a few thousand, I'll warrant."

"All right, Father," I said, and he lowered the staff and walked to his place at the head of the main table.

We sat with the other instructors. Helga brought Portia over and sat quietly next to Claudia, taking in the jokes and stories that were passed around with the helpings of roast venison.

When the meal was over and the dishes cleared, we stacked the tables against the walls and pulled the benches into concentric rings, leaving a large space in the center. Normally, we had performances in the evening after meals. Sometimes the novitiates would demonstrate their new-learned skills, sometimes one of us would perform, showing how to handle insults from the crowd or to cover for a dropped club.

Father Gerald walked to the center of the room and waited for the hubbub to die down.

"I can hear you whispering, Thomas," he said quietly, and the boy clammed up immediately. "Better. Well, what shall it be tonight? Who will favor us with a performance?"

He turned slowly, his staff pointing outward, sweeping the room.

"I am in a permanent game of Blind Man's Bluff," he said. "With this humble piece of wood, I am dowsing for fools. Who shall the spirit of the First Fool choose?"

"Father?" asked Thomas.

"Yes, lad?"

"There's something unfair about your method," said the boy.

"Is there?" asked the priest. "I would have thought that random pointing by a blind man would be as fair a method as any that could be devised."

"But one person will never be picked this way," said the boy.

"And who is that?"

"Yourself," said Thomas. "Is that because you've never been a fool?"

There were some sharp intakes of breath from the older fools in the room.

"He's in trouble now," I muttered to Claudia.

Even in the firelight, I could see the priest's face darken.

"Never...been...a fool?" he repeated slowly. "Is that what you think?"

"You've never talked about it," said the boy.

"I've told my stories many times," said the priest.

"Not lately," called out Brother Timothy, our juggling master and second in command.

"Really?" exclaimed the priest. He considered for a moment. "I suppose it has been a while. Well, then, although I suspect that this is a ruse on the part of young Thomas to avoid being called upon, it is a ruse that I can respect."

"And it appeals to your vanity," teased Sister Agatha, our seamstress and the keeper of our wardrobe.

"Vanity have I none," said the priest. "I am too old to sin. Let me think. What extraordinary events in my life would be of interest to you young people?"

He stood still, pondering the question.

"He's playing the moment," I whispered to Claudia. "He knows damn well what he's going to tell us. Watch."

While he stood in thought, the staff appeared to slide upward through his gnarled hand with no perceptible assistance from the priest. When it reached the end, he held his palm out, and the staff traveled across it, still seemingly of its own volition, to the tip of his index finger. Then he flipped it once through the air and caught it on the bridge of his nose. The staff ceased all movement, as if it had taken root on that ancient face.

You have no idea how hard it is to do that. But we do, and the hall was filled with the respectful whistling of the gathered fools and troubadours.

Father Gerald smiled and let the staff topple back into his waiting hand. "I wasn't always old," he began.

"No!" "Impossible!" "Don't lie to the children!" and other such cries rang out from the older fools, the ones who knew him well enough to razz him.

"I was a fool like yourselves," he continued, ignoring them. "Trained at the Guildhall and sent out into the world on various missions. My last assignment prior to heading the Guild was as Chief Fool in Denmark."

I tensed suddenly. Claudia sensed it and turned toward me.

"What is it?" she whispered in concern.

"This is not a story I want to hear," I whispered back.

"Denmark," repeated Father Gerald. "A country of fragments, of scattered islands and soggy peninsulas, of pieces of land jutting into the sea and pieces of sea jutting right back into the land. A country of fragmented peoples, bound together by ancestral conquest, their individual resentment of each other exceeded only by their collective disdain for the rest of the world. Condescending Sjællanders, contentious Skanians, irresponsible Fyns, melancholy Jutes. Theophilos, you were from there originally. Wouldn't you agree?"

"I don't know," I said. "Some of my best friends were Jutes."

"The problem with Denmark," he continued, "is that unlike other countries, they had no law of primogeniture, which is what, Thomas?"

"Um, right of the firstborn to succeed to the throne," rattled off the boy.

"Very good, Thomas," said Father Gerald. "Or, for the common folk, to inherit. Now, that is not necessarily a bad thing. There's no guarantee that the firstborn will be a capable leader, or even old enough to be an adequate monarch. The Danes would select from the available candidates the man most suited for the position. However, there was not always strict agreement as to who this should be. Frequently, several contenders would arise, each backed by powerful factions and armies of mercenaries. During the early part of the last century, five different brothers from the same family ended up being king for a short while.

"So, it will not surprise you to know that the Guild was actively involved in trying to keep the country from falling into civil war. It will also not surprise you to know that, as in many things, we were only intermittently successful.

"But this is by way of background, a setting for my story. It is a long one to tell, and I am too old to sing it, so bear with me. I shall tell it from the vantage point of God in His Heaven looking down, yet without the benefit of His omniscience. Like the country itself, the story is pieced together from many fragments told by many different people. As their final repository, it falls to me to assemble them into a coherent shape. It is a motley story, as a result.

"It begins with two fools meeting at a crossroads."

ƮWO

Fardel, *n. 1. A bundle, a little pack; a parcel.*
2. fig. A collection, "lot," parcel (of immaterial things)
esp. *A burden or load of sin, sorrow, etc.*
　　　　　　　　　　—*THE OXFORD ENGLISH DICTIONARY*

South Jutland, 1157 A.D.

Two roads crossed on a slight rise from the surrounding heath. Although neither road was straight, each following the path of least resistance through the gently irregular landscape, the ancient builders had made some effort to make the crossroads a perfect perpendicular, perhaps to lend exactitude to the traveler searching for his way. At the center of the intersection, one could line up the four directions just as precisely as the ancients had with their stone circles marking the equinoxes and solstices.

A crossroads, properly constructed, reminds you that you are making a choice.

A huge standing stone, wrested from a granite boulder, stood by the crossroads, its face carved with runes. To the south, the road vanished into a forest of oak, the outer trees taking the brunt of the constant wind, bending slightly to the east. To the west, the heath descended into bog, only the road staying high enough to provide dry footing. To the east, a tiny but elaborately constructed stone bridge arched grandly over a brook that was all of four feet in breadth. The road followed the brook into the distance. Near the horizon, they met up with a small river running east, and the fickle road abandoned the weaker body of water in favor of the stronger, hugging the north bank.

To the north, the road snaked between regularly shaped mounds of turf, grouped in pairs or sets of seven, rising twenty feet or so into the air, culminating in flattened circles at their peaks. It was from this direction that a man could be seen, appearing around the edge of the farthest mound, following the windings of the road.

He was tall and lanky, a shabby gray cloak wrapped ineffectually around his body to ward off the ever-present wind. On his back were a bewildering variety of misshapen bundles, bound with string, twine, scraps of leather and cloth, holding them both to each other and to their bearer. They rose and fell with every step, some of them clanking as they did, others rattling or making odd clopping noises. The effect was a pleasing one, a regular rhythmic percussing, and the man sang along with it, an old Danish marching song that may have once cheered some Viking warriors on a rare occasion traveling by land.

A casual observer might have found this sight odd in such a desolate region of the country, although anyone taking the trouble to observe the man would have been anything but casual. But what would have caused absolute astonishment was that the traveler was walking the road backward.

He glanced over his shoulder periodically, more on the curves. At one point, he veered off the road and scampered to the top of one of the mounds. He surveyed the surroundings until he caught sight of the crossroads with the standing stone by it, then grunted to himself, satisfied. He slid lightly back down to the road and trotted, still backward, until he came to it.

He shed the collection of bundles with an exaggerated groan, then leaned over, his knees perfectly straight, and touched the backs of his hands to the ground facing the east. He stood up, then bent over backward and touched the ground behind him. Then he stripped his cloak off, revealing a muddied motley tunic and leggings, and a face that had been powdered to an unnatural paleness. He started to swing his arms about, slowly at first, then faster and in larger circles until they were a blur. Then he made several shrugging motions while rolling his head in different directions until his neck made a series of cracking noises. He sighed with pleasure, then dug a cap and bells out of one of the many pouches at his belt and placed it carefully on his head.

He was intrigued by the runestone, and stepped forward to examine it more closely. It was taller than him by the length of his arm, and the worn inscription was a jumble of scratches to his eyes, as incomprehensible as was the Latin alphabet in his early years. At the base of the stone, the inscriber had gouged a cross, delving a little deeper into the rock so that the last thing to fade would be Christ's symbol.

"Can you read them, then?" came a voice directly behind him.

The fool swiveled his head carefully around to see a priest standing in the crossroads, wearing a plain brown cassock, unadorned by any order's emblem. He was lightly holding an oaken staff that he did not seem to need for support. The fool cursed himself in his thoughts for letting the other man come behind him so easily, but the priest seemed good-natured enough.

"I don't have the reading of the runes," said the fool. "Do you?"

"Let me look," said the priest, and he stepped forward and squinted at the scratches. " 'I, Gustav Andersson, own the lands within view of this stone. I have built this bridge for the glory of Our Savior, so that pilgrims may use it to travel to the Holy Land. May all who do so pray for my soul as I have prayed for theirs. Thus I do penance for my sins.' It seems to be dated from early in the last century."

The fool looked at the bridge, which was made of stones that had to have been brought at great expense from other lands. All to span a brook that a child could have jumped.

"It's really not much of a bridge," said the fool.

"I suspect this Gustav Andersson was not much of a man," said the priest. "His monument is larger than his penance."

"Perhaps his sins were small as well," said the fool. "Let's think the best of him, having never had the chance to meet him."

The priest and the fool stepped back from the stone and looked at each other.

"I didn't hear you approach," said the fool finally.

"No, you didn't," agreed the priest. "So, they're letting fools into Denmark now, are they?"

"It's worse than that, Father," replied the fool somberly. "They're letting the Irish in, too."

The priest's eyes widened, then he threw back his head and guffawed to the heavens.

"You insolent toad," said the priest. "My Danish is perfect. How did you know I was Irish?"

"It's not the accent," said the fool. "But you have the map of Ireland writ large on your visage. I have seen enough Irishmen in my life to spot one in a crowd. And the two of us are not exactly a crowd, so it's all the easier."

"Have you been to Ireland?" said the priest, a soft glow in his eyes.

"Aye, that I have. It's a fine country for fools. They blend right in."

The priest laughed again.

"That they do, that they do," he agreed, and held out his hand. "*Stultorum numerus . . .*"

"*Infinitus est,*" replied the fool, clasping it. "Terence of York, at your service. Nice outfit. Looks authentic."

"Gerald," said the priest. "Father Gerald. It is authentic. I am a priest as well as a jester."

"Are you?" said Terence in surprise. "Then forgive me, Father, for I have sinned."

"Your penance is to live in Denmark," said Father Gerald. "I am the Chief Fool for the country. I am living in Roskilde right now, but I make the rounds periodically. Did you have a good journey?"

"Not bad at all," replied Terence. "Landed in Ribe last week. The local fool put me up."

"Kanard," said Father Gerald. "Invaluable man for a small town."

"Yes, well, he was kind enough to walk me to the right road and point me south. Told me to count twelve villages and then look for a crossroads with a stone that's too large and a bridge that's too small. Said I would meet a fool there. I was expecting a little more motley and makeup, I must say."

"Oh, I have it handy," said Father Gerald, pulling up his sleeve to reveal the diamond patterns on his tunic. "But it's convenient to travel like this. Why on earth were you walking backward, by the way?"

"It's that damn wind of yours," replied Terence. "It never stops. I figured that if I let it blow on my right side the whole journey, I would be permanently bent by the time I got here. So, I spent half the trip walking backward so I would come out even."

The priest shook his head in amazement.

"I know some fools take their roles too seriously," he said. "But this is absurd."

"Of course, it is," laughed Terence. "I figured you were watching from somewhere. I just wanted to give you something to think about." He stretched his arms to the skies, then pulled his right foot up to his chin. "My boots are in a shocking state," he observed. "All that walking."

Father Gerald smiled and lifted his cassock to reveal a pair of callused feet inside an ancient pair of sandals, held together by bits of string. The soles were worn parchment-thin. Terence inspected them critically.

"I hope you won't start complaining," he said. "Or that fellow with no feet is going to show up and top us both."

Father Gerald lowered the cassock.

"Where did you learn your Danish?" he asked.

"There's plenty who speak it in York," replied Terence. "My grand-father was a Danish sailor who lost a leg and settled there. He taught me how to curse like a Danish sailor, and I've been fluent ever since."

"And you speak German as well?" asked the priest. The fool nodded. "Good. You'll need them both. I am sending you to Slesvig. Stay in the town, but get in good at the castle. The King's name is Ørvendil—"

"King?" interrupted Terence. "I thought there were three kings already in Denmark."

"Well, he fancies himself a fourth," said Father Gerald. "But you're right. At the moment, there are three kings, and they come bearing swords, not gifts. Knud Magnusson has the islands. He's just a youth, nothing much, but the islands are not much to rule. Valdemar is the son of Knud Lavard, who actually was king for a while before he got himself murdered in the woods somewhere. And then there's Sveyn Peder—he's a bad one. The Sjællanders pushed him to power, and now they are sorry they did. He's brought in Wend mercenaries, and they are running riot taking tributes. He's even trying to trade favors with the Germans, and people around here don't like the Germans much."

"So, the Guild favors Valdemar?"

"I favor Valdemar," said Father Gerald. "But just because he's the best man doesn't mean he can take power from the others. The Guild's interest at the moment is in keeping him alive, something I suspect Sveyn Peder opposes."

"How does Ørvendil fit into all of this?"

"He was Valdemar's man for a while, but when Valdemar put him in Slesvig, he started getting ideas. Slesvig is border country, practically independent. Tell you what, Fool. Stand with me and I'll give you a demonstration."

Terence came to the priest's side.

"Look south," commanded Father Gerald.

Terence gazed upon the forest.

"That's trouble," said Father Gerald.

"Is it?" asked the fool. "I only see trees."

"Very good," said Father Gerald. "What you can't see is beyond the trees. South of here is Holstein. They speak a different language, they have different loyalties, and they look at Jutland as a way to gain control of the northern seas. Look east."

"That's where I'm going," said Terence.

"Look farther," said Father Gerald. "That's trouble."

Terence stood on the tips of his toes. "No, still can't see anything but road and river," he said.

"Out east is Wendish territory. Nasty folk, available to be nasty for hire, as long as they can lug their seven-headed idols around. Now, look west. That's trouble."

"That's where I came from," said Terence.

"Not that far," said Father Gerald.

"I don't suppose you mean the bog," said Terence.

"I like the bog," said Father Gerald. "It slows down the armies."

"Whose armies?"

"Flanders. Normandy. Maybe even your King Henry will send a fleet out to do a little fishing. Now, look north."

Terence turned to face the ancient mounds.

"Let me guess," he said. "That's trouble."

"Up north, they are looking south and thinking this is trouble," said Father Gerald. "An upstart duke who might switch allegiance to the Germans if it will make him a Danish king."

Terence looked north.

"And they'll all be joining those fellows under the mounds," he said quietly. He shuddered suddenly. "Too many dead people in this country already, if you ask me. I've never seen so many barrows and monuments in one place."

"That's Denmark for you," said Father Gerald. "It hasn't been Christian that long. The Vikings are just beneath the surface, waiting to burst forth. There's been war in this country ever since the old king died. There is a tenuous peace in the land right now, but the balance could tip at any moment."

"What do you want me to do?" asked Terence.

"Deflate Ørvendil's ambitions. Teach him to be happy with his lot, and remind him that the favor of Valdemar may very well be worth more in the long run than any attempt at the throne."

"It is better to serve in Slesvig than to reign in Roskilde," said Terence. "Very well. Any other information about the town?"

"Ørvendil's drost, his second in command, is named Gorm. He's probably the man to see about entry into Valdemar's inner circle, but you may also want to try with the soldiers there. Ørvendil's wife is named Gerutha."

"You've forgotten the most important thing," said Terence.

Father Gerald grinned. "There are two taverns, both near the wharves. One is called The Red Pirate, and the other is The Viking's Rest. I recommend the ale in the latter. Do you need money?"

"I earn my way," declared the fool. "Will you be making the rounds with me?"

"Go in on your own," ordered the priest. "I don't want anyone connecting the two of us yet."

"But you'll be my contact?"

"I'll pop up when you least expect it," promised the priest.

"Yes, I've seen that already today," said the fool dryly. "If I have to run, which is the safest direction?"

"Away from the trouble," said the priest.

"Ask a stupid question," muttered the fool. He picked up his collection of bundles, then stopped, looking again at the runestone.

"What is it?" asked the priest.

"Just a whim of mine," replied the fool. He looked around until he found a small gray stone the size of his hand. He picked it up, slid a dagger from his sleeve, and started scratching letters on the stone.

"Terence was here," he said when he was done. He embedded it firmly in the dirt by the runestone, then stood back to survey his handiwork.

"Will anyone ever notice?" asked the priest, smiling.

"Will anyone ever notice anything we do?" replied the fool. "At least I have a stone, now. That's probably all that Gustav fellow wanted when all was said and done."

He held out his hand. Father Gerald clasped it firmly, then the two thumbed their noses at each other. The priest watched as the fool strode east, the wind at his back. Terence walked firmly to the middle of the bridge, then stopped and looked around.

"I take it back," he called. "It's an excellent bridge."

"What changed your mind?" asked the priest.

"My feet aren't wet," replied the fool, and then he turned and kept walking.

The priest watched him until he reached the distant river, then turned north and vanished amidst the mounds of the ancient dead.

Terence walked for an hour before he saw his next living soul. An earthen ridge stretched north from the road, planted with bushes at the top. Past it lay a farm, with regular rows of barley and wheat laid out. The farmer was watering his oxen at a pond near the road.

"Hail, good fellow," called Terence. "Is that water fit for a fool?"

"The oxen like it well enough," replied the farmer amiably. "Come over, if you like."

He was a stocky man with massive arms and a slightly bent back. He wore no shirt in the summer sun, and his skin was nut brown. He looked at Terence curiously as the fool removed a skin from his belt and filled it from the pond.

"My name is Terence," said the fool as he tied the skin shut.

"Magnus," replied the farmer. "What are you, some kind of pilgrim?"

"A performer," said the fool.

"Singer?" asked Magnus. "Musician? Dancer? Tumbler?"

"Yes," said Terence. "Among other things." He looked back at the ridge. "Tell me something, if I may be so bold as to ask. What is the purpose of that ridge? It seems too low to be of much use in repelling an army."

"It shields us from our greatest enemy," replied Magnus. "Step over here a little and you'll see."

Terence came over to him and looked at the ridge. "I confess, I do not see anything," he said.

"Close your eyes," suggested the farmer.

"I will see better with my eyes closed?" laughed the fool. Nevertheless, he closed them and listened. The sun beat down upon his face, warming him. Suddenly he smiled.

"Well?" asked Magnus.

"I am hot," replied the fool. "I am hot because the sun is shining on my face, but also because the wind is no longer cooling me. The ridge is a windbreak."

"Without that ridge, the good soil would be floating on the Baltic inside of a year," said Magnus. "My ancestors built it long ago, and we spend as much time tending to it as we do these crops."

"You are a worthy descendant of such wise men," declared Terence. "Thank you for educating a fool like me."

"Not at all," said Magnus. "Any kind of conversation is welcome out here. Where are you headed?"

"East," said Terence. "Is there a decent-sized town nearby?"

"Stay on the road another two hours and you will reach Slesvig," advised Magnus.

"I am your servant," said Terence, bowing. "And if conversation with you is always so enlightening, it will be well worth the occasional visit, if you wouldn't mind."

"I would be glad to," said Magnus. "I'm always interested in hearing about the world, even if it's just Slesvig."

Terence waved and walked on.

Nearly two hours later he came up against a more serious earthenwork wall, patrolled by soldiers. One stopped him.

"What are you?" he said, looking at his motley.

"A humble fool, good soldier, seeking to exchange amusement for sustenance," replied Terence.

The soldier looked at him some more.

"Where do your loyalties lie?" he asked.

"To whoever will be buying my next drink," said Terence. "I will follow that man with more devotion than a puppy, and speak his praise to all and sundry. Do you know where I can find this man?"

The soldier laughed.

"If it's drunken charity you want, try The Viking's Rest," he said. "Off the middle wharf. They have rooms, too."

"Sounds like heaven," said Terence. "A fool's blessing upon you, my friend."

The soldier waved him through.

The river widened, then split around an island, a ragged rectangular chunk of land that he paced off at about three hundred yards. Around its edges ran a wall of tree trunks packed tightly together, with wooden towers encased in layers of hide at random intervals. At the eastern end, where the river spilled into the fjord, there were three levels of platforms with archers keeping a relaxed watch. He couldn't see over the stockade wall, but guessed that it surrounded a great hall, some barracks, and Ørvendil's quarters. Some bleating noises escaped from within, joined by hammers hitting anvils, the shouts of soldiers being drilled, and the loud sobbing of what sounded like a child.

He wondered at this last. Father Gerald hadn't mentioned whether Ørvendil and Gerutha had any children. He decided he had better learn more in town before approaching the island fortress. Besides, the sun was beginning to set, and already he could see the drawbridge being raised from the northern shore to cut off the island from the rest of the world.

The fjord stretched out in front of him to the horizon, yet was no more than half a mile wide. The main part of town was a few hundred yards ahead of him on the north shore. Watch fires were being lit in the distance.

He hurried along the shore, marking wharves, fishing boats in abundance, nets drying on skeletal wooden frames. There were longboats of a more martial mien as well, at a wharf that was fenced off and bristling with guards. He reached the middle wharf, looked left, and saw a welcoming sight—a tavern, with a sign depicting a Viking of old, asleep at a table with a tankard spilling onto the floor by him.

He bounded in, his bundles swinging merrily about, as the sailors and salt packers in the room turned in astonishment. He held up a hand in greeting, dropped his bundles to the floor, and rummaged through them hastily, finding a number of odd objects: a stuffed sparrow hawk, a drum, a tankard, a small saw, and a lute. Placing the last carefully aside, he tied the drum at his waist and started juggling the other three, marking each rotation by slapping one hand or the other on the drum. He started tossing them higher, increasing the frequency of the drumbeats until it looked like he was simply a drummer with the ability to levitate strange objects about his head. He caught all three, waited for the applause to die down, then searched through the bundles some more, diving under some of the larger ones in his quest. He emerged holding six brightly painted wooden balls, which he sent into a strange circuit, both into the air and bouncing off the drum back into his hands, which were darting about like flies. When he finished up this routine, he put the drum on the floor and picked up his lute.

"I am Terence the Fool, my friends," he proclaimed to the room. "I am here to sing for you."

By the end of the song, which he accompanied both by lute and drum, playing the latter with his left foot, the room was his. At the end of the evening, having fed and drunk, he reached an agreement with the tapster to provide entertainment in exchange for a small room in the back and regular meals.

The next night, the tavern was packed as Slesvig crowded in to see the only fool within miles. Terence was patient, and waited a week without approaching the island. Then, one morning, a summons reached him.

He scrubbed his motley so that the colors reemerged from the dinge, and pulled out a small glass to make sure that his makeup was less haphazard than usual. Then he shouldered his collection of bundles and walked up to the drawbridge.

Inside, he came upon a group of four rectangular barracks, laid out in a square so that they could present another level of defense in the unlikely event that the enemy came inside the stockade. Beyond them stood a great hall, two levels high and taking up nearly half of the enclosed land. A small flock of goats was grazing to the left of it, and there were stables behind them. Several smaller buildings lay scattered beyond the hall, with gardens laid out around them.

A squat man stood at the entrance to the hall, watching him carefully. He had a misshapen head, as if he had been assembled hastily by an indifferent sculptor, with the features smeared on as an afterthought. He beckoned to Terence, and the fool came up to him and bowed.

"You are the fool," said the man.

"I am, milord. My name is—"

"I know your name," snapped the man. "I am Gorm Larsson, the drost to Ørvendil."

"How do you do, milord."

"Do not speak unless you are bidden to do so," thundered Gorm.

"I cannot do that, sir," said Terence mildly.

Gorm stared at him, momentarily speechless despite his mouth being fully open. Terence memorized the expression and stored it for future use.

"You will . . ." Gorm began.

"No, I won't," said Terence.

"You . . ."

"No."

There was stifled laughter from within the hall behind the drost, who was nearly apoplectic with rage.

"How dare you address me so!" he shouted.

"Because I am a fool," replied Terence frankly. "That's why you sent for me. If you want predictable conversation, and only when bidden, then you can get yourself a courtier. They cost more, and they are truly boring people despite their magnificent clothing, but they will know their place. But I am a jester, Lord Drost. I will speak when I am spoken to, and when I am not spoken to, and at random moments. Sometimes, I make no noise at all, just to see what it's like. May I come in?"

Gorm stepped back, momentarily stunned by the onslaught. Terence stepped past him and looked around. The room was almost empty, table-tops, trestles, and benches stacked against the walls. The far wall was over a hundred feet away, and some women were standing by it.

"Listen to me, Fool," said the drost urgently as he hurried to keep pace with the taller man. "This is a real lady here, none of your Danish peasants. She's been to the courts of France, visited Rome. She knows what a real court is like, and you shall treat her accordingly."

"If she knows what a French court is like, then she will know how fools behave," said Terence. He strode up to the women firmly, then stumbled at the last second, tumbling end over end into a splayed heap amidst his bundles.

"Hello, ladies," he said, waving merrily, and was met with a collective giggling from the group.

The woman in the center smiled. She was almost as tall as he was, a commanding, raven-haired beauty in her early twenties. She stepped forward and held out her hand to the fool. Terence seized it and allowed her to haul him back to his feet, to the appalled gape of the drost.

"Welcome, Fool," she said. "I am Gerutha, wife to Ørvendil."

"Milady," he said, executing a proper bow with elaborate arm flourishes, sending the other ladies into fits of giggling again. He looked up suddenly with an expression of alarm and held a finger to his lips. "Careful, milady," he said in an exaggerated whisper. "There is some sort of creature clinging to you."

"Amleth," she said. "Don't hide. Come and meet the jester."

A small boy peeped timidly around her skirts, thumb in his mouth. He was about two, with jet-black hair from his mother and skin almost as pale as the fool's, only without the help of powder. He looked up uncertainly at the apparition in motley.

"Amleth, is it?" said Terence gently. "A pleasure, milord. I believe I have something for you." The boy watched him as he reached into his pouch and produced a brightly painted ball like the ones he used for juggling. He held it out. The boy hesitated.

"Take it, Amleth," urged Gerutha, but the boy held back.

Terence smiled, and sat down on the floor so that he was looking directly at the boy. He held the ball out again. Slowly, the boy detached himself and approached the fool, suspecting a trick. He reached for the ball, and took it, taking his thumb out of his mouth to turn the plaything over and over, watching the patterns.

"Hello, Amleth," said Terence, holding out his hand. "I am Terence of York."

The boy looked up from the ball to the good-natured face of the fool.

"Yorick," said the child.

[25]

Terence shook his head. "Terence," he repeated. "Of York."

Amleth looked at him and darkened, his expression suddenly combative.

"Yorick," he insisted stubbornly.

Terence smiled.

"Well, then," he said, "Yorick it is."

ℭHREE

"But look, amazement on thy mother sits."
                    —*HAMLET,* ACT III, SCENE IV

Slesvig, 1157 A.D.

D id you see him?" Gerutha said to her husband as she undressed
that night. "I have never seen Amleth take to anyone as he took
to that jester. He is usually so frightened of strangers."

Ørvendil grunted, watching her as he lay under the covers. He was a
large bear of a man, scarcely distinguishable from the pile of furs that
served as their bed.

"I don't like it," he said as she slid next to him, wrapping her limbs
around his body for warmth. "He is surrounded by warriors, men of
arms, great men. Yet he hides behind his mother's skirts and only comes
out when some painted freak throws a ball to him. Is this the future
king of Denmark?"

"Maybe you should throw a ball to him once in a while," said Gerutha. "He's only two. The way you storm around, it's no wonder that
he's frightened. Grown men are frightened of you."

"Yet you are not?" he said. He rolled quickly, pinning her under him.
"Not frightened of a king?"

She smiled up at him.

"I would be unworthy of your attentions if I was," she whispered. And you are not a king yet, she thought, and then closed her eyes as they began to make love.

"Who is he?" Ørvendil asked idly the next day as he surveyed the fjord from atop the archers' nest at the eastern wall.

"An irritant," replied Gorm. "A powdered scarecrow who makes his living from cheap tricks and ballads."

"Where is he from?"

"He says York. The guard at the western wall said he came from that direction."

"And before he reached the wall?" asked Ørvendil. "West, north, south, what? You're supposed to be my spymaster. What else do you know about him? Could he be a spy?"

"He hasn't been behaving like one," said Gorm. "He's been entertaining at The Viking's Rest ever since he arrived. He hasn't been wandering about the town asking questions."

"He doesn't have to if he's at the tavern," snapped Ørvendil. "Everyone goes there. All the information anyone could possibly need will come spilling out by the third drink. And now he's wormed his way onto the island. How did that happen?"

"Your wife invited him," said Gorm. "She thought it would make it more like a real court."

Ørvendil turned to him in rage. Gorm didn't flinch.

"A real court!" shouted Ørvendil. "What does . . ."

He stopped as a high shriek pierced the air. Around him, archers notched arrows, calling to each other as they frantically searched for the source of the sound. Ørvendil held up his hand, and the chatter ceased.

The shriek echoed through the island. Ørvendil and Gorm turned to the rear of the platform and looked down. Terence suddenly appeared, galloping out of the great hall, Amleth on his shoulders, the boy clinging tight to the head of the jester. The shrieks were coming from the child—

repeated, uncontrollable howls of delight. The jester lengthened his stride and leapt over the backs of a pair of startled pigs, scattering a small flock of chickens that were pecking at the ground near the stockade wall.

Ørvendil looked around, noting the grins on the faces of the archers, the laughter of the guards patrolling the walls. Beside him, Gorm was red-faced with fury.

"I'll have him thrown out on his painted head," he growled. "A complete collapse of military discipline, milord. Shameful."

"No, no, it's not worth the trouble," said Ørvendil.

Gorm turned to him in confusion.

"But, milord?" he asked. "Don't you think he's a problem? You wanted me to find out more about him."

Ørvendil looked at his spymaster.

"Yes," he said. "Speak with him. Find out what you can."

"And then?"

Ørvendil looked back down at his son, who was bouncing happily on the fool's shoulders.

"Then report what you have learned back to me," he said. "But let him stay for now."

"But why, milord?"

"I've never heard Amleth laugh like that before," said Ørvendil, half to himself.

Gorm started to say something, then thought better of it and descended the ladders to the ground.

"You there, Fool," he called. Terence turned and galloped up to him, Amleth still riding merrily along.

"My Lord Drost," said the fool, bowing low, the child hanging on for dear life as he did so. "How are you on this fine day?"

Gorm looked at him with contempt. "Is that how you treat your master's son? Is that any way to handle a child?"

"Child? What child?" asked Terence innocently. Amleth giggled, and the fool looked up to him and put a finger to his lips. "Hush, Amleth," he whispered. "If you're quiet, then no one can see you."

"Can't see him?" protested Gorm. "He's . . ."

Terence winked at him. The drost stared at him stupidly, then took a deep breath.

"Why, where did he go?" exclaimed Gorm woodenly. "Young Amleth has completely vanished. And I could have sworn he was here a minute ago."

Amleth's eyes grew big, but he kept silent.

"Quite the talented lad, isn't he?" said Terence. "One second he's there, the next he's gone. He's a veritable magician, if you ask me."

"Amleth," called Gerutha from inside the great hall. "Time to eat."

Amleth turned with a disappointed moan, and Terence immediately plucked him from his shoulders and plopped him down on the ground.

"I have found you, milord," he said to the boy. "The moment you made that sound, you became visible again. Now, run along to your mother, or I'll be in trouble."

"Bye, Yorick," called the child, and he waved as he ran inside the hall.

"Well done, my Lord Drost," commented Terence as he waved back. "With a little practice, you would have the makings of a fine fool."

"It doesn't take much to amuse a child," said Gorm.

"You would think so," said Terence. "But it must be extremely difficult in truth, for no one here has done it. Thank goodness I arrived when I did, or Amleth could have ended up like . . ." He stopped, looking pointedly at the drost. "Well, let's just say it's a good thing I'm here."

"Good for you, certainly," said Gorm. "How is it that you happened to come to Slesvig? It's a long way from York."

"That was part of its appeal to me," confessed Terence. "I had tired of York, and York had tired of me. I needed a new audience, so I sailed the seas. I fetched up in Ribe, but there was already a fool there. Nice fellow. He showed me around, we did a couple of two-man shows, then he kicked me out and told me never to come back. He suggested Slesvig."

"Why?" asked Gorm.

"He said there was no fool here, so I would have the place to myself. He did not know about you, unfortunately."

"Cease, you grow tiresome," said Gorm. "Must I be the endless butt of your japes?"

"It's large, certainly," said Terence, craning his neck to look at the ample rear of the drost. "But I wouldn't call it endless. In fact, if one's butt is one's end, then it can never—"

"Enough!" shouted Gorm, and he stormed away, muttering.

There was a chuckle from above. Terence looked up, shading his eyes from the noon-high sun, to see Ørvendil watching him from the top platform.

"Milord, I am literally dazzled by your presence," called Terence.

"Are you?" replied Ørvendil. "Come, join me. You'll like the view."

Terence scurried up the ladders to the top, then looked around. The fjord stretched out in front of him. Even at this height, he couldn't see its end.

"How far is it to the sea?" he asked.

"Two days with a willing crew," said Ørvendil.

"And with an unwilling crew?"

"One, if they want to live," said Ørvendil.

"And which do you prefer?" asked Terence.

"It depends how quickly I need to be at sea," replied Ørvendil. "Sometimes you have to take the unwilling crew."

Terence shook his head.

"It seems to me," he said, "that you would want the willing crew no matter what, even if it means arriving later."

"Why?" asked Ørvendil.

"Because when you get there, they will be your allies, while the unwilling crew could turn on you at any moment."

"Perhaps," said Ørvendil. They stood for a while, watching the fishing boats in the distance. "They tell me that you're a fool. I don't believe it."

"They tell me that you're a king," said Terence. "I don't believe that, either."

"Who tells you that?" asked Ørvendil.

"Idle gossip," said Terence. "The word is that you see Slesvig as a stepping stone to higher things. But how high can you rise in such a low country?"

"Idle gossip can be dangerous," observed Ørvendil.

"Yes, it can," agreed Terence. "But to whom? If a pathetic fool like me has heard it, then it is likely that smarter, more powerful men have as well. Does that put the gossipers in danger? More likely, the subject of the gossip."

"Are you saying that I am in danger?" asked Ørvendil.

Terence shrugged. "As I understand it, there are already three kings in Denmark. Three is an uneven number. I can juggle three of anything, but I can't make them balance. One will rise and the other two will fall, dragging each other down."

"A fourth could even the scales," observed Ørvendil.

"If he picks the right one to join," returned Terence. "If he guesses wrong, however, then he shall fall as well. And the chances of guessing wrong are two out of three."

"Then your counsel is to wait and see?"

"My counsel?" laughed Terence. "I am a fool, milord, playing with words. Who would take counsel from such a man?"

"If I thought the counsel worth taking, then I would," replied Ørvendil.

"Would you indeed?" said Terence, amused. "Well, if you thought the counsel worth taking, then I daresay it's because you have already thought of it yourself."

"How much do you charge for counsel?" asked Ørvendil.

"My advice is always free," said Terence. "That's why no one ever thinks it's worth anything. No, milord, pay me for folly, and nothing else. Allow me food and drink while I am here, and anything else that suits your mood will be ample remuneration. And if you have no stomach for fooling, then I will go to those who do."

"Like my son," said Ørvendil.

"He's a fine boy," said Terence.

"I want him to be a man," said Ørvendil.

"He's already a boy, so you're halfway there," said Terence. "He doesn't have to be a man right away. Let him be a boy for a while longer. Do you know what he needs the most right now?"

"You, I suppose," said Ørvendil.

"No," said Terence. "He needs other children to play with. He's a two year old inside a fortress, with his view of the world cut off and nothing but armored legs to bump into. He's made friends with the animals, did you know that? He has names for each of them. Put him with other boys, his spirit will fly. He'll learn how to play, how to make friends, how to fight, how to forgive. He needs to run through the woods, paddle in the water, scrape his knees, and roll in the mud. If a man did those things with a sword in his hand, you would think him an exceptional soldier. If you truly desire to make Amleth a man among men, let him be a boy among boys first."

"A lengthy bit of free advice," said Ørvendil. He looked across the fjord, then turned and looked down into the enclosed island. "All right, I agree. Do you know any children?"

"Milord, there is a town filled with children right there," laughed Terence. "Walk through it with your eyes and ears open, and you may spot a few. That's where a fool has an advantage over a lord."

"How, Fool?"

"I can leave this island and wander the world without fear, and the children will flock to me. A lord must hide behind walls and men, and rarely ventures out for fear."

"Are you calling me a coward?" thundered Ørvendil, his hand on his sword.

"I have only seen you in here," said Terence. "It was my understanding that King Valdemar made you his representative in Slesvig when he was elected by the Jutland *thing*. I assume that he chose you because you are a brave and capable leader, and worthy of his trust."

"Well?" roared Ørvendil, slightly mollified.

"A leader leads," said Terence. "His people must see him do so. Not just in the cathedral on Sundays."

"There are men who wish me dead," said Ørvendil.

"If you stay in here, then they will have a following out there," said Terence. "But if the people are yours, then your enemies will be alone and easier to face."

"You seem intent on making an enemy of my drost," observed Ørvendil.

"He is a man who needs a fool," said Terence. "He has forgotten what it was like to be a boy. Oh, and there is something he needs even more than a fool, in my opinion."

"What is that, Fool?"

"He needs a woman," said Terence. "He has forgotten what it is like to be a man, too."

"With all of this wisdom at your beck and call, I wonder that you should choose to remain a fool," said Ørvendil slowly, staring at the painted man.

"I lack ambition," said Terence, bowing slightly. "Now, if you will pardon me, milord, I have to perform at the tavern tonight. Come by if you have a mind to do so. The ale is outstanding."

"Who sent you, Fool?" asked Ørvendil.

"Why, you did, milord," replied Terence. He turned and slid down one of the platform poles, then trotted across the drawbridge, waving to the soldiers as he did so.

Ørvendil watched until the fool vanished into the town. Then he stepped toward the ladder, and hesitated. As his men watched curiously, he stepped to the platform pole that had served Terence as transport, grasped it firmly, swung out over the edge, and slid to the ground, landing with a thud that momentarily knocked the breath out of his body. He gasped, sucking in air, then laughed.

Gorm watched him with astonishment from the barracks. "Milord, are you all right?" he called.

"Never better," replied Ørvendil. "I haven't done that since I was ten. Not as easy as it looks, I must say."

"God in Heaven, you could have broken your leg," said Gorm sternly.

Ørvendil walked up to the drost and clapped him on the shoulder hard enough to send him staggering.

"Gorm, my friend," he said, "we are going to find you a woman."

He walked away, leaving the drost standing with his mouth hanging open.

Gerutha was tending her flower garden in the rear of the compound, pruning a pair of rosebushes that cowered by the palisade. She looked up in surprise as her husband, who rarely came to the garden, strode up, grinning like a maniac.

"I like this fool," he said. "He gives better advice than many a university-educated sage. Tell me, my Queen. Have you any unmarried cousins?"

"Let me think," said Gerutha, putting down her blade. "Signe still lacks a husband. She is my mother's cousin Harald's daughter."

"From outside of Flensburg," remembered Ørvendil. "Skinny, with ratty hair."

"A cruel but accurate description," said Gerutha. "She must be about seventeen now."

"Yet unmarried?"

"Yes," said Gerutha. "She has always been a little odd. She kept to herself as a child. She never liked decent society."

"Perfect," said Ørvendil. "Send for her immediately."

"Very well, husband," said Gerutha. "I take it that you have found a suitable husband for her."

"Gorm," said Ørvendil.

"Gorm," said Gerutha thoughtfully. "Yes, that just might work. You realize, of course, that this will make him family."

"The better to bind him to us," replied Ørvendil. "Good. Now, where's Amleth?"

"Having a nap," said Gerutha. "He should be waking about now."

Ørvendil walked to their quarters, a two-story building with one small room on each floor.

"Amleth?" he called softly.

The boy appeared in the doorway, rubbing his eyes. He looked up to see his father and flinched.

My son fears me, thought Ørvendil.

He did not want that. He looked down at the quivering shape of his son, and held out his hand.

"I understand that you have a new ball," he said gently. "May I see it?"

Amleth slowly reached into his pouch and produced the ball his new friend Yorick had given him. Resigned to never seeing it again, he handed it to his father.

Ørvendil inspected it carefully as Amleth watched, the boy's eyes never leaving the ball.

"Sit down," commanded his father abruptly.

Amleth looked at him in confusion, wondering what strange behavior was called for.

"Sit," repeated his father. To illustrate, he plopped down on the path before his son, his legs spread in a vee before him.

Slowly, carefully, Amleth sat on the ground opposite his father.

"Legs like mine," said Ørvendil.

Amleth, beginning to think his father mad, copied him.

Ørvendil took the ball and rolled it to his son, the ball coming up against the boy's right thigh. Amleth looked at the ball suspiciously, searching for any sign of betrayal. But the ball just sat there, resting against his leg. He leaned forward and grabbed it.

"Good," said Ørvendil, applauding. "Now, roll it back to me."

The boy hesitated.

"Don't worry," Ørvendil assured him. "You'll get it back. I promise you."

Amleth rolled the ball to his father, who plucked it from the ground and sent it rolling back.

Amleth smiled. Ørvendil smiled back.

Gerutha rounded the corner, a basket of flowers in her hand. She stopped and watched in pleased astonishment as her husband and son sat in the dirt as equals, rolling a painted wooden ball back and forth, back and forth.

ƒOUR

"Beware of entrance to a quarrel."

—*HAMLET*, ACT I, SCENE III

Roskilde, 1157 A.D.

A priest walked behind a hedge on the outskirts of Flensburg. A minute later a jester walked out, an oaken staff in his hand, the priest's cassock folded neatly and packed inside his bag.

At the wharves, he took passage on a German *cog* that was leaving for Sjælland. The crew negotiated the straits between Langeland and Lolland with ease born of long practice, and put in at Vordingborg. He left them on merry terms and walked briskly to the northern road.

Two days later, walking a little less briskly, he reached the moat and earthenwork wall enclosing Roskilde. The city was about three times the size of Slesvig, surrounding a bustling harbor at the southern end of a wide fjord. Already there had been talk of building a new cathedral to handle the burgeoning population, awaiting only some resolution to the long civil war that had sapped the riches of the island. In the meanwhile, watchtowers lined the coast, ready to ignite the bonfires that would signal the approach of a hostile navy.

Gerald kept a room on the second floor of a boardinghouse at the eastern end of the city. He arrived there shortly after sunrise, having walked through the night. As he came to his doorway, he was mildly irritated to hear someone snoring inside.

Noiselessly, he entered to find another fool stretched out on his pallet, the source of the snores. Smiling, Gerald carefully extended his staff until the end was about to poke the sleeper's nose. Suddenly the other fool grabbed the staff and wrenched it out of Gerald's hands.

"Just because you consider yourself the master of stealth doesn't mean I don't know when you are there," said the fool. Then he opened his eyes and grinned.

"Larfner, would you mind heaving your wretched carcass out of my bed?" said Gerald. "I need it more than you do at the moment."

"Debatable, considering how much I had to drink last night," said his colleague, but he complied, rolling across the room. He was a robust, stocky man in his midforties, and wore a motley favoring patches of brown and green.

Gerald lay down with a sigh, peeling off his sandals and wiggling his toes. Larfner watched him with disgust.

"Truly, you have the ugliest feet known to mankind," he said. "It's a wonder that you can pass for human. Hunters crossing your trail must think they've found some forgotten monster of yore."

"They get me from one place to another, and that's all that I ask of them," said Gerald. "What are you doing in Roskilde? You're supposed to be with King Knud."

"And so I am," said Larfner. "He is in Roskilde."

Gerald sat up in alarm. "What's happening?" he asked. "Is he allying with Sveyn against Valdemar? Damn you, man, how could you have let that happen?"

"There's an alliance," said Larfner. "But of all three of them. They've finally agreed to the treaty."

"Have they at last?" exclaimed Gerald. "Then praise the First Fool, Our Savior. Brilliant work, my friend. When did this miracle come about?"

"Three days ago in Lolland," replied Larfner. "Very little to do with us, I'm sorry to say. The proposal came out of the blue from Sveyn's camp. The documents have made the rounds to the others for signatures and seals, and tonight there's going to be a celebratory dinner. With entertainment, by the way, so you and I can do some two-man work."

"Only two?" asked Gerald. "Where's Leif?"

"Laid up in Odense, I heard. I don't have the details. But he and I have made one small contribution to the peace. There's going to be a marriage."

"Of whom?"

"Valdemar and Sophie, that Russian half sister of Knud's. Ever seen her?"

"Let me think," said Gerald, frowning slightly. "Yes, I remember her. And I remember why I didn't want to remember her. A remarkably unpleasant woman in every aspect. Does Valdemar really want to marry her?"

"He wants the alliance," said Larfner.

"I wonder if that's wise under the circumstances," mused Gerald. "The treaty would keep things balanced for a while, but if Sveyn sees this marriage as a threat . . ."

"I think he'll thank Valdemar for saving him from having to marry her," chuckled Larfner. "Anyhow, he's as tired of this war as anyone. He would rather settle things locally than have Barbarossa summon everyone to be told what to do."

"That didn't work so well the last time," remembered Gerald.

Larfner picked up a wineskin, took a swig, then offered it to Gerald.

"A bit early for that," observed the priest.

"It's daylight, isn't it?" replied Larfner. "Suit yourself. What's the new fool like?"

"Tall," said Gerald sleepily.

"A little more information, please."

"Extremely tall," Gerald elaborated. "And skinny. We could plant beans by him if he was willing to stand still that long. His Danish is good, and he seems to know what he's about. I'm sorry I didn't know about Leif. I would have brought the new fool here. We could use three fools for three kings."

"Ah, the two of us are worth a company of fools," said Larfner. "Get some sleep, or I'll have to carry the act. Not for the first time, I might add."

"Get on with you," grumbled Gerald. "Come by at noon and wake me, would you?"

"Very good, milord," said Larfner, bowing until his head was looking out between his legs. He left the room in that position. A moment later there was a shriek from a maidservant downstairs. Gerald grinned and fell asleep.

Larfner returned at noon and kicked him on the hard side of gently several times until Gerald sprang to his feet, ready to wrestle the other fool to the floor. Larfner stepped back into the doorway, poised for flight.

"Think you could take me?" growled the priest.

"I could, but we both would be in wretched shape before it was over," said Larfner. "Here's bread and herring for you."

The priest ate hurriedly and threw his makeup on, then put on his sandals and picked up his staff.

"We should do the Two Brothers tonight," he said. "That's always a good one for reconciliation."

"Nothing combative," agreed Larfner. "Goes against the grain, but it's good for me to be good once in a while, just for the practice."

They walked out into Roskilde, heading toward the center. The town itself being fortified, the King's hall was not otherwise enclosed. It was a circular building, about twice the size of its counterpart in Slesvig, and had sleeping quarters attached on either side, with the King's quarters in the rear.

"Knud's on the left, and Valdemar's on the right," Larfner informed him.

"Got it," said Gerald. "Attend your master. I'll pay my respects to the other kings."

He went through the door at the rear of the hall and ducked behind a tapestry into the King's quarters. A pair of guards intercepted him, but let him pass upon seeing his face. He had spent many years cultivating relationships on every level of Roskilde, from the highest of magnates to the lowest of thralls, and he was a particular favorite of the Danish garrison in Roskilde. Sveyn Peder was seated at a low table with two of his captains. He was a tall man in his forties, with a sallow complexion broken by a livid scar on his chin. He looked up with irritation when Gerald came in.

"Where the hell have you been hiding yourself?" he demanded. "I haven't had any entertainment in a week."

"Visiting a relative, Your Highness," said Gerald, bowing. "A song, sir? Something to lighten the mood?"

"My mood is fine," snapped the King. "Go play for our guests until dinner. Keep them out of my hair."

"Very good, milord," said Gerald. "I shall be here during dinner as well."

"No surprise. I never knew you to miss a free meal," said Sveyn. "Get out of here."

Having expected this reception, Gerald sought out Valdemar. The Jutland king was twenty-six, powerfully built, with flaxen hair and eyes the color of the sea. He looked at the fool with delight as he entered.

"Look, everyone, it's what's his name, Gerald," he said to the two men with him. "Come to juggle for us?"

"If that's what you wish, milord," replied Gerald, bowing. "My heart-felt felicitations on this occasion of peace, if I may be so bold. A great day for Denmark."

"Let us hope so," replied Valdemar. "Do you know these fellows, Fool?"

"I recognize the one by your side," said Gerald, marking a slender, spry-looking man. "Esbern the Quick, is it not?"

"Esbern Hvide to you, Fool," said Esbern.

"Of course, sir," said Gerald. "Well met, young Esbern. How is your family?"

"They are well, thank you, Fool," replied Esbern. "My brother Axel is back from Paris."

"Is he here?" asked Gerald. "I would enjoy seeing him again. His conversations are always on such a high plane that I end up dizzy after them. Has he finished his studies?"

"Finished, and entered the priesthood," said Esbern. "Before, he was just an annoying brother, but now he's become quite the sanctimonious pain in the ass."

"He already has his sights set on a bishopric," laughed Valdemar. "I told him he's not old enough yet. Do you know what he said?"

"That you're not old enough to be a king?" guessed Gerald.

Valdemar roared with laughter, joined by the others.

"But, good sir," said Gerald, turning to the third man. "I do not believe that I have had the pleasure. I am Gerald the Fool."

"Fengi of Slesvig," said the other man. He was short and remarkably hairy. There was something about the glowering eyes that reminded Gerald of someone.

"I know who you are," he said suddenly, snapping his fingers. "You're Ørvendil's brother. You look like him done in miniature."

"Bastard of a fool," muttered Fengi as the other two laughed.

"He makes up for his stature with his greatness of heart," said Valdemar, throwing his arm around him. "I would rather have him at my side on a battlefield than any man I have met. He has saved my life on more than one occasion."

"Then welcome, milord," said Gerald. "I do not apologize for my jibes, for they are how a fool shows respect, as well as how he makes his living. But let me perform nonverbally for you."

"What can you do with that?" asked Valdemar, pointing to the staff.

"This?" replied Gerald, spinning it rapidly with his right hand. "Anything I like. Observe."

He kept it spinning as he passed it from hand to hand, then behind his back. He then placed it upright on the hard clay floor. He put his right hand on top and grabbed it firmly in the middle with his left, then jumped lightly, ending upside down in midair, supporting himself with the pole. He breathed in, exhaled, then pushed up with his right hand so that he was now balanced in a one-hand stand, his feet pressed against the ceiling.

Valdemar and Esbern clapped, while Fengi nodded approvingly.

"Can you fight with that?" he asked as Gerald dropped back to the floor.

"If I had to," said Gerald. "Generally, it comes in handy deflecting thrown vegetables, which means I have used it far too often."

Fengi took a knife out of his belt. "Could you block a thrown knife?"

"If I saw it coming, yes," replied Gerald calmly. "It's just like a thrown carrot, only sharper. Care to essay a throw?"

"Put up your weapon," commanded Valdemar. "We don't want to damage our host's property."

"Oh, I am no man's property but my own," said Gerald. "I am a free fool. If I choose to have a warrior's knife thrown at me, then it is a fool's choice."

He stood facing Fengi, holding the staff vertically with both hands near the middle, separated slightly.

Fengi weighed his knife for a moment, looking at Gerald, then put it back in his belt.

"I don't know whether you're a brave man or a foolish one," he said.

"There's a fine line between the two," said Gerald. "In the heat of battle, it can be crossed many times in either direction. Let us hope that no man will have to put it to the test again in our lifetimes."

"Amen," said Valdemar. "I believe that was adequate entertainment for now. Give us leave, good Fool, and we will see you again at dinner."

"Thank you, milords," replied Gerald, catching the penny tossed to him by Esbern.

He wandered around the great hall, where the tables and benches were being set up by the serving thralls around a central fireplace. He paced the distance between the central fireplace and the tables, rehearsing routines in his mind for the space available. Each king would be at his own table, with Sveyn Peder at the rear and the two visitors by their respective guest quarters. He took three clubs from his pack and ran through some juggling maneuvers, marking where he needed to stand to gain the higher parts of the slanted roof while avoiding the crossbeams. The thralls stopped their labors for a moment to watch him until a soldier came in and barked at them.

Gerald, not wishing to cause the thralls any more trouble, nodded at the soldier and wandered outside, noting with approval that Valdemar's men were chatting amiably with the ones who had come with Knud.

He decided to walk about the town until it was time for him to perform again. At the wharves, he marked the boats of the two kings, guarded warily by their crews who spent half their time watching each other and the other half watching the skies.

Gerald looked up at the clouds gathering in the distance. There's going to be a storm later, he thought. He turned back toward the King's hall, wondering if he should try to wangle a bed for the night there rather than trudge through the rain back to his room. A pair of soldiers passed him, wearing Sveyn's colors, but speaking Slavic.

"Wends," muttered Gerald in disdain. "What are they doing here?" Then he pondered that question more seriously. "Why would Sveyn Peder have Wends in Roskilde when he's trying to make peace?" he said to himself.

He followed the pair, reaching into his bag for his lute. They turned before reaching the King's hall and entered a nearby building. Gerald took a deep breath, and leapt through the doorway, announcing his presence with a mighty strum.

Startled soldiers leapt to their feet, reaching for weapons. Gerald stilled them with another chord, and proclaimed in Danish, "Greetings, friends. Your King has sent me to entertain you for the afternoon. What shall I sing for you?"

A group conferred with each other hastily, then one stepped forward. "No one invited you here," he said in heavily accented Danish.

"No one invites me anywhere," replied Gerald. "But I promise you that by the time I have finished singing, you'll be begging me to stay."

"Do you know any songs in our language?" asked the soldier curiously.

"I am afraid that I do not speak your language," said Gerald. "But I could sing you something in Danish or German if you would like. Or would you prefer juggling?"

"We would prefer that you get the hell out," said the soldier, and a few of the others chuckled in agreement.

"Very good, milords," said Gerald, bowing low. He turned and left.

He lurked outside a window, trying to pick up snatches of conversation. Despite his protestations, he spoke fluent Slavic, but kept that to himself. He learned nothing useful, and it was getting toward dinnertime, so he hied himself back to the King's hall.

Larfner was already at work, strolling about the hall playing his lute. He raised an eyebrow at Gerald, who joined in from the other side of the hall. The two fools sauntered to the center of the room by the fireplace.

"Anything amiss?" asked Larfner.

"Nothing in particular," said Gerald. "When do the festivities begin?"

"They're waiting for the Archbishop to show up and bless everything," said Larfner.

"Eskil's come all the way from Lund?"

"No, apparently he was in Roskilde already. The Bishop here has been ailing, and Eskil wanted to make sure the local magnates don't put in someone loyal to them and not to Rome."

"Well, he's . . . wait, they're coming in."

It had been agreed that the three kings would enter the hall simultaneously so as not to assert any claim to superiority. In actuality, although the three doors were flung open by the serving thralls at the same time, Valdemar and Knud were the ones who came into the hall, accompanied by their men. As all eyes turned toward the rear of the hall, Sveyn Peder made his entrance, Archbishop Eskil of Lund at his side. Knud looked troubled by the apparent endorsement of his rival by the Church, while Valdemar smiled, amused by the petty display.

Sveyn held his arms out to the assembled diners.

"Good friends, my brother kings, you are welcome in Roskilde," he said. "Our responsibilities are great, and our burdens heavy. Let this night mark the easing of our spirits, the removal of care and woe, the lifting of the dark cloud of war from our great lands. Gentlemen, I ask His Holiness to give a benediction."

Eskil stepped forward. "In the name of the Holy Father, I bless this union of former rivals. Let peace come to us all, in the name of the Father, the Son, and the Holy Spirit."

"I thank our host and His Holiness," said Knud. "And I have one more piece of joy to bring to the table. I am pleased to announce that my sister, Sophie, is betrothed to my brother king, Valdemar. May the joining of our two families mirror the reconciliation of all the Danes."

"I thank you, my brother," replied Valdemar courteously. "For so I must call you now with all my heart."

"Well," said Sveyn. "Such tidings are ever welcome. Our feast is thrice blessed. Let it begin."

Goblets were lifted and toasts drunk, and the fools began to perform in earnest. The serving thralls moved in and out of the room, bringing heaping plates of stew and bread, keeping the ale flowing freely.

Gerald and Larfner finished the Two Brothers to applause from all sides, and stepped over to a side table near Valdemar's group to partake of what was set out for them.

"A happy room, I think," said Larfner. "It's going quite well. I told you that we could get by without Leif."

"Did you see Sveyn's face when Knud announced the marriage?" chuckled Gerald. "He hadn't a clue that that was in the works. You're right, I think he was relieved."

He put down his cup and slung his bag around to the front to pull out his juggling clubs. As he did so, one of the serving thralls collided with him.

"I beg your pardon, good sir," said Gerald jovially.

The thrall shot him a nasty glance, then looked back down at the floor and walked off. Gerald felt a chill run through his body as he saw the man's face. He glanced about the room at the other servants.

"Still think the two of us are enough?" he asked Larfner softly.

"What are you talking about?" asked Larfner.

"The serving thralls," said Gerald. "I know every one of them, and none of them is here. They've been replaced by Wend mercenaries. Are two fools enough to face a company of Wends?"

Larfner looked around the room, doing a quick count.

"There's at least twenty of them," he said. "We have to warn the kings. I'll take Knud."

He struck up a tune and ambled toward the far side of the room. Gerald casually took up his staff that was leaning against the wall, then walked along the sideboard until he was behind Valdemar. He leaned forward.

"Be on your guard, milord," he muttered. "This is a trap."

Valdemar's expression never changed, but he quietly loosened his sword in its scabbard and shifted his stool back from the table.

Gerald was about to alert Valdemar's companions when he saw the Wend who had confronted him earlier in the day. Now, he was approaching with a platter of freshly baked loaves of bread.

The knife on the tray looked much sharper than a bread knife.

Gerald stepped toward him, sliding the end of his staff in front of the Wend's feet. The soldier tripped, the platter went flying. Gerald caught the knife.

"I believe you lost this," he said in Slavic, holding it away from him.

"I have another," snarled the Wend, reaching for his waist.

Gerald brought his staff up into the man's groin, then stepped forward and felled him with a blow to the head with the haft of the knife.

"Milords, save yourselves!" he shouted as the disguised soldiers rushed into the room.

Valdemar was already up, throwing his cloak over the head of an onrushing soldier. He grabbed his stool and broke it on the man's skull. Esbern was up, sword drawn, as were the rest of Valdemar's men.

Gerald threw his knife into the throat of the nearest Wend, then suddenly lunged forward. A dagger hurled from the center of the room stuck in the end of his staff, inches from Fengi's chest. Fengi shot a look of appreciation toward the fool, then picked up his stool with his left hand and used it as an improvised shield.

On the other side of the room, Knud was having less success. Despite

Larfner's warning, his men had not reacted as quickly as had Valdemar's. Larfner himself was beset by three soldiers, and was laying about with a knife in one hand and his lute in the other.

Knud went down, a knife in his back. Sveyn stood behind him, teeth bared. The Wends from that side of the room started toward Valdemar.

"Fall back!" yelled the Jutland King. "Make for the door."

His men retreated into his quarters, Gerald with them. They tried to shut the door, but the Wends were massed on the other side. Suddenly there was a discordant twang, accompanied by the splintering of wood, and Larfner pulled one of the soldiers away and pushed into the room. He, Gerald, and Valdemar managed to shove the door into place and secure the bar.

In the great hall Sveyn picked up the treaty, crumpled it, and tossed it into the fire. Then he gestured to his men to break down the door to Valdemar's quarters.

"That door won't hold for long," said Valdemar as he and his men hastily threw on what armor they could.

"Out the window, milord," said Larfner. "We'll hold them for a few minutes."

"Right," said the King. "If you get out, make for the wharves and join us. Our thanks, gentlemen."

Valdemar, Esbern, Fengi, and the three other men who had made it inside went out the window. The barred door started shivering under the repeated crashes.

The two fools looked at each other.

"That was my favorite lute," said Larfner. "Now, I'm angry."

"You're wounded," said Gerald suddenly, looking at a section of the other's motley that was rapidly changing color.

Larfner looked down at his side.

"Strange," he said. "When did that happen?"

Then he sagged to the floor, still staring at the stained motley.

Gerald felt for a pulse, then gently closed Larfner's eyes.

"We could have used that third fool, old friend," he said. "No time for extreme unction. I'll pray for you later, if I'm lucky." He pulled Larfner's pack from his shoulders and added it to his own, then took the knife from his hand.

The door crashed into the room. The first Wend through took Larfner's knife in his heart. The next two went down under two quick blows from Gerald's staff. As the rest stumbled over the bodies, Gerald ran to the window, hurling his staff ahead of him. Then he dove through, somersaulting in midair and landing on his feet. He picked up his staff and ran north.

He heard a commotion from a nearby street, and veered toward it. Up ahead of him, Valdemar's party was backed against a warehouse wall, weapons up, surrounded by a squad of Wends wielding axes. Gerald rammed his staff into the back of the neck of the nearest, tripped up two more, and picked up an ax from the ground. Emboldened by his arrival, the Jutlanders attacked. Within a minute, the Wends had fled, leaving nine of their number on the ground.

Valdemar looked at Gerald, who had accounted for two more during the fighting.

"Your friend?" he asked.

"Dead," replied Gerald.

"He died well," said Valdemar.

"Not if they catch you," said Gerald. "Make haste, milord."

"Come with us," urged Valdemar.

"I have no other choice," said Gerald.

They ran to the wharves, then pulled up short. Valdemar's boat had been seized, his crew taken.

"That's not good," said Fengi.

"Well, there's six of us," said Valdemar. "Seven, counting the fool. Let's grab that small boat over there."

"Rowing," sighed Esbern as they climbed into it. "I do detest rowing."

"It's better than dying," said the King as he cut loose the ropes. "Pull for the open sea."

They stayed to the far side of the harbor, hoping to sneak out under the cover of darkness. The alarum was sounded as they were some two hundred yards from shore, and a cluster of torches moved onto a larger boat. But it remained at its wharf.

"Wonder why they aren't following us," said Fengi.

"Well, no matter," said Valdemar. "Considerate of Sveyn to wait until we were done eating before he attacked. At least we'll have enough strength to get out of here. I wish we had some stars to steer by."

"Milord, I think I know why they aren't following us," Gerald began with a sinking feeling.

Then, the storm hit.

ƒIVE

"You cannot speak of reason to the Dane,
And lose your voice."

—*HAMLET*, ACT I, SCENE II

Slesvig—Fyn, 1157 A.D.

They had captured him when he was young. He didn't remember much about the trip north, just a vague memory of being blindfolded and taken onto a boat. They landed after two days at sea, and he was bound and put on a wagon. Throughout the journey, he had but a single thought in his mind: home.

He spent most of his time behind bars. On the rare occasions when they allowed him in the courtyard to exercise, they would blindfold him again and tie a rope to one of his legs so that he couldn't escape.

Then one day, without explanation, they took him out without a blindfold and without a rope. He immediately thought of flight, and waited for a moment when their attention was lax. Then he took off without a second thought.

They did not pursue him. They stood there watching, almost as if they had expected him to do what he was doing.

He didn't know where he was, but his instincts shouted south. He took his bearings from the morning sun and headed in that direction.

He was weak. His muscles were unused to this much exertion. He stopped when he safely could, stole moments of sleep, foraged for what food and water he could find undetected.

Finally, the landscape began to look familiar. Then the long, narrow fjord opened up in front of him. There was an island at its western end that he knew was his destination. He was exhausted, and there was something wrong with his leg, but with one final surge of energy he made it onto the island. His family was there, overjoyed to see him after having given him up for good. A man came in, patted his head, and fiddled with his leg for a moment. It felt normal again. They gave him food, and although he was once again behind walls, his heart surged within his breast because he was home again, and that was the most important thing in the world.

Gorm unrolled the tiny scroll that the carrier pigeon had brought him from his spies in Roskilde. He read it, grunted with surprise, and rushed to find Ørvendil.

From a discreet distance, Terence watched him. He had been trying for several days to devise a way of reading the scrolls before the drost started his daily rounds. The pigeon coop was on top of Gorm's quarters, accessible by a ladder. Unfortunately, this meant that it was visible from just about every watchpost on the island.

Terence sighed, then looked down as something tugged on his hand. Amleth was by his side, looking up at him solemnly.

"Have you been there long?" exclaimed Terence. The boy nodded. "Well, my friend, that was most excellent sneakery. I never even heard you come up. Show me how you did that."

Amleth, delighted to have a skill that Terence didn't, demonstrated his tiptoeing, giggling as the fool tried it, tripped, and fell headlong.

"Not like that?" asked Terence from the ground.

Amleth shook his head. The fool held out his hand for the boy to pull him to his feet.

"All right," said Terence. "You teach me how to do that, and I will show you something in exchange. Let's try it over there." He pointed to Ørvendil's quarters, which Gorm had just entered.

The drost climbed the steps inside and knocked softly on the door.

"What is it?" came the voice of Ørvendil.

"It's me, milord," Gorm whispered.

"Can it wait?" said Ørvendil.

"It's urgent news, milord," said Gorm. "From Roskilde."

There was a rustle of clothing, then the door opened and Ørvendil stood in front of him, looking disheveled.

"What?" he said.

"Milord," began Gorm, then he stopped and gawked as he saw the nude form of Gerutha as she slid her gown on.

Ørvendil glanced behind him, then chuckled.

"The fool was right," he said.

"The fool, milord?" said Gorm in confusion.

"Never mind. What is so important that you must interrupt my slumbers?"

"Begging your pardon, milord, and milady," stammered the drost. "I received word from my man in Roskilde. The whole city is talking of it. King Sveyn has killed the other two kings."

"What?" exclaimed Ørvendil as Gerutha, now dressed, came up to join him. "How?"

"By treachery, milord, and violation of all that is holy. He invited them to dinner to celebrate a duly signed treaty, and had his men attack them."

"And he killed them both there?" wondered Ørvendil. He began pacing in the tiny room.

"Actually, he only killed Knud there," said Gorm.

Ørvendil stopped. "What happened to Valdemar?" he snapped.

"He fought his way clear with a handful of men, but his boat had been taken. He tried to escape in a small boat, but a fierce storm blew up. There was no sign of him after that, but no one could have survived it, according to my man."

"No one but Valdemar," said Ørvendil. "Best seaman I ever saw. It would be easier to drown a fish than to capsize him."

"I am of your mind, milord," said Gorm.

"Was my brother with him?" asked Ørvendil, looking away for a moment.

"I do not know, milord," said Gorm. "I've heard nothing otherwise."

"If Valdemar's alive, then he's on the run," said Gerutha. "Where will he go?"

Ørvendil looked at his drost.

"You're Valdemar, you have no men, and the King is on your tail. Where would you go?"

"Here," said Gorm simply.

Ørvendil nodded. "My thinking as well. Then we shall have to be ready for him."

He turned suddenly and strode over to the window. He looked out to see Terence standing just under it, teaching Amleth the rudiments of juggling with three silk handkerchiefs that wafted slowly in the air.

Amleth looked up and saw his father. He waved merrily. Terence turned and called, "Good day, milord. The boy shows promise. We'll make a fool out of him yet."

"A worthy ambition," replied Ørvendil. "Keep at it, son."

He turned back to his wife and Gorm.

"We will speak of this further," he said. "I'm going to inspect the outer walls. We're vulnerable from several directions now. I don't want to make a move until I know what's become of Valdemar."

"Does anyone," asked Valdemar moodily, "have the slightest idea where we are?"

They had made it through the storm, rowing and bailing without cease as the waves sent them soaring and crashing. Somehow, they had kept the boat from capsizing, but they had been carried into the open sea. It was two days after their escape from Roskilde, and they had yet to see a trace of land or a navigable star. The sun had finally emerged from the banks of clouds that had so recently attacked them, and the Jutlanders squinted and peered at the horizon.

"We've come south, I think," said Fengi. "Judging by the sun, anyway."

"There's something to the west," called Esbern, pointing. "I can't see if it's island or mainland."

"Westward it is," said Valdemar. "Let's take inventory. What supplies have we?"

Sheepishly, the men in the boat held out pouches of gold. Valdemar laughed.

"We are rich indeed," he said. "All we need is someplace to spend it. At least we have weapons and armor. What about water?"

"I filled the skins while I was bailing," said Gerald. "There's enough."

He looked haggard, his makeup for the most part gone, leaving only a few white streaks on his face. The King looked at him thoughtfully.

"You were the only one to think of that, Fool," he said. "We were all remiss."

"Sometimes, when you think you are going to die, you forget what you will need if you are wrong," said Gerald.

"Have you any food?" asked one of the soldiers.

"Let's see," said Gerald, rummaging through his pack and the one he had taken from Larfner. "Here's a loaf of bread. Let me pass around half of that for now. And I will put the rest to good use."

He pulled a length of twine and a small metal hook out of his bag, then attached them to the end of his staff. He baited the hook with a morsel of bread, and dangled it over the side. A minute later he was hauling a good-sized cod into the boat.

"Hope you like it raw," he said, gutting it with his knife.

"You are proving remarkably useful," said Valdemar. "Are you ambitious?"

"I confess to one ambition," said Gerald.

"Out with it."

"I wish to be fool to the king of all the Danes," he said.

"God grant your ambition, Fool," said Valdemar with a smile.

They ate in silence, then picked up their oars.

"Land fall by sundown," said the King. "Then comes the real work."

They made it ashore as the sun hit the far horizon, pulling the boat across the mud flats as shorebirds screamed and flapped furiously about them. When they reached higher ground, they dragged the boat into a thicket and did their best to erase their tracks. Then, to a man, they collapsed.

"Anyone know this place?" asked the King.

"I'm not certain, but I think somewhere on Fyn," said Esbern. "It has the look of the eastern shore."

"Should we make for Odense?" asked Fengi.

Valdemar shook his head. "Sveyn will have sent messengers out yesterday morning. Fyn is under his dominion as much as Sjælland is. If we go to Odense, our heads will be on display in the market by nightfall."

"Where then?" asked Fengi.

"We could take to the water in the morning," said Valdemar. "Head south to Slesvig. With luck, we could reach your brother before Sveyn's messengers do."

"My brother will know by now," said Fengi.

"How?" demanded Valdemar.

"His drost has a spy in Roskilde who sends him messages by pigeon."

"Does he?" mused the King. "Very interesting. Let's assume he does know. Ørvendil is still my vassal."

"Of course," said Fengi, but there was doubt in his voice.

"Either he's still loyal to me, or he will betray me to Sveyn," continued the King.

"Or he'll take advantage of the situation to make his own bid for the throne," said Esbern.

"He wouldn't do that," protested Fengi, but without enthusiasm.

"Do you trust your brother?" asked Valdemar.

Fengi was silent.

"So, there are three possibilities, and two of them are fatal to our cause," concluded Valdemar. "Shall we hazard a throw of the dice on Slesvig?"

"If you do not make the throw, are you still in the game?" asked Gerald.

The others looked at him.

"I don't recall hearing that the fool is part of this council," said Fengi.

"The fool has saved our lives three or four times in the last two days," said Valdemar. "He has earned the right to speak."

"I have a tendency to speak whether I have the right to or not," said Gerald. "I ask you again, if you do not go to Slesvig, can you still survive?"

The others looked at Valdemar.

"If Slesvig is faithful, then I have the best chance of prevailing," said the King. "If not, the rest of my forces would be caught between Sveyn on the north and Slesvig on the south. I would not do well fighting on two fronts."

"Then one out of three is better odds than nothing at all," said Gerald. "Perhaps I could weight the dice in your favor."

"How?" asked Valdemar.

"This had best not involve killing my brother," said Fengi, lurching to his feet.

"If your brother has turned traitor, then his life is forfeit," said Valdemar. "But as deadly as our foolish friend has proved to be, I suspect he has something else in mind."

"I have a friend in Slesvig," said Gerald.

"Let me guess," said Valdemar. "Another fool."

"Yes, sire," said Gerald. "Another fool."

Slowly, a grin crept across Valdemar's face.

Four nights later, Terence helped the tapster heave the last drunken fisherman out of The Viking's Rest, then went to his room in the back, counting his money as he walked. This was why he failed to notice the end of the staff held across his doorway at midshin.

"Careless," commented Father Gerald as Terence went sprawling.

"They would make you sweep out the Guildhall for a month if they caught you like that."

Terence picked himself up, then held up his hand.

"At least I didn't drop any money," he said. "I wasn't expecting to see you so soon. What's up?"

"What have you heard about events in Roskilde?" asked Father Gerald, sitting on the edge of Terence's pallet. He was in monk's garb again, the better to skulk around at night.

"Nothing specific," said Terence. "Gorm got a message by bird a few days ago that sent him scurrying around like a man possessed, and Ørvendil has stepped up the patrols and reinforced the garrison, but no one knows why."

"Any unwinged messengers come in?" asked the priest.

"No, and I've been watching like a hawk," said Terence. "What happened in Roskilde?"

Father Gerald filled him in briefly. Terence gave a low whistle when he heard about Larfner.

"I didn't know the man, of course," he said. "But Kanard spoke quite well of him. I know he's an old friend of yours. I'm sorry, Father."

"So am I," said Father Gerald. "We'll mourn him properly when this is over. In the meanwhile I have become more actively involved than I anticipated when I last spoke to you. Despite the Guild's admonitions, I have become one of Valdemar's protectors."

"Where is he now?"

"In a monastery about five miles from here, along with Ørvendil's brother Fengi and three men. Esbern the Quick is living up to his name by running north to rally the troops and bring his family's power into play. But the key to success may be right here in Slesvig. If the King comes here, will he live through the night?"

Terence frowned.

"I haven't been here that long," he said. "But if I was a betting man, I would say yes."

Father Gerald seized the fool's hand, covering the coins in it.

"Bet," he commanded.

"Maybe I could level the field first," said Terence. "Do you want to stay here?"

"No, I need to report back," said Father Gerald. "I will return tomorrow night."

He opened the shutters and peeped outside, then climbed through the window

"Where shall we meet?" asked Terence.

"I'll find you," said the priest as he vanished into the night.

"I'm sure of that," muttered Terence as he closed his shutters. He yawned. One day's notice to save the world, he thought. Better get some sleep.

He came to the island just before dawn, much earlier than his usual time. The guards at the drawbridge were surprised to see him at that hour, but admitted him without question.

Instead of heading toward Ørvendil's quarters in the rear of the island, he climbed the ladders to the top platform at the front, greeting the archers by name as he passed them.

Ørvendil was on the top platform, as Terence expected, looking across the fjord at the rising sun. Mists billowed across the waters, broken by the masts of the fishing boats. Gulls swooped in and out of sight, calling to each other.

Terence joined Ørvendil and looked east.

"I can't see him," he said.

"See who?" asked Ørvendil without turning his head.

"Whoever it is that you think is coming," said the fool.

"Who do I think is coming?" asked Ørvendil.

"The rumor is that it's Valdemar," said the fool.

"The rumor is wrong," said Ørvendil.

Terence shrugged.

"It matters not to me," he said. "But if Valdemar is on the way, I would be glad to entertain at the feast."

"There is no feast," said Ørvendil.

"Then I'll entertain at the famine," said Terence. "I am not particular."

"I say again that Valdemar is not coming," said Ørvendil.

"I will make a wager that you are wrong," said Terence.

"Are you a betting man?" asked Ørvendil.

"Not until just recently," replied Terence. "Would one as mighty as you take a fool's wager?"

"Hmm," mused Ørvendil. "I have learned in my life that betting with men that I do not know well is a losing proposition."

"Wise policy," said Terence. "So, you reject a fool's gold. Copper, anyway."

"I am saving you from folly," said Ørvendil. "Valdemar will not be coming here or anywhere ever again. I have information that he is dead."

"Do you?" said Terence. "And if that is the case, how does Ørvendil? Aren't you honor bound to avenge him?"

"He charged me with the care of Slesvig and its people," said Ørvendil. "I would be betraying that trust if I led them into a futile battle."

"Wise politics," said Terence. "I see that you have become something other than a simple warrior."

"War is never simple," said Ørvendil.

"What if Sveyn brings the war here?" asked Terence.

"Are you planning to flee?" asked Ørvendil.

"My instinct is to run from war," said Terence. "But my loyalty is to a two-year-old boy."

"Would you risk your life to save Amleth?" asked Ørvendil in surprise.

"He is worth saving," said Terence simply. "He will become a great man, and a good one. Given the right man to emulate, of course."

"Meaning you, I suppose."

"No, milord," said Terence. "Meaning yourself."

Ørvendil looked out across the fjord. The mists began to dissipate as the sun rose higher in the sky.

"You overpraise me, Fool," he said softly. "Why are you here so early? You're never up before midmorning. What is your mission here?"

"To remind you of your true self, milord," said the fool. "That is the mission of every fool."

"Is it?" wondered Ørvendil. "Are there many like yourself?"

"There are fools beyond counting in this world," said Terence. "But only a few like myself. Coincidentally, I spoke with one of them just last night."

"Where was he from?" asked Ørvendil.

"Roskilde," replied Terence.

Ørvendil looked at him sharply, but the fool stood smiling serenely, his eyes closed, as the sunlight warmed his limbs. Then he opened them and looked at the lord of the stockade.

"I rarely see the sun rise," he said. "It's a wondrous thing to see a new day, is it not? Well, milord, I must go see my master. He tells me that there will be some other boys coming to play today. I have brought a football along for the occasion. Things should be quite lively. Come and join us, if you can spare the time."

He stepped over to the pole supporting the platform and slid down.

Ørvendil watched the fishermen ply their nets as the mists cleared, then turned and looked north across the town that was beginning to wake, and beyond to the outlying hills where the shepherds had been up since dawn, and past them to where he knew his outposts had been watching through the night. No signal fires on the horizon. Not yet.

He climbed down the ladders, not wishing to imitate Terence's methods this time. The cooking fires were going, and the smell of fresh baked bread pervaded the fortress. He swung by the kitchen to grab a piece, then went to his quarters.

Amleth was already out and running, kicking the ball to Terence. The fool could juggle with his feet as well as his hands, observed Ørvendil. He watched Terence kick the ball in the air a dozen times without letting it touch the ground. Amleth looked at him in awe.

Gorm emerged from the great hall. Ørvendil beckoned to the drost, and they entered Ørvendil's quarters.

Gerutha was there, gathering flowers she had picked into a vase.

"What is it?" she asked, catching sight of Ørvendil's expression.

"Valdemar is coming here, possibly today," said Ørvendil.

"How do you know this?" asked Gorm. "I've had no information about it."

"You have your birds, I have mine," said Ørvendil. "It was an unusual source, but one that I trust. So we must choose our path."

"Choose?" exclaimed Gerutha. "You have already chosen. You wanted to become king. There were three kings in the way. Now, one of them is gone, and one is about to place himself in your hands. Give him to Sveyn, and you eliminate your greatest rival."

"And Sveyn will become your ally," said Gorm. "Which will give you access to Roskilde, something that is denied to you now."

"The path is not yet chosen," said Ørvendil. "There have been things said, desires expressed, all as to what if? It is easier to speculate when the choice is not available, the paths yet unseen."

"But this was what you wanted," urged Gerutha. "This is what we all wanted. We have been waiting for years for just such an opportunity, and now it has been placed before you."

"It can only be the divine will of God at work," said Gorm, clasping his hands piously.

"For God's sake, just make up your mind," said Gerutha.

Ørvendil looked back and forth at the two of them, their faces distorted in his eyes by their ambition. Do I look like that? he wondered.

"Sometimes I think that God gives us choices only to test us," he said. "When I had no choice, I wanted what I did not have. Gorm, my friend. You said that Sveyn had violated all that is holy when he betrayed his brother kings, and more importantly his guests. What will be said of me if I betray the man who trusted me with part of his kingdom?"

"That you slew a traitor," said Gorm. "And in doing so removed the last obstacle to peace in Denmark, something that has eluded us for years. You will be praised. The people will carry you on their shoulders to Roskilde."

"Perhaps," mused Ørvendil. "Or perhaps they will rise against me as a despot."

He heard a movement behind him, and turned toward the doorway. His son stood there, looking at him, hugging a football to his tiny chest.

"Hello, son," said Ørvendil, squatting down to face him.

"Play with me?" pleaded the boy.

There were shouts of children outside.

"Your friends are here?" asked Ørvendil.

Amleth nodded solemnly.

"It's good to have friends," said Ørvendil. Suddenly he placed his hands on the boy's shoulders. Amleth, startled, looked up at his father's eyes.

"Friends are important, Amleth," said Ørvendil. "A true friend will stand by you under any circumstance, no matter what. And all you have to do in exchange is exactly the same. Do you understand me?"

Amleth shook his head. Ørvendil smiled sadly.

"You will in time," he said. "Run out and play. I'll be with you shortly."

Amleth dashed outside, and his shrieks soon joined those of the other two boys. Ørvendil stood and faced his wife and drost.

"I've made my decision," he said.

Outside, Terence crouched by Amleth as they faced off against the other two boys in a game they had devised on the spot.

"Did you go see your father like I asked?" he whispered.

Amleth nodded.

"Is he coming out to play with us?"

Amleth nodded again.

Terence smiled, satisfied.

"Well done, my boy," he said. "Well done indeed."

Ⓢ IX

*"When the blood burns, how prodigal the soul
Lends the tongue vows."*

—*HAMLET*, ACT I, SCENE III

Slesvig—Viborg, 1157 A.D.

Valdemar, Fengi, and the three soldiers trudged toward Slesvig's east-ernmost gate, weapons loose in their belts. Ahead of them an unusually large number of soldiers manned the earthenworks, watching them approach.

"Are you quite sure this is a good idea?" muttered Fengi to the King.

"The fool said it was safe," said Valdemar.

"And you trust the fool," said Fengi.

"Don't you?" asked Valdemar.

"No," said Fengi. "And even if I did, I would wonder if he himself had been fooled."

"Always a possibility," said Valdemar cheerfully. "Let's go."

Suddenly a company of horsemen poured through the gates, fully armored, their spears leveled. They galloped toward the King's party.

"Milord?" said Fengi, reaching for his sword.

"Be still," commanded the King, and he stepped forward to face the oncoming troops.

The horsemen wheeled and encircled the party, then came to a stop. Their leader looked at Valdemar, then dismounted and removed his helm.

"Sire," said Ørvendil, kneeling and holding his sword hilt-first to the King. "Welcome home. Praised be to God that you lived."

Valdemar took the sword and held it aloft. There was cheering from the horsemen, echoed by the soldiers on the walls.

"Rise, my friend," he said. "I trust that everything is well?"

"I have kept your birthplace safe for your return," said Ørvendil. "Please, take my horse."

He led the steed to the King and handed him the reins. Valdemar mounted, then started toward the town. The three soldiers mounted behind three horsemen, and the company followed the King.

"And what about me?" demanded Fengi, still standing.

Ørvendil looked at him in surprise.

"Oh, so you're here now?" he said. "Sorry, I didn't bring enough horses."

Then he roared with laughter at the chagrined expression on his brother's face.

"Come, little brother," he said, throwing an arm around the latter's shoulders. "I shall walk with you. I want you to tell me everything about your adventures since we last saw you."

His brother stood rigid at the touch, then slowly relaxed.

"Well, we were on Lolland when we heard about the treaty," he began, and the two of them walked into Slesvig.

At the great hall on the island, dinner was waiting. Gerutha herself waited upon Valdemar, selecting the choicest morsels for his bowl. The two brothers flanked the King, and Ørvendil's men filled the room.

"I must say that I have become chary of dinners in great halls," commented Valdemar.

"One could scarce blame you after your recent perils," said Ørvendil. "If you like, I will taste your meal for you."

"No need," said the King. "If I was meant to die at your hands, it would have happened before now."

There was a brief hush at these words as the soldiers looked to the head of the table. Gerutha went pale for a moment, then regained her composure.

"Let me be the taster to the King," she said softly, plucking a piece of bread and dipping it in Valdemar's bowl. She popped it into her mouth, swallowed it, and smiled.

"Forgive me, lady," said the King. "I am weary past exhaustion, and my thoughts were not meant to insult your hospitality, however clumsily they were expressed. My love and trust have not been misplaced in your good husband."

There was a commotion at the other end of the room, and a pair of fools burst in.

"I told you there was food!" cried Terence in delight. "Look, Gerald, a feast!"

"But is there ale?" wondered Gerald. "I have been forced to drink water for several days running, and that is hard on a man."

"If you were running for several days at sea, then you deserved what you got," scoffed Terence. "Despite your good opinion of yourself, you can't run on water. Next time stay on the boat." He walked to the head of the table and bowed to the King. "Your Majesty, you are welcome in Slesvig. I have heard that you brought a fool with you on your journey, and he did not entertain you even once. He is a disgrace to our entire profession, milord, but I propose to make up for it now."

"Very good, Fool," said Valdemar. "We could use a laugh or two."

"Two, milord?" said Gerald. "We shall have that in a matter of seconds."

And they did, followed by many more.

For the finale, Terence stood in the center of the hall with his drum at his belt.

"Milords and miladies," he said, beginning a drumroll. "It is my pleasure tonight to introduce to you a performer of such skill, such courage, and such precocity that I myself must kneel before him."

Gerald stepped forward and began to bow. Terence grabbed him by the seat of his motley and pulled him back.

"Not you," Terence said, and Gerald made an expression of exaggerated bewilderment. "May I present to you the astonishing skills of . . . Amleth!"

Amleth ran to the center of the room, stood before Terence and Gerald, and bowed to the head of the table. The room applauded, laughing at the child before he had even begun.

With a look of intense concentration, he took the three silk handkerchiefs that Terence had given him and held them up. Then he tossed one into the air over his head. As it floated down, he tossed the second, then the third. He caught the first, tossed it again, and repeated the action with the others. After five rounds of this, he plucked them from the air, then held his arms out, grinning madly.

"Well done, boy!" shouted his father, beating his fists on the table.

"Very impressive, child," applauded Valdemar. He dug into his pouch and pulled out a penny. "Come, you have made your mark as a performer."

"That's no mark, that's a penny," said Gerald.

Amleth walked up and took the coin, his eyes wide as it caught the light. Then he scampered back to the fools.

"Look, Yorick," he said excitedly.

"Congratulations," beamed Terence, hugging the boy. "You were superb."

"Quite promising," said Gerald. "You should go to your mother now. Buy some sweets in town tomorrow. You've earned them."

Amleth ran under the table to the other side and hugged his mother. He waved to the room as she carried him out.

"Now that the entertainment is over, we must to business," said Valdemar. "It is only a matter of time before Sveyn sends his troops across the straits to Jutland. We must make ready for them."

Terence, now playing his lute softly at the other end of the hall, nudged Gerald as Gerutha silently slipped back in.

"More interested in the war council than in her own son," he muttered.

"So I see," said Gerald. "Interesting."

"How soon before Sveyn makes his move?" asked Ørvendil.

"My source says he's spent the last three days celebrating his victory," said Gorm. "It will be at least that long before he learns that you are still alive, sire."

"Good. That will buy us some time to put our armies together," said Valdemar.

"I will lead the army of Slesvig north," declared Ørvendil.

"No, you won't," said Valdemar.

Ørvendil sat there, looking stunned.

"But, sire," he protested.

"Hear me out," said Valdemar, silencing him with a gesture. "I must think of all of Denmark, not just myself. Word will reach the Holsteiners and the Wends of what has happened here. They may take advantage of our disorder to attempt to seize Slesvig. I need you here, Ørvendil. It will do me no good if I defeat Sveyn and have nothing left to rule. Give me half your troops, but keep the other half and defend our borders."

"Half my troops are yours," said Ørvendil. "And I will give you a man worth all of them. Gorm, you are to go with the King."

"Good, milord," replied Gorm. "I shall serve him as I do you."

"Better, we hope," muttered Terence. Gorm looked around uncertainly for a moment, then turned back to the King.

"Then we leave in the morning," said Valdemar. "We shall unite at Viborg with my men and those loyal to Esbern and the Hvides."

"That won't give you enough to meet Sveyn head on," said Ørvendil.

"No," said Valdemar. "But I shall double the size of my army by just one day's work."

"What sorcery will you use to accomplish that trick?" asked Fengi.

"Just watch," said Valdemar. "You'll see."

Valdemar slept in Ørvendil's bed, while the lord of the fortress made his preparations in the room below.

"One door closes, and then the other one closes as well," said Gerutha bitterly as they spread fresh straw on the clay floor and covered it with a woolen blanket. "Now, you can never gain Sveyn's love, and you seem to have lost Valdemar's trust as well. Protect our borders my foot. He doesn't want you anywhere near him. Instead of having one or the other, now you have neither."

"At least I have you," said Ørvendil sleepily.

She snorted and rolled onto her side, her back to her husband.

She woke with the sunrise, slipped on her gown, and left her husband snoring on the floor. She walked back to her flower garden and stared moodily at the roses. They were spindly things, clinging to a dilapidated trellis, fighting for their few minutes in the sun. She sighed and began pulling weeds.

"Good morning, sister," said Fengi, standing at the foot of the garden.

She stood hastily, wiping her hands on her apron.

"Good morning, brother," she said. "I did not hear you approach. You are up early. The other men are all sleeping off the feast."

"I never sleep well here," he replied. "I decided to walk around the place. Those platforms at the front are new."

"Yes," she said. "They can hold more bowmen than the old ones. He's even thinking of building a catapult."

"But where will he get the stones to throw?" asked Fengi. "Just like big brother to come up with a grandiose plan like that without thinking it all the way through."

"And that's not even the most . . ." she stopped herself in midthought.

He looked at her curiously.

"You seem almost . . ." he began, then he stopped as well.

"Seem what?" she asked.

"It is not my place to say," he said.

"You are my husband's brother," she said. "Speak your mind. I seem almost what?"

"Disappointed," he said.

"How could I possibly be disappointed? I have all of this," she laughed, sweeping her arms over the garden.

"Still," he said.

She looked at him. So like his brother, she thought, yet so unlike as well. A leaner man, a shorter one, certainly, yet he exuded an aura of power far beyond that of her husband. It was no surprise that, of the two of them, Fengi would be the one at Valdemar's side.

"I remember the day you first came here," he said suddenly.

"It wasn't that long ago," she said.

"Six years," he said. "I was seventeen, in charge of the patrols on the western road. I was there when your carriage came up."

"I remember," she said. "You escorted us to town."

"One carriage holding a lady, and three carts carrying her belongings. I remember thinking to myself, 'Three carts! She owns more things than half the women in town put together. Won't she be in for a shock when she gets to Slesvig!' You came to the front of the carriage as it drew near, and I got a good look at your expression when you saw the town for the first time."

"What was it like?" she asked.

He looked at her.

"Like the one you had last night when Valdemar told my brother to stay behind," he said softly.

"Is it wrong to want glory for one's husband?" she asked stiffly.

"Is that what it was?" he asked in return.

"Of course," she replied.

"Then forgive my curiosity, sister," he said, bowing slightly. "Now, I must beg my leave. There are preparations to be made."

He turned to leave.

"Fengi," she said softly.

He turned back to look at her, and she found herself blushing.

"God be with you," she said, holding out her hand. "You will be in my prayers."

He took it, then brought it to his lips.

"Thank you, Gerutha," he said, holding her gaze with his own. Then he let go of her hand and walked away.

Unseen by both of them, Amleth watched from the rear doorway of the great hall, munching on some fresh baked bread with honey. As his uncle passed the corner, the boy took off through the interior of the building, emerging from the front entrance. He rounded the corner just in time to collide with Fengi.

"Uncle!" he said gleefully, holding up his arms.

Fengi looked down at him curiously.

"You have my mother's face, did you know that?" he said.

Amleth shook his head. Fengi squatted to face him.

"She died when I was a boy, not much older than you," he said. "But I remember her. Your smile is like hers."

He gave the boy an awkward pat on the head, then straightened up and continued walking. Amleth scampered alongside of him, laboring to keep pace.

"I enjoyed your performance last night, nephew," said Fengi. "You and that fool must spend a lot of time with each other. What's his name?"

"Yorick," said Amleth.

"Yorick," repeated Fengi thoughtfully. "What's he like?"

"He's a funny man," said Amleth enthusiastically.

"So you like him," said Fengi. "He's a fool, you know."

Amleth nodded.

"Do you want to be a fool or a warrior when you grow up?" asked Fengi.

Amleth looked confused.

"Oddly enough, in the last few days, I have met warriors who were actually fools, and a fool who was actually a warrior," said Fengi.

They had reached the drawbridge, which was being lowered. They watched it together.

"Good-bye, nephew," said Fengi. "Say your prayers and mind your mother. Give her a kiss from me, will you?"

"I will," said Amleth. "Bye, uncle."

He waved as Fengi walked across the bridge. His uncle did not look back.

Amleth ran back to the garden where his mother had finished with her flowers. He threw his arms around her. Laughing, she picked him up and hugged him. He kissed her on the cheek.

"And good morning to you," she said, kissing him back.

"That was from Uncle Fengi," he said proudly.

She smiled. "Was it now?" she said. "Well, this is from me."

She kissed him again, and all was well with his world.

Ørvendil and Gerutha escorted Valdemar to the head of the company assembled for him. Gorm and Fengi stood at the front. Valdemar turned to his hosts.

"I thank you, my friends, for your hospitality," he said. "It shall not be forgotten."

"We are but servants in your house, sire," said Gerutha.

"We will keep your kingdom safe," said Ørvendil. "God be with you."

Valdemar embraced them, then mounted his horse. "We march north to Viborg," he told the men. "There we will be joined by our brothers. Together, we shall meet the Devil on the field of battle. When victory is ours, Denmark shall be one. Are you with me?"

"Milord, not since Jason set sail on the *Argo* has such a band of heroes assembled," cried Gorm. "Praised be our Lord and King, Valdemar!"

"Valdemar!" shouted the men.

"Listen to Gorm," marveled Terence at the rear of the crowd. "He had the makings of a military toady all this time, and I never knew."

"Denmark shall be one," said Gerald. "One what, I wonder?"

"Well, good luck, fellow fool," said Terence. "I'll stay here where it's safe."

"Thank you," said Gerald. "One bit of advice."

"What?"

"Be careful about Amleth. It's good that you've taken to each other so well. But don't forget that he already has parents. For better or for worse, they should be the ones raising him, not you."

"I know," said Terence. "I just want..."

"You want them to raise him the way you would if you were his

[72]

father," said Gerald. "I understand. But you could end up driving a wedge between them, especially when the boy is this young."

"I'll be careful," promised Terence. "You be the same."

"I'm marching headlong into war," grumbled Gerald. "The time to be careful has long passed."

They clasped hands, and Gerald hurried to catch up with the army.

Ørvendil and Gerutha watched from the foot of the drawbridge until the last soldier had disappeared, then walked back into the great hall, now deserted. He took her hand. She pulled it back and walked away from him.

"I will build you a castle," he said. "I promise."

"Out of what?" she said. "There's not enough stone in Slesvig, and you don't have the money to bring it in."

She went out the rear door. He watched her, then turned toward the front. Then he stopped and looked down at the hard clay floor.

"Maybe not," he said. "But there are other ways."

Two armies assembled outside the cathedral in Viborg that October, eyeing each other uneasily. Many had faced each other on the field of battle, and were tensed for another fight now.

Inside, the banns were read, and a young priest stepped forward and presided over the marriage of a couple who had met only minutes before. He took their hands and pressed them together, then blessed the union before a heavily armed congregation.

When it was over, Valdemar stepped into the aisle. He was joined by Esbern, Fengi, Gorm, and several captains from the army that had served the late King Knud.

The young priest joined them.

"Not bad for your first wedding, Axel," said Valdemar. "Thank you for performing it."

"Impressive command of Latin, little brother," said Esbern. "Father will be pleased that your studies were not wasted."

"The Bishop didn't look too happy that I was performing his duties in his cathedral," observed Axel, who was strapping armor over his cassock.

"Don't worry," said Valdemar. "If I become king of all Denmark, I will make you bishop here."

"If you become king of all Denmark, I will be going with you," replied Axel. "I don't want to miss the fun."

"Then I'll make you bishop of Roskilde," promised Valdemar. "As soon as the old one goes to Heaven."

"I hear he is ailing," said Axel. "I will pray for his recovery."

A throat was cleared behind them. Valdemar glanced back and managed not to wince.

"I almost forgot," he said. "Will you excuse us for a while?"

They bowed, and he beckoned to his new bride. She took his hand with a look of wolfish anticipation, and he led her out of the cathedral to the cheers of both armies.

"Did you see her face?" said Esbern. "He must really want to be king."

"Sacrifices must be made when you take the throne," said Axel. "Let us await the consummation."

They stood outside with the men, watching a small house near the cathedral. About half an hour went by, then Valdemar emerged, fully armored, and waved a bloody sheet. The men cheered.

"Men of Denmark," cried Valdemar. "I have taken the Princess Sophie to wife."

There were more cheers at this statement of the obvious.

"The making of this match was the last action of the late King Knud," he said. "His sister is now my wife, under my protection. His family is now mine." He stopped and looked at the army of the late king. Then he took a deep breath and shouted, "And the debt owed to his blood is now mine!"

There was a deep-throated roar of approval.

"South of here lies the moor known as Grathe," continued Valdemar. "Our scouts report that Sveyn Peder, the murderer, is hoping to lead his army through there in the hope of catching us unawares. We shall meet him on Grathe Moor. Our armies combined cannot be anything but victorious. And when we are, peace will be celebrated across all of Denmark. Go bravely into battle, not for revenge, but for peace, my friends, and we shall begin a new golden age together."

He strode through the armies, banging his sword on his shield. Behind him, his new bride watched from a window, a slight smile upon her lips.

A day later, King Sveyn Peder staggered through a bog, his shield gone, his sword notched, an arrow wound in his thigh. His men had been routed, and he himself had turned and run in full view of the opposing armies. He had somehow managed to evade capture, but was lost on ground that was both hostile and unpleasantly soggy.

He cried out with relief when he reached solid ground, and nearly collapsed in exhaustion. There was a road ahead. Roads were good things. It meant he could escape back to the harbor where his navy awaited him, and once he had reached them, he could reassemble his men. He wasn't defeated, not yet.

He knew that there would be patrols searching for him. He thought of waiting until darkness to continue, but then he saw salvation in the guise of an old monk, plodding along the road, leaning heavily on an oaken staff.

Sveyn burst out of the woods, his sword out.

"Hold, Father," he commanded.

The monk stopped.

"How can I help you, my son?" he asked solicitously. "You are wounded. I have some small skill in healing, if you will permit me."

"You have something I value even more highly," said Sveyn.

"What could that be?" asked the monk.

"Your cassock and cowl," said the King. "Give them to me."

"That I cannot do, my son," said the monk. "They are the uniform of my order. I cannot let another take them."

"I was not asking," snarled Sveyn, bringing up his sword. Then he howled in pain as the monk, with speed belying his years, stepped inside his swing, seized his sword hand with one hand and his elbow with the other, then twisted the arm back. There was a crack, then Sveyn dropped the sword, clutching his now useless right arm.

"Broken, I should think," said the monk. "How about some of that healing I mentioned?"

Sveyn growled and reached for the sword with his left hand. The monk sighed, then picked up his staff and swung. There was another crack, and Sveyn fell to his knees.

"Instead of the healing, sire, perhaps you should consider confession," said the monk.

Sveyn looked up at him, comprehension dawning on his face.

"You know me," he said.

"Yes, milord," said Gerald, pushing back his cowl. "And you know me as well."

Sveyn stared dumbly.

"You're the fool," he exclaimed in bewilderment.

"When I was with you, I was a fool," said Gerald. "But I am also a priest. I will give you the opportunity that you did not give so many that fatal night in August—to clear your soul and make your peace with God. Will you make confession, milord?"

"Damn you!" shouted the King, trying to pick up the sword once again.

"Your death is required, I'm afraid," said Gerald gently as he snatched the King's sword from the ground.

"I thought that priests were not allowed to spill blood," whined the King in desperation.

"I'm not that kind of priest," replied Gerald. "Please believe me when I say that revenge for my friend Larfner is not my reason for killing you."

He swung the sword once, and Sveyn's head was separated from his neck.

"But, sadly enough, vengeance has been satisfied," said Gerald. He knelt by the corpse and administered extreme unction. Then he tossed the sword by the body, pulled his cowl back over his head, and walked away.

$\mathcal{S}$EVEN

"Or if thou wilt needs marry, marry a fool..."

—*HAMLET*, ACT III, SCENE I

Slesvig, 1157 A.D.

There are times when people become weary of fools. Terence knew this well enough to make sure that he occasionally spent time outside of Slesvig, wandering the villages under its dominion, juggling for meals and singing for a night's lodging in a hayloft. He would return from these sojourns refreshed, and the quiet in the town left by his absence made the noise of his presence all the more welcome.

And there are times when fools become weary of themselves. When he wanted peace and quiet, he would make the two-hour trek west to Magnus's farm. There he would walk with the farmer and discuss whatever topics came to mind without feeling the need to perform. Or he would share the chore at hand, basking in the simplicity of accomplishing a necessary task. Gorm had arranged for him to be followed on these occasional visits, but the spy observed nothing illicit, and casual questioning of the farmer revealed only information about growing barley and rye. A great deal of information about growing barley and rye, as Magnus was a garrulous man on that subject. The spy eventually gave up.

Terence knew about the spy, of course, but worried neither about him nor any other attempt by Gorm to learn more about him. A handful of people now knew of his connection to the Roskilde fool, but few knew more than that, and those who did found it useful to keep that knowledge quiet.

On an unusually moderate day in early December, Terence lay his cloak down on the meadow near the watering hole where he first met Magnus, then stretched out on his back. Magnus was in his barn, slaughtering pigs for the smokehouse, a task Terence begged off from joining. He lay there, half asleep, listening to the breeze whistle through the brush on the windbreak.

When the woman first appeared, Terence thought that he dreamt her. She was looking behind her as she clambered up to the top of the windbreak, and the wind was sending her hair streaming toward him, almost as if the hair itself had taken her captive and was dragging her away. She turned to look ahead too late to avoid an exposed root directly in her path. It sent her somersaulting through the high grass and weeds anchoring the windbreak on the side by the farm, her arms flailing about in an effort to slow her fall. She met the level ground with a thump.

By that time Terence was up and running to her aid. She was sprawled on the ground, her eyes closed, breathing rapidly. He felt for her pulse, then looked down at her face that, despite being smudged and slightly scratched, or possibly because of being smudged and slightly scratched, appeared to him to be quite lovely.

At that moment her eyes opened to behold the whiteface of the fool, his hair sticking out at odd angles from beneath his cap and bells. She looked at him quizzically.

"Have I stumbled upon some hidden fairyland?" she asked him. "Or is this a dream?"

"I know it isn't a fairyland," he replied. "I'm no longer certain about the dream, but which of us is the dreamer?"

"I did bump my head, I think," she said. "That would make me the more likely candidate."

"Ah, but I am a fool," he said. "We never know the difference, anyway."

"I have never dreamt of a fool before," she said. "Do you ever dream of women?"

"Often," he replied, laughing.

"Then perhaps this is your dream," she said. "Rather ungallant of you to cause me to trip and fall like that."

"My apologies," he said. "Are you all right?"

"I think so," she said, sitting up and rubbing her head ruefully. "My pride is hurt."

"I think that you no longer have any pride," he said.

"Why is that?"

"It is said that pride goeth before a fall," he replied. "Since you have just fallen, your pride must have gone on ahead."

"Alas, I am a fallen woman," she sighed. "How embarrassing to tumble like that before a professional tumbler like yourself. You must teach me how to do it better."

"It wasn't bad for an amateur," he said critically. "Remember to tuck your head under next time, and practice, practice, practice."

She started to laugh, a deep merriment from within. He held out his hand and pulled her to her feet.

"Is this your farm?" she asked, looking around.

"No," he said. "It belongs to my friend Magnus. But I'm sure that he wouldn't mind you falling on it."

"Could he hide me, do you think?" she asked, suddenly serious. "I could earn my keep. I know farms. I grew up on one."

"Why do you need to hide?" he asked.

"I ran away," she said. "They'll find me. They always do."

"Who?" he asked.

"My family," she said. "They are escorting me to Slesvig to marry me to someone I have never met."

"Without your consent?" he exclaimed.

She looked down.

"I did consent," she said in a small voice. "I thought I would be out from under my father's thumb at last. But I didn't want to come here so soon. I wanted to spend one last Christmas with my sister and her children. They are the only ones I really cared about, and now I may never see them again. And I miss the fields and the forests near my home. I have spent so much time wandering them on my own that I am fearful of being in a city with so many people."

"Slesvig isn't that large," he said.

"Do you know it well?" she asked.

"I am the town fool," he said.

"Then why are you here?"

"Obviously, so that I may come to your aid," he replied.

She smiled shyly.

"Maybe Slesvig will not be such a terrible place after all," she said. "If a man of this quality is only the town fool, what paragons must the others be?"

"Never judge a town by its fool," he admonished her. Then he stopped as the sound of hoofbeats came from the distance.

"Damn," she muttered. "Time to face my fate. It has been a pleasant idyll with you, good sir. What is your name?"

"It depends on who is talking to me," he said. "Most of Slesvig calls me Yorick. It's not my name, but it stuck."

"What do you wish me to call you?" she asked.

He hesitated. "Terence," he said. "It would sound lovely coming from you."

"Terence," she repeated. "My name is Signe. And that is my father galloping toward us."

Signe's sire was clearly a man given to temper, and the sight of his runaway daughter brushing grass and leaves from the back of her gown while in the company of a strange man did nothing to improve his disposition.

"Get away from her, thrall!" he shouted, uncoiling a whip as he directed his horse toward them.

"I'm not a thrall, I'm a fool," protested Terence as he stepped to the side.

The father turned his attentions to Signe.

"Is this the sort of man you consort with when you run away?" he snarled. He snapped the whip toward her. She stood without flinching, awaiting contact, but Terence stepped between them and blocked it with a juggling club.

"Don't do that," he implored the man. "Your daughter is innocent of any dalliance, you have my word."

"The word of a fool?" laughed the father. He lashed out at Terence. The fool ducked quickly under the whip and jumped up on the horse behind him.

"Don't do that again," he said quietly, pinioning the man's arms with his own. "It would be a simple thing for me to inflict a great deal of pain upon you right now, but I do not wish to distress this lady any further. Drop the whip."

The father hesitated, then yelped suddenly and let the whip fall to the ground. Terence smiled.

"There," he said. "Now we can all get along."

"I will report your insolence to the Duke," sputtered the father.

"If you are referring to Ørvendil, I can assure you that he is quite used to my insolence," replied Terence. "I am in the garrison every day, solely for the purpose of being insolent. His son Amleth regards me as a personal favorite. If you wish to report to Ørvendil how you were bested by an unarmed fool on the road, be my guest. Is that still your wish?"

The other remained silent.

"Good," said Terence. "I take it that you have more people coming?"

"I left them about a league back," muttered the father. "They should be here shortly."

"Then I suggest for all of your sakes that you put a good face on this," suggested Terence. "You don't want a scandal involving your daughter to precede her into Slesvig, do you?"

"No," said the father.

"I didn't think so," said Terence. "I am going to release you. Don't try anything funny. That's my job, and I dislike competitors."

He let the man go and jumped off the horse. He picked up the whip and hefted it. Then he flicked it forward. The end stopped just in front of the man's nose.

"I'm a little rusty," said Terence to Signe. "I meant to be half an inch closer." He coiled the whip and tucked the end into his belt.

"Would it be unfilial of me to say that I am sorry that you missed?" whispered Signe.

The rest of her party arrived before Terence could reply. The female thrall in the carriage looked at her mistress and clucked in distress.

"Better get in, lady," she said. "I'll have you presentable by the time we reach the town."

Terence held out his hand. She took it and climbed into the carriage, sighing reluctantly.

"Will I see you in Slesvig?" she asked as they pulled away.

"I will be back on the morrow," he called. "I am in the fort most days, and The Viking's Rest most nights. Tumble in anytime."

He heard her laugh, and watched the carriage until it disappeared around a bend. Magnus came up, wiping his bloody hands with a rag. He looked at the retreating carriage.

"The meal is ready," he said. "Who was that?"

"That was trouble," said Terence admiringly.

Signe and her father reached the island fort later that afternoon. Gerutha hurried to greet them.

"My dear cousin," she cried upon seeing Signe. "How you have grown since we last met."

"Greetings, Gerutha," said her father. "Here is my last daughter. Take her off my hands with my thanks."

"And mine," muttered Signe.

"We were expecting you yesterday," said Gerutha. "Was there any trouble?"

Signe's father started for a moment, then looked at his daughter, who smiled at him.

"No," he said. "No trouble. I must be on my way."

"Surely you could stay the night," protested Gerutha.

"No, cousin," he said firmly. "I have wasted enough time on this journey. Take your things, daughter, and I will take my leave of you."

"A fair exchange," said Signe as a soldier took two small trunks from the rear of the carriage. "Good-bye, father."

He raised his hand in a halfhearted salute, then turned his horse and trotted off, the carriage and escort following.

"Come, cousin," said Gerutha, taking the younger woman's arm. "I have put you in our lower room for now. Come wash the dust off your face, and we shall talk until dinner."

"I should pay my respects to your husband," said Signe. "And to my own, I suppose."

"Ørvendil is supervising repairs on the southern earthenworks," said Gerutha. "He should be back for dinner. As for your husband-to-be, he is at the coronation of King Valdemar in Roskilde. We expect him to return in a day or two."

There was a basin and a clean cloth on the table in the lower room. Signe scrubbed her face clean as Gerutha watched her.

"You've turned out prettier than I thought you would," said Gerutha. "All that walking about in the woods must agree with you."

"I shall miss my walks," said Signe. "Are there any woods nearby?"

"My dear girl, you are going to be married to the drost," laughed Gerutha. "Someone in your position can hardly go traipsing about unescorted."

"I don't traipse," said Signe.

Gerutha sighed.

"Listen to me," she said. "Since we are to be living together inside these walls, I want you to regard me as a sister and a friend. You are no longer a little girl who may do as she pleases. You are becoming a wife to a man of considerable rank who is respected by all. You must respect him as well and do his bidding. You were lucky I thought of you when my husband decided to arrange his marriage."

"Thank you," said Signe. "What may I do to help you around here until that happy day?"

"Let me show you my gardens," said Gerutha cheerfully.

She led Signe to the rear of the fort and pointed proudly to her roses.

"These were next to nothing when I first arrived," she said. "Now, see how they thrive. There's no flowers right now, of course, but in the spring, they should be glorious."

"They are very nice," said Signe politely. She looked over at the herb garden, which was desiccated and strewn with dead weeds. She knelt and crumbled some soil between her fingers.

"With you doing so much work on your flowers, perhaps I could help with this garden," she said.

"That one is yours," said Gerutha. "I never bother with herbs. That's the sort of thing a kitchen wench does. But if it appeals to your farm-bred sensibility, be my guest."

"Thank you," Signe said. "Thank you, sister."

Ørvendil returned for dinner and greeted his wife's cousin cordially.

"Looks like we did better for Gorm than I thought," he said to Gerutha that night. "She's vastly improved her appearance since I last saw her. Looks positively healthy."

"She's still strange and willful," said his wife as she undressed for bed.

"Then one of them will tame the other," he said, grinning as he pulled her down to him. "Care to wager which one will win?"

"A soldier usually tames a maid," she said, kissing him.

Usually, she thought. But not always.

In the room below, Signe heard them moan with pleasure, and shivered slightly.

Gorm returned the following night. His first act was to speak to the man he had detailed to spy on Terence. After learning of his failure, he dressed him down bitterly and dismissed him from service. When Terence returned to The Viking's Rest later that evening, he bought the fellow a drink to ensure that there were no hard feelings.

Gorm went straight to bed without meeting his bride. Their first encounter was early the next morning. He emerged from his quarters to see a young woman working on the herb garden, breaking the hard soil with an iron-shod spade. She was sweating heavily despite the cool of the early morning, and her hands were covered with dirt, much of which she had transferred to her cheeks and brow. She looked up at him and nodded pleasantly, then went back to work. He grunted, then went to the kitchen.

Ørvendil was already up and eating.

"Well, look who's back," he said, holding up his hand. "How was the coronation?"

"Too soon over," replied the drost. "I was hoping for more of a feast after everything we went through."

"You'll get one here soon enough," said Ørvendil. "Let your belly be patient."

"Who's the new kitchen wench?" asked Gorm. "I saw her in the garden just now."

Ørvendil stared at him for a moment, then started guffawing.

"You simpleton," he bellowed. "That's the new wife we picked out for you. Go introduce yourself, and for God's sake don't let her know that's what you thought she was."

Gorm nearly fled in embarrassment back to the garden. Signe was still there, covering it with dried leaves. She stood as he approached, wiping her hands on her apron.

"You're . . ." he began, then he stopped. "Damn me, I was never told your name."

"I am Signe, sir," she replied. "I am Gerutha's cousin. I've come here to marry Ørvendil's drost, Gorm."

"Yes, I am," he said, stammering. "I mean, that is to say, I know. And I am. Gorm, that is."

"Oh," she said, momentarily taken aback.

He was not at his best, having traveled for several days on little sleep. His eyes were bleary and his skin already wrinkled despite his being just a few years older than Ørvendil.

Still, those were just appearances, she thought. She held out her hand. "I am glad to meet you at last," she said. "And glad that we met before we married. It might have been awkward otherwise."

"Yes," he said. "It's awkward enough now without anyone watching, isn't it?"

"There's that boy who keeps peeping around the corner," she said, pointing.

He turned around to see Amleth ducking back behind Ørvendil's quarters.

"Milord's son, Amleth," he said. "Has all the makings of a fine irritant when he grows up."

"He's quite curious for such a little one," she said. "He seems a little frightened of me for some reason."

"He's frightened of most people at first," he said. "The only one he ever took to right off was that fool."

"Oh, I've met him," she said. "He was quite nice."

Gorm snorted.

"A fool's a fool, no matter how nice," he said. "Come, let me carry your spade for you. We should get to know each other, I suppose."

"Thank you," she said, handing it to him. "That would be most welcome."

When Terence arrived at the island midmorning, Gorm was standing at the foot of the drawbridge. Terence nodded to him, intending to walk by, but to his surprise the drost put a finger to his lips and beckoned to him.

"Good morning, milord," said the fool. "Welcome home. How was your journey?"

"Wearisome," said Gorm. "Walk with me for a while, Fool."

"Very well, milord," said Terence, wondering what was up.

They walked upstream for a hundred paces before Gorm spoke.

"What do women want, Fool?" he asked.

Terence chuckled.

"My Lord Drost, if I knew, I would be a married man by now," he said.

"Have you never wooed a lady, Fool?" asked Gorm.

"No lady wants a fool for a husband," said Terence. "Although many get them in spite of their desires. But my life has been one of constant movement. That does not leave much room for romance, at least not one lasting more than a drunken night's worth."

The drost looked glum, and Terence decided to take pity on him.

"On the other hand, milord," he said, "I have been called upon to woo on behalf of others."

"How does that work?" asked Gorm.

"Through the power of music," said Terence. "A woman will be won by song, and not necessarily by the singer. If there is some lady whose favors you seek, send me to her on your behalf, and stand by me in fervent suppliance so that she knows that I am but the vessel pouring forth your love."

"And there will be a fee for this service, I suppose," said Gorm.

Terence shrugged.

"I cannot work for love when I work for love," he said. "But you will find me to be quite reasonable for a fool."

"Done," said the drost. "She will be at the evening meal tonight. Please stay for that before you go to your tavern duties."

They returned together. Amleth was standing at the entrance, jumping up and down with glee.

"Yorick!" he cried. "You're back!"

"Hello, my little fool," said Terence, scooping the boy up and swinging him by his arms around and around. Gorm shook his head at the familiarity and walked away.

The evening meal was convened at sunset, and Terence duly made his entrance with Amleth. He had spent the day teaching the boy some new songs, and handed him a small tambourine for the occasion. They strolled around the room together, Amleth singing one verse, Terence the next. It wasn't long before they ran through Amleth's repertoire, so the boy contented himself by keeping the beat with his new instrument.

Terence had left Ørvendil's table for last, waiting for Gorm's signal, and in the uncertainty of the firelight had failed to note the new arrival. When Gorm stood and waved to him, he and Amleth approached that end of the room. The drost joined them, facing Ørvendil, Gerutha, and Signe, and bowed.

"Milord," he said as the soldiers behind him exchanged knowing winks and nudges. "I have requested your fool to make a special performance on my behalf, but it is not meant for you."

"Guessing something of the nature of the performance, I am relieved," said Ørvendil. "Pray, continue."

Gorm turned to face Signe.

"My bride, this song is my first gift to you. Yorick, if you will."

There was a brief lull in the music as Terence stared at Signe in surprise.

"My Lord Drost, you have captured a fair prize," he said, regaining his voice. "May my music be equal to her love."

He sang, his eyes never leaving hers, an old ballad of a couple who swore undying love, but who were separated by the vicissitudes of fate, remaining loyal throughout until they were reunited by sympathetic higher powers. His voice caressed her, and though Gorm stood by the fool throughout, his hands clasped almost in prayer, it was the fool that she watched, though none in the room marked her. Except for Amleth, who sat at Terence's feet, looking back and forth between the two of them.

When Terence finished, the soldiers, who had become so entranced with the song that they had ceased drinking, pounded the tables and roared their approbation. The fool bowed to Signe, then to Gorm.

"Let me reward you for that, Fool," said the drost, reaching for his pouch.

"Stay, milord," said Terence. "Let it be my gift to you and your lady. May happiness be yours forever."

"Give him the money anyway, Gorm," called Ørvendil. "You owe him something for this lovely creature. It was at his suggestion that we arranged it."

Signe looked at Terence in shock, then stood.

"I would like to thank all of you for making me so welcome in Slesvig," she said. "Husband, come sit by me. Fool, please play some more."

"Your servant, milady," said Terence, quietly strumming his lute.

He wandered through the room, Amleth by his side. He looked back at Signe, who was chatting with the drost. Gorm remained stiff and ill at ease.

"My fault," muttered Terence. "All my fault. Forgive me, milady."

Amleth looked up at him, puzzled. Terence smiled at the boy and patted his head.

"Where's my accompaniment, little fool?" he said.

Amleth started shaking the tambourine.

The wedding was the next day. The cathedral, the largest building in Slesvig, was filled with every soldier not on patrol, along with some curious townspeople. Ørvendil, Gerutha, and Amleth sat together in the front. Terence sat in the last row, feeling miserable and hungover. He had drunk more than usual at The Viking's Rest after he left the island, so much so that he dropped several balls during his juggling routine to the derision of the locals.

The banns were read. Signe wore a dark blue velvet gown that had been lent to her by Gerutha, and a circlet of evergreen twigs on her head, set off well by her auburn hair. Gorm was in full armor, the leather straps worn and cracked from long use, the buckles inadequately polished. The bishop presided over the ceremony, joining their hands before the altar and blessing the union. Then the couple turned and faced the congregants, smiling bravely as all but one in the room stood and cheered. Signe looked out upon the sanctuary of strangers, and saw the lone seated man, the fool who was hunched on a bench at the rear, looking down at his boots.

The soldiers carried their drost and his bride on a platform from the cathedral all the way back to the great hall. The feast had been in preparation all day, cattle whipped across the drawbridge to be cut down inside the fortress and roasted in great pit fires. Fresh rushes were strewn throughout the hall, and extra thralls were brought in to supplement those of Ørvendil's household.

Ørvendil himself stood for the first toast.

"My friends," he said, "I drink to my right hand, a man who has given his life to serve, and who has finally been persuaded to accept some happiness of his own. I drink to his new bride, a lady who brings a breath of country air into these soldiers' quarters, whose beauty and grace are second only to that of the woman who shares my life." Gerutha smiled and bowed her head. "To Gorm and Signe!"

"Gorm and Signe!" shouted the soldiers. "Speech! Speech!"

Gorm stood and cleared his throat.

"My lord and lady, my brothers in arms," he said. "I thank you for the dangers that we have shared and the love that you bear me." He stopped, took a deep breath, then continued. "I have wanted to memorialize the events of recent months, to make the appropriate tribute to those brave men who fought for our King and brought peace and unity to all of Denmark. I have long fancied myself a poet..."

"Oh, dear God," sighed Terence as the drost launched into a recitation of bad verse that lasted nearly an hour.

When it was over, those who were still paying attention respectfully thumped the table, waking the rest who joined in as soon as they realized it meant the continuation of the meal.

"Well, that was inspiring," said Ørvendil. "I had no idea you had this skaldic side to you."

"Did you like it, milord?" asked the drost.

"Oh, yes," said Ørvendil. "You should teach it to Amleth someday."

Amleth, who was busy running under the tables, stopped and turned pale.

"But if you want the opinion of a professional, perhaps we should ask friend Yorick," said Ørvendil.

Terence, who had been nursing a wineskin throughout the recitation, stood unsteadily and staggered toward the main table.

"Why, sir," he cried. "You have completely missed your calling. You should have been a warrior-poet, going into battle with ax in one hand and harp in the other, a battling bard. What did you say when you first left us for the wars? That not since Jason and the Argonauts set off in search of the Golden Fleece had such a group of worthies gathered? I forget which hero was meant to be you. Not Jason, certainly, for the wife he brought back was not the equal of the one you have now. Not Herakles, for he deserted his comrades to chase after a boy. Neither Castor nor Pollux fits your singular self, nor Orpheus, despite your poetic prolixity, for you are no singer, sir." He stopped for a moment, considering, then brightened. "I have it. You are the one who watches and records the great deeds of others, and lives to write them down. As Appollonius of Rhodes did for Jason and his band of heroes, so you have done for Valdemar the Great. I hereby dub thee Appollonius the Second, and I promise to study thee anon, along with all of the other fusty, musty, crusty poets of yore."

There was laughter at this. Gorm was indignant, and turned to complain to Ørvendil. But his lord was chuckling right along with them, attempting to cover his mouth with his hands.

"To bed!" came a shout from the soldiers, and the rest picked it up. An impromptu escort formed, a squadron of drunks, and Gorm and Signe were bustled into their quarters while the soldiers camped expectantly outside.

The couple closed and barred the door to the ribald hoots of the men, then wearily climbed the steps to the upper room. Signe looked around. Crude shelves lined the walls, covered with old books and tattered scrolls. A new pallet, a gift from Ørvendil and Gerutha, was in a corner, covered with the linens she had brought from home.

"I did not know that you were a scholar as well," she said.

"I studied in Paris when I was young," he said. "I never wanted to be a soldier. I wanted to be a poet, or an actor. But I was a bad actor, and a worse poet. I made a fool of myself tonight, didn't I?"

"No, certainly not," she said reassuringly.

"I became a soldier," he said. "A strategist, a spymaster. It is the only thing that I do with any proficiency. I have always been comfortable with men. I do not know what sort of husband I will turn out to be."

"I have never been a wife before," she said nervously. "We will make the best of it."

There was chanting from outside. Gorm sighed.

"Come," he said, leading her to the bed. "We must produce a bloody sheet for them."

"There will be blood?" she asked.

"Yes," he said, nodding his head sadly. "There will be blood."

€IGHT

"And let those that play your clowns speak no more than is set down for them, for there be of them that will themselves laugh, to set on some quantity of barren spectators to laugh too, though in the mean time some necessary question of the play be then to be considered. That's villainous and shows a most pitiful ambition in the fool that uses it."

—*HAMLET*, ACT III, SCENE II

Roskilde—Slesvig, 1158 A.D.

The Bishop of Roskilde lay still on his bed. It was a proper bed, with an ornately carved oak headboard depicting scenes from the life of Christ. Silk coverlets were laid out to keep his body warm, but they could do little for him. He had breathed his last the night before.

In a large room below, the members of the diocesan chapter sat around a large table. The chair at the head of it was left empty in tribute to the late bishop. A priest, representing the cathedral, rapped his knuckles on the table to command attention.

"A prayer first," he announced, and heads bowed. When he was done, he rapped the table again. "We will follow the procedure set forth at the Concordat of Worms. Nominees will be proposed by this chapter, after which we will vote. A representative of the Emperor may observe. Is there a representative of the Emperor here?"

"Not in years," said a deacon. "Barbarossa prefers to look south, fortunately."

"Very well," said the priest. "Is there a representative of the Archbishop of Lund present?"

He looked around and saw none.

"Unfortunate," he said. "I know Archbishop Eskilde has had his differences with the King, but..."

"He's fled to France," interrupted a lay member. "If he gave a damn, he would come back and stand up for himself."

"Just as well he stays there," said another. "We don't need anyone stirring up trouble again."

"Fine," sighed the priest. "Is there a representative of the King here?"

"Will I do?" said Valdemar, standing in the doorway.

The chapter members stood hastily and began bowing. Valdemar motioned them to sit.

"I hope you don't mind," he said genially, looking around at the group. "Hmm, not enough seats. Mind if I take this one?"

He sat at the head of the table in the late bishop's seat. There were stifled gasps among the chapter members.

"My lord," said the priest. "You do understand that you have no voting privileges here."

"Of course I understand," said Valdemar, leaning back and propping his boots up on the table. "I just came to make sure that protocols are honored, and that this will be a proper election, untainted by outside influences."

"Of course, Your Majesty," said the priest, stammering slightly.

"In fact, I would like to suggest that you use a secret ballot," continued Valdemar. "That way, everyone may make his choice from his own conscience without fearing the criticism of the rest."

"An admirable idea, milord," said the deacon. "We were about to propose nominees."

"Good," said Valdemar. "I will go wait outside the cathedral, so that my presence does not in any way hinder the fairness of this process. I will be in the courtyard, anticipating the divine choice. My prayers are with you, my friends."

He stood and left the room.

"What was that all about?" asked a lay member.

"Take a look," said the priest, standing by the window overlooking the courtyard.

The chapter crowded around him, peering down.

"Odd place to drill soldiers, isn't it?" remarked the deacon.

"Yes, and so many of them," said the priest. He turned to face the others. "Secret ballots, gentlemen. Vote your consciences, and pray for our salvation."

"But we haven't had nominations yet," protested one of the lay members.

"I think we have, don't you?" said the priest, passing around slips of paper.

A few minutes later the priest emerged into the courtyard and approached Valdemar. The two conferred for a moment, then the King turned and signaled to his men to disperse.

From there, he returned to the great hall that had once been his rival's. He kept his quarters in the same rooms from which he had once fled as a besieged guest. He felt safer in them, knowing the value of a good escape route.

Axel was sitting there, playing chess with Gerald. The two looked up as the King entered.

"Congratulations, you are now the Bishop of Roskilde," said the King.

"Good," said Axel. "We'll be needing a larger cathedral."

"Rather cheeky bringing that up before you have even been installed," said Valdemar. "What's wrong with the cathedral we have now? It holds everyone who actually shows up for services."

"But there will be a lot more people in Roskilde by the time you and I finish our plans," said the new bishop. "I have been thinking that I should change my name to something more suited to my new office."

"What did you have in mind?" asked Valdemar.

"Something biblical, but close to my own name," said Axel. "Someone beloved of a king. How does Absalon strike you?"

"Bishop Absalon," said Valdemar. "Sounds important."

"I like it," said Axel.

Gerald shook his head. He wondered at the new bishop who had forgotten the story of the betrayal and revolt of King David's favorite son.

"I will announce it after the old bishop's burial," said Axel. "That's going to be tomorrow, by the way. You should be there. I will be giving the eulogy as my first act as bishop."

"Tomorrow?" exclaimed Gerald. "Will you have enough time to write it?"

"I wrote it months ago," said Axel. "The old bastard took forever to die, didn't he?"

He unrolled a map of Denmark and spread it out on a table.

"Do you mind ending our game?" he said to Gerald. "You were gone in five moves."

"So I see," said Gerald, bowing. "Well played, Your Holiness."

"I like the sound of that," chortled Axel, taking pieces from the board and using them to anchor the corners of the map.

"Congratulations, Axel," said Fengi, entering the room. "Must I genuflect before you now?"

"Later," said Valdemar. "Let's see what this schemer is proposing."

"Just what will be needed to keep your kingdom," said Axel. He took the castles from the board and placed them at different points on the map.

"That's where we need strongholds," he said to Valdemar.

"Strongholds," said Valdemar. "A new cathedral and several stone castles. How on earth are we going to pay for all of that?"

Axel pointed to the straits between Skaane and Sjælland.

"With the sea, Valdemar," he said. "We control the straits now. We tax everything that passes through them. We take a percentage from the fish markets. And we set up a new market here."

He stabbed a finger at the eastern end of Sjælland.

"It's ideally located," he said. "There's a decent harbor, and it's sheltered from the worst of the winds."

"But not the worst of the Wends," said Fengi. "When are we going after them?"

"We just finished a war," said Valdemar. "The people won't put up with another one so soon."

"They will if it puts an end to Wendish raiding," said Fengi. "If we wait . . ."

"We're not ready yet," said Axel.

Fengi swept the chess pieces from the table.

"Who is 'we,' Axel?" he said. "When did you start making decisions for the King?"

"When did you?" retorted Axel. "I am the Bishop of Roskilde, and with the Archbishop in exile, the See of Lund might as well be mine. The Crown must work with the Church in Denmark if there is to be any hope of survival."

"But the Wends respect neither Church nor Crown," said Fengi. "What other option do we have?"

"Peace," said Gerald.

The others turned to look at him.

"Of course, it's not my place to say," he said.

"Oh, stuff it, Fool," said Fengi. "That act grows tiresome."

"You forget your place, Fengi," said Valdemar quietly. "Our love for you is of long standing, but our patience is not infinite."

"I see," said Fengi. "Of the three men before you in this room, I am the one you chastise for speaking freely. Very good, milord. If you have no further need of me, I will take my leave of you."

He bowed briefly and left the room. Gerald followed him.

"I did not mean to drive a wedge between you and the King, milord," he said.

"Of course not," said Fengi. "You're just a fool. A fool can have no influence in the affairs of the great. Whereas a soldier such as myself is of immense importance."

"The most difficult time for a soldier is during peace," said Gerald gently. "You must learn to make your own peace with it."

"What would you have me do?" demanded Fengi. "Plant a garden and raise flowers?"

"A man of your talents and intelligence should be able to find a worthwhile office," said Gerald.

"Unfortunately, the position of King's Fool has been filled," snapped Fengi. "Tell Valdemar that I have gone to visit my brother. I will be back in time for the next war."

He stormed away.

"Then, God willing, we shall not see you again," muttered Gerald.

Signe lay on her pallet, a rag clenched between her teeth, waiting for the pain to subside. The contractions were coming more quickly now, to the satisfaction of the midwife who sat placidly knitting on a stool by the window.

This should be easy, thought Signe. I've seen cows drop calves in the middle of a field and keep on grazing. Mares who bore foals nearly as big as me without a nicker of pain. If such lowly creatures can manage this, surely I can.

But the labor had gone on for most of the day, and she was weak from it.

"Eggs," she gasped.

"What, dear?" said the midwife.

"We should lay eggs, like chickens," said Signe. "It would be so much easier."

"Yes," chuckled the midwife. "But then I would be out of a job, wouldn't I?"

The next onslaught came sooner than Signe expected, and the midwife stood, holding a knife and a clump of dried moss.

"Here it comes at last," she said cheerfully. "Start pushing, dear."

Signe started to scream.

Outside, Amleth stared up at the window, trying to understand the sounds. They had told him she was having a baby, and he had seen the swelling of her belly and felt the kicks, but he still did not know how this child was going to get out of its tiny, warm prison. He thought of nuts being cracked open to reveal their treasures, and wondered if the other lady would be doing the same to Signe. If so, it was no wonder that she was screaming.

Gorm sat in the great hall, a nearly empty wineskin on the table before him. With each of his wife's screams he shuddered and took another swig. He had been drinking for a long time.

Ørvendil poked his head through the doorway, saw the drunken drost, and clucked disapprovingly.

"Come, man, is that any way to behave?" he said, sitting by him. "I've seen you go into battle against heavy odds without blinking. What's the matter with you?"

"I can face my own death without fear," said Gorm. "But she's in such agony, and it's all my fault."

"It's no fault, it's the way of things," said Ørvendil. "All women go through this, yet we all get born somehow. I think it's mostly show, anyhow. That way, they make us feel guilty so we end up pampering them for a while."

There was a shriek that dwarfed all that had gone before, and Gorm turned deathly white. Then there was a slap and a baby crying.

"You see, my friend?" said Ørvendil, clapping the drost on the back. "There was nothing to worry about."

Gorm staggered to his feet and lurched toward his quarters. The midwife met him at the entrance.

"A girl, more's the pity," she pronounced. "Nothing but trouble in the long run."

"And Signe?" asked Gorm.

"She lost a lot of blood, but I finally stopped it," said the midwife. "She should live. Give her plenty of wine for one week, and keep your filthy hands off her for a month or so. She can't do this too often."

"Yes, all right," said Gorm. He moved as if to enter, but the midwife stood blocking the door, her hands on her hips.

"Well?" she said.

Gorm looked at her uncertainly.

"Thank you?" he said.

She held out her hand.

"Oh, of course," said Gorm, quickly thrusting some coins into it. She stuck them in her pouch and stood aside.

He took the steps two at a time, then stood at the door to the bedroom, reeling slightly with exhaustion and wine. Signe lay on the pallet, holding the newly swaddled infant against her breast. She looked up at Gorm and smiled weakly.

"Here she is, husband," she said. "How do you like her?"

He plopped down by her and looked at his daughter. She was already sleeping, as worn out from being born as her mother was from bearing her.

"She's so small," he whispered, touching her hand with his finger.

"She'll grow," said Signe. "What shall we call her?"

"I was thinking of Alfhild," said Gorm. "From my studies of history, she was a woman known for her chastity and her courage as a warrior. These are qualities I would fain see in my own daughter."

"Chastity, yes," said Signe wearily. "We'll leave warfare to the men."

"I just meant. . . ." he stammered. "Is the name all right?"

"It's fine," said Signe, closing her eyes.

"Can I get you anything?" he asked, but she had fallen asleep. He watched the two of them lying there, the baby nestled in her mother's arms, rising and falling with each breath. He did not notice Amleth, who had crept silently up the steps to look at the new child, wondering how she had escaped.

When Gorm came down later, the men at the rear posts cheered him from on high. Ørvendil came out of the great hall and clasped his hand.

"A daughter, eh?" he said. "Well, too bad about that. Better luck next time. How's the wife?"

"Tired," said Gorm. "So am I. Is there any dinner left?"

"Dinner, and more importantly ale," said Ørvendil, leading him inside.

Signe lay on the pallet, trying to get Alfhild to nurse. Such a pale girl, she thought. Like the moon.

She sat up, wincing in pain. The midwife had left her little instruction on how to take care of either herself or the baby, and her husband had not thought of arranging for any help. She wondered where he had gone.

She started, seeing Amleth peering at her from the steps. She had thought that he was there before, sometime after the baby was born, but her mind was in such a confused state that it might have been a dream. He looked frightened, and she realized that she must be a haggard mess. She beckoned to him.

"Would you like to see the baby?" she whispered.

He nodded solemnly, coming forward, holding something in his hand. She smiled when she saw that it was a bouquet.

"Are those for me?" she asked.

He nodded again, handing them to her. She pulled him to her and kissed him on the forehead.

"Thank you," she said. "Those aren't from your mother's garden, are they? She'd be angry if you picked them without her permission."

"Yorick and I picked them on the moor," he said, his eyes never leaving the little girl.

"Did you?" she said softly, looking at them more closely.

They were wildflowers, violets, crowflowers, and dandelions, and their fragrance eased her pain for the first time that day.

"Thank you," she said. "And thank Yorick. They remind me of home."

Gerutha looked at her garden in frustration. Despite her best efforts, her roses failed to produce more than a pair of wan blooms, while the lilies came out misshapen and yellowed. She looked over at Signe's herb garden, which was thriving, and sighed.

"Manure," said Fengi, standing behind her.

She squealed in surprise, then surprised both of them by turning and giving him a quick embrace.

"But we had no word of your coming to visit," she said. "And what do you mean by manure?"

"It's what I say whenever people discuss gardening," he said. "I look as knowing as possible and say, 'Manure. It needs more manure.' I may be right, for all I know, but mostly I just enjoy saying the word. Sorry about the unexpected visit. Shall I go away and come back again?"

"You're being naughty," she scolded him. "It's good to see you under any circumstances. How long will you be staying?"

"Until I'm needed elsewhere," he said. "I have been thinking of seeing more of the world. Perhaps I'll try my luck with the Varangians in Constantinople."

"Don't say that," she said. "We need you here in Denmark."

"We?" he said. "You and who else?"

"If it were only me, then that should be enough," she said, then thought, I'm flirting with him.

"It is, of course," he said, laughing. "You've talked me out of Constantinople. Thank you. Where's my brother?"

"Supervising more earthenworks north of the town. You should go greet him."

"I will immediately. What news before I leave you?"

"Gorm and his wife had a baby girl," she said. "Sickly looking thing, but it survived. Signe barely made it through."

"Thank God for that," he said, crossing himself. "How does Gorm like fatherhood?"

"He doesn't know what he should be doing," she laughed. "Men are so useless about babies."

"And Amleth?"

"Ask him yourself," she said. "He's standing right behind you."

It was Fengi's turn to whirl around in surprise. His nephew stood before him, grinning and holding his arms out. Fengi lifted him up and tossed him high, then caught the shrieking child.

"Hello, nephew," he said.

"Hello, uncle," replied Amleth.

"I never heard you approach," said Fengi. "With stealth like that, you'll be working for Gorm soon."

Amleth shook his head violently at that prospect. Fengi put him down, and the boy dashed away.

. . .

If Ørvendil was surprised to see his younger brother ride up, he did not show it. He was standing on a newly constructed ridge while teams of thralls dug up dirt, loaded it into carts and barrows, hauled it to the ends of the ridge, dumped it, and tamped it down with small logs. He waited for his brother to reach him and locked him into an embrace in full view of everyone, then walked with him along the length of the construction.

"What trouble are you in?" he asked quietly.

"Is that the first thing that crosses your mind?" laughed Fengi.

"Given where you were, yes," said his brother. "You wouldn't leave Roskilde when things are going so well for you unless they weren't going so well for you. What happened?"

"I left of my own accord," said Fengi. "The new regime is shaping up in ways that I do not like. Axel Hvide has just become Bishop of Roskilde."

"Little Axel?" exclaimed Ørvendil. "Esbern's brother? But he isn't even old enough to grow a beard."

"He is now," said Fengi. "The little bastard may end up running everything if we're not careful."

"If we're not careful," echoed his brother thoughtfully. "When did you and I become a we again? You left to follow your ambitions years ago."

"And you stayed to follow yours," retorted Fengi. "Why are you building fortifications here? Which of your enemies would attack from the north?"

"We have had Wends raiding the coastline north of us," said Ørvendil. "I thought that since the earthenworks south and west of Slesvig have been completed, it would be worth building up our northern defenses so that they can't slip around us in that direction."

"It seems to me that you've turned Slesvig into a nice little defensible territory," said Fengi. "Defensible from every direction."

"What are you getting at?"

"Given how well I know you, I thought you might have given up on being king of Denmark, but thought you might set up your own kingdom. You could get a little support from Holstein in exchange for access to the northern seas, maybe even reach out to Barbarossa before Valdemar does."

"What you are talking about is treason," said Ørvendil.

"Which I am certain you considered ever since Valdemar put you in here," said Fengi. "I'm still wondering why you didn't take advantage of him when we showed up last year. He wouldn't have been the first king to be murdered in Slesvig. Do you mean to tell me that this is what you've settled for? No more ambition?"

"There comes a time when you settle for your lot in life," said Ørvendil. "I've lived a little longer than you, and I know that now. You still have to learn it. Get married, have children. It will make more sense to you once you've done that."

"Rubbish," said Fengi. "You have to keep moving or you'll die. Look, we could do this together. You're squeamish about taking on Valdemar, fine. There's Wendish territory to the east, and no one would complain if we attacked them. You know that they are looking at us and drooling in anticipation."

"No," said Ørvendil. "If you're spoiling for a fight, go somewhere else."

"Coward," muttered Fengi.

"Be careful what you say, little brother," cautioned Ørvendil.

"What are you going to do about it, big brother?" taunted Fengi, his hand drifting toward his waist.

"If your hand gets one inch closer to your hilt, you'll find out," said Ørvendil pleasantly. "You know you can't take me in combat."

Ørvendil's guards were moving closer, sensing the menace within the two brothers. Fengi looked around and let his hand fall to his side. Ørvendil laughed and put his arm around his brother's shoulders, and the guards relaxed their vigilance.

"Have a nice visit with your family," said Ørvendil. "Then go back to Roskilde. Or go to Barbarossa, or France, or wherever you can find a real battle. When you've conquered this restlessness, come back here and we'll find you a wife. We're good at that."

Terence had finished performing at The Viking's Rest when, to his surprise, he saw Gorm sitting alone at a table, watching him. He filled two tankards with ale and brought them over.

"We rarely see you in here, my Lord Drost," he said, placing one of the tankards in front of him.

"I came to see you," said Gorm. He picked up the tankard and drained it in one gulp. "Is there someplace we could talk?"

"A moment, milord," said Terence. "My gullet is not as expansive as yours, and I prefer to taste the brew when I drink it."

He finished his ale, then stood.

"Let us walk. The evening is still young."

They left the tavern and ambled along the shoreline. The moon was full, and its sister shone from the depths of the fjord.

"I need to talk to you," said Gorm. "You did me great service when I did so last year, and the matter is again one that is deeply personal."

"Why not a priest, Sir Appollonius?" asked Terence. "I am flattered that you would come to me on a personal matter, but I am not sure that we could even call ourselves friends, much less confidants."

"I think that is why I can come to you," said Gorm. "Anyone else who heard this would laugh at me. Imagine, the one person I thought wouldn't laugh would be a jester. This is a matter of marriage, and I don't think a priest could help with that."

"Given the number of concubines and bastard children they have, you might be wrong," said Terence.

"But that isn't marriage," said Gorm. "That is simply carnality. Fleshly desire."

"True enough," agreed Terence.

"And yet, it touches upon my own concern," said Gorm. "I never asked to be married, you know."

"I know," said Terence.

"The embrace of a woman . . ." began Gorm, then he turned crimson.

"You may speak, milord," said Terence. "I am not unaware of such things."

"I have long prayed for my freedom from sin," said Gorm. "The feelings of carnality disturb me."

"But they are not sinful within the sacrament of marriage," protested Terence.

"That's how we are taught," said Gorm. "But I am uncertain of it. The consummation was . . ."

"Was what, milord? Successful, surely, for we have that delightful little Alfhild in the world with us now."

"Successful in that sense, of course," continued Gorm. "But it nearly killed Signe to have that baby. It nearly killed them both. And that midwife warned me away from her."

"Just for a while, I'm sure," said Terence. "To give your wife a chance to recover."

"I want her, Fool," Gorm burst out. "I cannot control these feelings. Yet my lust mortifies me, and the venting of it could kill her if she goes through another childbirth."

"These things do happen, milord," said Terence. "It is the way of the world."

"I could not live with myself if I caused her death through my own sinful desires," said Gorm miserably. "I know that I would be perceived as unnatural if I withheld myself from her, but it does seem to be the best course of action. Do you see that?"

Terence walked on with the drost. Poor man, he thought. He comes to me for advice on his future, yet it is Signe's happiness that I care about. It would be better for everyone if I refused to counsel him on this matter.

"Appollonius, my friend," he said. "I agree with you."

Gorm gave him a look of gratitude, and Terence felt sick inside.

𝔑INE

"I find thee apt."

—*HAMLET*, Act I, Scene V

Slesvig, 1161 A.D.

Yorick, may I ask you a question?" asked Amleth.

"Certainly," replied Terence. "Let me just finish what I am doing."

The two of them were sitting by the ruins of an old Viking tower on a promontory south of the mouth of the river. The fool was busy whittling the head of a straight branch that he had hollowed out. A small campfire burned behind them on which they had cooked a fish that Amleth had netted. Terence took a small, thin iron rod from one of his pouches and laid it so that its end was nestled on the embers, then turned his attention back to the boy.

"Your question, my young lord," he said.

"Why do fools wear whiteface?" asked Amleth.

"Do we?" exclaimed Terence. He peered into the water and cried out in shock when he saw his reflection. "Why didn't you tell me? I look ghastly."

"I'm serious," said Amleth, giggling nonetheless. "I want to know."

"There are many reasons," said Terence. "Let me ask you this. What happens to your room every spring?"

"It gets swept out," replied Amleth.

"And?"

"They put on a new coat of whitewash."

"Aha!" said Terence. "Why is that?"

"It looks nicer," said Amleth. "It makes the room brighter when the sun shines in."

"There you have it," said Terence. "My job is to make the world a little bit brighter. To bring the sun into the darkness. What better way to do that than with a whitewashed face?"

"Is that the real reason, Yorick?"

"What better reason could there be, my young friend?"

"I thought that it might be a mask," said the boy.

"Why would a fool need a mask?" asked Terence, smiling.

"Maybe because he doesn't want anyone to know who he really is," Amleth replied.

"But you know who I am," said Terence. "You can see my every expression from miles off, even in the dead of night. I am an open book, written on white paper so that I am easier to read."

"So it's not a mask?"

"Every face is a mask, white or not," said Terence. "I've seen you at times with complete clarity, just as I can see to the bottom of this fjord right now. Other times, however . . ." He stirred up the mud from the bottom until the water was completely murky. "And all of that was based on what you chose to reveal to me with your expressions. The only difference is that your mask resembles the face of a boy named Amleth. It's an uncanny likeness, milord."

"Should I always reveal my thoughts, Yorick?"

"Of course not," replied the fool. "Especially in the world you live in. You are growing up inside a fortress inside a city encircled by walls which are surrounded by earthenworks. Everyone here is concealing something all of the time. The man who is open about everything will be a man in great danger. If you are going to rule Slesvig someday, you must learn how to hide your thoughts, and to recognize when others are doing the same."

"I don't want to rule here," protested Amleth.

"You are Ørvendil's son," said Terence. "That is your father's wish for you."

"Can't I become a jester instead?" pleaded the boy.

"A jester? That's much harder work than being a duke," said Terence. "You have to learn so many different things to become a jester."

"Really?" teased Amleth. "I thought all you had to do was act foolish all of the time."

"As if that wasn't difficult enough," said Terence indignantly. "To suppress my vast intelligence in the cause of foolery. You cannot imagine the effort it takes. I lie down at the end of a long day and suddenly start spouting epic poetry and complicated logical proofs, just to make up for all of the stupidity I force myself to utter. No, Amleth, stay with your destiny. You'll be better off."

"But I would make an excellent fool."

"Alas, the demand is slight and the supply is great. However, there is no reason not to keep practicing. Something might open up somewhere. Work on your juggling."

He tossed four balls to the boy who caught two in each hand. Amleth had mastered three balls by the time he turned five, but the fourth had been causing him difficulty. He muttered to himself in frustration every time one fell.

"Relax, breathe, find the rhythm," counseled Terence. He gingerly took the iron rod out of the fire, holding the cooler end with a cloth. He then carefully burned several holes through one side of the piece of wood he had been whittling.

"Will Rolf and Gudmund be coming to play with you today?" he asked.

"Maybe later," said Amleth. "I don't care much."

"You don't? Why not? Aren't they your friends?"

"I think that they only play with me because their parents want favors from my father," said Amleth. "They always act so strangely when they come to the island. I think it would be easier if I just lived in a normal house like they do."

"Maybe," said Terence. "Maybe you should ask your father if you could live in town."

"I did. He says as soon as the castle is built. I'll be an old man before that happens."

Terence placed the carved end of the hollowed-out piece of wood in his mouth and blew into it. A slightly fuzzy piping emerged. He frowned and peered down the end of it, then took the metal rod and smoothed out the bore. He sounded the flute again, and the tone was clearer. He ran his fingers up and down the scale. It sounded true, and he played an old Yorkshire tune.

"That one came out well," commented Amleth. In his fascination with Terence's labors, he had forgotten that he was juggling, and the four balls jumped through their patterns perfectly. He realized what had happened.

"I'm doing it!" he said excitedly.

"Good, Amleth," said Terence. "You've found the rhythm. Four will be second nature to you from now on. Say, isn't it your sixth birthday today?"

"You know it is," said Amleth.

"I know it is," said Terence, reaching out and plucking the balls from over Amleth's head. "And this is for you."

He handed him the flute. Amleth seized it eagerly, turning it over and over. Then he piped a few notes.

"It's glorious!" he cried, hugging the fool. "Thank you, Yorick!"

"It's another thing to practice," warned Terence. "You'll be a busy little boy."

"Show me the fingering," said Amleth.

Terence taught him some simple tunes, and the boy played them over and over while the fool doused the fire and packed their gear.

"Come, child," he said, looking up at the sun. "It's almost noon. We have to meet your father."

. . .

North of the town, a kiln had been constructed, the labor supervised by several men brought in from Tuscany, most of whom spoke little Danish but gesticulated quite fluently. Clay was dug up from the riverbed and trundled to the yard next to the great oven. There it was mixed with straw and pressed into crude wooden molds, then turned out onto stone slabs.

It was the day of the first firing, and Ørvendil needed to be there despite the arrival of his son's birthday. Amleth was happy and excited to see this new magic in action. He and Terence had watched the kiln's construction, and he had been impressed to learn that the fool spoke the Tuscans' language. The brickmakers had become regulars at The Viking's Rest as a result, and brought their strange, lively music with them. Terence began teaching the boy Tuscan.

The Bishop himself had come from the cathedral to bless the new enterprise. Then he stayed on, as curious to see it as the six-year-old boy. Other children were crowded behind the fence, envying Ørvendil's son who got to get so close to the fire.

"We do one first," said Carlo, the master brickmaker. A single brick was put inside the kiln, and then the opening was sealed off. Everyone stared at it, watching every wisp of smoke as if it were a portent. Then, the master declared that enough time had passed. The seal was cracked open, and the finished brick was plucked from the embers by a pair of iron tongs and plunked down on the ground. The master walked slowly around it, inspecting it from every angle, then tapped it several times with a wooden mallet.

"It's good," he pronounced finally, and a cheer went up from everyone. He picked up the cooled brick, walked up to Ørvendil, and knelt, holding it before him.

"First one is for you," he said. "Be careful, still hot."

Ørvendil took it from him and bade him stand, then looked at it curiously. He turned to the crowd and held it aloft.

"The first of many," he cried. "And with them we will build Slesvig into a great city!"

There were more cheers at this, and Ørvendil smiled. Then he turned to his son.

"Here, Amleth," he said, handing the brick to him. "Happy birthday."

"Thank you, father," said the boy, delighted with it.

"And thank Carlo for making it," added his father.

"*Grazie*, signore," said Amleth, bowing.

"You are most welcome, most learned child," said Carlo as the other Tuscans laughed in delight. "May I present my brothers, Reynaldo and Phillippo. They don't speak Danish yet, but your Tuscan is getting better all the time."

"Yorick taught me," said Amleth proudly. "Thank you for the brick. It's wonderful."

"That's not your only present, you know," laughed Ørvendil.

"There's more?" asked his son.

"Come with me. We'll walk for a bit. Yorick, you come along, too."

"Very good, milord," said Terence.

The three of them walked to the outskirts of town into a slight declivity in the landscape that hid them from view. Ørvendil stopped, turned, and put a finger to his lips. Then he reached into his pack and pulled out a long, narrow object wrapped in cloth and handed it to the boy.

"What is it?" asked Amleth as he unwrapped it, then he gasped. He was holding what would have been a man's short sword. For the boy, however, it was the equivalent of a longsword, and he swung it clumsily through the air, causing the two men to jump hastily back.

"Hold, hold," laughed his father. "That's a real sword, and it will draw real blood. Here's the scabbard. Put it in there."

He handed the boy an ancient scabbard, its leather cracking.

"My father gave me this when I was your age," said Ørvendil. "And his father gave it to him. Your education from now on will include the proper methods of fighting. Here is the first lesson. You never remove your sword from your scabbard unless you are prepared both to kill and to die. Nothing less than that. Do you understand me, boy?"

Amleth nodded solemnly.

"But how do I practice without taking it out?" he said.

Ørvendil pulled two wooden swords from the pouch.

"With these," he said. "They are weighted differently, and they won't cut anything, but we'll start you out with them. Fool, are you acquainted with the techniques of fighting?"

"I have lived most of my life in taverns," said Terence. "I've had my share of fights."

"Any with swords?" asked Ørvendil.

"Milord, I carry no sword," replied Terence. "Mostly they were fist-fights and wrestling matches."

"Perfect," said Ørvendil. "Any fighting begins with a knowledge of wrestling. Then you add in the weapons. Catch, Fool."

He tossed him one of the wooden swords.

"Now, Fool, when I tell you to, attack me," commanded Ørvendil. He stood with his left hand raised, the weapon in his right held low, his weight on his back foot. "Now."

Terence lunged forward, and Ørvendil easily parried the thrust.

"I'm sorry, milord," said Terence. "I did not do that very well."

"Nor will many you encounter in life," said Ørvendil. "But there will be some formidable foes. When you attack, thus . . ."

He stepped forward, his sword thrusting up toward Terence's stomach. The fool quickly stepped back and parried it. Ørvendil looked at him in surprise.

"Did I make that attack so obvious?" he wondered. "You blocked it quite skillfully."

"Mere luck, milord," said Terence. "I was just . . ."

Ørvendil struck again, and the fool blocked it.

". . . defending myself," Terence continued, and suddenly found himself facing a hailstorm of blows. He kept backing away, ducking and blocking. Amleth watched the two men in fascination. Finally, his father broke through the fool's guard and landed a blow on his shoulder. Terence winced in pain and lowered his sword, holding his palm out in surrender. Ørvendil stepped back and scrutinized him.

"There is not a soldier in my entire garrison who could have matched me as well," he said softly. "Where did you learn to handle a sword like that?"

"I am an entertainer," explained Terence. "We used to stage mock sword fights at festivals. We had to know how to handle the weapon just as well as a soldier does."

"Somehow, I doubt that's the true explanation," said Ørvendil. He tossed his practice sword to his son. "Amleth, stand there and get a feel for this. I will talk with this entertainer for a moment."

The two men walked some distance away and watched the boy go through his paces, imitating both his father and Terence.

"Talented boy," said Terence.

"Yes," said Ørvendil. "I would give my life to keep him safe."

"Yes, milord."

"Would you?" asked Ørvendil. "Give your life for him?"

Terence looked at him, his face expressionless.

"I need to know the answer," said Ørvendil.

"Yes, milord," said Terence. "I would give my life for him."

They watched Amleth some more.

"Thank you, Yorick," said Ørvendil. "I hope that that time never comes."

Gerutha looked at her garden in frustration.

"Manure," she muttered.

"What, cousin?" asked Signe, working in the herb garden nearby while Alfhild toddled about, trying to catch a white butterfly that had drifted into the fort.

"I am thinking of tearing out everything and starting all over again," said Gerutha. "Perhaps make a walled garden dedicated to the Holy Mother, where we could sit and devote ourselves to prayers."

"It sounds too much like a convent for my taste," said Signe. "It's bad enough living behind high walls. Why build more?"

"But that would be the charm of it," said Gerutha. "A place where women could be at peace, undisturbed by the rudeness of men."

"I wouldn't mind being disturbed a little more," said Signe. "I think my husband is frightened of me for some reason."

"Really?" said Gerutha. "Why do you think that? Is he cold to you?"

"He's kind enough," said Signe. "And he's completely devoted to Alfhild. But since she was born, he's been reluctant to . . ."

She blushed and fell silent.

"He's an odd one, no question," said Gerutha thoughtfully. "I don't think he's seeing anyone else."

"Gerutha!" exclaimed Signe. "He would never do that."

"Oh, any man would do anything," said Gerutha. "Any woman would as well, given the opportunity. There's no shortage of bastard children in Denmark, that's for certain. But I don't think that's your husband's problem. Have you tried . . ."

She whispered something in her cousin's ear, and Signe's eyes grew wide.

"Can one do that?" she asked in wonder.

"Oh, yes," said Gerutha. "Once they get over the shock, they quite enjoy it. Gorm's always been timid about women and love. He needs to be jolted out of it, if you ask me. And maybe you'll get a son out of it this time."

"That would please him, having a son," said Signe. "He was mocked so badly by everyone for having a daughter. Except by Terence, oddly enough."

"Terence? Oh, Yorick," said Gerutha. "I'm so used to hearing Amleth call him that that I've quite forgotten his true name."

"Where is Amleth? I thought we were going to celebrate his birthday today."

"We will. He went to see the opening of the new kiln with his father. He was quite excited about it."

"Oh, dear," sighed Signe. "It's finally ready. Now all of my precious trees will be cut down to feed the fires."

"They are not your trees," said Gerutha sharply.

"No, I know that," said Signe. "It's just that I so much enjoy walking among them."

"If we are going to have a proper castle around here, then the trees will have to go," said Gerutha. "That's just how things will be."

There was a commotion nearby, and Amleth burst into the rear of the fort, waving his new treasures.

"Look, mother!" he cried. "I got a brick from the kiln, and I thanked Carlo in Tuscan, and he said I spoke it really well, and father gave me the sword his father gave him, only I can't take it out until I learn how to use it better, but he's going to teach me, and Yorick gave me this wonderful flute, and I can already play some tunes, come and listen..."

"Wait, wait," protested his mother, laughing as he pulled her by the skirt of her gown into the great hall.

Signe laughed as she heard the amateur piping inside, then looked up to see Terence smiling at her.

"Hello, Terence," she said.

"Milady," he said, bowing. Then he squatted in front of Alfhild who sucked her thumb and looked at him shyly. "No hug, Princess?"

She ran up to him and threw her arms around him, then shrieked giddily as he held her high in the air.

"Can you see over the walls, Princess?" he said.

She shook her head.

"You will in time," he said. "You are growing like one of your mother's odoriferous weeds. Truly, milady, you have a gift for gardening."

"Not so loud," cautioned Signe. "Gerutha gets so jealous about my little accomplishments."

"That's new, isn't it?" asked Terence, pointing to one plant.

"Oregano," said Signe. "My husband got it from one of the brick-makers. It smells wonderful."

"May I?" he asked. She nodded, and he sat by the plant and buried his face in it as Alfhild giggled. "Pungent. A good herb for a lamb stew."

"That's what I think," said Signe. "But try and get them to cook with it here. The recipes haven't changed since the cooks' great-grandmothers handed them down."

"Then you should command the kitchen for an evening and perform culinary miracles," declared Terence.

"Ah, such an act of rebellion would put me in the stocks," said Signe.

"Then you would be a true cook, for they say that the measure of a cook is in her stocks," said Terence.

"I want Gorm to set up a house in town so that we may have our own kitchen," said Signe. "But he will not leave his men. I would like Alfhild to grow up in a more normal place, although she absolutely adores being around Amleth. Don't you, my sweet?"

Alfhild nodded.

"And I was hoping you would marry me," said Terence to the little girl. "Do you know this garden as well as your mother does?"

"Let's show him," said Signe, gathering the little girl onto her lap. "Tell Terence where the fennel is."

Alfhild pointed the stalks out.

"And the marjoram?" asked Terence.

Alfhild looked around, then pointed.

"Impressive," said Terence. "Of course, I haven't the slightest idea which herb is which, so she could be pointing to daisies for all I know."

"Sit here," said Signe, patting the ground next to her. The fool joined the two, and Signe put Alfhild's hand in his. "Alfhild, show him lovage. That's right. And thyme. Mint, horseradish, and dill."

"Dill I know well," said Terence. "I have eaten my share of pickles."

"How about this one?" said Signe, plucking a narrow leaf from a plant with clusters of light blue flowers. She rubbed it between her thumb and forefinger, and held it out to the fool.

Instead of taking the leaf, he took her hand and brought it gently to his face. She started at the contact, but did not stop him. He bowed his head and inhaled deeply.

"It's wonderful," he said. "But I don't know what it is."

Signe started to answer, then faltered.

"Rosemary," said Alfhild.

Gorm sat in a corner of The Viking's Rest an evening later, watching Terence perform. No, he was watching the Tuscans watch him perform.

As Ørvendil's spymaster, he had to check them out thoroughly, and none of his men spoke enough Tuscan to eavesdrop adequately.

There were six of them, including the three brothers. If they were brothers. They had been recommended by someone at Barbarossa's court who had been passing through Slesvig on the way to Roskilde the previous year. Gorm had independently verified that they had constructed kilns in Lübeck and Holstein, but that in a way made them more suspect. They were only hired men, after all, and hired men from Holstein could still be in its pay.

Terence spun a ribald yarn that sent the Danes in the room into hysterics. Gorm grimaced at the subject matter, then narrowed his eyes as he noticed that both Carlo and Reynaldo were laughing along with the Danes and translating the punchline to the rest of the group.

Carlo had said that he was the only one who spoke Danish. Gorm decided to have Reynaldo watched more closely. He finished his ale and left the tavern.

He was unusually irritable this evening. His wife had tried to do something unspeakable to him earlier, something that he had only heard of in his soldiers' recountings of their adventures in whoring. He slapped her when she tried it, then shoved her to the pallet with a curse. She wept, saying that all she wanted to do was to please him, to give him a son. One part of him wanted to weep with her, to take her into his arms and let her comfort him. But he knew that to be weakness.

He came back to the fort and detailed a man to follow Reynaldo. He did not want to return to his room just yet. Salvation came to him in the form of his master, who was coming in late himself.

"Good evening, old friend," said Ørvendil. "What news?"

"I have been investigating your brickmakers," said Gorm. "I have my suspicions of Reynaldo."

"You suspect most people," said Ørvendil.

"That's why you need me," said Gorm. "To balance your trusting nature."

"Maybe," said Ørvendil. "Speaking of which, I need to send someone to Roskilde to represent us at the military council. How about it?"

"It would be an honor, milord," said Gorm, bowing. "I will leave first thing in the morning."

"Good," said Ørvendil. "See what kind of trouble my brother's been getting into lately, won't you?"

"Yes, milord," said Gorm.

"Now, get back to that pretty wife of yours," said Ørvendil.

Gorm winced, and hoped Ørvendil did not see it. He climbed quietly up to his room where Signe lay sleeping, curled away from the doorway. He packed his gear as quietly as possible, then sat in the lower room, watching Alfhild sleep in her little bed, until the first crowing of the cock told him it was time to leave. When Signe rose, he was long gone.

That evening, Terence finished his evening performance and staggered off to his room. He had been invited to join in many rounds of ale, and had accepted far too many of the invitations. Now, he was feeling their effects.

He had also noticed Reynaldo's fluency with the local tongue the night before, and waited for the all too predictable appearance of Gorm's man tonight. He wondered what he would find out about the brickmaker. Terence's own conversations with them had not turned up anything suspicious, but the Tuscans were a private group. Not surprising, given that they were foreigners here. The Jutlanders did not like foreigners, despite their show of good cheer at the construction and opening of the kiln. They grumbled about having to do the hard labor at low wages while the Tuscans earned masters' fees for watching bricks bake.

He yawned and stretched out on his pallet. Suddenly he was aware of someone else in the room, standing silently by the window. Slowly he reached for the dagger he kept under the pallet.

"Who's there?" he said.

"I am," came a woman's voice. It was pitched low and soft, with the tone of a silver bell.

"And who might you be?" asked Terence, sitting up.

"A gift, Fool," she replied. "One sent by a grateful patron who wishes to remain anonymous."

"What have I done to merit such a token?"

"You brought cheer to a lonely heart," she said. "I am the recompense."

"Show yourself," he said.

She stepped forward into the slim, slanted stream of moonlight that slipped through the shutters. She was wearing a dark green gown covered by a hooded black cloak. Her face was obscured by a mask over her eyes.

"You are masked," he said.

"So are you," she replied.

"Forgive me, but how do I know this isn't some trick?" he asked. "A lulling prelude to a robbery, for example."

She shrugged, and the cloak and gown tumbled down around her.

"I am unarmed," she said.

"I would hardly say that," he said. "What is your name?"

"No more questions," she said as she knelt down to kiss him. "No more words."

When he woke the next morning she was gone. He thought for a moment that he had dreamt her in his drunken state, but as he smelled the morning air, he picked up her fragrance. It was an odd one, not the sickly cheap perfume favored by the women of the town. He searched for it, breathing reverently with his eyes closed.

"Rosemary," he said.

Ten

" 'A is far gone, far gone. And truly in my youth I suffered much extremity for love, very near this."

—HAMLET, ACT II, SCENE II

Roskilde, 1161 A.D.

Upon his arrival in Roskilde, Gorm sought out his longtime informant and handed him a cage containing three more carrier pigeons. The birds were jessed and hooded, and not at all happy about it. They protested loudly as the cage rocked back and forth during its transfer. The drost caught up on the latest gossip of the city, then rode on to the great hall.

He was quartered in a barracks, where he was recognized and welcomed by a sergeant who knew him from the civil wars. Back in the company of soldiers, Gorm relaxed and chatted away, happy to be in a place where the war stories were actually war stories.

He presented himself to the King in the morning, handing over his credentials to the Royal Drost with all due ceremony. His presence was noted by all, as was Ørvendil's absence.

"Does your master so disdain military matters that he will insult the King rather than attend this council?" asked Bishop Absalon.

"Quite the contrary," said Gorm. "He is busy supervising the construction of stronger defenses at the southern border of your kingdom. What could be more military than that?"

"Our southern borders haven't been attacked in years," said Absalon.

"Thus proving the efficacy of the defenses," said Gorm. "The moment we let down our guard is the moment that we will be attacked."

"I was once sold a charm at an absurd price," drawled a voice from the sideboard. "The crone who foisted it upon me assured me that it would keep away dragons. Do you know, to this day I have never seen one?"

Several men guffawed at that. Gorm peered across the fire to see a fool leaning against the wall, a lute cradled in his arms.

They're everywhere, Gorm thought to himself.

Valdemar motioned everyone to their seats. The fool remained standing against the wall, softly playing his lute. Gorm found the music irritating, but the rest of the company didn't seem to notice it.

"We will hear first from our ambassador to the court of Frederick Barbarossa," said the King. "Welcome, Fengi. What news?"

Fengi stood, and Gorm leaned forward to get a better look. The onetime warrior had exchanged his armor for the rich vestments of a courtier, and his body had filled out accordingly as a result of carrying so little weight.

"The Emperor sends his greetings," he said. "He wonders when you will get around to recognizing him as your liege lord. He wishes you to stand by him in his selection of the Pope."

"Does he?" smirked Valdemar. "Well, perhaps we should consult with the Church first. Is there a representative of the Archbishop of Lund here?"

"No!" shouted several in the room, roaring with laughter.

"Oh, dear," said Valdemar. "How will we be counseled if such a high prelate prays from so far away for so long? I suppose that we will have to turn to the Bishop of Roskilde in his absence. Absalon, how says the Church on the Emperor's request?"

"The Church notes that Rome is far away, but the Emperor's dominions are close by," said Absalon. "As are his armies."

"Geography is destiny," said Valdemar. "Tell the Emperor that we will recognize him as liege lord, in exchange for his support, or at least his lack of interference in local matters."

"Done, milord," said Fengi.

The rest of the council was given over to reports on castle building, shipbuilding, the plans for the new merchants' town, and the relative merits of importing salt from Lübeck versus manufacturing it from the sea. Gorm followed it all with interest, contributing little. When the meeting was over, the men at the table rose, many adjourning to the nearby taverns. Before he could leave, Gorm was summoned to approach the King. He did so with trepidation. Valdemar crooked a finger at him, and the drost leaned in to hear what he had to say.

"Tell your master that I expect him in person the next time," said Valdemar. "Remind him that he rules at my pleasure. If my displeasure is incurred, I will call an assembly of the Slesvig *thing* and replace him."

"I will, milord," said Gorm, bowing.

He turned to leave, then saw Bishop Absalon speaking with a small group of men. He hovered at their perimeter, waiting patiently until they had finished. When Absalon turned to leave, Gorm tapped him on the shoulder. The Bishop turned toward him.

"What?" he said in irritation.

"Your Holiness, I wonder if I might have a word with you," said Gorm humbly.

"About what?"

"It's a religious matter," said Gorm.

"Then go find a parish priest with some free time," snapped the Bishop. "Can't you see that I'm busy?"

"Now, I can," said Gorm. "Forgive me for disturbing you."

Fengi watched him from the door. As the drost turned, he smiled broadly and waved to him.

"Come, dine with me, old friend," he called. "There's an inn near the western wall that sets an outstanding table."

Gorm fell into stride by him.

"Seeking confession from our bishop?" asked Fengi jovially. "He won't tend to anyone unless he thinks they're useful."

Stung, Gorm looked away for a moment.

"Oh, my dear fellow, I apologize," said Fengi quickly. "That was meant as a joke. I didn't think that you really were seeking...Look, I meant that Absalon only counsels those he thinks useful to his own ambitions. I never meant to imply that you were useless. Quite the contrary, my friend. I regard you as one of the ablest men in Denmark."

"Do you really?" said Gorm, flattered.

"Absolutely. Why else would my brother send you to check up on me?" laughed Fengi. "He has, hasn't he?"

"It was not the essential part of my mission," said Gorm. "But he did ask me to see how you were."

"As well as what I was up to, eh?" said Fengi. "So, what have I been doing?"

"After leaving Slesvig, you traveled to Italy," said Gorm. "You spent some time in service in Ferrara, training the local garrison. You left in a hurry amidst rumors of an affair with a countess who also was the Bishop's mistress, much to the distress of the count. You then spent time at the court of the Emperor, working your way into his inner circle, and then used that connection to win your way back into Valdemar's favor, becoming his ambassador. You have amassed a small group of men who act as your spies, both in Denmark and in Holstein. Two of them are in Slesvig."

"You are extremely well informed," said Fengi, surprised and impressed. "And my brother knows all of this."

"Not all," said Gorm.

The two walked along in silence, Fengi deep in thought, Gorm waiting. When they arrived at the tavern, they took a small table in the far corner and ordered a meal.

"There's a rumor going around that my brother is planning to break off from Denmark," said Fengi suddenly.

"I haven't heard that," said Gorm.

"I'm surprised," said Fengi. "Valdemar knows. He wasn't happy at all about big brother's failure to come here today. He's had his doubts ever since Ørvendil built the defenses at the northern border of Slesvig. They are too far inland to be of any use in repelling the Wends. No Wend would ever venture more than two hours' run from the coast. They're cowards."

"But ..."

"Has he been bringing any foreigners into town?" asked Fengi. "Perhaps in the guise of skilled labor? Artisans?"

"There's some brickmakers from Tuscany," said Gorm. "Six of them."

"Tuscany, eh?" said Fengi. "Is their leader a swarthy fellow called Carlo? And were they in Holstein before coming there?"

"How did you know about that?" asked Gorm.

"They're mercenaries," said Fengi. "Paid killers. Didn't you check them out?"

"I did," said Gorm miserably. "My contacts in Holstein are limited, unfortunately."

"I think Ørvendil's up to something," said Fengi thoughtfully. "He's kept you out of things, hasn't he? And that's why you haven't told him everything that you know, isn't it?"

"I've always kept some information to myself," said Gorm. "You never know what it may mean until you have all of the facts."

"Smart man," said Fengi. He leaned forward. "But you are wrong about one thing. I actually have three men in Slesvig."

"Who is the third?" asked Gorm.

"You," said Fengi.

"What?"

"Look," Fengi said urgently, leaning across the table. "I don't know enough about his plans yet to go to Valdemar. But we cannot have another civil war in Denmark. It would be horrific, coming so soon after the last one, and we need to present a strong front to the rest of the world. Valdemar wants me to stay in Roskilde for a while, so I can't investigate Slesvig myself, and my men, as you well know, are not privy to what's happening inside the fortress. But you are."

"Not according to what I've heard from you today," said Gorm.

"No, but you can be," said Fengi. "Now that you understand the situation, you can be on the lookout for anything suspicious."

"God knows that I can do that," said Gorm bitterly. "It seems that I have suspected everyone but the man I should have suspected the most." He drained his goblet, then set it carefully down on the table. "All right, I will report to you. But if I think that you are wrong, then I want you to take no action against your brother."

"Of course not," said Fengi, holding out his hand.

Gorm clasped it, shaking slightly, then left the tavern, his plate untouched.

A man who had been sitting nearby, his back to them, stood, came over to Fengi's table, and took the recently vacated seat.

"How did it go?" he asked.

"Like a charm," said Fengi. "Nothing easier than playing on the suspicions of a naturally suspicious man. You know what to do?"

"Of course," said the man. "When does he return to Slesvig?"

"The council meets for two more days," said Fengi.

"Then I will leave this evening," said the man. He gestured at Gorm's plate. "Do you mind? No point in wasting food."

"Be my guest," said Fengi.

As Gorm left the tavern, his mind teemed with recrimination and doubt. His failure in properly investigating the bricklayers gnawed at him. His inability to gauge his master's intentions shook him to his foundations. He barely noticed the man he bumped into. Then he saw the cassock, and stopped.

"My apologies, Father," he stammered.

"Not at all, my son," said the priest.

Gorm hesitated for a moment, then plunged in.

"Father, I wish to make confession," he said. "Would you hear it?"

"Alas, I am on my way to minister to a poor soul on his deathbed," said the priest. "But there is a parish church not two hundred paces south of here, just beyond the gate. Someone there should be able to assist you."

"Thank you, Father," said Gorm gratefully, and he set off in that direction.

Gerald watched him thoughtfully. His priestly side regretted not being able to help the man himself, but he did not want Gorm to know about his other identity, and a confession at close quarters would easily have led the drost to make the connection between the priest and the fool. Something had upset the drost, that was plain to see. Gerald wished he knew what it was. He had seen him leave with Fengi, which aroused his curiosity, but by the time he had removed his makeup and donned his cassock, it was too late to hear what they had to say to each other. It occurred to him that he could have heard the drost's confession to gain the information, but he had sworn long ago never to abuse that sacrament.

He entered the tavern and immediately spotted Fengi eating in the corner with another man he had never seen before. He bought a pitcher of ale along with some cheese and pickled herring and sat near them, trying to overhear their conversation, but they were merely eating. When they left, Gerald followed. The two split up outside the tavern, Fengi heading back to the great hall and the other man walking south. Gerald hesitated, then followed the stranger. He thought that he might have been staying at one of the boardinghouses outside the southern wall, but the man simply passed through the gate and kept going.

Gerald was not prepared to trail him all the way across Sjælland. Sighing, he abandoned the quest and returned to his own room to prepare himself for the evening's entertainment. He sketched the man's face on a scrap of paper, jotting down what he could about his description, and added it to a large sheaf of similar drawings that had grown steadily since he had been in Roskilde.

"Too many spies and not enough fools," he muttered. He wished, not for the first time, that Larfner were still alive to help him.

. . .

Gorm grew more hopeful about the small parish church with every step he took toward it. It was ideal for his purposes—out of the mainstream of Roskilde society, and with no connection at all to Slesvig. Perhaps there he could find the spiritual comfort and guidance that he desired. He conjured up visions of how the priest might look—a kindly man, spiritually pure, imbued with the inner light brought on by years of monastic asceticism, yet tempered with a worldly knowledge of human affairs. A man that would see into his heart and his inner conflicts, understand, forgive, and prescribe the correct path through the sin-ridden thickets that blocked his view of paradise.

The church was a small, rectangular affair, built of crudely worked blocks of tufa with a wooden roof that looked badly in need of repair. He pushed open the door to find a single aisle with benches on either side leading to a simple nave with a cross nailed against the wall. There was no one there.

"Hallo!" he called. There was an indistinct noise from inside a wooden door at the rear. He strode toward it and opened it.

A sleepy priest was standing there, hastily knotting the cord around his cassock, his hair long and unkempt. He waved peremptorily at the drost.

"Be right with you," he muttered.

"What is it?" said a woman's voice.

Gorm peered around the priest to see a slatternly female lying on a pallet, a naked breast visible under the partially thrown covers. She had a wineskin in one hand, and given its depleted appearance had been sampling it heavily.

"Just a lost soul, I expect," said the priest. "Go back to sleep. I'll be with you when I'm done."

He motioned the astonished drost back into the nave.

"Who was that?" spluttered Gorm.

"My housekeeper," said the priest. "Now, what may I do for you, my son?"

"How can you...?" Gorm began, nearly choking. He took a deep breath. "How can you help me?"

"I don't know," said the priest. "What is the problem?"

"The whole world has become corrupt!" screamed Gorm. "Nothing is pure. No one can be trusted."

"That, I'm afraid, is beyond my simple capabilities," said the priest. "I can pray for you, my son."

"Pray for yourself!" snapped Gorm, and he stormed out of the church.

"Probably too late for that," muttered the priest.

"Are you coming back to bed?" called the woman from inside the outer room.

"Yes, my dear," replied the priest.

He turned, crossed himself briefly out of habit, and went back inside.

Fengi knocked respectfully on the door to Valdemar's room.

"Come," said the King from inside.

Valdemar was seated, his feet propped up on a cushioned stool.

"Am I disturbing you, milord?" asked Fengi.

"I am in need of disturbance," said Valdemar. "My fool wandered off after the meeting, just when I was in the mood to be amused."

"I can offer little in the way of entertainment," said Fengi. "My thoughts lay in rather a different direction."

"Share them."

"I want to apologize on behalf of my brother," said Fengi. "He should have been here."

"It is not for you to apologize," said Valdemar. "These words should be coming from his own mouth."

"True, milord."

"In any case, I am surprised to hear you speaking up like this. He is your brother, after all."

"You are my brother," said Fengi. "My loyalties are here."

"Nobly spoken," said Valdemar. "What do you want?"

"Nothing more than what I have said," replied Fengi. "My brother does act on Denmark's behalf in building these fortifications. I saw them the last time I passed through Slesvig. They are very impressive. I daresay they are strong enough to withstand an attack from any army around."

"Including mine, I suppose?"

"Why would you attack Slesvig?" asked Fengi. "It is already yours."

"What are your brother's intentions?" asked Valdemar bluntly. "Stop these hints and speak plainly."

"I do not know his intentions," said Fengi. "I have no proof that they are anything but what they should be in such a loyal soldier."

"No proof," repeated Valdemar. "But you have your suspicions."

"No more than do you," said Fengi. "Suspicions are dangerous things, milord. Anything can be suspect. Or anyone. But the truth is often harder to come by."

"But if you do come by it, you will let me know immediately," ordered Valdemar.

"Of course, milord."

"Well, off to Barbarossa with you," said Valdemar. "Keep me informed."

"I will, milord," promised Fengi as he turned to leave. The King stopped him with a gesture.

"Of everything," said Valdemar.

"Yes, milord," said Fengi.

He left the King's chambers, a smile playing on his lips.

Gorm returned to Slesvig several days later. As he rode through the gates in the eastern earthenworks, his practiced eye saw the defenses anew. He noticed the effort put into them, the thickness and height of the ridges, larger than anything the Wends ever had to contend with in their lives.

All around him he saw soldiers. The same soldiers he had seen for years, had drilled mercilessly at dawn, had led on patrols. The soldiers he had molded into a top fighting unit.

He and Ørvendil.

He rode past the kiln, which was going full blast. Red roof tiles were piled neatly next to it, the cathedral renovations having taken precedence over the building of the new castle.

The new stronghold.

He fancied that people were eyeing him strangely, although when he looked directly at them, they were looking elsewhere, seeming to pay him no mind. He doubted that. He was a danger now, armed with newly opened eyes of his own. He would increase his spies in the town. Not a bird would fly over the city, not an insect crawl through it without his knowing it. He would never be caught by surprise by anything again, and those who attempted to deceive him would be dealt with.

He walked across the drawbridge to the island, grunting at the greetings of the men on the platforms. It was evening, already past the last meal, but he had no appetite. He entered his quarters and went upstairs without even glancing at his sleeping daughter. Signe was still up, combing out her hair. She turned with surprise when she heard him.

"You're back," she exclaimed. "We had no word that you were returning."

"Are you displeased?" he said.

"Why, husband, of course not," she said. "How was your journey?"

He looked at her. She was in her nightgown, her feet bare, her unplaited hair reaching down to the small of her back.

"Lie down," he said.

"Don't you want to tell me about Roskilde?" she asked him.

He stepped forward and shoved her down to the pallet. She landed hard, tears coming to her eyes.

"I told you to lie down," he said.

"What is the matter?" she said. "Why are you behaving like this?"

He unbuckled his sword belt and let the weapon clatter to the floor. Then he knelt by her feet.

"The world is corrupt," he said. "Everything is rotten."

"But . . ."

He heaved himself onto her, knocking the breath out of her. His hands scrabbled for the hem of her nightgown, then he grew impatient and simply ripped the fabric apart. She was struggling, writhing beneath him, which only added to his rage. He slapped her hard, then did it again. She was crying now, which infuriated him.

"Wait," she pleaded. "I'm not . . ."

She cried out with pain as he entered her. He was in a frenzy, coarse grunts erupting from him with every thrust.

It was over in a minute, and he lay on top of her, panting, his heart pounding. Then he saw her face, the tears streaking her cheeks as she looked away from him.

"Why are you crying?" he asked. "This is what you wanted. This is what husbands and wives do, isn't it?"

She would not look at him. He stood, walked to the doorway, then turned to look at her again.

"Isn't it?" he screamed. Then he fled down the steps.

Two months later, she realized that she was with child.

ELEVEN

"Like sweet bells jangled, out of time and harsh..."
—*HAMLET*, ACT III, SCENE I

Slesvig, 1162 A.D.

When will the baby come?" asked Amleth as he pulled weeds out of the herb garden.

"I don't know," said Signe, sitting with her back against the wall, her hands resting on her swollen belly. "Soon, I think."

"Is it a boy or a girl?" asked Amleth.

"I think perhaps a boy," said Signe. "But I don't know for certain."

Amleth looked at her in puzzlement.

"You had a baby before, didn't you?" he asked.

"You know that I did," said Signe. "You may have noticed her chasing after you for the last few years."

"So, if you have done this before, how come you know so little about it now?" asked the boy, a sly grin on his face.

Signe looked at him openmouthed, then burst into laughter.

"Come here, you scamp," she said, holding her arms out.

He came to her shyly, and she hugged him, ruffling his hair, then kissed his forehead.

"Thank you," she said.

"For what?" he asked.

"For making me laugh," she told him. "It's been a while since anyone has done that."

"I could fetch Yorick," he offered.

"No," she said, shaking her head. "He's so busy of late. I don't wish to take him away from those who are in need of cheer."

"But . . ."

"Besides," she said, hugging him again. "I have his most talented student to entertain me. Now, run along, little cousin. It's time for your lesson with your father."

"Bye, Signe," he called, snatching his sword belt from the ground and running.

"Good-bye, cousin," she said softly. "I wish I had better answers for you. I wish I had some for myself."

Terence reached out and swept the boy into the air as he came dashing through the great hall. Amleth shrieked as he sailed up near the crossbeams, but kept his body in the right position for the fool to catch him.

"You shouldn't scream like that," said Terence sternly. "It gives people the impression that I could actually let you fall."

"There's always a first time," said Amleth as the fool put him back on the floor.

"So, how does your cousin?" asked Terence casually.

"Fine," said the boy. "I made her laugh."

"Did you?" exclaimed Terence. "Well done, my student. Nothing coarse, I hope."

"I don't know anything coarse," declared the boy with the most innocent look he could muster.

"Of course not," said Terence. "Does she need any further entertainment?"

"She said that she didn't," said Amleth. "She said she didn't want to take you away."

Terence looked out toward the rear doorway, but could not see Signe's garden. He sighed.

"Very well," he said. "Your father is waiting at the usual place. Don't let him cut you in half."

"I won't, Yorick," promised the boy. "Bye!"

He ran off.

Gerutha looked at her garden in disgust.

"Rip everything out," she commanded the thrall standing by her.

"Everything, milady?" he asked warily. "Even the roses?"

"The roses have given me nothing but trouble for all of my hard work," she said. "It's time to begin anew. Rip them all out and toss them into the woods somewhere. Maybe Nature will take pity on them and let them grow."

The thrall shrugged and commenced digging up the garden.

"I never thought that I would live to see this day," said Ørvendil as he and Amleth came up behind her.

"When we build the new castle, we will have a proper courtyard with a proper garden," she said. "Somewhere with good light and healthy soil.'

"When we build the new castle, we will," he said. "Would you like to see Amleth in combat?"

"Show me," she said, turning to watch.

Amleth and his father faced off against each other, the wooden practice swords in their hands. Ørvendil took a step forward, menacing the boy. Amleth stepped backward, keeping his weight on his back foot, his sword held low and behind him. His father lunged suddenly, and the boy sidestepped the thrust and brought his weapon around to clang off his father's left shoulder.

"Good, Amleth!" shouted one of the soldiers on the wall.

"Watch your post," called Ørvendil. "If you want entertainment, go see Yorick at the tavern."

"Yes, milord," said the soldier, winking at the boy.

"Well done, boy," said Ørvendil, clapping him on the back. Amleth beamed with pride.

"That was wonderful, Amleth," said his mother, smiling. "Run and find your friends until dinner."

Amleth needed no second invitation. He took the practice sword from his father and ran off.

"I hope he and his friends don't use those practice swords on each other," said Gerutha.

"I hope they do," said Ørvendil. "He'll pass on the learning to them, and have a good time doing it."

"When will you begin work on the new castle?" asked Gerutha.

"When the roof on the cathedral is done," said Ørvendil. "Be patient, love. What's another year when the end is in sight?"

"Could I get some bricks for a Mary's garden, then?" she asked, a wheedling tone entering her voice.

"Church first, wives after," said Ørvendil. "Not yet."

"I have lived my entire life with 'not yet,' " she said.

"I'm sorry."

"And with 'I'm sorry.' "

He looked over at Signe's herb garden, searching for a new subject.

"I swear, the woman has a golden touch," he said. "She must be descended from some fertility goddess of yore."

"Unlike me," snapped Gerutha.

"I didn't mean that," he said hastily, coming over to embrace her. She stiffened in his arms. After an awkward hug, he released her.

"It's not always the richness of the soil that makes the garden grow," she said. "Sometimes it's the quality of the seed."

She turned back to the thrall, who was desperately trying to look unconcerned.

"I am going out for a walk," she said. "When I return, I want to find nothing but freshly turned dirt here. I want it to look like a new grave, do you understand?"

"Yes, milady," said the thrall, shoveling frantically.

"Would you like me to . . . ?" began Ørvendil.

"No," she said, walking away.

Alfhild skipped through a meadow, chasing the butterflies that flitted among the flowers. Signe watched her from a low rise, resting against a large cushion that a thrall had carried for her. She plucked a blade of grass from the ground and brushed it across her face, smiling as her daughter stopped to peer at her reflection in a small pond.

A shadow fell over her, and she looked up to see Terence standing behind her.

"Fancy meeting you here," she said.

"I was just passing through," he replied. "May I join you?"

"How does one just pass through the middle of a meadow?" she asked.

"I'm a fool," he replied. "If I started giving reasons for everything that I did, I would be out of a job."

"True enough," she said.

They sat in silence for a while, watching Alfhild.

"She grows more like you every day," said Terence. "A good thing, in my opinion."

"Thank you," she said. "I wonder what the new one will be like?"

"So do I," he said. "Is it a boy or a girl?"

"A boy, I think," she said. "He feels much different than Alfhild did. He's very active."

"Still, I hope that he also resembles his mother," said Terence.

"What do you have against his father?" she asked.

He looked at her for the first time since he joined her, studying her face in every detail.

"Nothing," he said finally. "I like his father."

"So do I," she said. "So do I."

She went into labor three weeks later, the contractions jolting her into consciousness in the middle of the night. She turned instinctively to her husband, but Gorm had taken to sleeping on a thin blanket in the lower room.

She thought that she would have more time, but the pains were of a greater intensity than anything she had experienced with Alfhild. Her breath came in short, shallow gasps, and the sweat was already running in rivulets. She felt dizzy, and suddenly terrified that the baby would come without anyone there, or that she would die before that, trapping him inside her.

There was a moment of calm between the assaults. She remembered that she had been given a cowbell for just such an emergency. Her hands scrabbled along the base of the wall until they met up with it, and she shook it hard, finally getting enough air into her lungs to cry out.

For the first time since she had come to Slesvig, she was grateful for living in an armed camp. The patrols were out and alert, and from their vantages high above her had watched the progress of her pregnancy through the months with interest. She had become a favorite of the men posted at the island, and they had quietly promised each other to keep an eye out for their leader's quarters in case anything like this happened. They quickly sounded the alarum.

Ørvendil and Gorm dashed out of their respective quarters, swords in hand, searching for information. The soldiers on the walls were shouting and pointing at Gorm's home. The drost ran back inside, past a startled Alfhild who had been in the middle of a bad dream, and dashed up the stairs. He was back out in a trice.

"It's her time," he told Ørvendil. "I must fetch the midwife."

"Go," said Ørvendil. "I'll send Gerutha up to stay with her until she arrives. Godspeed."

With a speed that belied his girth, the drost made for the drawbridge, calling for it to be lowered. He stood impatiently for nearly ten minutes as the guards struggled with the windlass. Finally, he ran up the incline of the partially lowered planks and vaulted the remaining gap over the river.

Amleth was awake with the first sounding of the alarum, and as his father ran upstairs to get his mother, he sneaked into Gorm's quarters. Alfhild was hiding under her sheets, sobbing with terror. He went over to her and whispered, "It's all right. Everything is all right. Go back to sleep. When you wake up, you will be a sister."

He rubbed her back, and the sobbing subsided. Exhausted, she fell back asleep. He heard Signe shriek from upstairs, and ran to be with her.

"Who is it?" gasped Signe as he came in.

"It's Amleth," he said. "Gorm went to get the midwife. Mother is coming."

"Thank you," she said, tears streaking her face. He took her hand, then winced as she crushed his with the coming of the next contraction.

"I'm here, Signe," called Gerutha as she came up the steps, a lit torch in one hand and a small basket in the other. She stopped for a moment in surprise.

"Amleth," she exclaimed. "What are you doing here?"

"He's comforting me," said Signe, managing to smile at the boy.

"You're a good child," said Gerutha briskly as she came over. "But you shouldn't be in here now. This is woman's work."

"But can't I watch?" pleaded Amleth.

"Go," commanded his mother, jamming the torch into a sconce.

Amleth went down the stairs, and his mother turned her attention to Signe.

"So," she said, smiling and patting her cousin's belly. "How does your garden grow?"

The midwife was in a drunken sleep and not easily roused. It took the repeated pounding on her door by the drost, followed by his threats to kick it in when her head finally appeared at the window, to put her into some semblance of haste. She stumbled along slowly while Gorm gritted his teeth and tried not to shove her ahead of him.

"I can't help it if they come in the middle of the night," she complained. "Can't she wait until morning?"

"No!" shouted Gorm.

"Well, you might at least have sent a cart for me," she grumbled.

"There wasn't time," he said. "Please, for the love of God, can't you move any faster?"

"This is how fast I walk," she said. "No point in yelling at me about it. I'm old."

They finally arrived, and the midwife went slowly up the steps while the drost remained below, pacing. When she reached Signe's bedside, Gerutha was kneeling by her, wiping her brow with a wet cloth.

"Ah, yes, I remember this one," said the midwife, rolling up the sleeves of her blouse. "A world of trouble with her first baby."

She felt Signe's brow, then reached for her wrist and checked her pulse. She looked over at Gerutha in alarm.

"What is it?" asked Gerutha.

"You'd better send for a priest," said the midwife.

Gerutha turned pale, then ran down the steps. The midwife turned back to Signe.

"All right, dear," she said cheerfully. "Let's get this baby out."

Ørvendil himself went to the cathedral, not wanting Gorm to leave the island again while his wife was in extremis. Gerutha stayed with the drost, heating up some wine with spices to keep him from storming everything in sight. Unlike with Alfhild's birth, there was no regular series of shrieks from the upper room.

"I should never have done this to her," said Gorm dejectedly. "She warned me that another birth could kill her."

"Who, the midwife? Don't be ridiculous," protested Gerutha. "She's gotten by on luck and volubility for years. There's no woman in town who takes her seriously. I'm sure Signe will be fine."

"But listen to her suffer," said Gorm. "It's all because of me."

"That is her wifely duty," said Gerutha. "The suffering that we all bear as Eve's daughters. Please, stop blaming yourself. Whatever happens is God's will."

Ørvendil returned, priest in tow.

"What's happening?" he asked.

Before anyone could respond, the midwife's voice sounded from up-stairs.

"Is that priest here yet?" she called.

Gorm thundered up the steps, followed more slowly by the priest.

The midwife held a baby in her arms. It was a boy, crying weakly, still bloody. Signe lay nearly still on the bed, only a slight heaving of her breast indicating that she was alive.

"The baby?" she asked, her voice hoarse.

"A boy," said the midwife loudly. "He's fine."

Signe smiled, her eyes closed.

"Better hurry," muttered the midwife.

The priest knelt beside her.

"Milady, do you wish to make confession?" he asked.

"What?" she said, opening her eyes again.

"Confession, milady."

She focused on her husband for the first time.

"Gorm," she said, sounding almost puzzled.

He threw himself down by her, clumsily clutching her hand.

"Stay with me, Signe," he said, sobbing. "You mustn't go. I need you. I love you."

She looked at him as though seeing him from the bottom of a deep pool of water.

"I'm sorry," she whispered.

Then she was gone.

The priest patted Gorm gently on the shoulder.

"I think that, under the circumstances, the Church would regard that as an acceptable confession," he said gently. "Her soul is in Heaven. I'll administer extreme unction and stay with her. My condolences, milord."

Gorm didn't move. Then the baby started crying louder, and he stood to look at it more closely.

"Looks more like her than you, that's for certain," commented the midwife. "You'll be needing a wet nurse, and soon. Try Margaret, the potter's wife. She's still nursing. Here, take him."

Gorm received the boy awkwardly, and turned to look at his wife. The midwife stayed there, an expectant look on her face, but the drost continued staring at the body. Finally, she cleared her throat.

"I get paid either way," she said. "Extra for the middle of the night."

Numbly, he reached into his pouch with his free hand. He had no idea how much he handed her, but she was more than satisfied.

"Well, I'll stop by Margaret's for you," she said. "Sorry about your wife. I thought she might pull through. There was much less blood than with the first one. I guess some women just aren't strong enough to bear children."

She left quickly. Gorm slowly descended the stairs, the baby mewling in his arms. Gerutha and Ørvendil were waiting for him.

"I'm sorry, old friend," said Ørvendil. "But at least you have a son, now. What are you naming him?"

"I thought Lother," said the drost.

"A good king in his time by all reports," said Ørvendil. "You should get him christened quickly."

"Let me take him," said Gerutha kindly. "You've done enough."

"I have," said Gorm. He handed the boy over to her, and lay down on his blanket, staring at the ceiling. "She's in Heaven now."

"Of course," said Gerutha firmly. "But you still live, and you have two children to raise. You must honor her memory in being their father."

"I shall never have another wife," said Gorm softly.

"We won't talk about that," said Ørvendil. "Get some rest. We'll get Lother to that wet nurse as soon as possible."

He left to await her arrival. Gerutha sat on a chair and rocked the baby, watching Gorm and Alfhild sleeping. Suddenly her eyes darted over to the steps where Amleth was creeping down.

"Were you hiding up there?" she whispered. He nodded. "The entire time?" He nodded again, miserably. She beckoned to him, and he came over to her.

"I should punish you for your disobedience," she said, pulling his head to rest on her bosom. "But there is enough sorrow here tonight. Go to bed, and this will be our secret."

He left, staggering from the lack of sleep, and went to find the comfort of his pallet. But sleep would not come to him. The image of Signe's body floated above him, her face over his, her mouth still open, as if she still wanted to take one more breath.

He wasn't frightened by the image. He had seen dead people before. He just couldn't understand why Signe chose to be one of them.

The cock crowed, and he sat up, having lain awake the entire time. His mother was still with the baby, and his father was busy making arrangements for the funeral. He walked about the island, but a pall had fallen across it, Even the animals were subdued, sensing the sadness of their keepers. He walked silently by the chickens, not bothering to chase them for once.

He wanted to talk to Yorick, to have the fool explain everything to him. He did not understand everything that he saw. He didn't know why having a baby killed the mother. He didn't think that that happened all of the time. His mother was still alive. Most of his friends had living mothers. Why should this baby be so deadly?

He slipped through the gate over the drawbridge and walked into town. He knew where Yorick had his room, and found the back way into the tavern without difficulty. He heard a sound from within that was unlike anything he had ever heard coming out of the fool's mouth before. He peeped cautiously around the doorway.

Yorick was huddled in a corner of the room, an empty wineskin at his feet. He was moaning, a low, guttural sound, and clutching his head to his knees.

"Yorick?" said Amleth softly.

The fool looked bleakly up at the boy.

"What are you doing here?" he said. "It's too early for you. And it's too late for me."

"I wanted to know something," said Amleth. "Everyone at the island is too busy to tell me."

"What, child?" said the fool.

[143]

"Why did the baby kill his mother?"

The fool stared at the boy, then beckoned him closer. He wrapped him in an embrace, his wine-drenched breath coursing over the little one's neck.

"He didn't kill her," said the fool, his whiteface streaking anew from his tears. "She died. It is something that happens sometimes with women. That is why we should honor all of them. She was a good woman."

"I liked her," said Amleth.

"So did I," said the fool. "But liking someone never stopped them from dying. How is the boy?"

"They were fetching a wet nurse from town," said Amleth. "They think he'll live."

"Thank Christ for that," said the fool. "What will they name him?"

"Lother," said Amleth.

"Lother," repeated the fool. "I like it."

He released the boy and pointed to his pallet. There was a bunch of flowers lying there, tied loosely.

"Take those, and put them by her," he said. "Tell no one. It will be our secret."

"That's my second secret today, and the sun is still low," said Amleth.

"What was the other one?" asked the fool.

Amleth told him how he had sneaked back into Signe's room to watch her give birth to Lother. The fool listened intently, asking a few questions, then sat back in his corner at the end of the narrative and closed his eyes.

"That's a good secret to keep," he said.

"Is it still a secret now that I've told you?" asked Amleth.

"You can trust me with anything," said Terence. "You know that."

Amleth returned to the fortress with the bouquet in his hands. As he came to the drost's quarters, his mother grabbed him by the wrist.

"Where did you vanish to?" she said angrily. "I have been looking everywhere."

"I went to get these," said Amleth, holding the bouquet up. "I wanted to give these to her."

Gerutha snatched the flowers from him and threw them on the refuse heap.

"To your room," she commanded him. "I'll deal with you later."

He looked at her in astonishment.

"Well?" she snapped.

He turned and fled inside.

Alfhild was there, sitting by the window. She turned when she heard him come in.

"Mama is dead," she said, sniffling. "And they won't let me hold the baby."

She started to cry. Amleth wanted to do the same, but he looked at the little girl, then sat next to her, his arm around her.

"Everything will be fine," he said. "I'm here."

The midwife woke around noon, feeling ravenous. She had been overpaid for her services, but felt that the indignities to which she had been subjected merited the additional remuneration. She prepared a meal, then cursed as she realized she was out of wine. She was about to go out when there was a knocking at her door.

She knew of no other imminent births. Puzzled, she opened the door to see that tavern fool standing before her, grinning maniacally.

"What do you want?" she asked abruptly.

"To know everything," he said. "Is not that the goal of any fool?"

"What do you want to know from me?" she asked.

"About Signe and Lother, a birth and a death in the same hour," he said.

"Those are personal matters," she said. "Hardly the subject of common gossip."

He held up a wineskin and jiggled it so that a pleasant sloshing noise came from within it.

"Well, in that case," she said, holding the door open.

He smiled and went in.

TWELVE

"They fool me to the top of my bent."

—*HAMLET*, ACT III, SCENE II

Slesvig—Roskilde, 1162 A.D.

The midwife had no friends or family in Slesvig. The general suspicion that she may have been a witch kept most of the townsfolk away. It may have been because of this that her absence from view caused no notice. It was a lovesick farmer's daughter who found her, stretched out on her pallet with several knife wounds in her chest. The girl had wanted a love potion to win the affections of a neighboring shepherd, but ended up fleeing the house, screaming at the top of her lungs. Strangely enough, the story she told, enhanced by repetition and her fertile imagination, eventually so enthralled the shepherd that he fell for her charms without any occult enhancement.

"The last person who was seen talking to her was Yorick," said Ørvendil to his wife as they undressed that night.

"Yorick?" said Gerutha. "What possible interest would he have in a midwife?"

"I asked him that very question," said Ørvendil. "He protested up and down that he had nothing to do with her death. He only wanted to hear about poor Signe's last moments."

"He did? Why?" wondered Gerutha.

"Curiosity, I suppose," said Ørvendil. "Too morbid for my tastes, but a jester dines out on stories and gossip, so that would have been meat for his stew."

"And you believe he had no part in her death?" asked Gerutha.

"The midwife? No," said Ørvendil. "What reason would he have for killing her?"

"I frankly do not know," admitted Gerutha. "But to be the last to see her alive..."

"He was the last anyone else saw seeing her alive," her husband corrected her.

"Still, it makes you think, doesn't it?" asked Gerutha.

"Not of Yorick," said Ørvendil. "I trust him."

"He may have murdered a woman, and you trust him to play with our son," said Gerutha.

"I'll have one of my men look into it tomorrow," he said.

"Not Gorm," she said.

"Hm? No, I take your meaning," he said sleepily. "He's having enough troubles as it is right now."

"You missed my meaning," she said. "Wouldn't you consider him a possibility?"

He sat up.

"No," he said. "Not Gorm."

"Yet you sound less certain about him than you did about Yorick," she said. "Gorm has been completely distraught since he lost Signe. He may very well have held the midwife responsible for the death of his wife."

"I pray that wasn't what happened," said Ørvendil. "But I'll put a different man on it."

"Good," said Gerutha. "I want to get to the bottom of all this."

The next morning Gorm staggered into the great hall, dark patches under his eyes. He saw Ørvendil speaking to a captain of the guards. The Duke glanced over at the drost, whispered something hurriedly to the captain, then clapped him on the back and sent him on his way. Then he turned to Gorm, smiling broadly.

"You look like hell," he said.

"I was up with the baby all night," groaned Gorm. "It's difficult when the wet nurse isn't here. Thank you for letting Alfhild sleep with Amleth."

"Thank my wife for that," said Ørvendil. "She figured you had enough on your mind right now."

"I heard about the midwife," said Gorm. "I'll start looking into it today."

"No need," said Ørvendil. "I just sent Lars to do it."

"You did?" said Gorm. "But that should be my responsibility."

"Your responsibility right now is to that baby," said Ørvendil. "Lars will handle it just fine."

Gorm looked at his master closely.

"You think I had something to do with it, don't you?" he said.

"No," said Ørvendil. "I honestly don't. But we have to make sure that the investigation . . ."

"You think I had something to do with it!" Gorm repeated loudly.

Ørvendil's face darkened. He walked quickly up to the drost and grabbed him by the shoulders.

"Now, you listen to me," he said quietly. "If I put you in charge of an investigation while the town gossip already has you as a possible murderer, then no one will trust whatever conclusions you reach."

"But if you don't put me in charge, then everyone will know that you don't trust me," said Gorm.

"Everyone knows that you are in mourning and that you are taking care of that baby," said Ørvendil. "No one will think that I don't trust you."

"I will," said Gorm. "Do you wish me to resign from your service?"

"Not in the least," protested Ørvendil.

The drost sat down at the table, resting his head in his hands.

"I'm sorry," he said, beginning to weep.

"Look," said Ørvendil more kindly. "If that wet nurse won't move in here, why don't you take a place in town near her?"

"In town?" said Gorm. "But my post is here. My men are here."

"You would come in here first thing in the morning," said Ørvendil. "It's not as if you're patrolling with the night watch, and this way you could get out of your quarters until the memory fades from them. I'm sure Alfhild would prefer staying somewhere else."

"She'll stay where I tell her to stay," said Gorm. "She's my daughter."

"It's just a suggestion," said Ørvendil. "If you'd rather stay, then stay."

"I'll think about it," said Gorm wearily.

Amleth was juggling with Terence, tossing four clubs back and forth. Alfhild sat on the ground nearby, watching the boy in admiration. When Gerutha came out of the great hall, Amleth was the first to espy her.

"Mother, look!" he cried. "Look what I can do."

"Very good, Amleth," she said, coming up to Terence's side. "Go play with Alfhild for a minute. I want to speak with Yorick."

"All right," he said to Alfhild's delight. He started rolling a ball to her.

"So many 'Mother, looks' to get through," said Gerutha, watching them play. "What with you teaching him juggling and his father teaching him swordplay."

"Both useful skills," said Terence. "With swordplay, you can survive in wars. With juggling, you can survive in taverns."

"It's almost as if he has two fathers," said Gerutha. "He dotes so much upon you."

"I am merely a friend," said Terence. "He knows who his father is. He adores him. And you."

"I wonder if I have been the best mother to him," she said. "Perhaps I have indulged him, letting him be with you so much."

"If you consider that an indulgence, so be it," said Terence. "Have your husband say the word, and I will stop coming here. The children would be disappointed, though."

"They would get over it," said Gerutha.

"You seem anxious to have me go," said Terence.

"I am trying to protect my son," said Gerutha.

"From me?" laughed Terence. "I am also his protector. I keep his mind from knotting up too tightly."

"It's just that," she said, hesitating for a moment, "you were seen visiting that poor midwife."

"Her name was Thora," said Terence. "She complained about always being called the midwife rather than by her actual name. Funny how your profession can disfigure you for life like that. Midwife. Thrall. Fool. Before you know it, everyone's forgotten your true name, including yourself. Queen is another one like that."

"Did you kill her?" asked Gerutha.

"I had no reason to, although a fool always lacks reason, so maybe that is no excuse. No, I am no more likely a candidate for the gallows than you are, milady."

"I am glad to know it, Fool," she said, turning to leave. Then she turned back. "I wouldn't become too enamored of this protector role," she said, smiling pleasantly. "I take care of my own."

"I am certain of that, milady," he said, bowing.

The next day Gorm walked back from inspecting the northern defenses, which seemed more formidable every time he saw them. Lother seemed as if he wanted to live, to the drost's relief. He had taken to the wet nurse with enthusiasm, and was considered by her to be a good-natured baby, something Gorm himself felt unqualified to say.

He noticed, as he neared the brickyard, that Reynaldo was walking on a path that would soon intersect his own. The Tuscan nodded curtly at the drost.

"Good morning," said Gorm in Tuscan.

Reynaldo looked at him in surprise.

"I did not know that you spoke our language," he said.

"I spent some time there when I was younger," said Gorm. "I don't have much of an opportunity to speak it around here."

"You speak it well," said Reynaldo.

"Thank you," said Gorm. "You speak ours well, too."

"I do all right," said Reynaldo, then he stopped, his face turning crimson.

"I thought as much," said Gorm, switching back to Danish.

"You think you are so smart," said Reynaldo. "You follow us around, and listen to our conversations, and act like you know everything. Well, I tell you right now that you know nothing."

"I may know more than you think," said Gorm. "But if there is any matter on which you would enlighten me, feel free."

Reynaldo looked around quickly. There was no one else within earshot.

"There is something you might be interested in," he said. "For a price, I might tell it to you."

"Or I could torture it out of you for nothing," said Gorm. "In my present mood, I may do that anyway. I suggest that you start talking before I change my mind."

"It is information that could put me in grave danger," said Reynaldo. "And you."

"Don't worry about my life," said Gorm. "I place little value on it. What do you have to say?"

"It is a strange thing, living so far from home," said Reynaldo, sighing. "I thought when I left Tuscany that the farther north I went, the colder the people would be. But now that I am in Slesvig, I find that the people here are the same as my own. They are fairer, they eat different foods, much worse food in my opinion, but they are still the same. There are passions here, ambitions, love, hatred. I am a passionate man. I left behind a woman that I loved who was forced to marry another. I buried my heart in Tuscany and thought I would never see it again."

He sighed again. "I say all this to you because I know that you understand great passion. I have seen what you have gone through with the loss of your good wife, may her soul find Heaven. I know that you will understand what a momentous thing it is for me to say that I have found my heart again."

"Are you saying that you love a maid?" asked Gorm. "Is that what this is all about? Hardly worth payment or torture."

"It is that, but much more," said Reynaldo. "I am a constant man. When I have a passion, it is for the person, and for everything around her. I have fallen in love with a Danish maid, and with this country, with these strangely shaped waters and constant winds. And it is because of this love that I now wish to protect what I had been brought here to destroy."

"I take it that you are not talking about brickmaking anymore," said Gorm.

"We are the first recruits for what will become a much larger army," said Reynaldo. "You don't need so many Tuscans to supervise a kiln. One skilled brickmaker is enough. I know that you have suspected us for some time. You were correct to do so. I could show you where we buried our cache of weapons."

"But who do you work for?" asked Gorm.

"Surely you have guessed by now," said Reynaldo. "Who but the man who brought us here?"

"Ørvendil?" said Gorm.

"The same," replied Reynaldo. "Already, he has begun transferring the men he cannot trust to posts outside of the island. I am surprised that he has not suggested that you leave there yet."

"Ørvendil," said Gorm in despair. "But why?"

"A man with an army may do what he wishes," said Reynaldo. "I was not trained to ask questions. I could make my guesses, but you know your master better than I do."

"I thought I did," muttered Gorm. "And now you have come to me because you have had a change of heart."

"No," said Reynaldo. "When I came here, I was a heartless man. My heart has not changed so much as it has been rediscovered. Now, I fear bloody war and the death of all that I want to live. I cannot run away and leave my beloved behind again. I cannot afford to spirit her out of here. So, I must change what will happen before it is too late. The only person I could think of coming to with this information was you."

"Because I am a passionate man," said Gorm.

"And a brave one. And one who loves his country. And his children."

They walked along in silence, Gorm thinking, Reynaldo watching him think.

"Tell no one else about this," said Gorm. "I must find out who among my soldiers I may trust. I will get word to a man I know who has the ear of the King. Do not speak to me again."

"Thank you, milord," said Reynaldo fervently. "When our first son is born, he shall have your name."

"No," said Gorm sadly. "It would be like naming him Judas."

He turned toward the island. Reynaldo watched him. Then he walked to the house of his Slesvig maid. She was passionate. After he paid her.

Valdemar read the letter that Fengi handed to him. Then he reread it.

"I think that we have moved beyond suspicions," he said.

"Yes, milord," said Fengi sadly.

"You trust this man?" asked the King.

"You know him as well as I do," said Fengi. "He fought well for you on Grathe Moor while my brother sat on his fortified island, waiting to see who would win."

"He stayed because I told him to," said Valdemar.

"Yes, and with remarkably little protest," said Fengi. "All I am saying is for a man like Gorm to approach you like this without his master's knowledge . . ."

"It must be tearing him apart," said Valdemar.

"He may rather have himself torn apart than see his country suffer the same fate," said Fengi.

"All right," said Valdemar. "We will remove Ørvendil from power. But we will do it properly, by Danelaw. We have long delayed the convening of the Slesvig *thing*. I think that it is time we called it."

"My brother will think that it's being called to formally elect him," said Fengi.

"We will let him think so," said Valdemar. "But when the time comes, you will denounce him in my name and seize him."

"Me, milord?" exclaimed Fengi.

"You," said Valdemar. "I am proposing that you assume the reins of power in Slesvig. With my backing, you will be selected. I want to have someone in there that I can trust."

"You would trust a man who would betray his own brother?" asked Fengi.

"I would trust a man who is bound to me, not by petty ties to his family," said Valdemar.

Fengi knelt before him and kissed his ring.

"I shall do your bidding," he said.

As Fengi left the King's chamber, he saw Gerald heading toward him.

"So long, Fool," he said. "I am off to Slesvig."

"Ah, to visit your brother," said Gerald. "Always good to see family. Have a pleasant journey."

"Oh, I will," chuckled Fengi. "The best ever."

Gerald watched him as he walked away, suddenly suspicious. Then he knocked respectfully on the King's door.

"Enter," said Valdemar.

Gerald came in to find his master in a foul mood, his eyes perusing a letter in his hand.

"Fengi was in good spirits when he left here," said Gerald. "Did he steal yours?"

"Don't attempt to cheer me, Fool," said Valdemar. "I have no taste for it right now."

"What is the matter?" asked Gerald.

"Nothing that concerns you," said Valdemar. "I've taken care of it already. Go amuse someone else."

"Very good, milord," said Gerald, bowing and retreating from the room.

He wished he had a glimpse of the letter in Valdemar's hand. He walked quickly until he reached Fengi's lodgings. He knew that the man's room was on the second floor, out of earshot. He ducked down an alley, laid his staff on the ground, and climbed a water barrel. Then he jumped, his hands catching the edge of the roof. He pulled himself on top, hoping that no pedestrian would bother looking up. He crawled to a spot over Fengi's room, then pressed his ear to a crack between the wooden planks that covered it.

"Pack everything," he heard Fengi say.

"Everything, milord?" replied a thrall. "Are we staying for a while in Slesvig?"

"Oh, yes," said Fengi. "For a very long while."

Gerald listened for a while longer, but heard nothing of use. When he heard the door close, he inched backward to the side of the house and dropped back onto the water barrel. He jumped down and grabbed his staff, then ran to his own quarters to fetch his gear. Then he started to run.

Before Fengi's thralls had finished packing, the priest was several miles south.

He reached Slesvig five days later, hoping he had a lead on Fengi. He rummaged through his pack and pulled out some suitably rustic garb, hoping to pass for a farmer on a rare jaunt into town. He stowed his motley, picked up his staff, and walked to The Viking's Rest.

It was late afternoon, and the fish packers, smelling about as one would expect, were on their first round of ale. A group of brickmakers entered, chattering away in Tuscan. Gerald was wearing a broad, floppy cloth hat that kept his face partially concealed. He scanned the room from under it, looking for his colleague but not finding him. Something about one of the other patrons jolted his memory. He desperately wanted to talk to Terence. He was about to inquire of the tapster as to his whereabouts when he heard a drum beating outside. He turned just as Terence staggered in, looking gaunt underneath his whiteface.

"Entertainment!" cried Terence as the drunken denizens turned and cheered. "Where is the entertainment?" He tripped over a stool and his head slammed into the edge of the bar as the room laughed heartily.

"Oh, wait," he said, straightening. "I am the entertainment."

He began juggling clubs, but the past proficiency was not there. The third or fourth time he dropped them, he just let them lay on the floor. Gerald saw with alarm that the fool's forehead was gashed from when he had hit the bar, the blood dripping into his eyes. Terence dabbed at it ineffectually with his sleeve.

"Now, where was I?" he said. "Was I telling the one about the maid and the ass, or the ass and the maid? Neither of them has a happy ending. Where's my drink?"

"Ten rounds of juggling without a drop first," said the tapster. "Pick up your clubs."

Terence picked them up and held them in front of him. "If there's a drop, then there won't be a drop," he said. "But if there is no drop, then there will be a drop. Is that the challenge?"

"That's it," said the tapster.

"Count for me, everyone," said Terence, and as the fish packers took up the count, he began juggling three clubs.

He made it through to the end to the cheers of the room, and seized his mug of ale with a flourish. But Gerald saw the effort it had taken him for a feat that any ten year old at the Guild could do with his eyes shut. He watched with dismay as Terence floundered through a ribald ballad. When the fool retired, Gerald slipped around to the back and caught him sagging to the floor.

"What in the name of the First Fool is wrong with you?" said the priest, helping him to his pallet.

"Performed at a party," said Terence. "Too much to drink."

"I've never heard of you letting your drinking get in the way of your performing," said Gerald.

"A drunk can get as many laughs as a fool around here," said Terence. "It's much easier and a lot more fun. What are you doing here? I wasn't expecting you until next month."

"I think Fengi's up to something," said Gerald. "He's on his way here."

"When?" asked Terence sleepily.

"Maybe in the next two days," said Gerald. "But I have to ask you something. What do you know about those Tuscans?"

"Brickmakers," said Terence. "Maybe spies, who knows?"

"More than maybe," said Gerald. He dug into his pack and pulled out a sheaf of papers, shuffling through them until he found the one that he wanted. "Who is this man?" he demanded.

Terence squinted blearily at it.

"I know him," he said. "When did he sit for his portrait?"

"In Roskilde," said Gerald. "He was dining with Fengi."

"Well," said Terence. "That's odd. Must be one of Fengi's spies."

"Why didn't you know that?" said Gerald.

"I don't know lots of things," said Terence. "And the things I do know, I can't do anything about." Then, to Gerald's shock, he curled up on his pallet and began to weep.

"Stop this," said Gerald, pulling him upright and cuffing him about the head.

"Quit it," cried Terence, feebly shielding himself with his arms.

"What is the matter with you?" asked Gerald.

"Secrets," said Terence. "Too many of them. I can't prove anything. I can't tell Amleth what I suspect, and I can't protect him from it."

"Amleth?" asked Gerald. "Protect him from what?"

"He couldn't possibly understand," blurted out Terence. "He'd turn on me."

"What are you talking about?" asked Gerald in bewilderment.

Terence suddenly knelt before Gerald, clutching at his tunic. "You're still a priest, aren't you?" he asked.

"Yes," said Gerald.

"Help me," begged Terence.

"What is it?" asked Gerald.

Terence looked up at him, the blood drying on his brow, his whiteface crosshatched with tear tracks.

"Forgive me, Father," he whispered. "For I have sinned."

Father Gerald looked out at us. No, he couldn't look out at us, we all knew that, yet it seemed in that moment that his gaze had returned to him, filled with sadness and compassion. Portia was long asleep in her mother's arms, but she was the only one not held captive by the old priest's tale.

"There are disadvantages to being a man in holy orders," he said. "Especially when one's natural inclinations to storytelling become subservient to the most sacred of confidences. What I heard that night, I cannot say, even now after so many years.

"But what was to come, I can tell you. Even in my final darkness, I can see it. I cannot tell you how often I wish that I could not."

THIRTEEN

"Let the doors be shut upon him, that he may play the fool nowhere but in's own house."

—HAMLET, ACT III, SCENE I

Slesvig, 1162 A.D.

Gerald left early the next morning to avoid being seen in town by Fengi. Terence, despite his hangover, rose and walked with him to the northern gate.

"Are you sure you can handle this by yourself?" asked Gerald.

"No," said Terence. "But having you here will probably just make things worse."

"I could send another fool in," said Gerald.

"You don't trust me," said Terence.

"Not in your present state of mind," said Gerald.

Terence put his left hand on his cap and bells and thumbed his nose with his right.

"I swear by the First Fool, Our Savior, by David's lyre and Balaam's ass that I will not get drunk until you see me again," he said. "And only then if you drink along with me. Will that suffice?"

There was something in his look, bloodshot though his eyes were, that reassured the priest.

"Yes," he said. "That will suffice. *Te absolvo.*"

"Nice that you can do that," said Terence. "Go talk to your king."

There was a cry from the guards at the drawbridge the next day as Fengi and his retinue arrived. Gerutha hurriedly presented herself to greet him.

"My dear brother," she scolded him. "Again you arrive without warning. We would have prepared a proper feast for you. Whence comes this discourtesy?"

"Forgive me, sister," he said, bowing and kissing her hand. "My news demanded haste, and my anticipated pleasure at giving it transcended the ordinary courtesies. Where is my brother?"

"Inspecting the southern earthworks," she replied. "He will be home this afternoon. Let me escort you to your room."

He took her arm and walked across the drawbridge onto the island, a satisfied smile on his face as he passed through its gate. Gorm was standing inside with an honor guard. As his eyes met Fengi's, he nodded slightly.

Fengi greeted him, then embraced the drost.

"My friend, we have heard of your loss," he said. "No words can possibly console you for that, but the King himself wished me to express his love and condolences to you on his behalf."

"I thank you, milord," said Gorm.

"How did Fengi know about that already?" wondered Terence, who was watching from a short distance away.

"Why?" asked Amleth, who was standing next to him.

Terence looked down at the boy and patted his head.

"Forgive me, young lord," he said. "I hadn't realized that I was speaking aloud. Forget that I said it."

They watched Fengi approach with Gerutha. Fengi smiled broadly when he saw the boy.

"Has he doubled in size since my last visit?" said Fengi, holding his arms out. Amleth ran and leapt into his uncle's embrace, Fengi staggering slightly from the impact.

"Hello, uncle," said Amleth. "I have a sword now. Would you like to see it?"

"I certainly would," said Fengi, prying the boy loose and lowering him to the ground.

"Look!" said Amleth proudly, drawing it and shoving it almost in his uncle's face.

Fengi stepped back hastily.

"Take heed, boy," he said. "Even toy swords may wound. Hand it over." He took it and examined it, nodding before giving it back.

"I remember when your grandfather gave that to your father," he said. "Ørvendil chased me all over the grounds for the rest of the day, waving it around and screaming bloody murder. I hope that he has taught you better than that."

"Oh, he teaches me every day," said Amleth proudly. "Someday, I will be as good a swordsman as he is. He's the best there ever was."

"That's what everyone says," said Fengi. "And I see your friend the fool is still lurking about."

Terence bowed.

"Milord, it is good to see you again," he said. "If there is any entertainment that you desire, it will be my pleasure to provide it."

"I am hoping to be the entertainment," said Fengi. "But that must await my brother's arrival. Sister, I am at your service."

He offered Gerutha his arm, and the two of them walked into the great hall.

Terence watched Fengi's thralls unload his bags from a wain.

"Looks like an extended visit," he commented to Amleth.

"Good," said Amleth. "I like Uncle Fengi."

"Doesn't everyone?" observed Terence.

When Ørvendil returned to Slesvig, he observed the fool sitting cross-legged on a large boulder near the ruins of the Viking tower.

"Hail, Yorick," he called, heading his horse in that direction. "What brings you here?"

"The winds of rumor," said the fool. "Fortunately, I had my sails set to catch them."

"What news do these winds carry?" asked Ørvendil.

"Suspicions only," said the fool. "Improbable threats, yet were they to prove true, then there is one here who will prove false."

"I am too tired for riddles," said Ørvendil.

"So am I," said Terence. "Your brother is arrived from Roskilde. He took enough time to get here to allow my brother fool to beat him in a race that he knew nothing about. He thinks that your brother means you harm."

"This is the same fool that sits at the throne of Valdemar?"

"Yes, milord."

"What does Valdemar say about Fengi?"

"We don't know, milord," admitted Terence. "But your brother has the King's trust, and you don't. Now, Fengi arrives with no advance warning, promising to entertain you tonight."

"So he's a threat to your job as well, is he?" chuckled Ørvendil. "Is that all you could come up with?"

"There's one more thing," said Terence. "He already knew of Signe's death. He publicly embraced Gorm and consoled him. Only a pigeon could have gotten word to him that quickly, and there's only one man in Slesvig who uses them."

"So Gorm is in communication with someone in Roskilde," said Ørvendil. "There's nothing odd about that."

"But . . ."

"Cease, enough," said Ørvendil. "My brother and I have had our differences, but those were long ago. We still share the same blood."

"Then pray that none of it is shed," said Terence. "Please take precautions, milord. They can be done quietly, and if I'm wrong, then there's no harm done."

"You waylay me and accuse my brother and my drost to my face," said Ørvendil. "Next thing you'll be telling me is that my son is part of the conspiracy."

"Of all the people in Denmark, your son is the one you may trust the most," said Terence. "I would that you considered me as loyal and honest."

"I do," said Ørvendil. "But you are trying to frighten me with trifles. Even if I doubted my brother, I would not fear him. He has never been able to defeat me in any form of combat."

"He's a cunning man, milord," said Terence. "I wish you had his subtlety. He may defeat you by connivance rather than combat."

"Let him try," declared Ørvendil grandly. "Now, let's go have dinner."

Ørvendil embraced his brother at the entrance to the island while the soldiers applauded from the walls.

"Good to see you, little brother," he said. "What brings you at such speed to our home?"

"Nothing but the best of news giving my horse wings," said Fengi, pulling a scroll from his pouch. He held it aloft so that all could see the royal seal, then he opened it.

" 'By order of Valdemar, King of all Denmark,' " he read, bellowing the words to the four corners of the island. " 'The position of Duke of Slesvig has never been formally confirmed. Therefore, we call an assemblage of the Slesvig *thing*, so that the citizens of which it is composed may vote upon the matter. Thus decreed, Valdemar.' " He rolled up the scroll and handed it to Ørvendil with a flourish. "Congratulations, my brother."

Ørvendil drew his sword, stuck it in the ground, and knelt before it, his hands clasped before him.

"I give thanks to Almighty God," he said. "To His Son and the Holy Spirit, to His Blessed Mother and all of His saints. May I prove worthy of His trust and of the King's."

"Amen," said Fengi, kneeling by his side.

"Gorm, my friend," called Ørvendil, rising.

"Here, milord," said the drost, coming forward.

"Will you arrange for the assembly? Two nights hence, on the Sacred Hill. Let a bonfire be built that will be seen throughout the land."

"It will be done, milord," said the drost. "Soldiers, give up your voices for your lord and master."

The cheers filled the island. Ørvendil acknowledged them with a nod, then turned and smiled at his wife and son, who were standing in the entrance to the great hall. As he and his brother walked in for the feast, Ørvendil saw Terence leaning casually against the wall, his arms folded, his face expressionless. He winked at the fool and vanished into the hall.

"Come on, Yorick," urged Amleth, tugging on the fool's arm. "It's time for dinner."

Terence smiled.

"Do you know what the first rule of fooling is, Amleth?"

"What, Yorick?"

"Always take your meal when you find it, even if you're not hungry. You never know if it's going to be your last."

"That's not much of a rule, Yorick," said Amleth as they went in.

"What do you want from me?" asked Terence. "Wisdom?"

"You see?" crowed Ørvendil to his wife as they prepared for bed. "Things have worked out after all."

"I see that after all these years of loyalty and hard work, you are in exactly the same place as yesterday," said Gerutha. "What difference does a title make?"

"It makes you a duchess," said Ørvendil, bowing playfully to her.

"When I could have been a queen," she replied bitterly.

He lunged forward and slapped her face.

"How dare you?" he shouted as she sank to her knees in terror. "Will you never be satisfied?"

Not by you, she thought, but she held her tongue this time.

Ørvendil climbed to the top of the archers' platform just before dawn. The night watch was thinly manned due to the celebration the previous evening. He found only one person at that post, seated in the center of the platform, silhouetted against the first glimmerings of the sun. Then the figure turned, causing a faint tintinnabulation with his cap.

"Yorick?" exclaimed Ørvendil.

"My name is Terence," said the fool quietly. "Everyone's forgotten that. Except for one."

"Who is that?" asked Ørvendil, sitting beside him.

"Doesn't matter," said Terence. "Dead, now. Maybe you shouldn't use my name. It may bring bad luck."

"My luck seems good right now," said Ørvendil.

" 'Seems,' " said Terence. "That is such an unreliable word. So is 'luck.' "

"So is 'fear,' " said Ørvendil. "Your fears are more unfounded than my luck."

"So it seems," said Terence. "Keep your sword loose in its scabbard, just in case."

"I always do," said Ørvendil.

Gorm stood at the foot of Signe's grave. Someone had left a bunch of wildflowers on it, tied with a long blade of grass. Already, small plants were sprouting from the earth, as if her gift for growing continued beyond death.

"Thought I'd find you here," said Fengi.

The drost turned. The other man was seated on a grave stone behind him.

"I'm sorry to invade your privacy, but this seemed like the best place to talk to you," said Fengi.

"She's dead because I failed her," said Gorm bleakly. "It is appropriate that she witness my betrayal."

"It is you who are betrayed, my friend," said Fengi. "You are the one who is loyal to the King, not your master."

"Very well," said the drost. "You know my conditions."

"I do," said Fengi. "And I welcome them."

. . .

All through the next two days, thralls chopped down trees and carried them to a great, flat-topped hill south of the town. They piled them together, then more on top, until a pyramid of wood soared fifty feet into the air. Amleth and Terence watched them from a safe distance.

"What is so sacred about this hill?" asked Amleth.

"I don't know," said Terence. "I asked one of the priests about it, but he just muttered something about sacrilege and walked away. I guess that the *thing* has been coming here since before the Church came to Slesvig."

"Were there human sacrifices here?" asked Amleth, his eyes wide.

"Maybe," said Terence. "But we don't do that anymore."

The sun was beginning to set. From their vantage point, they could see men streaming toward the hill from every direction. The thralls were rolling barrels of pitch up the hill now. When they reached the top, they upended them and poured their contents over the newly hewn logs so that they would burn more readily.

"All right," said Terence. "I promised your mother that I would bring you back before sunset."

"Can't I stay and watch?" pleaded the boy.

"This is man's business," he said. "No place for you yet."

Back at the island, Ørvendil was ready. His armor was burnished to a dull gleam, and his horse had been brushed until its coat shone as well. Amleth held the horse's reins for his father as he mounted, Gerutha emerged from the great hall, holding an enormous golden goblet with both hands. She stood before him and offered it up.

"Mead," she said. "Brewed as our ancestors did to honor the gods."

"The gods?" he said, laughing. "Don't let the priests hear you. Those days are long past."

"Tonight's ritual is from the old days," she said. "Sometimes, the old ways are the best ways. To you, my lord and husband."

She drank from the goblet, then handed it up to him. He downed it in three gulps, then held it aloft.

"For Slesvig!" he shouted, and the men picked up the cry and sent it over the town.

He handed the goblet back.

"Thank you, Gerutha," he said. Then he seized the reins of the horse and galloped over the drawbridge.

Gerutha and Amleth watched him depart.

"Where's Yorick?" she asked him.

"He went back to watch the *thing*," said Amleth. "I wish I could see it."

"Just as well," said Gerutha. "They are really long, boring ceremonies from what I have heard. I'm tired. I am going to lie down for a while. Wake me when your father comes back."

"Yes, mother," he said.

She kissed him, then went inside.

He stood looking at the drawbridge. Then he looked up at the guard standing over it. The guard saw him, then grinned and nodded.

Ørvendil caught up to the fool at the base of the hill.

"Well, Terence?" he said, dismounting. "What do you say now?"

"Maybe Terence shouldn't be my name either," said the fool. "I've been thinking of changing it."

"To what?"

"Cassandra," said Terence, watching the last rays of the sun disappear.

There was a roaring noise, and the two men looked up to see flames shoot into the air as the gathered men cheered.

"Let's go," said Ørvendil.

The elders of Slesvig and the surrounding villages stood in front of the fire. The oldest stepped forward.

"As our ancestors did, as our children will do, I call upon the men of Slesvig to ascend the Sacred Hill," he intoned in a hoarse voice. "Are you here, men of Slesvig?"

"We are!" shouted the men.

"As Danelaw sets forth, and by decree of the King, we are gathered to elect one of us to be our ruler. Is there any man here who would assume that great burden?"

"I will," said Ørvendil, striding into the center of the circle.

"Give us your name, candidate."

"I am Ørvendil Gervendilson."

"What are your qualifications?"

Ørvendil turned and faced the assembly.

"For many years I have been the steward of your fortunes, the watcher of your borders, the builder of your defenses, and the protector of your children. I have been placed here at the behest of the man who is now our king, and have his love and trust. I ask that I may continue to serve you."

The respectful thumping of staves and swords on the ground met this speech, and Ørvendil bowed to the elders.

"Well spoken, milord," said the leader. "Is there any man who challenges this candidate?"

"I do!" shouted a voice from the back.

There was a murmuring among the men, and a portion of the crowd parted. To the astonishment of everyone but Terence, Fengi strode into the circle.

"State your name," said the elder.

"Fengi Gervendilson," he replied.

"What are your qualifications?"

Fengi smiled, and turned to face the crowd.

"My qualifications are that, unlike my brother, I am not a traitor to the crown of Denmark."

"What?" shouted Ørvendil. "You call me traitor, brother?"

"I do," he said. "And I have proof of your treachery. Citizens of Slesvig, this man has conspired against the very life of our King. In doing

[168]

so, he has brought in mercenaries to form the core of an army so that he could set himself up as a king in Slesvig, one to rival Valdemar himself. He has made overtures to the Wends, our sworn enemies, and threatens to bring us into another ruinous civil war not five years after the last one."

"Lies!" shouted Ørvendil. "Hideous and base deceptions. Do not believe this man. It is his own ambition that drives this attempt to unseat me."

"I cannot unseat you," said Fengi. "You do not possess the throne yet. Not without the consent of the men here."

"What proofs have you?" demanded the elder.

"A Wendish spy," said Fengi. "Captured with letters to Ørvendil acknowledging his complicity in this endeavor."

"An obvious ruse," said Ørvendil.

"A Tuscan mercenary, disguised as a common brickmaker," said Fengi. "He has turned on you, my brother, despite your payment. He has revealed the cache of weapons you had buried, deadly seeds awaiting the spring of your ambitions."

"Nonsense," said Ørvendil. "None of these is trustworthy. They are not even Danes."

"There is one more man," said Fengi. "A Dane. A trustworthy one. Will you hear him, milord?"

"If such a one exists, let him stand before me," said Ørvendil. "I fear no one."

"It is I, milord," said Gorm, stepping beside Fengi.

Ørvendil stared at his drost in shock.

"*Et tu*, Brute?" he said softly.

Gorm winced, but stayed by Fengi.

"Well?" demanded Ørvendil. "What do you have to say?"

"I know you to be false," said Gorm. "I know that you conspired against the life of Valdemar during the civil wars, and that only through my intervention did he live through the night upon his arrival in Slesvig after his flight from Roskilde. I know that you have brought mercenaries into Denmark, and have attempted to sway the loyalties of the Danish soldiers here. I know that you love not our king, and intend to destroy him. I know that you desire nothing less than a throne to sit upon and a crown for your head, and for that you are willing to sacrifice anyone and anything."

"You know nothing," growled Ørvendil. "Men of Slesvig, this man is nothing more than a common Judas, seeking to line his pockets with the thirty pieces of silver promised him by my brother. He has recast history in a new mold. It was he who wanted me to slay Valdemar and curry favor with Sveyn. He has been nursing his disappointment well, so that it has grown and flourished. Men of Slesvig, you know me. You must believe me."

He looked around at the faces, the features harsh in the firelight. They began to swim in front of him. He drew his sword.

"Soldiers," he cried. "My comrades in arms. Stand by me."

The soldiers present took up a position behind the drost.

"Gorm, you inspire loyalty even to a perverted cause," said Ørvendil.

"Give up your sword, milord," said Gorm.

"Is there no one here who will stand by me?" Ørvendil shouted.

There was silence, then the sound of a single sword being drawn from its scabbard. A small figure emerged from the crowd and walked into the circle to take up a place by Ørvendil.

"Amleth, no," breathed Terence.

Amleth held his sword in front of him, his weight on his back foot, a flawless copy of his father.

"I stand by you," he said.

Swallowing hard, Terence stepped into the circle.

"And you, Fool?" asked Ørvendil. "Do you stand by me?"

"I stand by the boy, milord," said Terence.

Ørvendil knelt to look at his son, placing his hands on Amleth's shoulders.

"I have never been prouder of you nor loved you more than I do right now," he said. "But this is not your battle. Not yet. Fool, I invoke your promise to me."

"Yes, milord," said Terence. "Come, Amleth."

"No," said Amleth. "I am staying with my father."

"Go, son," said Ørvendil, rubbing his eyes. "That's an order."

Amleth sheathed his sword, looking up defiantly at the wall of men surrounding him. Then he surrendered himself to Terence, who picked him up and carried him out of the circle.

Ørvendil held his sword aloft.

"I call upon the ancient Danelaw," he said. "I stand ready to meet my challenger here and now. Trial by combat, brother."

Fengi drew his sword and walked toward him.

"I accept," he said.

"This is what you wanted all along, isn't it?" said Ørvendil, softly so that only the two of them could hear.

"For a long time now," replied Fengi.

"You never could beat me," said Ørvendil, bringing his sword back and his free hand up in front of him.

"You've grown soft and complacent, brother," said Fengi, his sword waving slowly back and forth. "You are not the swordsman you think you are."

The faces of the men in the circle were a blur in the distance to Ørvendil. All he saw was his brother, silhouetted against the bonfire. He stepped to his left, his sword coming up to chest level.

From the edge of the circle, Amleth watched, held by Terence. The fool had thought of taking the boy out of there, but knew that no matter what happened, Amleth must see it or forever hate the world for hiding it from him.

"Father will win," said the boy confidently. "You'll see."

Ørvendil did not move with his son's confidence. He kept blinking, as if something were in his eyes. The noise of the flames was as a roaring of the sea in his head. As he circled around his brother, he stepped awkwardly for a moment in a hole in the ground. Fengi immediately swept his sword across, keeping it low. Ørvendil stepped back hastily, but cursed as the tip of the blade caught his right shin.

"First hit to me," taunted his brother.

"A scratch," growled Ørvendil. "Enough playing."

He attacked, each blow meeting Fengi's sword with a loud clang. Fengi fought defensively, conservatively, but the onslaught drove him back toward the bonfire. He could not risk glancing behind him to gauge the distance, but the heat and the crackling of the logs were too close for comfort.

"You see?" said Amleth.

Something's wrong, thought Terence.

Ørvendil had paused, his breath coming heavily. He rubbed his brow with his free hand. Fengi attacked, and Ørvendil's sword barely parried him in time. The older brother suddenly thrust at the chest of the younger, but Fengi anticipated the move and stepped quickly to the side, with a thrust of his own at Ørvendil's waist, piercing his stomach just below the breastplate. Ørvendil hacked at the blade with his own, and Fengi's sword broke at the hilt. The younger man stepped back, drawing his knife from his waist.

"Father!" cried Amleth.

Ørvendil glanced out at the boy and the fool, then pulled the broken blade from his side and threw it into the bonfire. His own sword seemed absurdly heavy in his hand. He raised it and staggered toward his brother, screaming as he came. His legs gave out just before he reached him, and as he fell, Fengi grabbed his hair, pulled his head back, and cut his throat.

"No!" screamed Amleth.

Terence picked him up and dashed down the hill.

Fengi looked down at his brother's body, then picked up his sword and looked out at the *thing*.

"Any other candidates?" he asked quietly.

There was silence.

"Then make your election," he said.

Terence loped through the darkness, his long legs putting Slesvig far behind. The boy sobbed as he clung to the fool, riding his shoulders. When they reached a bulge of forest that provided some cover, Terence ducked behind a clump of bushes and sat down for a moment to catch his breath.

"Listen to me," he said, panting. "Your father charged me with keeping you safe if anything happened to him. I don't know how far Fengi is taking this, but I have to assume that your life is in danger. I'm getting you to a place where you can be hidden, then I'm going back to Slesvig to find out what's going on."

"What about my mother?" sniffled the boy.

Terence hesitated.

"I hope that she's all right," he said. "Was she still at the island?"

"Yes," said Amleth.

"How did you manage to sneak out without her noticing?"

"She went to lie down after father left," the boy explained. "The guard at the gate knew I wanted to see the *thing*. He let me go."

"I'm sorry," said Terence. "It was a terrible thing for you to see, and you may have put yourself in danger by standing up for your father like that." He ruffled the boy's hair. "But it was brave and wonderful of you, Amleth. You made your father proud. I know that."

He stood up and beckoned to the boy.

"Remember what I once told you about being silent?" he whispered. Amleth nodded, and the fool placed him back on his shoulders.

He ran into the night.

The soldiers at the island listened with varying degrees of shock, anger, and grudging acceptance as Gorm told them what had transpired at the *thing*. When Fengi rode in, they stood at attention and saluted him. He leapt from his horse and strode to the rear of the island.

He didn't knock when he entered Ørvendil's quarters. He walked by Lother's cradle and the sleeping Alfhild and up the steps to the room of his late brother. He stopped, seeing the nude form of his sister-in-law, the thin blanket covering it rising and falling slightly. He sat by her head and stroked her hair lightly. She stirred, then settled back to sleep.

He chuckled softly, then took her chin in his hands and shook her, first gently, then with increasing force until her eyes opened and focused on him in confusion.

"Fengi?" she said.

"The same," he replied. "I have come to bring you some news."

"What is it?" she asked.

"Your husband is dead," he said. "At my hands."

She sat up suddenly, the blanket sliding from her. He gawked for a moment, then recovered. She looked at him steadily.

"You know my conditions," she said.

"Oh, yes," he said, taking her in his arms. "And I welcome them."

ƒOURTEEN

"Denmark's a prison."

—*HAMLET*, ACT II, SCENE II

Slesvig—Roskilde, 1162 A.D.

Terence stood at the edge of the river, trying to gauge its depths in the darkness.

"I wish that old Gustav had built his bridge here," he muttered.

He looked down at the sleeping child at his feet, then pulled a piece of cord from one of his pouches. He sat by Amleth, crossed the boy's wrists, and tied them together. Amleth woke as he finished, saw that he was bound, and started to scream. Terence quickly clapped a hand over the boy's mouth.

"Quiet!" he commanded. "We are on the wrong side of the river from where we need to be, and there is no safe crossing for us. There's nothing to do but to swim for it. I tied your hands so that you could hang on to me better. I am going to uncover your mouth. Will you remain silent?"

The boy nodded. Terence let him go, then hauled him to his feet and picked him up. Amleth swung onto the fool's back and placed his hands over Terence's head.

"Don't strangle me, boy," warned Terence. "Or it will be a watery grave for both of us."

He waded into the river until the water was up to his waist, then lunged forward, kicking hard. He was a good swimmer from childhood on, and had kept it up most days in the fjord, to the amusement of the town children and the irritation of the fishermen. He had taken Amleth on his back more than once, but this was different, laden as they were with clothes, bundles, and weapons. The currents were tricky. Terence was dragged and turned around more than once, but there was enough of a moon out for him to keep his bearings. After about fifteen minutes, he was able to drag himself and the boy onto the opposite bank.

"I'm glad I left my lute at the tavern," he said as he untied the boy. "I'd never get it in tune after this."

Amleth's teeth were chattering. Terence, who was no drier or warmer, hugged him hard and rubbed his limbs. He took a wineskin from his waist and pulled out the stopper.

"Here," he said, offering it to the boy. "Pray that it is wine rather than river, or we will have to send to Cana for a miracle."

The boy swigged it, then lurched forward and spewed everything left in his stomach onto the ground.

"Well done," said Terence cheerfully. "I was wondering when you would get around to that."

The boy looked up at him mournfully.

"Come on," said Terence. "Wash your mouth out, and we'll move on. It isn't far, but we need to get you to a warm fire."

"No more fires," said Amleth, taking the fool's hand.

They reached Magnus's farm long after midnight. As Terence neared the farmhouse, a pair of hounds started barking, charging him as they did so. They scented the fool before they reached him, and knew him as a friend. The boy clung to Terence's leg as the two dogs nosed him curiously.

"Who's there?" called Magnus, standing in the door with a lantern in one hand and an old spear in the other.

"It's me," said Terence. "I need help."

"Who's that with you?" asked the farmer, peering at Amleth.

"A boy," said Terence. "He needs help, too."

"You had better come in, then," said Magnus. He went inside.

"Who is he?" asked Amleth.

"A friend," said Terence. "Now, I want you to listen to me carefully. I am going to leave you with him and return to Slesvig. If I am not back by sunset, assume that your safety cannot be guaranteed there. Make for Ribe. There's a fool there named Kanard. When you see him, tell him . . ." He hesitated. "Tell him '*stultorum numerus.*' He will say '*infinitus est.*' These are the passwords from one fool to another. He'll take care of you." He fumbled at his waist for his purse and handed it to him. "That should be enough to get you there."

"But then what?" asked Amleth.

"Make for England," said Terence.

The boy slept, and the two men sat nearby and watched him. Terence related the evening's events to the farmer.

"If what you say is true, then your own life may be forfeit the moment you step foot in town," said Magnus.

"Seems likely," agreed Terence. "Nevertheless, I have to find out what's going on, especially with his mother. He must know that."

"How did the town turn on Ørvendil so readily?" asked Magnus. "Especially his own soldiers."

"He had Gorm arrange the assembly," replied Terence. "Gorm must have handpicked every man there. Ørvendil never had a chance."

"Yet it was his brother who killed him, not the *thing*," said Magnus. "That puzzles me. Fengi is a capable soldier, no question, but I have never heard that he was his brother's equal with a sword."

"Neither have I," agreed Terence. "But Ørvendil wasn't himself tonight. He fought like a sleepwalker. I wonder what affected him like that."

Amleth's eyes opened for a moment, then closed again.

"It makes no difference anymore," said Magnus. "He wasn't himself. Now, he isn't anything. God have mercy on his soul. You look done in. Grab yourself some sleep. I'll keep watch with the dogs."

"Thank you," said Terence. "Thank you for everything."

"No one should be killing children," said Magnus. He picked up his spear and went outside.

"Did you find that fool and the boy yet?" asked Fengi.

"Not yet," said Gorm miserably. "So many people ran in so many directions last night that it was impossible to trace his tracks. I've sent patrols in every direction."

"Good," said Fengi. "His mother will be frantic if we don't find him soon."

"How did she take it?" asked Gorm.

Fengi snorted for a moment.

"She took it well enough," he said. "Don't worry about her."

"But..." Gorm began in confusion.

"Fengi," cried Gerutha, running out of the great hall. "I can't find Amleth anywhere."

"I know," he said, taking her hands in his. "We're looking for him. I've sent patrols out in every direction."

"Why isn't he here?" she demanded. "How could you let him slip out like that?"

"Now, my dear, the boy is understandably upset," he said, leading her back into the hall.

Gorm watched them in astonishment.

"Doesn't seem to be mourning much, does she?" said Lars, his captain.

"They are all whores, no matter how fancy the trappings," spat Gorm. "Each and every one of them."

He stormed off.

"Amen, and thank God for it," said Lars, and the soldiers laughed.

Alfhild sat watching the wet nurse feed her brother. She was hungry. In all of the morning's excitement, no one had bothered to feed her. She didn't know what was going on. When she woke up at dawn, she heard noises from the upper room. That wasn't unusual. She was used to hearing Ørvendil and Gerutha making those noises. But although she recognized Gerutha's noises, the man was different. She crept upstairs just as that brother of Ørvendil's opened the door while throwing his cloak on. They looked at each other in surprise.

"So, you are the one I heard coming up," he said, kneeling to face her.

She nodded.

"You're a pretty little thing," he said, patting her head. "You look like your mother."

She nodded again, her thumb in her mouth. Behind him, she could see Gerutha asleep.

"Where's Ørvendil?" she asked.

"He's not here anymore," said Fengi. "I am."

"Oh," she said, and went back downstairs.

Now, she sat by her brother, who didn't even know enough to know that things were different. Through the window she could see the soldiers running more than they usually did. She realized that she hadn't seen Amleth this morning. Or Yorick. They could explain things to her, especially Yorick. It was strange for them to be out this early in the morning, but maybe they had gone fishing. She decided to go out and wait for their return.

She cut through the great hall. Gerutha and Fengi were in there. Gerutha was yelling something about an agreement, something about Amleth being missing. Fengi kept nodding. She wondered why Ørvendil wasn't there. Maybe he was out looking for Amleth. That's what fathers were supposed to do when children got lost.

There was a commotion by the gate as she came out of the great hall. She went over to a corner by one of the barracks and watched. Soldiers on horses were dragging in somebody in a net. When the horses halted, the person in the net rolled a few feet, then tried to stand up. A soldier went over to the man in the net and kicked him hard. The man fell down.

Her father walked up to the man, his sword in his hand, looking very

[179]

angry. He was angry a lot, ever since her mother died. She had often tried to comfort him, but every time she hugged him or sat in his lap, he would push her away and say mean, horrible things. She wondered what the man in the net had done to make her father so angry. He was kicking the man in the net, too. She had never seen him do that to anyone. She inched closer, then with a small shriek saw that the man in the net was Yorick.

"Where is he?" shouted Gorm. "Talk."

"My dear Appollonius," gasped Terence, struggling to his feet. "For so many years, you have begged me to shut up. Now that I finally have, you want me to speak. Make up your mind for once."

"Tell me where Amleth is, or I will rip out your tongue," said Gorm.

"A counterproductive measure, don't you think?" replied Terence, then he spat blood as the drost's fist crashed into his jaw. "I had no idea how much you enjoyed this sort of thing."

"I will put myself into the very ecstasy of torture if you don't tell me where to find the boy."

"I speak only to Ørvendil's brother," said Terence. "Not his brother's fool."

Gorm turned nearly purple and raised his sword. Before she even knew what she was doing, Alfhild ran forward.

"Don't hurt him!" she screamed, clinging to her father.

He looked down at her, then back at the fool.

"Have you turned even my daughter against me?" said Gorm.

"She lacks your capacity for betrayal," replied Terence. "She is trying to save you from yourself, Signor Appollonius. Listen to her."

Gorm felt his rage draining, replaced by a dull weariness. He sheathed his sword.

"Get the Duke," he said. One of his men went running.

"Oh, was there an election?" asked Terence innocently. "I missed that part. Must have been right after the murder."

"Father?" said Alfhild, still hanging on to Gorm's leg.

He pried her off, then handed her to Lars.

"Take her back to my quarters," he ordered. "Wait with her there. I don't want her to see any more of this."

Lars led Alfhild away.

"Judas had no family, as I recall," said Terence pleasantly. "That must have made things easier for him."

"You're making things easier for me every time you open your mouth," said Gorm.

Fengi came out and stood in front of Terence.

"Well?" he said.

"Where's Gerutha?" asked Terence. "Is she alive?"

"See for yourself," said Fengi, beckoning for her to come out.

She walked forward, looking at Terence with hatred.

"Where is Amleth, Fool?" she asked.

Terence looked at her, then at Fengi.

"Milady, I am glad to see you well," he said, managing to bow despite the net. "My condolences on your loss."

"Where is my son?" she screamed.

"Alive and safe," replied Terence. "I take care of my own."

"Tell us where he is, Fool," said Fengi.

"Not until I know that he will live," said Terence.

"And if I have the information tortured out of you?" asked Fengi.

"I will die first," replied Terence. "Amleth will be on his way out of the country before you get anything out of me. The arrangements have already been made. Only I can stop them."

"He's bluffing," said Gorm.

Fengi walked around the fool, examining him. Terence ignored him, even when Fengi put a sword to his neck.

"Speak, Fool," he said.

"Whose sword is that?" asked Terence. "Your brother broke yours last night. You have taken everything else that belonged to him. Is that his as well?"

Fengi grabbed Terence's neck.

"What do you want? Money?" he said.

"I want your oath in front of everyone here that you will guarantee Amleth's life," shouted Terence. "Nothing else."

Fengi stepped back and swung the sword with all of his might. Gerutha screamed, and every man present flinched.

Except for Terence, who stood calmly as the net separated around him.

"A good trick," he said. "You missed your calling. You should have been an entertainer."

Fengi walked back to Gerutha and took her hand.

"To assure an easy transition, I have agreed to take my brother's widow to wife," he said.

"Given the family alliances that she brings to the table, a powerful match," said Terence.

"Do you really think that I would let any harm come to her son?" asked Fengi.

"Did you love your mother?" asked Terence. "For you killed her son last night. I take little stock in blood ties in this part of the world."

"But you would trust my oath?" asked Fengi.

Terence spread his arms and indicated the soldiers surrounding them.

"I trust the soldiers," said Terence. "Make your oath to them, and they shall be honor bound to enforce it."

There was a murmur of approval at this.

"Very well," said Fengi. He stuck the sword in the ground and knelt before it. "I swear on the honor of all the soldiers present that I shall guarantee the life of Amleth, or my own blood be forfeit by their swords. Will that suffice?"

"It will," said Terence. "Now, get me a fast horse."

"Where is the boy?" asked Fengi, rising to his feet.

"I will return with him," said Terence. "But I am weary. I need a horse, and I want no one to follow me. Is that understood?"

"Give him a horse," commanded Fengi, and a soldier took Terence by the arm and led him away.

"When he returns with the boy, I want the fool's throat slit," said Fengi to Gorm.

"No," said Gerutha. The other two looked at her. "Amleth has lost his father, and will take our alliance ill. If he loses Terence as well right now, it may destroy him. I can't let that happen. Let him have this fool until he's older. Then do what you want."

Fengi bowed slightly.

"I am your servant in this as in every matter," he said.

Alfhild sat on her pallet while Lars made funny faces at her. She was too distracted to laugh at him. She had not only made her father angry, she had made him tired. She had seen him when he was tired like that before, and it never boded well.

Lars stood as he heard Gorm's footsteps approaching the door. The drost entered, nodded at his captain, and sat down on a bench opposite his daughter.

"That will be all, Captain," he said.

Lars left, winking at Alfhild. Gorm looked at his daughter, his eyes sunk deep into their sockets, his expression bleak.

"You are still young," he said. "You must learn this, and learn this now. Never disobey me. Never disrespect me. Never dishonor me. If you ever do anything like that again, I will make sure that no man ever looks at you again. Do you understand me, daughter?"

She nodded.

"Good," he said. "Now, come here."

She got up and ran forward, arms extended. As she reached him, he slapped her once across the face. She stumbled and fell, crying. He left her there and went to wait for Amleth's return.

Terence galloped along the river road, bouncing awkwardly on the saddle. He wasn't used to riding, and the horse sensed it, taking every opportunity to pull against the reins and go its own way. By the time he reached Magnus's farm, it was past noon.

Magnus was tending his vegetable gardens near the house, an innocent activity that allowed him to keep a sturdy spade handy. His spear was leaning against the front of the house. He nodded with relief when he saw that the rider was Terence.

"Everything is well?" he asked. Then he got a closer look at the fool's face, the bruises clearly visible under the remains of his whiteface.

"Everything is not well," said Terence. "But Amleth will be safe."

"What about you?" asked Magnus.

"Who knows?" replied the fool. "It doesn't matter much what happens to me. Where's Amleth?"

"Hiding in the barn," said Magnus. "Come, I will take you there."

The barn was a few hundred paces back from the road, a simple wooden structure with a thatched roof. There was hay piled into the rafters, and it was there that they found Amleth, burrowed into the deepest part of it. He cried out with joy when he saw Terence and swung down into the fool's arms.

"I thought I would never see you again," he said, hugging him tightly.

"No fear of that," said Terence cheerfully. "It takes more than a mere army to slow me down."

"Is my mother alive?" asked the boy.

"She is."

"And is she all right?"

Terence hesitated. "Yes," he said. "A little too all right."

"What is it?" stammered Amleth. "What's wrong?"

Terence put him down, then sat next to him.

"Amleth, there is no easy way to tell you this," he said. "Your mother has agreed to marry Fengi."

Amleth turned pale.

"But she can't," he whispered. "She is married to father. She can't marry anyone else."

"I'm sorry," said Terence.

The boy sat next to Terence in silence. Slowly, his body sagged against that of the fool, but he did not weep.

"Take me to England," he said suddenly.

"What?"

"Take me to England. I'll learn how to be a fool. I'll be your son." He looked forlornly up at the fool. "I can't go back there. Not now."

Terence looked at the boy, and thought his heart would break.

"I cannot," he said softly. "I have to go back to Slesvig."

"But why?" wailed the boy.

"I have my reasons," said Terence.

"My uncle will be there?" asked Amleth.

"Yes."

The boy fingered the sword at his waist.

"All right," he said. "Let's go."

Gerald found Valdemar in much the same position as when he had left him, and in much the same mood.

"Ready to be cheered up yet?" asked the fool.

"Where have you been?" responded the King. "No one has seen you for days."

"I am surprised anyone even took notice of my absence," said Gerald. "I count for so little around here."

"Well?" said Valdemar.

"I have been to Slesvig," said Gerald. "You have to stop Fengi."

"What do you know about it?" demanded Valdemar.

"Enough to know that you are making a grievous mistake," said Gerald. "Ørvendil is loyal to you."

"Not according to his drost," said Valdemar.

"His drost has been deceived or corrupted," said Gerald. "Fengi has had a spy in Slesvig for months. I suspect that he is the one working on the drost's sympathies."

"You suspect," said the King mockingly. "Everyone tells me to suspect everyone else but them. It is a miracle that I can govern the household thralls, much less the entire kingdom, given the reputed disloyalty of men who have served me for years."

"I am one of them," Gerald reminded him.

"But you don't serve me," said Valdemar. "You are like some cat who has taken up residence, and wanders in and out as he pleases. Very entertaining creatures, cats, but no one ever thinks them loyal."

"Cats are good at catching rats," said Gerald. "That's why most people keep them around."

"And you say that Fengi is a rat, to continue the metaphor," said Valdemar.

"Yes," said Gerald.

"I say that you are wrong!" shouted Valdemar. "Get out of here, Fool. I have depended upon you too much. I should have remembered my history. There have been kings in Denmark before me who were deceived by mimes and jugglers. Find some other household to amuse. Worm your way in, build up your favor, then turn on someone else. I don't need your help ruling my kingdom."

"Very good, sire," said Gerald, bowing stiffly. "Should you ever require my services, you know where to find me. But I urge you to reconsider your actions as to Ørvendil."

"I considered them carefully before I made them," said Valdemar. "What's done is done. Leave me, Fool."

The fool left.

Terence and Amleth rode into Slesvig, the boy sitting behind the fool. They ignored the stares of the curious, the sympathetic, and the hostile as they passed, the fool fixing his gaze on the road ahead, the boy watching the river flow by on the right. When the island fortress came into sight, the fool slowed the horse down to a walk.

"Your safety depends upon your mother," he said quietly, feeling Amleth tense behind him. "I suggest that you humor her for now, and keep your head down. I will protect you as much as I can, but I don't know how much I can protect myself anymore."

"Then I will protect you," said Amleth. "As much as I can."

"I accept," said Terence, smiling wryly. "And no matter what, keep up the juggling. It helps concentrate the mind."

They turned onto the drawbridge and rode into the fortress. Gerutha rushed forward and hauled him off the horse, embracing him and covering his face with kisses.

"I thought I might never see you again," she said, sobbing.

"I know," said Amleth. "I'm back, mother."

"Did he tell you?" she asked. "I must marry Fengi."

"Must you?" he asked.

Terence, getting down from the horse, winced at the boy's tone, but Gerutha either did not notice it or chose to disregard it.

"I am doing it to protect you," she whispered. "You will become Fengi's son and heir this way. He is going to be a great man, even greater than he is today."

Amleth suddenly pushed himself away from her, his face seething with hatred.

"You!" he shouted, pointing at his uncle who stood watching from the entrance to the great hall. "You killed my father."

"Yes," said Fengi. "I had to. He challenged me. I wish that there had been some other way."

Amleth drew his sword and faced his uncle, who watched him with barely concealed amusement. Terence leaned over and plucked it from his hand.

"Your father taught you better than that," he said to the boy. "You cannot kill him, and you should not be prepared to die so young." He stuck the boy's sword back in its sheath.

Amleth looked around him. Everywhere there were adults looking down at him, betraying him. He bit down hard on his lower lip to keep himself from bursting into tears and ran toward the rear of the island.

"Well, Fool, you kept your end of the bargain," said Fengi. "I shall keep mine. Unless, of course, the boy ever comes near me with that blade in his hand."

"He won't," said Terence.

"Will you take an oath as to that?" asked Fengi.

Terence smiled and handed the horse's reins to a soldier, but said nothing.

Amleth sat with his back against the palisade between Signe's herbs and the bare patch that had been his mother's flower garden. There was a piece of wood about the length of his forearm lying nearby. He picked it up, pulled out his sword, and started whittling the twigs and bark from it. After a while, he got up, ran into his room, and returned with the brick his father had presented to him on his birthday. He continued working on the end of the wood until it made a sharp point. Then he took the brick and hammered the newly made stake into the ground by his side.

There was someone standing over him. He looked up through his tears to see Alfhild watching him, a serious expression in her eyes.

"What are you doing?" she asked.

"Making my own fort," he said. "A place to protect me from my enemies."

"I can get you some more wood," she offered.

"All right," he said. "Thank you."

She ran off, then returned with several pieces from the pile of firewood near the kitchen. She dumped it on the ground before him, then sat next to him and watched as he carved another.

He was determined to make this one perfect. He turned the piece around several times before making each refinement with the sword, holding it up to the light and examining it from every angle. The second stake took him nearly two hours to complete.

Gerutha watched him from her room.

"Look at him," she said to Fengi when he came up. "The entire afternoon wasted in carving two stakes."

"It's the shock," said Fengi. "Several shocks. He's a boy. Boys are resilient. He'll get over it in time, you'll see."

"I hope so," she said doubtfully.

Terence had been watching as well, holding a cold, wet cloth against his jaw that ached considerably. He saw Gorm walk up to the children and say something in a sharp tone to his daughter. She jumped up immediately and ran to their quarters, the drost following her slowly.

The sun was beginning to set. Terence walked over to Amleth and sat next to him.

"Building your own fort?" he asked.

"Yes," said Amleth.

"Taking your time, I see," said Terence.

"All I have left from my father is this sword and this brick," said Amleth.

"And those eyes, and that mouth, and that chin, and those arms," said Terence. "Your nose is from your mother, I think."

"Maybe I'll cut it off," said Amleth.

"Don't," said Terence. "Your nose is blameless."

"If I spend each day building this fort, then I will spend each day with the things my father gave me," said Amleth. "I suppose that seems crazy."

"It does," agreed the fool. "And that is why you should keep doing it."

The boy picked up another piece of wood and began carving it.

"You think that I am still in danger," he said. "Even with my mother protecting me."

"We have to think about what happens if you were to lose her," said Terence. "I was watching your uncle when you drew your sword. He fears you."

"He fears a boy?"

"He fears the man you shall become," said Terence. "He fears his brother's image. But he will not fear someone whose mind is addled."

"So, you want me to play . . ."

"The fool," said Terence. "Yes, Amleth. I want you to do that. It's an old trick, but it just may keep you alive."

They sat together in silence, the boy holding up the wood and inspecting it closely in the waning light.

Fengi watched the two of them, barely aware of the man who came up by him.

"Congratulations, milord," he murmured.

[189]

"Thank you," said Fengi. "I have your next assignment."

"Yes, milord?"

"I want you to keep an eye on that fool," said Fengi.

"Very good, milord," said Reynaldo, smiling slightly.

ҒIFTEEN

"Madness in great ones must not unwatched go."
———*HAMLET*, ACT III, SCENE I

"ime passed." said Father Gerald. "*There have been worse times in Denmark for fools. They say that when Starkad became king, he routinely had us beaten for licentiousness. A fool may not beat a king for that same crime, which was lucky for Starkad. But 1162 marked the beginning of bleak days for us, for we had lost what influence we had. I have often wondered who turned Valdemar against me, whether it was Fengi or Absalon, or simply the fickle nature of a man in power. I juggled in the streets and taverns of Roskilde, made the rounds of the rest of the cities, and collected what information I could. But I never got back into the inner chambers of the King. I wish that I had. A new war was brewing, one that should have been avoided. And Fengi, who had so long been a proponent of this war, saw a way to turn it to his vantage.*"

Rügen——Slesvig, 1166 A.D.

Three longboats cut through the seas, the oarsmen pulling hard. Occasionally, the sound of a lash would echo across the waters as a soldier in the stern would catch a thrall lagging for a moment.

Fengi stood at the prow of the lead boat, leaning into the wind, feeling the spray in his face. Ahead, the white cliffs of Rügen grew larger. The small cove that was to be their meeting place came into sight, and Fengi smiled.

The Wends regarded their villages as places to stay between seagoing raids, and paid little attention to matters of architecture. Their huts were slapped together, and their great halls had dirt floors and leaky roofs. Yet their armor was fierce and impressive-looking, and their military discipline the equal of any of their neighbors. The Slesvegians were not deceived by the small size of the party that greeted them at the shore. They knew that bowmen lurked in the darkness, their arrows ready to be loosed.

"Welcome, Lord of Slesvig," said the Wend leader, speaking in fluent Danish. "Our home is yours."

"Thank you, Lord of Arkona," replied Fengi in Slavic. "We are honored by your hospitality."

The Wends brought them to the hall, where the meal was waiting. In the center of the room stood a wooden statue of Svantevit, the seven-headed god, each head bearing a different expression, all of them frightening.

"You may offer your own prayers, if you wish," said the Wend leader.

"My prayers are for all of us," said Fengi.

"Then let us eat," said the Wend.

Women silently filed into the room, depositing platters of fish and buckets of ale on the tables, then as silently filed out. The men set to the meal.

When they were done, Fengi stood.

"It is good that former enemies such as we can sit down to a good meal together," he said. "I know that we have been at odds in the past." He paused for effect. "But that is nothing compared to what we will be facing in the future."

"Do you repay our generosity by threatening us?" said the Wend leader, standing and turning dark red.

"I do not threaten," said Fengi. "I merely warn. There is a gathering of Danes taking place, the building of a navy greater than any in the northern seas, and their first purpose is to put an end to you. They see you as an annoyance, and they intend to swat you right off this island."

"Then we shall meet you in battle," declared the Wend.

"The combined forces of every Wend on this island cannot possibly be enough to face the Danes," said Fengi. "You will die bravely, I am sure, but you will still die."

"Why do you tell us this?" asked the Wend. "Are you not one of the Danes?"

"I am, or was," said Fengi. "Which brings me to my offer to you."

"Offer?" said the Wend suspiciously.

"Yes," said Fengi. "You think that your only choice is to die in battle. I offer you life instead. Not only life, but employment and Christianity if you want it."

"Employment," said the Wend. "You want us to work for you."

"You are warriors," said Fengi. "I need warriors. I have a little project of my own. It will take a few years to put together, but when it comes to fruition, we all may do very well by it."

"You wish us to become mercenaries for you," said the Wend.

"That's it in a nutshell," said Fengi. "There will be pay, shelter, the odd battle, and all you have to do is go to church on Sundays."

"Church," said the Wend disdainfully.

"Just make the weekly appearance like the rest of us. But you could still bring this lovely creature with you," said Fengi, patting Svantevit on the nearest head. "Just so long as you keep it out of sight."

"And then?" asked the Wend.

"And then you get to do what you like doing the most," said Fengi. "Killing Danes."

The Wend conferred with two of his captains, then turned back to Fengi.

"I was in the battle of Grathe Moor, serving Sveyn Peder," he said. "I saw you fight there. If it were not for that, we would cut your throats right now for appealing for our help in a matter of petty ambition. But I know you to be a warrior, Lord Fengi. We respect that. I will not go with you to Slesvig. My place is on this island with my people, defending them. But if any of my men wish to live on in service to a foreigner, I will not stop them. I fear that you will not get the best of the Wends. But even the lesser Wends are still great warriors."

"I can ask for nothing more," said Fengi. "Those who join me will be treated well. And the rest of you will be in my prayers."

"So be it," said the Wend. "Go in peace."

When the longboats pulled up to the docks in Slesvig, Gorm was standing there, waiting. He personally tied the line from the bow of Fengi's boat, and extended a hand to his lord.

"Our lookout saw several boats returning with you," he said. "But they landed somewhere on the southern shore. I take it that means you had a successful journey."

"Not bad," said Fengi. "About eighty armed men and their families. More will join them, especially once the island is taken. They'll be in a camp near the church of St. Andreas. I want them kept out of sight for a while. Valdemar and Absalon would not appreciate their presence on Danish soil. Arrange for some supplies, especially ale. They can outdo the Jutes in drinking."

"There may not be enough ale in Christendom if that's the case," said Gorm. "But I'll see what I can do."

"How was everything in my absence?" asked Fengi as they walked back to the island.

"Uneventful," said Gorm.

"Good," said Fengi. "Thank you. How does your family?"

"Lother gains speed daily," said Gorm, chuckling. "He lives to run. Do you know that he turns four next month?"

"Really?" exclaimed Fengi. "Time passes so quickly. I cannot believe that four years have . . ." He stopped short, remembering.

"Four years since she died, yes," said Gorm. "I cannot believe it either, but there is the constant evidence of my son to prove it."

"And Alfhild?"

Gorm sighed. "She still dotes on Amleth, despite my discouragement. I do not know what she finds appealing in that sullen monster. He sits in that little pen of his, reading and brooding, cursing at anyone who approaches. Except for her and Lother."

"And Yorick," said Fengi.

"Yes, and Yorick. Fools and children, those are all who his mind encompasses among the living. The rest is on manuscript. I daresay he has read everything that I own, and everything that the Bishop has as well."

"It is an odd sort of madness," agreed Fengi. "But he may still grow out of it. Let's hope so, for his mother's sake. And how is my lady wife?"

"She's been spending the day preparing for you," said Gorm. "Make sure you notice."

"As ever, you are invaluable," said Fengi. "Tell me, have you considered remarrying? It seems a waste to languish alone."

"Do I languish, milord?" asked Gorm. "I think that I do not. Nor am I alone, thanks to my children. But I cannot go through marriage again. The first was too happy and too painful a bond to relive, even in my memories. I would rather heal an old wound than incur a new one."

"Suit yourself," said Fengi as they crossed the drawbridge.

Lother came running full tilt, careening into his father, then hugging Fengi around his legs.

"Hello, Fengi," he said.

"Hello, Lother," said Fengi, fondly tousling the boy's hair. "Look how he's shooting up. Like a bean in May, isn't he?"

"Yes, he is," said Gorm.

"Must get his height from his mother's side of the family," commented Fengi. "What does he get from you?"

"His mind," said Gorm proudly. "He's learning Latin already. The priests say he has a real knack for it."

"Well, don't let them take him," said Fengi. "I'll need Gorm's progeny to fight battles as his father did."

"I'm a good fighter," said Lother.

"I'm sure that you are," said Fengi. "Maybe we should teach him Slavic, Gorm."

"Not so loud, milord," cautioned Gorm.

"Yes, quite right," said Fengi. "Well, I am off to compliment my wife. I will see you at dinner."

"Very good, milord," said Gorm, lifting his son into the air and putting him on his shoulders.

Amleth sat with his back to the stockade wall, smoothing his latest stake with a rough stone he had picked for that purpose. He heard footsteps running lightly toward him. It was Alfhild, a book clutched in her hand.

"It's from Yorick," she whispered furtively. "He says it's a play by someone named Plautus. He says it's funny. Will you read it to me?"

"It's in Latin," said Amleth, looking at it. "I'll do my best. It may not be as funny in Danish. I finished another stake today."

"Could I see it?" she said, plopping herself down next to him. He handed it to her. She held it up to the light, running her fingers across the surface. "You really got this one smooth. It practically shines." She touched the tip gingerly. "And it's sharp, too. How long have you been working on it?"

"About three weeks," he said, handing her his brick.

She took the stake and pounded it expertly into the ground next to the last one he had done, then reached over the tiny wall and plucked a sprig of oregano from the garden and rolled it under her nose.

"This smells so good," she said, sighing. "I think it's my favorite."

"Yesterday, you said sage was your favorite," he said.

"Read to me," she said, snuggling up against him.

"All right," he said. "It's about these twin brothers."

"Look at Alfhild with Amleth," said Fengi, watching the two children from his room. "Completely innocent of the world. Were it not for her mother's garden, I doubt that she would even know what a plant looks like. Her father does her wrong to keep her shut away from the town. It's unnatural."

"I think he intends her for the convent when she's old enough," said

Gerutha, lolling on the bed. "She, of course, thinks that she will marry our son."

"Your son," said Fengi. "He will be none of mine." He turned to look down at her. "When will I have a son of my own?"

"It is in the hands of the Holy Mother," she said piously.

He grimaced and turned back to watching Alfhild and Amleth.

"He's no match for her," he muttered.

"No, he can do much better than that," said Gerutha, thinking that she was agreeing with him.

The next morning, Terence showed up on the island. Amleth was waiting for him.

"Good morning, milord," said Terence, bowing to the boy.

"Good morning, Yorick," said Amleth, bowing back.

They started to leave.

"Just where do you think you are going?" demanded Gerutha, standing behind them.

"By your leave, madam," said Terence. "The boy needs some sun and exercise. I am taking him swimming."

She walked up to her son and turned him around.

"Give it to me," she commanded him.

"I don't know what you're talking about," he muttered.

"Yes, you do," she said. "Hand it over, or you won't walk off this island."

Reluctantly, he reached into his pack and handed over his sword.

"Now, don't get into any trouble," she said, kissing his forehead.

"Don't worry, he's with me," said Terence.

"Back by noon, Amleth," she said.

"Yes, mother," he called as he ran across the drawbridge.

The pair ran south until they reached the old Viking tower, then stripped to their linens and dove into the water.

"To the rock and back," said Amleth. "Loser has to make the fire."

"You're on," said Terence, and they kicked out into the fjord, swimming to a rock that stuck out of the water a hundred yards from shore. Amleth churned the water furiously, and had fifteen feet on the fool by the time he reached the rock, but he started tiring on the return. The fool passed him just before they reached the shore.

"I almost beat you that time," gasped Amleth.

"Slow and steady wins the race," said Terence, flopping onto the ground. "Go gather some wood, boy. I brought some sausages today."

Amleth soon had the fire blazing, and the two of them put sausages on sticks and started to toast them. The heat worked its way into their bones, warming their bodies and drying their linens.

"It's too bad Gorm won't let his children join us outside the island," said Terence.

"He thinks I'm crazy," said Amleth. "And he doesn't like you much, either. I don't mind. It's nice to relax and be normal. Playing the fool is hard work."

"Don't I know it," laughed Terence. "And you've only been at it a few years."

"How long until I am safe, do you think?" asked Amleth.

"When your uncle is in the grave," said Terence. "Maybe not even then. There may be no safe life for Amleth in this world."

"Will they let me go to Paris when I am old enough?" wondered Amleth.

"Your mother will," said Terence. "She still has ambitions for you, and a Parisian education would fit in just fine with her. Fengi would be worried about having you out of his control. But by the time you are old enough, you will have been out of trouble for seven years. Maybe that will be long enough."

"It seems so far away," sighed Amleth.

"Tomorrow is far away," said Terence. "Get through today first."

"What will you do if I go?" asked Amleth.

"Stay," said Terence. "My work is here. There will always be drunks and children to entertain. Maybe Gorm will relent and allow me to play with Alfhild and Lother some more. Now, there are two people who will miss you when you go. Have you proposed to her yet?"

"I'm only eleven," protested Amleth. "And she's eight."

"I realize that the age difference can be a hindrance to a marriage," said Terence with a serious expression. "But you can overcome it if you try."

"Stop it," laughed Amleth. "I am not going to marry anyone. Ever."

"Don't base your sense of marriage upon what you've seen inside that fortress," advised Terence. "There are plenty of happy ones, and the rest are more or less tolerable."

"Then why aren't you married?" teased the boy.

"I have decided to lead a life of celibacy," said Terence.

"Like a priest?" asked Amleth.

"No," said Terence. "I mean a life of celibacy. And thank you for the straight line. So, what was your uncle up to on this little vacation of his?"

"I don't know," said Amleth. "He hasn't talked to anyone but Gorm about it. Why?"

"He didn't take any Danes with him, only mercenaries," said Terence. "That interests me. Keep your ears open, all right?"

"I will," promised Amleth. "Shall we juggle?"

"Let's," said Terence, standing and pulling on his motley.

As they passed nine clubs between them, they heard a distant rumbling. Terence turned in the direction of the sound.

"Just a supply convoy," he said. "Oh, look. There's Gorm on horseback. Better get back into character in case he sees you."

Amleth hastily stuffed his clubs back into his bag and sat down, staring moodily at the dying embers of the fire. The drost spotted them, and rode up.

"Amleth, your mother bids me remind you that noon fast approaches," said Gorm.

"Hail, Lord Drost," said Terence.

Gorm looked him up and down, a pained expression on his face.

"I have never seen you without your whiteface on, Fool," he said. "I understand now why you wear it. Your face is quite hideous without it."

"Feel free to borrow it anytime you like," said Terence. "How are your children today, milord?"

"They are none of your concern," snapped the drost. "Amleth, the sun . . ."

"I know where the sun is," said Amleth. "Tell my mother I will be there anon."

The drost sniffed and rode away. Terence began applying his makeup, looking at his reflection in the water.

"I like your face," said Amleth.

The fool shrugged.

"It's a face," he said. "Just another prop for a fool to work with. All right, let's get you back."

Fengi and Gerutha stood looking over a great excavation at the edge of town. At one end, thralls were carrying out sacks of dirt. At the other, masons were laying brick as a foundation.

"At last," said Gerutha. "How long will it take?"

"A few years," said Fengi.

"Years," she said. "I want my Mary's garden."

"You will have it," he said.

"And will there be balls? With musicians and lovely gowns?"

"Every fortnight," he said, putting his arm around her. "And all of our children shall be raised as royalty."

"All of them," she said dully. "There's just one, and he spends his days sitting in the mud."

She walked away suddenly.

"There can be more," he called after her. "Mary didn't stop with just Jesus, you know. She had a whole brood of them. With a different father."

Gorm rode up, dismounted, and approached Fengi.

"I sent the supplies," he said.

"Good," said Fengi. He looked across the crowd of laborers working to build his castle. "We need more money. I may have to raise taxes again."

"There are complaints about the level of taxation as it stands," said Gorm.

"There are always complaints," said Fengi. "What does it matter? Do me a favor and escort my wife home."

"Yes, milord."

Gorm left his horse with a soldier and trotted after Gerutha.

"Milady," he said, gasping a bit. "I am to accompany you."

"Thank you, Gorm," she said. "You know, you really should call me Gerutha after all this time. We are family, after all."

"Only by marriage, and that connection is lost, alas," said Gorm.

"Never," said Gerutha. "Blood ties outlast death. And who knows? Maybe there will be another marriage someday."

"I thank you, Gerutha," he said, stumbling slightly over the name. "However, I am not interested in marrying again."

"I was not talking about you," she said. "But your daughter seems to have set her mind on my son."

"It is but a childish affectation," protested the drost. "As the only boy she knows, he naturally would become the object of her love. But I expect that she will grow out of it."

"Perhaps," said Gerutha. "But you must consider the effect that living isolated in a garrison will have on a young girl. Not to mention the effect a pretty girl might have on a garrison."

"I have instructed her on the ways of virtue," said Gorm stiffly. "She will remain a chaste and obedient daughter."

"Easily said of an eight-year-old girl," said Gerutha. She smiled at Gorm, which unnerved him. "She so reminds me of her mother, don't you think?"

He did not reply.

Seeing the drost personally oversee the supply convoy's departure had whetted Terence's curiosity. Although he had lost an hour on them by the time he had returned Amleth to his mother, the fool's long legs were able to close the distance on the slow-paced mules in no time.

His suspicions increased when the convoy turned east and followed the southern bank of the fjord rather than continue to the southern fortifications that protected Slesvig from Holstein. The wains passed the church of St. Andreas and continued on to a small farm. One of its fields was dotted with tents and campfires, and the wains were greeted by armed guards.

Terence hopped a fence enclosing a herd of cattle and crouched down. Then he ran, keeping low and using the cows for cover. They ignored him. When he reached the fence near the encampment, he flattened himself on the ground and peered cautiously through the tall grass that bordered it.

He could hear snatches of conversation, but he couldn't understand what was being said. It wasn't Danish, and it wasn't German. He suspected that these were new mercenary recruits, but was puzzled why they were being kept out of sight. Fengi had more than his share of mercenaries, something that was beginning to alarm the fool.

He thought they might be speaking Slavic, which meant that they had come from the east. He noticed that many of them made for one large tent in particular, carrying things in, then coming out several minutes later empty-handed.

The sun set, and the people were gathering by a central bonfire, sharing provisions and singing. He decided to chance getting closer, crawling on his belly the entire distance. He came up behind the tent that had caught his attention, and with his dagger cut a tiny hole in it. Then he pressed his eye against the opening he had made. A hideous face peered back at him, and he almost shouted, but it was carved from wood. Beyond it was another, and another...

"Wends," he breathed.

He crawled back to the fence, slithered under it, and made his escape through the cow pasture.

· · ·

The next morning Reynaldo approached Fengi as the latter rode by the brickyard.

"I have something to tell you," he said softly.

"What is it?" asked Fengi.

"That fool knows about the Wends."

"What?"

"I followed him yesterday when he went out of town. He tracked the supply convoy."

"Well," said Fengi thoughtfully. "That is unfortunate."

"Yes, it is," agreed Reynaldo, smiling.

Amleth thought little of it when Terence failed to come to visit him that day. When a second day passed with no appearance by the fool, he was curious and a little irritated. He got up from his tiny enclosure and wandered around the island.

"Have you seen Yorick?" he asked Gorm in the great hall.

"No, and I do not care to," said the drost frostily.

He sought out his mother.

"Have you seen Yorick?" he asked her.

"Yorick?" she said, puzzled. "No, now that you mention it. Maybe he's gone off wandering again. You know he does that."

Not without telling me first, he thought.

He asked a few of the soldiers, ones that he knew frequented The Viking's Rest after the end of their watches. None had seen the fool.

It was after noon. He waited for a group of wagons to cross the drawbridge into the fortress with fresh supplies, then slipped out and walked into town.

He didn't see the fool performing anywhere at the market or near the cathedral, his two favorite street locations. Amleth had been forbidden by his mother ever to enter a tavern, but he reasoned that by going in through the back entrance directly to Yorick's room, he would not be in violation of that maternal edict. Besides, he thought with a slight smile, he could always claim madness.

He walked casually into an alleyway off a street near the tavern, then ducked under a fence and ran silently to the back entrance. He listened at the doorway, holding his breath, but heard no one inside. The tapster was usually in the front room, and the other occupants of the sleeping quarters worked days. He opened the door a crack and peered in. Then he slipped inside, closing it quickly behind him. He crept down the hall until he came to Yorick's room. The door was ajar.

He tapped on it softly.

"Yorick?" he whispered. There was no reply. He pushed the door open slowly. "Yorick?"

The shutters were open, allowing the light to pour into the room. It was empty. He was about to turn and leave when a hand grabbed him roughly by the collar and spun him around. The man holding him appeared to be a monk, although his expression was not in the least one that inspired holy thoughts. In his free hand, he held an oaken staff.

"Who are you?" said the monk quietly, a trace of menace in his tone.

"Let go of me," said Amleth.

The monk shoved him into the room, came in, and closed the door behind him.

"I asked you a question, boy," he said.

There was something about him that seemed familiar to the boy. He glanced at the monk's sleeves, then suddenly blurted out, "*Stultorum numerus!*"

The monk arched his eyebrows in amusement.

"Come, child, he taught you better than that," he said. "You don't just throw passwords at any passing stranger."

"*Stultorum numerus,*" repeated Amleth, more confidently this time.

"*Infinitus est,*" replied the monk. "You must be Amleth."

"Yes," said Amleth.

"How did you know that I was a fool?" asked the monk.

"I've seen you once before," said Amleth. "When I was little."

"You have a remarkable memory," said the monk. "You weren't even three then."

"And I got a glimpse of your motley under your cassock," added Amleth.

The monk grimaced, shoving the sleeve back under his cassock.

"Now, that was careless of me," he said. "I must be getting old. My name is Gerald. I'm the Roskilde fool."

"You came with Valdemar and Fengi that time, before Valdemar was king. You and Yorick let me juggle silks in front of my father. How could I not remember that?"

"That's right," said Gerald. "I have heard much about you, young Amleth. My colleague sings your praises, sometimes literally, when we meet."

"Does he?" said Amleth, pleased.

"Yes," said Gerald. "Now, tell me where I can find him. I need to speak with him."

"I don't know," said Amleth. "Yorick usually comes to see me every day, but I haven't seen him since the day before yesterday, and he left me no note saying he was going anywhere. He . . ."

Amleth stopped. Yorick's collection of bundles were piled in a corner of the room. He went over to pick them up. Some of them rattled and jingled as he did. He looked at Gerald in alarm.

"He wouldn't go anywhere without these," he said.

Gerald knelt down by Terence's pallet and pulled back the blanket. There was a patch of blood staining the thin sheet covering the hay. He touched it, but could not judge whether it was recent or not. He put the blanket back before the boy could see it.

"Tell me everything you can remember about the last time you saw . . ." he hesitated for a moment. "Saw Yorick."

Amleth did, and Gerald nodded when he heard about the supply convoy.

"That must have been it," he said. "He's probably just gone in disguise to find out what that was all about. You say they went south?"

Amleth nodded.

"All right," said Gerald. "Meet me down at the docks tomorrow afternoon. You'll hear this song." He whistled a few notes. "Do you have it?"

Amleth nodded.

"Good," said Gerald. "Tell no one about this. And be careful with that password."

"Yes, Gerald," said Amleth.

He ran back to the fortress. No one had remarked on his absence, and his moodiness at the evening meal was nothing unusual by this time. He slept fitfully, then paced in his miniature stockade like a lion in a cage, waiting for the sun to reach its peak.

He wanted to run to the docks, to find Yorick waiting for him, a teasing smile on his lips as he would throw the boy high into the air and catch him at the last possible moment. But he forced himself to sneak out quietly and take the indirect route through the town first, making sure that no one was following him. He wandered the docks, keeping his head down and paying attention to nobody. He did not see the monk, but as he passed a sailor who was sitting on a bench, whittling, he heard him whistle the tune Gerald had given him the day before. He walked up to him.

"Sit down, Amleth," said Gerald's voice.

He sat next to the sailor.

"I didn't recognize you," said Amleth.

"Good," said Gerald. "I thought I might be slipping. I wanted to make it more challenging for you."

"Did you find Yorick?" asked Amleth.

"No," said Gerald. "Nor did I find what I think he must have found. There were tracks of a supply convoy that led to a farm near the church of St. Andreas, and signs that there had been some kind of encampment there, but there's nothing there now. I don't know who was there, or where they went. It could be that Yorick is following them."

"You think he's dead," said Amleth flatly.

Gerald looked at the boy. His eyes are too old for such a young face, he thought. No one should have to see what he's seen.

"Yes," said Gerald. "I do. We had an arrangement for times when he was going off on some journey knowing that I might be coming through Slesvig. A place where he would leave a message. There was none there."

"My uncle did this," said Amleth.

"Maybe," said Gerald. "But we cannot prove that."

"I don't need proof," said Amleth. "I swear by all that is holy that . . ."

"Stop it right now," said Gerald sharply. "Would Yorick be looking to you to avenge him? Is that what you have learned from him? He has devoted his life to keeping your life safe. Will you throw it away for him now?"

Amleth looked down at his feet, then slowly shook his head.

"What happens now?" he asked, looking back at Gerald.

The fool looked at the boy sitting next to him. He saw the intelligence in his face, the skills Terence had instilled in him for survival.

"I can't put another fool out here," said Gerald. "Fengi would immediately suspect him. But there is one person I could ask to keep an eye on things."

"Me," said Amleth. "You want me to spy on my uncle."

"If you are willing," said Gerald. "It would carry a great deal of risk."

"I don't mind," said Amleth. "I think that Yorick would want me to do it."

"I will not have you take any oaths to my guild," said Gerald. "You can back out at any time."

"How will I contact you?" asked Amleth.

"The second Wednesday of each month, wander by this dock. Listen for that song. Sometimes I will be there, sometimes I won't."

"All right," said Amleth.

Gerald reached down and handed him a sack.

"This is Yorick's collection of bundles," he said. "Keep them hidden away. He may turn up to claim them after all. If not, you might find them useful. Keep playing the fool at home, and keep practicing your skills. Oh, and he told me that you like these."

He handed him the piece of wood he had been whittling. It was carved into a stake.

"Thank you," said Amleth, taking it and getting up to leave.

"Amleth," said Gerald.

"Yes?"

"*Stultorum numerus . . .*"

"*Infinitus est,*" returned the boy.

He trudged back to the island, hiding the bundle in the rafters of a stable on the way. Then he walked back to his stockade and added the stake Gerald had given him to it.

Lother came running through, chasing a chicken. He stopped when he saw Amleth.

"Hello, Amleth," he said.

"Hello, Lother," said Amleth dispiritedly.

"What's wrong?" asked Lother.

"Nothing," said the older boy. He looked at the little one, then pulled out three silks from his pouch. "Lother, would you like to see me do a trick?"

Lother nodded, and Amleth started juggling the silks. The little boy's eyes grew wide.

"Can I try?" he asked, holding out his hands.

Amleth nodded.

"Here," he said, handing Lother the silks. "I'll teach you."

$\mathscr{S}$IXTEEN

"Cannot you tell that? Every fool can tell that."

—HAMLET, ACT V, SCENE I

Father Gerald?" called Thomas.

The priest turned toward him, frowning.

"What is it, my son?" he said.

"How do you know these things?" asked the boy. "I know you said that you pieced the story together from different sources, but how can you know them all?"

"Some of it came from refugees fleeing Rügen," said the priest. "The Danes overran the island. The Wends fought well, but were badly outnumbered. Many were enslaved, huddling in chains as their idols were chopped into kindling in front of them. Two sisters who served food at the meeting of Fengi and the Lord of Arkona provided me with details of the words exchanged. An aging mercenary years later gave me some of what transpired in Slesvig. And my best source of all, of course, was Amleth."

"But you still can't know everything that you've told us," insisted Thomas.

"I admit that some of this story is conjecture," said the priest. "Do you know what conjecture is, Thomas?"

"It means you're making it up," said the boy.

"Well, yes, in a way, but only based upon confirmed facts and details," said Gerald. "But, pray, let me continue. I spent some time searching for any trace of Terence, but found none. He had disappeared off the face of the earth. As I said, Amleth became my best source of information on Slesvig. He kept up his façade of moody silences and *bookish brooding so well that soon no one paid much attention to him. He would wander on his own through the town, a walking ghost, always with a manuscript in his hand for quick perusal should anyone stick their head out a window under which he was listening. The Danish soldiers who had been loyal to his father made him their mascot, teaching him fighting techniques and the use of bows. Often he would wander the docks, meeting traveling merchants and foreign sailors and learning their tongues, in the process collecting much useful gossip. Nobody would even wonder when, on the occasional Wednesday, he would sit down with one particular sailor who, oddly enough, hadn't been seen arriving by boat. I grew to look forward to these meetings . . ."*

Slesvig—Paris, 1171 A.D.

"Is that actually a hair sprouting from your chin, young man?" asked Gerald as Amleth joined him. "How old are you now?"

"It is seven hairs and sixteen," said Amleth. "And I wanted to talk to you about something."

"What is it?"

"You said that I could pull out of this anytime I wanted," said Amleth.

"I said it, and I meant it," said Gerald. "Do you want to stop now?"

"Not so much stop," said Amleth. "I still think that I want to join the Guild someday. But I want to go to Paris first. I want to go to the cathedral school and get a proper education."

"You can get a better education with the Fools' Guild than at any school," said Gerald. "Paris is an interesting city, of course, well worth the visit."

"Rolf and Gudmund are going, and they don't even care about it," said Amleth. "They just want to be away from their parents for a while so they can go drinking and whoring untrammeled."

"But wine and women do not interest you," said Gerald. "Maybe you have gone mad."

"Do they interest you?" asked Amleth.

"Not anymore," said Gerald.

"Would I have to give them up to be a fool?"

"No," said Gerald. "But you may choose to once you've had your fill of them."

"How can I have had my fill of something I haven't had yet?" wondered Amleth.

"Maybe you will learn that in Paris," said Gerald.

The following Sunday, Amleth fell into step besides Gerutha as they returned from mass. Fengi had already left to visit the southern earthenworks, and Gorm was hurriedly shoving Alfhild and Lother into a closed carriage before the girl could get a better look at the young men in the congregation.

"How is it with you today, mother?" asked Amleth.

"Mother," she repeated thoughtfully. "You haven't called me that in a long time. You must want something."

"I do," he said.

"Good," she said. "I feel better when you show signs of actual desire. It makes me think that you may be outgrowing these fits of madness."

"I find, madam, that they ease when I am out in the world," he said. "I think that the distraction does me good. It is the life on the island that I find oppressive."

"I understand completely," she said. "I so long for that castle to be built in town, but the funds keep running out. The more my husband raises the taxes, the less money there seems to be coming in. I suspect that the people are concealing their wealth, but it takes everything we collect just to maintain the army."

"I want to go to Paris," said Amleth.

She turned to him in amazement, then noticed for the first time that she was looking up into his eyes. There were dark circles under them, and a sadness in their depths that she recognized all too well. She thought she saw her own face in his, with few of the disturbing features of Ørvendil to haunt her. He was lean but wiry, lacking the bearish build of his father's family. He's my son, she thought suddenly. No one else's.

"The Holy Mother be praised," she said, taking his hands in hers. "I have dreamt and prayed that you would go there and learn to become an educated gentleman."

"Educated, I hope," he said. "A gentleman? It will take more than schooling to make me fit for proper society. But I feel that if I can instill the wisdom of the great in my mind, then I may be able at last to wrest control of it from the demons that have afflicted me."

"Oh, but you have greatness in you," she cried. "I have known this from the beginning. You are my only child, and you shall surpass all that came before you, I vow it."

She seized his head between her hands and kissed his brow fervently.

"Will you speak to . . ." he hesitated, almost choking. "Will you speak to father about it?"

"I will," she said, tears running down her face.

Amleth sat inside his stockade, knees drawn up so that he could fit comfortably. He worked at carving another stake, and so absorbed was he in the task that he did not notice his uncle approaching him until the latter's shadow fell across his face. Then he looked up.

"Paris," said Fengi. "You expect me to send a madman to Paris."

"They may not notice it so much there," said Amleth. "They get so many foreigners, they'll just attribute my behavior to my Jutland upbringing."

"What's wrong, boy? Have you read every book there is to be found in Slesvig?"

"I believe that I have," said Amleth thoughtfully. "But that's not saying much in a town this size. I crave more. I think that getting away from here would do me much good."

"What happens when you return?" asked Fengi. "Will you be back to your pile of mud and sticks, or will you be up to taking your proper place here?"

"I hope and pray that my affliction will abate," said Amleth. "It is in God's hands."

"You know, these are the most words I have heard out of your mouth in years," said Fengi. "I hadn't even noticed that your voice had changed. You're almost a man, now."

"Time passes," said Amleth. "Things grow. Things change. Things heal."

"And things die," finished Fengi. "Very well. You go to Paris. If I hear any report of you embarrassing our family, I will have you hauled back here."

"I won't embarrass you, father," said Amleth smoothly.

The word brought an unexpected smile to Fengi's lips.

"Thank you for that," he said, his voice softening. He squatted to look his nephew in the eye. "Things have been rough between us. I know it, I understand it, and I cannot blame you for it. But I would like them to be better, if only for your mother's sake. I know that it would please her for you to see her favorite place in the world."

"For my mother, then," said Amleth.

"Do you think he's up to something?" Fengi asked Gorm as they looked over the idled construction site. The vaults had been completed, but the brickyard had closed down when the money to pay the laborers had run out. Of the Tuscans, only Reynaldo remained, but his value to the two men had nothing to do with brickmaking.

"Amleth? Given his lack of reason, I doubt it," said Gorm.

"He's never lacked reason," said Fengi. "He's lacked control. He's spent all of these years thinking. People who think can also plan."

"Do you fear the planning of a lunatic child, milord?" scoffed Gorm. "He has no friends, no wealth or power of his own. Let him plan what he likes. He has been harmless for years, and he will be even more harmless in Paris. It would be good for him to go, and for my part, I would be happy to see the back of him."

"Why?" asked Fengi.

"Because my daughter is twelve, and soon will be thirteen," said Gorm.

"And grows prettier by the day," mused Fengi. "She does not know enough of men's ways to ware Amleth. I see why you fear him. I am convinced. It makes my wife happy, it protects Alfhild, it eases your mind, and it gets a constant irritant out of my sight. Maybe Gerutha will finally . . ."

He sighed rather than completing the thought.

"Speak to Rolf and Gudmund for me," he directed. "Suggest to them that it would be to their benefit to keep an eye on Amleth in Paris."

"Very good, milord," said Gorm.

"You're leaving," said Alfhild in disbelief.

"Paris," said Amleth. "You know, better than anyone, how much I want to go there."

"I never thought they would let you," she said. "I thought you would be trapped here forever. Like me."

"You won't be trapped here," said Amleth.

"You'll rescue me?" she asked, a sad smile on her lips. "Will you spirit me out of my high tower and carry me away on a white horse?"

"You live on the bottom floor," he pointed out.

"Father is going to have a tower built for me, I expect," she sighed.

"Then I will spirit you out of there and carry you away on a white horse," he promised, laughing. "Will you wait for me?"

"That's all I can do," she said. She seized his hand suddenly. "Come with me," she whispered. She pulled him through the door into her room.

"Where's your father?" he asked, nervously looking around.

"Hush," she said. She reached behind her neck and unclasped a silver chain with a cross on it. "Will you wear this for me in Paris? As a favor?"

"As a pledge to my lady," he promised solemnly, taking it and putting it on.

"Write to me," she begged him. "I know that they will be months in travel, but you are all I have of the world outside."

"There's your brother," he said, but she grimaced.

"He's annoying," she said.

"He's nine," he replied. "All boys are annoying at nine."

"You weren't," she said.

The day before his departure, he crept into the stables and retrieved Terence's collection of bundles from their hiding place. He sorted through them, smiling at the memories that some of the items brought back, wondering over what use the fool had made of some of the others. Then he stuffed them into a large sack that he had brought with him and went back to the island.

His mother had bought him a large trunk, with twice as much space as would be taken up by all of his belongings. He shoved the sack under the blankets she had packed, along with the sword his father had given him. The fearsome blade of his childhood was now barely even a short sword on his frame, and its edge had been dulled by the years of carving stakes.

He had one last task before he was ready to leave. He picked up another bag and poked his head into the kitchen. There, huddled in a corner by a heap of onions, Lother sat reading a book.

"Which one is that?" whispered Amleth.

"Aristophanes," said Lother, looking up.

Amleth winced in sympathy. There was a livid purple splotch on the left side of the boy's jaw.

"Gorm?" said Amleth, gently touching it.

Lother nodded, expressionless.

"What did you do?" asked Amleth. "Or, more to the point, what did he say you did?"

"I said something that made some of the soldiers laugh," said Lother. "I don't even remember what I said. Father said that I could not disrupt..."

"Military discipline," finished Amleth, sighing. "Come with me, Lother. Let's go disrupt something somewhere else."

The boy was on his feet in a trice.

Lother, unlike his sister, was allowed off the island by his father, and the drost reluctantly countenanced his companionship with Amleth, wanting to curry favor with Gerutha. The two of them loped along the shoreline to the Viking tower, Lother easily keeping up with the older boy's pace.

"You are going to be faster than me someday," observed Amleth, and the younger boy beamed with pride. Amleth pulled out two sets of juggling clubs and handed one to Lother. They each warmed up with some simple three-club routines, then began passing them back and forth with ease. Amleth added a seventh club to the pattern, then an eighth. Lother didn't miss a single pass, his eyes narrowed in concentration.

"I think it's about time we tried nine, don't you?" said Amleth.

Lother's eyes grew wide, but he nodded. The two of them caught the clubs in the air so that each held four.

"I'll start with five," said Amleth. "When you've matched my breathing, nod and I'll count it out."

They started their individual patterns, Lother watching the older boy, trying to match his four to the other's five. He started making his right-hand catches at the same pace as Amleth's, then synchronized his breathing. He nodded.

"On three," said Amleth. "One. Two. Three."

Nine clubs cleaved the air above and between the two boys for three circuits.

"Let's stop before we've pushed our luck too far," said Amleth, grinning.

They snatched the clubs from the air, Amleth ducking his head and taking his last on the back of his neck.

"We did it!" shouted Lother.

"A new combined record," said Amleth. "Congratulations."

Lother dashed forward and hugged the older boy tightly.

"Don't go away," he said, suddenly sobbing. "It will be miserable here without you."

"Then you will have to make things bright again," said Amleth, gently prying Lother's arms away. "Just don't make people laugh when your father's around. When you are with him, toe the line and play the obedient son."

"I hate that," said Lother.

"Just until you are a man," said Amleth. "It is hard living with grownups like these. I know that all too well. But study hard, and when you're old enough, you'll come to Paris and go to school with me."

"Can I?" asked the younger boy.

"Of course," said Amleth. "But you have to promise me something."

"Anything," said Lother.

"Take care of your sister for me," said Amleth. "Bring her tokens from the world outside. Flowers, frogs, books, something different every day. Make her laugh. You know how to do that. And protect her. That's your job as her brother."

"Will you come back to visit?" asked Lother.

"I'll be home in the summer," promised Amleth. "And keep juggling. You are much better at it than I was at your age. When I return, we'll go for ten. Here, take these."

He took half of the clubs and gave them to Lother.

"I can keep them?" said Lother gleefully.

"Yes," said Amleth. "Hide them well. Will you swear to me that you will keep your sister happy?"

"I swear," said Lother.

"Wake up, wake up, young masters," shouted a man, banging on the carriage door. "Welcome to your new home."

The carriage door swung open, and Amleth stepped down, looking around at his new surroundings.

"How do you do?" he said in langue d'oïl.

"Very good, young sir, and thanks for asking," replied the man. "I am Michel, the nuntius. I will be showing you around before you begin your schooling. Any more of you in there?"

"Two of my friends," said Amleth. "Sleeping off the journey."

"Sleeping off a drunk, if I know Danes," laughed Michel. "Rolf and Gudmund, if my information is correct."

"It is," replied Amleth. "I will attempt to rouse them."

By the time he accomplished this, Michel had carried all of their trunks up to their room. Amleth paid the driver and went inside, the other two straggling behind him. They had a single room, with the pallets laid out side by side. Michel had placed their trunks against the opposite wall, and set up three stools next to them so that the trunks would double as desks and tables.

The walls consisted of plaster mixed with small stones and coated with whitewash, although not recently. The wall facing the street had two large windows with shutters. Michel threw them open, and light streamed in.

"You are lucky, sirs," he said. "You will have good light for your studies. That will save you candle money."

"What is he saying?" whispered Gudmund in Danish.

"I thought you spoke langue d'oïl," said Amleth.

"I do," said Gudmund. "Just not that fast."

They looked out the window. Their immediate view was of a pig market.

"What we gain in sunlight, we lose in smell," said Amleth.

"Well, you can't have everything," said Michel. "At least there's fresh sausage to be had. Now, sirs, if you will follow me."

He led them back outside.

"They call this square Porceaux, for obvious reasons," said Michel. "If you lose your way, ask for the Porceaux, or just follow your noses. There's a stall here that sells fresh bread."

"What about wine?" asked Rolf.

"Every other shop," said Michel. "Now, first place I'm taking you to is the Blackfriars' Convent. Quickly, now."

"Why are we going to a convent?" muttered Gudmund once Amleth finished translating.

"Maybe it's a fancy name for a whorehouse," whispered Rolf excitedly.

Amleth merely smiled.

[218]

"Here we are, sirs," said Michel after they had walked half a mile. "A treat for the eyes and a drain on the purse, but you'll never find a better selection."

"Look at them," breathed Amleth in wonder. "Have you ever seen a more glorious sight?"

Spread out in front of the convent were tables of books, presided over by librarii, booksellers licensed by the school.

"Not a whorehouse at all," sighed Gudmund. "Only Amleth would be happy in a place like this."

"Come, Gudmund," said Amleth. "Our fathers sent us here for an education."

"There's education, and there's education," said Rolf.

Laden with used tomes, the freshly copied ones being too expensive for their budgets, the three Danes followed Michel to the neighborhood abutting the Grand Pont, where they met the banker to whom their fathers had entrusted their allowances. Then they crossed the bridge onto the island in the center of the Seine.

"Is that the new cathedral?" asked Rolf, pointing to a building surrounded by scaffolding.

"It will be when it's finished, and that won't be in our lifetime," said Michel. "The choir is done, and it's been dedicated to the Holy Mother. I am taking you to the cloister to register with the chancellor. After that, I will show you around the island to the houses where the masters teach, and then you'll be on your own."

Registration consisted of paying a fee and swearing an oath to the Church.

"Carry these with you at all times," advised the cleric who handed them the documents naming them as scholars. "If you get into any trouble, show them to the guards and they will turn you over to us for disciplinary procedures."

"So we have immunity?" asked Rolf eagerly.

"Only from the state," said the cleric. "The eyes of God are everywhere, and we carry out His dictates on earth. If we catch you, you will wish that the guards had jurisdiction."

They filed out somberly.

"Of course, the key phrase there is if they catch us," said Rolf.

"True enough," said Gudmund, cheering up.

The masters of the school kept small rooms scattered over the island, primarily near, and even on, the Grand Pont and the Petit Pont. The three split up to inquire as to classes. Amleth, having grilled Michel as to the relative merits of the scholars available, happily signed on for as much as he could handle.

Yet the experience proved a dry one. He would dutifully rise at dawn and join his fellow scholars, sitting on the floor of the rooms until an elderly man in a gown and biretta would shamble in and begin reading verbatim from a sheaf of yellowed pages. He would drone on without interruption until he reached the end, then assemble the pages back into their original order and walk out without further colloquy. The students were expected to take down what he said without question. As the weather cooled and their hands slowed in the unheated room, they soon mastered the technique of disrupting the teacher's rhythm by pelting him with rolls or even stones, allowing them to catch up in their note-taking during the ensuing tirades.

Amleth read on his own voraciously, seeking out booksellers through-out the city, both connected to the school and not. He soon realized that the cathedral school was rote learning throughout: grammar without literature, rhetoric without debate, philosophy without questioning, the-ology without spirituality. Knowledge without wisdom.

All the while, his jester gear lay untouched under the spare blanket in his trunk. One day, he realized with a pang that he had not practiced in over a month. It was early evening, and he was alone in the room. Rolf and Gudmund were out carousing. Having already run through their allowance, they were now borrowing from the moneychangers near the Grand Pont. The squealing of the pigs being slaughtered across the street had ended. He opened his trunk and pulled out his clubs.

He ran his fingers over their worn, familiar surfaces, then lay them on his pallet and began the stretching exercises that Yorick had taught him. Then he picked up three clubs and ran through the basic patterns until they were part of him again. He added a fourth club, then a fifth, breathing easily, his eyes focused on a point outside the window. He flipped a sixth club up into the air with his foot, and it too was sucked into the vortex of the pattern, the clubs seemingly moving on their own, unrelated to the blur of movement beneath them.

"I say, you are rather good at that," came a voice from behind him.

Amleth was startled, but managed to keep the pattern going. Slowly, he turned toward the door, the clubs still dancing over him.

There was a young man standing there, an amused smile on his face. Amleth had seen him before, a fellow student, but had not met him.

"How may I help you?" asked Amleth.

"Oh, it's not me that needs the help," returned the other. "I am here on a mission of mercy on behalf of your two mates."

"Are they in trouble?" asked Amleth.

"Yes," said the other. "My name is Horace, by the way."

"Amleth," said Amleth. "You are in my rhetoric class with Julien de Petit Pont."

"Yes. Ghastly, isn't it?" said Horace. "Anyhow, your fellow Danes are being detained in the Bishop's cells for the heinous act of throwing apples at a tradesman."

"Is that all?" said Amleth. "Why can't they just post . . . oh, I see. They've spent their money."

"With the last penny going for the apples," said Horace. "Come, I will take you there."

Amleth tucked his gear into his trunk, threw on his cloak, and followed Horace down the stairs.

"Where did you learn to do that?" asked Horace. "I've dabbled a bit, but you are really quite superb."

"Am I really?" asked Amleth. "I was taught by the town jester when I was younger. I have tried to keep it up."

"Well, it's quite marvelous," said Horace. "I've seen a few jesters in my time, and that was as good as any of them. Except maybe that fellow who performs over at the market at les Halles. Have you seen him?"

"No," said Amleth. "I would love to."

"I'd say you should pick up a little extra money performing, only I don't think you would," said Horace.

"Why not?" asked Amleth.

"You're a good juggler," said Horace seriously. "But you look like you haven't laughed in years. No one would find you entertaining."

"There's some truth in that," admitted Amleth.

Horace glanced about, then whispered, "The rumor is that you are mad. Is it true?"

"Would you like it better if I confirmed it or if I denied it?" asked Amleth.

"Oh, confirmed, definitely," said Horace. "So much more interesting, don't you think? Here we are."

With Horace's help, Amleth rescued his fellow Danes with profuse apologies and a small bribe, then led them home.

"Thank you," he said to Horace after they had laid the two inebriates out on their pallets.

"My pleasure," said Horace. "Nice meeting you. Say, if you are interested, come join us for dinner tomorrow night."

"Who are you with?"

"I'm a Norman," said Horace. "The Danish students eat with us a lot. You'll be right at home."

"All right, I will," promised Amleth. "And thanks again."

The next morning, he walked to les Halles. Just as Horace had said, there was a fool there, an aged fellow with a shaggy, gray beard whose motley resembled the markings on a cow, but whose patter was sharp and whose skills were exceptional. He did well with the morning crowd. When he took a break, Amleth went up to him.

"You are very good," he said. "What is your name?"

"They call me La Vache," said the fool. "Something to do with my motley."

"Did they name you that because of the motley, or did you get the motley to go with the name?" asked Amleth.

"It's been so long that I've forgotten," said La Vache. "But if you need me to entertain at one of your student affairs, I am available."

"How did you know I was a student?" asked Amleth curiously.

"You know that I am a fool by my dress," said La Vache. "Since you do not dress as a fool, you must be a wise man, hence, a student."

"I cannot argue with that," laughed Amleth. "Except to say that not every fool wears motley."

"True enough," agreed La Vache.

"After all, does not the Good Book say, '*Stultorum numerus*...'" He stopped.

La Vache's eyes narrowed.

"That would be from the Vulgate," he said quietly. "Not a phrase one generally hears on the street."

"It isn't complete, though," returned Amleth.

"What would you know about it?" asked La Vache.

"What is the rest of it?" asked Amleth.

La Vache glanced about the marketplace quickly. No one was watching them.

"*Infinitus est,*" he muttered. "Who are you?"

"My name is Amleth Ørvendilson. I am from Slesvig. I was wondering if you gave lessons."

"You're not with the Guild?" asked La Vache.

"No."

"Then how did you know the password?"

"It was given me when I was young by a jester who told me to use it for my protection if I needed it."

"Are you in danger now?" asked La Vache.

"Just from boredom," said Amleth.

"Well, we can't have that," said La Vache. "Especially in Paris. Do you see that large shed over yonder?"

"Yes," said Amleth.

"Meet me there at dinnertime on Thursdays. I'll show you a few things."

Amleth nodded and tossed him a penny.

He had done it all on an impulse, yet he found his thoughts racing toward Thursday, leaving the parts of his mind bent on study far behind. When the day arrived, he slipped away from the Porceaux square and walked quickly to les Halles, his gear slung over his shoulder. He saw La Vache going into the shed. He looked around, then followed him, stopping short when he saw what was inside.

Several jesters were stretching out in front of him, including La Vache. In front of them, in full motley and makeup, was Gerald.

"Welcome, Amleth," he said. "Now, the real education begins."

$\mathscr{S}$EVENTEEN

"Enquire me first what Danskers are in Paris…"
— *Hamlet*, Act II, Scene I

Slesvig—Paris, 1174–1175 A.D.

A letter has arrived, milord," called Gorm softly as Fengi emerged from his quarters at dawn.

"Who from?" asked Fengi.

"Rolf in Paris," said Gorm.

Above them, on the upper floor of Gorm's quarters, Alfhild crept to the window to listen.

"What's the gist?" asked Fengi.

"That French wine is superior to Danish ale," said Gorm. "That education is wasted on the young, and that…"

"He says all of this?" laughed Fengi.

"No, milord, I do," said Gorm. "When I think what I could do now when I should have done it then, I could weep."

"Don't weep now," said Fengi. "What of Amleth?"

Alfhild leaned as far as she could out the window without being noticed.

"He keeps to himself, apart from this Norman friend of his," said Gorm. "But he is still disappearing every Thursday evening, returning late, yet with neither wine on his breath nor book in his hand. He does not discuss where he has been, what he has been doing, or whom he has been with."

"What does Rolf think?" asked Fengi.

"He suspects that there is a woman," said Gorm. "Some French courtesan whose favors may be purchased with Danish coin."

Above them, Alfhild collapsed, clutching her hands to her mouth to keep herself from screaming.

"Very like," commented Fengi. "If it was true, then that would be the surest sign of sanity we have seen in him. It's about time. He's in Paris, after all. Not having a woman there would be like walking through a bakery without nibbling the pastry."

"Even so, milord," said the drost.

"I suppose even you ran wild when you were there," said Fengi.

"You may suppose as you like," said Gorm shortly. "I will not say yea or nay."

"Have they tried following him?" asked Fengi.

"A few times, just out of curiosity," said Gorm. "But he gave them the slip every time."

"Now, that's interesting," said Fengi thoughtfully. "Men's natures being what they are, I would think that he would want to boast of such a conquest rather than conceal it. This sounds more like something that he truly wishes to hide."

"Perhaps the lady is married," suggested Gorm.

Alfhild sank her teeth into her palm, tears running down her cheeks.

"That's a possibility," said Fengi. "One I would wish to be discouraged for the sake of his mother. She dislikes any hint of a flaw in his character. A scandal would be quite upsetting."

"We should send someone to follow him who knows how to do it properly," said Gorm. "Someone with discretion."

"Who do you have in mind?" asked Fengi.

"Reynaldo," said Gorm. "He speaks langue d'oïl fluently. And he knows when to be quiet."

"I know that well," said Fengi. "Send him."

. . .

On a sunny Thursday afternoon a few weeks later, Amleth and Horace emerged from the house of a master.

"Canon law does not become more interesting after three years," said Horace, yawning.

"I like it," said Amleth. "Once one pierces the fog, one can see how the Church really behaves."

"In the beginning was the Word," said Horace. "Then everyone started interpreting it. That's where the trouble began."

"We'd be better off without words," agreed Amleth. "No misinterpretations, no misunderstandings."

"No insults," added Horace.

"There are insults without words," said Amleth. "I have seen them often in Paris. You take your arms and arrange them thusly..."

"Stop," laughed Horace. "You'll get us both in trouble. I don't want to get thrown into jail just when spring is coming."

"What will you be doing this summer?" asked Amleth.

"Going home, having endless strolls with whatever prospective brides my mother is lining up for me," said Horace. "Dreadfully boring."

"Come with me, then," begged Amleth. "You've been promising to visit Slesvig for ages. I promise not to try to marry you to anyone."

"Your last argument is persuasive, Master Amleth," said Horace. "I will write my mother and tell her to bid the maidens adieu. Until tomorrow, then."

"Good-bye," said Amleth.

He dashed home and exchanged his books for his jester's bag, then wandered casually through the stalls at the pig market, greeting many of the vendors by name.

Behind him, Reynaldo followed, munching on a sausage. The young student seemed to him to be much more cheerful than the brooding boy of his memory. Perhaps it was the city, thought the Tuscan. Everything was better here—the food, the wine, the women. Especially the women, he mused, having already sampled enough to make the comparison.

He watched as Amleth ducked into a tavern, and took up a position across the street from where he could see inside. Amleth purchased a cup of wine and some cheese and mixed with a group of students, chatting away. Reynaldo sighed. He appreciated the faith his masters had shown in sending him here, but the assignment looked like it would be dull indeed, following a student to his mistress.

He finished the sausage and wiped his fingers on his sleeves, then looked up to see what Amleth was doing.

He wasn't there.

Reynaldo hurried across the street and looked around the tavern. The clump of students was still chatting away, but Amleth wasn't one of them. There was a rear door in the tavern, visible to him now that the students weren't standing between it and his observation post. He opened it and peered out. There was an alley stretching out in both directions, with many more turning off it. Amleth could have gone anywhere.

He slammed the door shut and went back to his inn, berating himself. It was going to be a long and irritating week.

"I was followed again," said Amleth as he ducked into the shed where they trained.

"Rolf or Gudmund this time?" asked La Vache, who was leading the stretching exercises.

"Neither," said Amleth. "My uncle must have become suspicious of me. He sent one of his spies from Slesvig. I lost him."

"Well done," said La Vache. "Good to know the training paid off. But I don't like having him poking his nose into the Guild's business."

"Neither do I," said Amleth.

"I'll get word to Gerald in Roskilde," said La Vache. "Meantime, we'll figure out something here."

The following Thursday, Reynaldo was ready. He followed Amleth from lecture to lecture just in case he was making an early start rather than coming home first. When his quarry emerged from his room and wandered through the pig market, the sausages, no matter how tempting, did not distract his pursuer. Amleth wove his way through the stalls, then entered the same tavern he had chosen the previous week. When he slipped out the rear door, Reynaldo was already in the alley, crouching behind a rain barrel. Amleth glanced around, but did not spot the Tuscan.

Reynaldo tailed him as he turned toward the Place de Greve. Amleth passed through the warehouses of the area to a neighborhood that gave even Reynaldo pause. In front of one of the smaller bawdy houses, a young woman stood in the doorway, a thin shawl draped around her bare shoulders.

"You are late, mon cher," she scolded him. He shrugged sheepishly, and she grabbed him by both shoulders, pulled him down, and kissed him hard as the other prostitutes and their patrons hooted from windows around them. Then the two of them vanished inside.

A gray-bearded porter standing nearby laughed.

"Every week, the same thing," he said to no one in particular. "You'd think that boy would be beyond shame by now."

"Excuse me," said Reynaldo. "Do you know that young man?"

"Him?" said the porter. "Don't know his name, but he's a regular in these parts. If he went to church on Sundays as much as he comes here on Thursdays, then his soul might be safe, but I doubt it. Students, pah!" He spat on the ground for emphasis.

"Thank you," said Reynaldo, tossing him a penny.

"Don't mention it," said La Vache, watching the Tuscan leave. "Or rather, do mention it."

Inside the bawdy house, the jester who had played the prostitute watched through the shutters.

"He's gone," she said, turning to Amleth. "I think he bought the act."

"Good," said Amleth. "Thank you."

"Oh, it was my pleasure," she said teasingly. She stretched out on the bed. "Sure you don't want to do anything else? We've already paid for the room. It would bring a touch of verisimilitude to your performance."

"I enjoyed the kiss," said Amleth sincerely. "But I wear the favor of another."

"Oh, la," she sniffed. "Spare me the chivalrous amateurs."

"Reynaldo has returned from Paris, milord," said Gorm a week later.

"Yes?" said Fengi.

"It was as we suspected," said Gorm. "A Parisian tarte for him to munch upon. Reynaldo was told that he makes weekly visits to bawdy houses in that district."

"How discriminating was his eye?" asked Fengi.

"Reynaldo said that she was very pretty," said Gorm.

"Good for Amleth," said Fengi. "Paris has been well worth the expense if it has brought him down to earth again."

"Yes, milord," said Gorm. "One less thing to worry about with all this other business."

"Let's not discuss that here," warned Fengi.

"Of course not, milord," said Gorm.

The drost went inside his quarters. He thought he heard his daughter weeping upstairs. He sighed with exasperation. She had been doing that a lot lately. He felt completely unable to address the needs of an adolescent girl. He had kept her shut up in the upper room for most of the day so that she might avoid temptation, but it did not seem to help.

He ascended the steps to the room and unbarred the door. She sat up on the pallet, her face so like her mother's that he turned pale for a moment, imagining Signe returning to haunt him.

"You wanted me to enter a convent," she blurted out suddenly. "When can I go?"

He knelt in front of her, taking her hands in his.

"Praise be to God," he said fervently. "I will arrange it forthwith."

He dashed down the steps in his haste.

Alfhild clutched an old, raggedy doll to her bosom and rocked back and forth, a low moan emanating from her.

"What's wrong?" asked Lother, poking his head through the door.

"I've decided to enter the convent," she said.

"Oh, no," he muttered. "Is that why father is looking so happy? He has finally broken you."

"He didn't break me," she said. "I just want to be away from everything. It's all too much for me."

"But a convent? And now? Can't you at least wait until Amleth comes back?"

She threw herself down and wailed.

"What on earth did I say?" asked Lother, rushing to comfort her.

"I never want to see him or hear his name again," she sobbed.

"Amleth?" he said, producing another wail. "But why?"

"He has been unfaithful to me," she said.

"Impossible," he said firmly.

"It's true," she said, shaking her head. "Father had him followed in Paris."

"Then it must have been a mistake," said Lother. "Or some kind of joke. He loves only you. You know that."

He took out a handkerchief and gently wiped the tears from her face.

"You can't go to a convent," he said. "I'd never get to see you there. Who would cheer you up?"

"You'll be gone in the fall anyway," she said. "You'll be in Paris studying, and he'll be in Paris whoring, and I'll be shut in here with father watching my every move. A convent would be paradise compared to that."

"Except that you'll become a nun," said Lother. "Amleth can't marry a nun."

"I can't marry him knowing what I know," she said. "Please, Lother. I've made up my mind."

"Let me talk to father," he begged her.

She smiled, and kissed his cheek, which still bore a recent bruise from his father's ministrations.

"I would rather be walled up in a convent until I die than let any more harm come to you," she said.

"I'm a man," he said. "I protect you."

"I know," she said. "I just don't know who will protect you."

"A convent," said Fengi when Gorm informed him of his decision. "And she actually agreed to go?"

"She is my daughter," said Gorm haughtily. "She does as I tell her to do."

"Of course," said Fengi. "Still, I shall be sorry to see her go. What with Amleth away, and Lother heading to school this fall, she would have been the only young person left on the island."

"She's almost a woman," said Gorm. "There are girls her age getting married."

"And you don't want her to marry," said Fengi.

"I cannot say that I see much in that institution," said Gorm. "At least I can preserve her from sin this way. There will be no temptation for her, and she will be none herself."

"Quite so," said Fengi.

"Impressive defenses," said Horace, looking out the window of the carriage as they passed through the gate in the southern earthenworks.

"My father built them," said Amleth.

"They keep the Holsteiners in Holstein," chirped Gudmund.

"Yes, the fearsome Holsteiners," added Rolf. "All our lives, we've lived in fear that the Holsteiners were going to invade us. Then our parents send us to Paris, and what's the first border we cross? Holstein!"

"We were terrified," said Gudmund. "We crouched down in the carriage, hoping they wouldn't see us."

"Except for Amleth," said Rolf. "But then, he's mad, isn't he?"

"Some of the time," said Amleth.

"What did you think would happen if they saw you?" asked Horace.

"Oh, something horrible," said Gudmund. "We'd be held for ransom, or flayed alive."

"Or eaten," laughed Rolf.

They crossed the river and headed east. Amleth grew quiet as they approached the town. The carriage stopped by the foot of the draw-bridge, and Horace and Amleth pulled their trunks from the roof and thanked the driver. It pulled away, Rolf and Gudmund waving from inside.

"God, did they even stop talking long enough to draw breath?" groaned Amleth.

"So, this is your island castle," said Horace, surveying the stockade.

"Don't call it a castle in front of my mother," warned Amleth. "She might take it as sarcasm."

"It was sarcasm," said Horace. "Ready to face the family?"

"No," said Amleth. "Let's go in."

They were greeted as they passed by the guards, but with little fanfare otherwise. A pair of thralls dropped whatever it was that they were doing and rushed to take the trunks from the two students. Gerutha appeared shortly thereafter, holding both arms out.

"My young gentleman has arrived," she cried, hauling Amleth into her embrace. He submitted with ill grace, then stepped back.

"Mother, this is my companion and fellow student, Horace," he said. "Horace, the Duchess Gerutha."

"Madame, it is an honor," said Horace in his best Danish, bowing low and kissing her hand.

"Ah, Parisian manners," she said, beaming. "It has been so long since I was at the courts there."

"Their present glory must be a pale shadow of when your magnifi-cence graced them," said Horace.

Amleth rolled his eyes as his mother simpered at the young man.

"Come," she said. "I will take you to your quarters."

"I know where I live," said Amleth, but his mother had already taken Horace's arm.

"This is the great hall," she said, leading him inside.

Amleth sighed and followed them.

The two students had missed the midday meal, so she left them in the kitchen. When they had filled their stomachs, they went back to the Duke's quarters.

"This is where you grew up?" asked Horace, looking around at the stockade walls.

"I'm afraid so," said Amleth.

"That explains a lot," said Horace.

"Quiet, or I'll tell mother that you are really a Norman, not a Parisian," said Amleth.

He stopped short as he entered his room. His mother was standing over his open trunk, holding a stuffed sparrow hawk, an expression of panic on her face.

"You have Yorick's belongings," she said in a near whisper. "Why? For God's sake, what are they doing here?"

"What were you doing in my trunk?" demanded Amleth.

"I was going to unpack your things for you," she said. "Why do you have Yorick's? Did you kill him?"

"For God's sake, mother!" Amleth shouted. She looked at him in horror. "How could you say that? You know how much he meant to me."

"More than I do," she said. She threw the stuffed bird back. "I'm sorry." She left.

Horace watched her.

"Will she tell your uncle?" he asked.

"No," said Amleth bitterly. "She's my mother."

He shut the trunk, taking care to bury the jester gear under the blankets. Then he turned to Horace.

"Let me show you my fort," he said.

He took him to the rear of the island where his stockade still stood between the herb garden and the bare patch that once had been Gerutha's. His brick still rested in the middle of it.

"Impressive," said Horace, surveying it. "There must be over two hundred stakes here."

"Over three hundred," said Amleth proudly. "It took me years."

"But will it protect you from your enemies?" asked Horace.

"Apparently not," said Amleth.

Horace turned to see a boy of twelve standing before them, a fierce expression on his face, his hand on his sword's hilt.

"Have you returned to face me at last, you coward?" shouted the boy.

"Have you grown so tired of life at such a young age that you would challenge me?" returned Amleth.

"Draw your sword and fight like a knight," said the boy. "Or I shall cut you down like the dishonorable dog that you are."

"Have pity, good knight," said Amleth. "I have no weapon as mighty as yours."

The boy reached into his pack and produced a wooden practice sword that he threw to Amleth. Then he drew his own.

They circled each other warily. Amleth feinted a few times, but the boy did not rise to the bait. Then Amleth stumbled for a moment over a rock, and the boy attacked. Amleth sidestepped and let the boy's momentum carry him over his outstretched foot. The boy leapt over it and whirled, sword at the ready. Amleth was already on the move, his sword coming in fast and low, but the boy blocked it easily, a grin on his face.

"You stumbled on purpose," he said. "That was a trick to lure me in. You almost had me."

"But I didn't trip you up this time," said Amleth. "You've improved quite a bit. Lother, meet my friend Horace. This is Lother, my cousin."

"Is it safe?" asked Horace.

"Not at all," said Lother. "I may have a quarrel with Amleth, you know. But I've been defending him just in case I was right."

"Right about what?" asked Amleth.

Lother beckoned them close.

"Alfhild thinks you were unfaithful to her," he said. "Reynaldo was spying on you in Paris. He came back and told father that you were visiting a brothel there."

"Alfhild heard about that?" said Amleth, turning ashen.

"I told her that it couldn't be true," continued Lother.

"It is, and it isn't," said Amleth.

"Which is it?" asked Lother.

"It was a trick we . . . I played on Reynaldo," said Amleth. "I wanted to give Fengi something to think about. But I had no intention of it getting back to Alfhild."

"That's the problem with jokes," said Horace. "They develop lives of their own."

"I have to see her," said Amleth. "I have to explain."

"Unfortunately, that may prove difficult," said Lother.

"Why?" asked Amleth.

"She entered the convent last week," he said gloomily.

"Oh, no," said Amleth. "Tell me she hasn't taken vows yet."

"She has to be a novice for six months, I think," said Lother.

"I have to see her," shouted Amleth, running toward the drawbridge.

He took one of his uncle's horses and galloped south. The convent was two miles past the church of St. Andreas, and it was midafternoon by the time he arrived. He leapt from the horse and banged on the front gate, his hair disheveled, his clothes dusty from the journey, and his face covered in sweat. The woman who kept the gatehouse took one look at the apparent madman and refused him both admittance and conveyance of any message to the inner sanctum.

Frustrated, he rode back. A nearby tavern beckoned, and he tasted Danish ale for the first time in months. It tasted good. He had a few more.

The sun was beginning to set when he emerged and, with great difficulty, climbed back on his horse. He wasn't paying any attention to the route home. A wrong turn brought him to an unfamiliar road that passed by a secluded area containing a large military encampment. The guards looked at him suspiciously as he rode by, singing a bawdy Parisian drinking song. One of them made some comment that he barely heard, and it was only when he had ridden some distance that it occurred to him that it had been in German.

He tied his horse up in a small copse of trees and walked back to the camp, staying off the road and out of sight. The campfires were burning brightly, and the soldiers were having their evening meal, a dozen conversations going on simultaneously. None of them was in Danish.

He ran back to his horse and galloped back to Slesvig.

His uncle was standing in the entrance to the stockade when he crossed the drawbridge. Amleth jumped down from the horse.

"She's locked away from me!" he shouted. "What harm did you think I would do her?"

"What is wrong with you?" demanded his uncle. "You barely arrive, then you steal a horse and vanish for the day? Your mother . . ."

"There is evil and sin everywhere!" shouted Amleth. "But you take the pure and put them in prisons filled with madwomen rather than letting them fight God's enemies on the battlefield. I say that these walls behind which you hide will no more protect you from the world than the ones I built by the garden. Yet I will be safe there, and nowhere else."

He fled to the rear of the island and jumped over his fortifications.

"What has happened?" asked Gorm, coming up to Fengi.

"He has relapsed," said Fengi. "Your daughter's absence seems to have deeply affected him."

"Praise be to God that I got her out of here in time," said Gorm.

"Praise be," said Fengi.

Amleth sat there day and night, refusing to join the others at meals. He accepted the food that was brought to him, and the use of a blanket, but otherwise remained. Sometimes Lother sat with him, sometimes Horace did. Gerutha came out to plead with him, but he sat stonefaced, and she walked away, weeping.

Two weeks after he began his retreat, Rolf and Gudmund came onto the island. They spoke briefly with Gerutha, then walked back to see Amleth. Horace stood nearby, watching.

"What cheer, fellow?" asked Rolf.

"None," replied Amleth.

"None here, that is certain," agreed Gudmund. "You are wasting away without entertainment."

"What do you propose to do?" asked Amleth. "Put on a puppet show for me?"

"We would, but we lack puppets," said Rolf. "But there is better entertainment to be had. We are going hunting this morning. There is good quarry to be had south of the fjord."

Amleth looked back and forth between the two of them, then over at Horace, who stood impassively, his arms crossed over his chest.

"Very well," he said, standing. "Perhaps it will ease my mind."

The three of them walked across the drawbridge where three horses stood waiting. Rolf and Gudmund bounded up on theirs, then turned to look at Amleth, and stared.

He was seated on his horse, but facing the beast's rump. He looked at them curiously.

"Why do you ride that way?" he asked.

"It is customary to face in the same direction as the horse," said Gudmund.

"But the horse is already looking that way," said Amleth. "This way, I protect its rear."

"How will you guide the horse?" asked Rolf.

"I don't know where I am going," said Amleth. "Therefore, there's no reason for me to guide it."

"But we are going hunting together," said Gudmund. "Your horse has to stay with ours."

"You lead," said Amleth. "I expect the horse will know what to do. It seems like an intelligent creature."

"Unlike its rider," muttered Rolf. "Very well. Let us be off."

The two of them trotted off. Amleth slapped his steed on the rump, and it trotted after the other two.

Rolf and Gudmund were grateful that their route took them south rather than through the town. The few passersby that they encountered nodded at the two, but then gawked in amazement as Amleth calmly rode by them, waving to them as he receded.

Amleth never once looked behind him to see where the other two were taking him, contenting himself to watch the landscape pass by on either side. Trees began popping into view, and soon he realized that he was in a forest a few miles south of the fjord, one that he had occasionally hunted in with his father. The sudden memory almost brought tears to his eyes, but he regained his composure before the others noticed. An advantage to riding backward, he thought to himself.

The horse stopped. He heard no other hoofbeats, so he gathered that his companions had stopped as well.

"Is this where our quarry resides?" he asked.

"Nearby," said Rolf. "Just down this path."

"For what do we hunt?" asked Amleth, turning for the first time. "It occurs to me that I have neglected to bring either spear or bow. And I don't observe any with you, either."

"Some prey must be taken bare-handed," said Gudmund, smiling. "I daresay that you will find this one worth the capture."

"Is it dangerous?" asked Amleth.

"Very," said Rolf. "So much so that Gudmund and I will not attempt to face it, for fear of being taken in its snares."

"But you have no compunction about sending me in there," observed Amleth.

"You are the only man we would send down that path," said Rolf. "And it is the love that we bear for you that keeps us here, for no man should face this creature alone."

"Yet you will thank us in the end," added Gudmund.

"This is not a hunt, it's a riddle," said Amleth. "You are being unfair to an addled mind such as mine."

"It is a riddle of sorts," said Rolf. "This is a prey that in the taking the taker will also be taken."

"Clear enough," said Gudmund, snickering. "Now, get you down the path, friend Amleth. Call if you need help."

Amleth looked at the two, then reached behind him and took his reins. He shook them slightly, and the horse walked down the path away from his companions. As it curved out of sight, he drew a short sword from his belt, the same one his father had given him on his birthday.

He kept his eyes open for traps and attackers hidden in the brush that loomed on either side of him. Then the path widened into a clearing. The trees surrounding it were old and majestic, and the sun only pierced them at the top of the clearing, making an uneven circle of light at its center.

Standing in it was Alfhild.

EIGHTEEN

"A dream itself is but a shadow."

—*HAMLET*, ACT II, SCENE II

Slesvig—1175 A.D.

This is a dream," she said. "I have had it before. I was lost in a forest, and you rode up on a white horse to save me. Only . . ." She looked at him, puzzled. "In my dream, you were riding properly. Why are you sitting on that horse backward?"

He slid down to the ground, speech deserting him. She waited, a touch of impatience in her eyes.

"This is not at all what is supposed to happen," she said. "Say something."

"This is no dream," he said, finding his voice at last. It sounded hoarse to him, the words slurring.

She lunged toward him and grabbed his hand.

"This is not what is supposed to happen," she hissed.

She pulled him with surprising strength to the edge of the clearing and pressed his hand against a tree.

"They are all around us," she whispered. "Just like at home, only these are alive. Can you feel it?"

She pressed her face against the rough bark, closed her eyes, and inhaled.

"All those years shut inside that fortress," she murmured. "Walled in by trees, jammed together, smelling of clay and pitch. Dead things. No wonder my mother couldn't survive in there. I think I died there years ago. I couldn't remember what trees were like anymore. Stockades, stone churches, closed carriages. One tomb after another. The smells here— they overwhelm me. The space, the size of it all. It's wondrous and terrible all at once. I cannot bear it. Too many scents, and I cannot recognize them. Wild, ancient smells. They were never in my mother's garden."

She leaned back, breathing deep, trying to take in as much air as she could. She had pressed her face against the tree so hard that her cheek was scratched and bleeding, bits of bark clinging to it. Amleth reached out to touch it, and she shied away.

"Don't," she cried. "Don't touch me ever again. Not after..." She looked down. "A French whore. That's what father said. We are all whores. He said that as well. He's been telling me that since I was a little girl. I never understood it until now."

"It isn't true," said Amleth.

"What isn't?" she spat. "That we are not all whores?"

"You are not a whore, and there was no other woman," said Amleth gently. "Your father was deceived."

"How can that be?" she scoffed. "Father is never deceived. He is never wrong."

"He was deceived because I deceived him," said Amleth, taking her hand again. "I never meant for it to reach your ears. He had Reynaldo follow me in Paris. I had a colleague play a farce with me for Reynaldo's eyes. He believed what he was meant to believe. But I would rather have died than let it get back to you, Alfhild. Can you possibly forgive me?"

She looked at him sternly.

"You speak words, and you sound truthful," she said. "But everyone says that you are mad. I have known you my entire life, and I thought that you were just feigning madness, but I don't know anymore."

She pulled her hand free from his grasp.

"Sometimes I think that I have gone mad myself," she said. "I cannot tell. I am no judge of what is true. My world is all walls, even here. You promised that you would rescue me."

"I did, and I meant it," he said.

She turned away from him.

"Father may have been right after all," she said softly. "I would give myself to you right now if you wanted me. If you would take me away from here."

"I cannot," said Amleth. He took a step toward her, placing his hands on her shoulders. She shivered at the touch, but whether it was revulsion or something else, he could not say.

"Why can't you?" she asked. "What chains you to this prison? We could run off to a place where nobody knew us and live our lives without fear."

"What about Lother?" he asked.

"We could take him," she said. "No one would think it unusual, a young married couple with her little brother in her charge. Let us exchange our vows here and now, before all of these witnesses, before they shut me up forever."

She threw herself at him suddenly, seizing his head with both hands and kissing him hard. He found himself kissing her back, unable to stop himself. Above him, the tops of the trees seemed to lean over them, shutting off the circle of sky, spinning faster and faster. He began to sink to the ground, taking her with him, when in the distance a raven cawed, once, twice, a third time.

He pushed her away roughly, gasping for breath. She fell back, her hands covering her face.

"What is wrong with you?" she screamed. "Am I so hideous?"

"How came you here?" he whispered.

"What?" she said, bewildered, tears filling her eyes.

"How did you get out of the convent?" he said. "Who brought you here?"

[243]

"Your friends," she said slowly. "Rolf and Gudmund. They said that you had sent them."

He stood and staggered around, looking up at the surrounding trees.

"You are all devils!" he screamed. "Why do you persist in tormenting me?"

He sank back down to his knees and grabbed her, pulling her face close to his.

"Listen to me," he whispered urgently. "Go back to the convent. Wait there. It may be days, it may be months, but do not leave unless I come for you myself."

"But why?" she asked.

"Foul temptress!" he shouted. "Take your wares to the market and peddle them there, but keep your claws off me."

She collapsed, sobbing, clutching her stomach. He leaned down and whispered, "Trust no one but me and Lother. There are tasks that I must accomplish before I leave here, but when I leave, I leave with you. Go back to the convent, Alfhild."

"But what if you never come?" she cried.

"Then find yourself a living man," he said, getting to his feet.

He jumped on the horse and galloped into the woods. She lay there, sobbing uncontrollably. She heard two horses approaching, and stood, expecting to see Rolf and Gudmund. But it was her father and Fengi instead.

She looked back and forth at the two of them, trying to comprehend what their presence meant. Gorm leapt down from his horse, his face red with anger.

"Whore!" he shouted, striking her across the face and sending her tumbling to the ground.

That, she understood. She curled into a ball, her arms covering her face, and waited for the beating to continue.

"Cease, Gorm," Fengi commanded quietly. "She did nothing more than she was meant to do."

"She offered herself to him right here," shouted Gorm. "In the middle of this filth, she desired to become the foulest part of it."

Fengi dismounted and knelt by the cowering girl.

"What did Amleth say to you?" he asked gently, patting her shoulder.

"What?" she whispered, looking up at him with an expression of sorrow and shame that nearly stopped his heart.

"What did he tell you?" he repeated, stammering slightly.

"Nothing but the ravings of a disordered mind," she said, sitting up slowly.

"I told you that this was a bad idea," said Gorm petulantly. "Putting her virtue into harm's way just to gain information. Let me take her. She must be chastised sufficiently before I turn her back over to the sisters."

"Gorm, you do all three of us a disservice by this behavior," said Fengi sharply. "Now, go and fetch those two idiot friends of Amleth and then find that lunatic before he comes to some harm."

"But ..." began Gorm, motioning toward his daughter.

"Now!" commanded Fengi. "I will escort her to the convent myself. Go!"

Gorm, his every movement betraying his reluctance, mounted his horse and rode off.

Fengi squatted down and looked at Alfhild, who was wiping her eyes with a kerchief.

"So," she said bitterly. "This was your plan all along. To transform me from an encloistered virgin to the spymaster's whore."

"You were safe," said Fengi. "We were watching you."

"I am the more shamed for it," she said. "Why have you used me thus?"

"To see if Amleth was truly mad," said Fengi. "Why wouldn't he leave with you? What reason did he give?"

"There was something he had to do first," she said.

"What was it?"

"He would not tell me," she whispered.

He held out his hand to help her to her feet. She took it hesitantly. They stood together, and she turned to go. He did not relinquish her hand.

"Truly," he said, then he cleared his throat. She looked at him fearfully, then down at her feet. "Truly, a man would have to be mad to reject you."

"Can you get me out of the convent?" she blurted out.

"Only with your father's consent," he said.

"Then you had better take me back there, hadn't you?" she said, looking him directly in the eyes.

His mouth was suddenly dry. He choked out something in response, then lifted her onto his horse and climbed up behind her.

The journey to the convent, with her jolting before him on the horse's back, was the most exquisitely agonizing experience of his entire life.

"There he is," called Rolf as he sighted Amleth galloping across a meadow, still sitting backward.

"How does he do that?" wondered Gudmund.

"Never mind," snapped Gorm. "Let's stop him before he does any real damage."

Amleth waved merrily to the three when he saw them in pursuit. He was determined not to look behind him until the ride was over. Occasionally the horse would leap some obstacle, and he would grip its flanks with his knees, clinging for dear life. He soon began anticipating when the steed was preparing itself to jump, which made the maneuver a little easier.

What he did not expect was the horse coming to a dead stop when confronted with a fence that was beyond its capabilities. Amleth flew backward over the horse's head. He had enough time to gather himself into a ball while he was flipping end over end, and in a brief moment of clarity saw the fence as he passed over it, along with the thorny brush that awaited his imminent landing. All right, bad idea taken too far, was his last thought.

"Well, at least the horse is none the worse for wear," commented Rolf as they rode up. "Looks like our friend will need some patching."

They looked across the fence at Amleth, who was ensnared in a tangle of branches, his clothes shredded in numerous places. He struggled feebly, and a branch gave way, sending him with a thud to the ground. He lay there, breathing hard.

"I should leave you there," said Gorm. "If I thought you would learn the error of your ways as you bled to death, I would. But I have been charged with bringing you back home."

"I will make my home here and you shall be discharged," said Amleth. "Have you been hunting in these woods as well, Appollonius? I saw prey worth the taking, but it was too young for serious sport. Perhaps I shall hunt here again in a year."

"A few more bruises and cuts would not be noticed on him, would they?" muttered Gorm, and Rolf and Gudmund smirked.

"Come with us, Amleth," called Gudmund. "We have had enough entertainment for one day. Let us go dine."

Amleth rolled out of the bush, stood, and brushed himself off.

"I am yours, gentlemen," he said.

Then he ran.

"Here we go again," said Rolf, spurring his horse on.

When they returned to the island, Rolf and Gudmund kept Amleth pinioned between them. Gerutha nearly fainted when she saw his scratched and bloodied face. He ignored her and shrugged off his two companions, then went back to his fortress of stakes and sat down.

Horace came up shortly thereafter and sat next to him.

"You do a very creditable raven," muttered Amleth.

"Thank you," said Horace. "I do some other birdcalls. Would you like to hear them?"

"Some other time," said Amleth. "How did you know I was being watched?"

"I've been keeping an eye on Rolf and Gudmund," said Horace. "When I saw the three of you go into the woods, I hobbled my horse and ran along the side of the trail. When you went on ahead, they started talking about whether Gorm and Fengi were in position or not. I circled around and saw their horses. I figured it was a trap of some kind."

"So you became a raven," said Amleth. "The bird of knowledge. A good choice."

"What exactly happened in there?" asked Horace.

"They tried to use Alfhild," said Amleth. "It almost worked."

"Is she siding with them, then?" asked Horace.

"I don't know," said Amleth. "I hope not."

Gorm sat with Gerutha at the main table in the great hall, quietly telling her what had transpired that day. Fengi joined them when he had reached the part about finding Amleth in the brush.

"It's that girl of yours," said Gerutha. "He's become obsessed with her."

"It didn't strike me as obsession," said Fengi. "If anything, he threw her off. There's something else."

"What?" asked Gerutha.

"I don't know yet," said Fengi. "But I cannot let him return to Paris in this condition."

"I agree, milord," said Gorm. "We cannot be sure how he will act, or what he will say. We don't even know what he knows about our plans."

"I was so hoping Paris would bring order to his mind," said Gerutha. "But you are right. We cannot risk it. Things are in such a delicate phase right now."

Gorm stood.

"By your leave, milord," he said. "It has been a wearying day. I wish to retire."

"By all means, my friend," said Fengi. "Your daughter is safely restored to her cloister."

"You have my thanks for that," said Gorm as he left. "Let her remain there until the Holy Mother takes her."

"A waste," muttered Fengi.

"What is?" asked Gerutha.

"Sending that girl in for her vows," said Fengi. "You should have seen her."

"I wish that I had," said Gerutha.

The combination of watching his daughter's near fall from grace and the pursuit of Amleth had left Gorm in a state of exhaustion. He was unprepared, therefore, for the small form that hurled itself across the room the moment he crossed the threshold of his quarters.

"Monster!" screamed Lother as he slammed his father against the wall. "Prostituting your own daughter. How could you!"

He struck his father with all his might, the blow catching the older man in the jaw and sending him reeling.

"Stop this," Gorm said weakly, but the onslaught continued. His training finally asserted itself. He blocked the next blow, then caught the boy's wrist and twisted it. Lother cried out in pain, but was forced to his knees by the older man.

"You can't take me yet," muttered Gorm, raising his free hand to strike the boy to the floor, but to his surprise, Lother swept his leg around to catch Gorm behind his left knee. The drost fell back, striking his head against the bench, and the boy pounced on him immediately, straddling the old man.

Lother held his fist, ready to bring it down.

"I'm faster than you, old man," he said. "I may not be stronger than you yet, but I will be soon. If you won't protect my sister, then I will, do you hear me?"

Before he could strike, he was seized from behind by two guards who had heard the commotion. He resisted for a moment, then subsided.

Gorm got to his feet and dusted himself off.

"If one of my men had behaved in this manner, I would have no compunction about having him beheaded on the spot," he said. "Don't think that I would treat you any differently merely because of familial obligation."

Lother looked at him defiantly.

"However," continued Gorm. "I believe that you acted this way out of genuine concern for your sister. There is honor in that, Lother, and that is a quality that I would not discourage."

"If only you could lead by example," said Lother.

Gorm reached forward and placed his hand around the boy's throat.

"Respect is another quality I would encourage in you," he said, then he squeezed slightly and Lother's eyes bulged. "And silence, when respect is not forthcoming, is another worthy attribute. Remember that."

He released his hold on the boy, and Lother gasped for air.

"Lock him up for now," Gorm instructed the guards. "I'll decide what to do with him in the morning. I'm not thinking clearly at the moment, and do not want to make a decision I might later regret."

The guards dragged the boy away, and Gorm fell into a fitful sleep.

"Lother attacked you?" laughed Fengi. "Never thought he had the balls."

"This is the age where they make their presence known," said Gorm. "I took that into account in my decision."

"Amazing," said Fengi. "You've beaten him on the slightest provocation for years, and when he finally does something significantly punishable, you let him off with a lecture."

"For the first time, I thought he had a just cause," said Gorm. "We acted shamefully yesterday."

"Perhaps," said Fengi. "Our goals were worthy, but we should have found another method. What do you intend to do with the boy now?"

"I was sending him to Paris this fall anyway," said Gorm. "I think I will send him earlier. He'll get a proper start on his education."

"A good thought, and a compassionate plan," said Fengi. "I have a suggestion."

Horace walked into the great hall with some trepidation. He had not spoken with Fengi or Gorm since he had spoiled their trap, and he did not know if they suspected him. The two were at the end of the main table, reviewing some documents. Fengi looked up when he entered and waved him over.

"Good morning, Horace," he said, offering him some wine. Horace shook his head politely. "Well, to the point. I have a favor to ask of you."

"Anything within my power, milord," said Horace.

"A most courteous reply," said Fengi. "You are aware of the malady from which my son suffers."

"I am, milord."

"Unfortunately, it appears to have worsened since he has come home this summer," said Fengi. "We cannot send him back to school anymore. We must tend to his needs here."

"I am sorry, milord," said Horace. "What can I do to help my friend?"

"Nothing," said Fengi. "We know you have your own studies to attend to. As it happens, Gorm's son Lother will be beginning his education this term."

"I am delighted to hear it," said Horace.

"Since Rolf and Gudmund will be entering our service, there will be no one else from Slesvig traveling to Paris," said Fengi.

"I would consider it a great personal favor if you would take my son there," explained Gorm. "He could benefit from your advice and instruction on the way."

Horace bowed.

"Of course, milords," he replied. "We have a few weeks until the term begins, so . . ."

"Actually, I am sending him early," said Gorm.

"Early, milord?"

"Tomorrow," said Gorm.

Horace looked at them for a moment.

"Very well," he said. "I will pack my bags."

Fengi waved to a corner of the room, where Horace's things rested against a barrel.

"We took the liberty," he said, smiling broadly. "You will leave at dawn."

"Very good, milord," said Horace, bowing again.

With Lother and Horace gone, Amleth retreated into his shell, reading quietly, occasionally sneaking into his room to juggle when Gerutha and Fengi were elsewhere. Once in a while Rolf and Gudmund would entice him outside the stockade, but these excursions invariably ended with them chasing him through the town, cursing both him and their new-gained armor for causing such excessive exertion.

In the meanwhile, more mercenaries assembled in the camp south of the fjord, while Gorm and his men led increasingly brutal tax collections to pay for the military upkeep. The elders gathered to elect one of their number to protest to Fengi on behalf of all. When he failed to return from his mission, the protests dissipated.

One day in late October, Amleth rose from his enclosure, stretched, and wandered toward the front of the stockade. The drawbridge was down, allowing a procession of wains to bring supplies onto the island. Amleth watched them with interest, then ambled toward the entrance. Suddenly he took off at full speed across the bridge. The alarum was raised, but by the time a patrol had been assembled and horses saddled, the lunatic was past the Viking tower. The patrol rode after him, but he vanished into the woods south of the fjord.

Search parties were sent out. A rider was sent to the convent, but came back with no report of him. Inside the great hall, Gerutha paced and fretted while Fengi conferred with one unsuccessful captain after another.

"If we had a proper castle by now, this wouldn't be happening," she wailed. "He'd be in a room in a tower with his books, safely locked up, rather than in this sieve."

"Quiet," said Fengi. "You're not helping."

There was a call from the archers' platform, and he ran out.

"Someone's coming from the south," cried the archer. "A rider, and he has Amleth."

Fengi climbed the platforms and looked. Amleth was slumped over the neck of a sorrel horse, held steady by the rider, an older man wearing Norman armor and colors.

"Does anyone know this young man?" called the rider. "I found him lying in the woods. He appears to be ill."

"Fetch him," commanded Fengi, and several soldiers ran out.

The Norman followed them in and removed his helmet, revealing a weathered face and steely gray eyes.

"I beg your pardon for this interruption," he said. "I thought from the quality of his garments that he might be of the nobility here."

"He is," said Fengi. "He is my son, and a duke's hospitality is at your command, kind stranger."

"Are you the Duke of Slesvig?" asked the Norman. "Then I have found my destination, or at least part thereof. I seek your drost, one Gorm by name."

"He will be returning shortly," said Fengi. "I am Fengi, lord of these parts."

"Lamord of Normandy," said the rider, dismounting and kneeling before him. "I am honored, milord."

"Are you the master swordsman?" asked Fengi in astonishment.

"I have that reputation," said Lamord, rising.

"The honor is mine," exclaimed Fengi, seizing the man's hand and shaking it heartily. "I saw you in battle in Flanders years ago, and thought that a warrior centaur out of legend had taken the field, so skillfully did you command both horse and blade. What brings you to Slesvig?"

"A detour from my journey to Roskilde," said Lamord. "I bring news to Gorm of his son."

"Is Lother well?" asked Fengi.

"He is well," said Lamord. "Indeed, he excels. But I would prefer to bring word to his father's ear first."

"Of course," said Fengi. "You shall be our guest tonight. Come, Master Lamord. I will show you to your quarters myself."

. . .

"Lamord wants to see me?" worried Gorm, turning slightly pale when he heard. "I sincerely hope that this does not involve a challenge."

"What, does my drost fear one of the greatest swordsmen in Christendom?" laughed Fengi. "No, old friend. He merely stopped on the way to Roskilde to bring you word of your son. It was fortunate that he did so, for he was the one who found Amleth."

"Where did he find him?"

"South," said Fengi. "Too close to the encampment for my part."

"How much does Amleth know?"

"I don't know, and that concerns me," said Fengi. "We have to have it out of him, and in some way that doesn't displease his mother."

"Perhaps your problem is also the solution," said Gorm. "I have an idea."

At dinner, Lamord was given the place of honor next to Fengi, and Gerutha herself served him.

"We have roasted a suckling pig to celebrate the safe return of my son," she said, carving him a choice cut. "It is a small token of my gratitude, but I beg you to accept it."

"More than ample reward for a plain soldier," said Lamord. "I have been in the wars enough of my life to appreciate hot food of any nature. I thank you, milady. How does the young man?"

"I am better, thank you," said Amleth. The assemblage turned and stared as he entered, blinking uncertainly in the torchlight. "Are you my rescuer, sir?"

"I am the one who found you lying on the ground in the middle of nowhere," replied Lamord. "If that be enough for a rescue, then I am your rescuer."

Amleth held out his hand.

"I am sorry to put you to that trouble," he said. "You must know by now of my affliction."

"I have been informed of it," said Lamord. "I am glad I found you before the wolves did. I urge you, sir, take some sustenance. It will do you good."

Amleth staggered to the table and took his seat. His mother immediately served him, and he began to shovel food into his mouth as if he had never seen a meal before.

There was an uncomfortable silence in the room, broken finally by Gorm's clearing his throat.

"I understand, good soldier, that you have word of my son," he said.

"Ah, the young prodigy," said Lamord. "I commend you as his teacher."

"I tried to educate him as well as I could," said Gorm. "He never had a living mother."

"Unnecessary," said Lamord. "The boy is a natural swordsman and a man of honor. If this be the result of motherless upbringing, then let all boys foreswear the teat."

"A swordsman you say?" asked Gorm.

"I hear his studies go well," said Lamord. "But it was in that martial capacity that I came upon him. Some quarrel led to a duel at dawn with a much older student."

"What caused the quarrel?" inquired Fengi.

"The older student insulted the honor of the Danes," said Lamord. "This boy Lother, without a hair on his chin, challenged him directly."

There was a cheer from the Danish soldiers at the table.

"Now, this older boy was a student of mine," continued Lamord. "Naturally, I went to see him put my teachings into practice. He did, but someone had taught this boy how to fight. Not only did he defeat my pupil, but several of his friends who joined in."

"I hope that no lives were lost," said Gerutha.

"Just some blood and a great deal of dignity," laughed Lamord. "I took the liberty of inviting young Lother to a class, and he shone. As I was journeying to Roskilde, I could do no less but to come here and congratulate his father for a job well done."

"One does what one can," said Gorm modestly.

"All you ever taught him was how to receive a blow from a fist," blurted out Amleth.

"Quiet, Amleth!" commanded Fengi furiously.

Amleth rose and pointed at Gorm.

"It was I who taught your son how to survive by the sword!" he shouted. "As my father taught me. My father was the only man in Denmark who could have stood up to this posturing Norman, and I am his son and heir."

"I defeated your father in fair combat," said Fengi softly. "Have you forgotten that?"

Amleth looked at him, then lowered his gaze.

"No," he said. "I haven't."

He turned and fled the room.

"I will not apologize for him," said Fengi. "He has insulted our guest by this behavior."

"Not at all," said Lamord genially. "I have seen lesser events make men mad. The source of his affliction is clear and understandable."

"You are most charitable," said Gerutha, holding back her tears.

The next morning Fengi had his horse saddled along with Lamord's.

"I will ride with you part of the way," he informed the Norman. "There is much that I would hear of Paris."

"I would be delighted," replied Lamord. "Milady, thank you again for your charming hospitality."

"Our home is ever yours, Master Lamord," she said. He bowed, then the two men mounted and rode off.

She watched them depart, then walked quickly to the rear of the stockade where Amleth was sitting behind his walls of stakes.

"I would speak with you in private," she said.

He patted the ground by his side.

"No," she said. "Not in earshot of the guards. Come with me."

He stood and quietly followed her. She led him into their quarters and up the stairs to her room. He looked around, curiously.

"I cannot remember the last time I came up here," he said. "Not since father was killed. Since you defiled his bedchamber."

She stepped forward quickly and slapped him hard.

"Think what you wish," she said. "But never dishonor me."

"Too late for that," he said.

"Why are you doing this?" she asked.

"Doing what?" he replied.

"Maintaining this pretense of madness," she said. "Don't you think a mother can see through it?"

"Everyone tells me that I am mad," he said. "How could I possibly disagree with what is common knowledge?"

"Because you are an uncommon man," she said. "You are smart enough and subtle enough to play a game of your own."

"My affliction . . ." he began.

"You have no affliction," she snapped. "This is part of some scheme. What do you seek? Are you a spy?"

"A spy from the land of dreams," he said. "I keep hoping they will call me back, but lately I have been having trouble sleeping."

"What do you know of Fengi's plans?" she asked.

"What do you know of them?" he returned. "I care not for his plans, or anyone else's. All plans lead to the same end."

"What end is that?" she asked.

"The grave," he said.

"Is that where your plans lead?" she asked.

He looked at her, an amused smile on his face.

"I have no plans," he said. "Therefore, I will outlive you all."

"Do you threaten me?" she asked.

He stepped toward her, and she flinched.

"Do I frighten you, mother?" he asked softly.

"I am frightened for you," she replied.

"But I have you as my protector," he said mockingly. "Wherefore should I be fearful when I know that you will always intercede on my behalf? Perhaps I have relied upon you too long. Maybe if I stood on my own, I would be free of all this."

"What do you know of Fengi's plans?" she repeated.

He placed his hands on her shoulders and looked into her eyes.

"Which of us is the spy here?" he asked, sliding his fingers toward her throat.

"Stop!" she spluttered.

He stopped, and there was a moment of silence, followed by a rustling noise nearby.

He whirled and seized a sword hanging on the wall, then plunged the point into the center of the quilt covering the bed. As it pierced the layers of bedclothes, there was a muffled grunt from under the piled straw at its base.

Gerutha screamed in horror. Amleth looked at her, a strange gleam in his eye.

"Excuse me, madam," he said. "Just ridding your bed of some vermin infesting it."

He stripped back the blankets and brushed away the straw until he saw Gorm's face staring up at him, the eyes bulging out slightly. He felt for a pulse, but the drost was dead.

"You should have known better, old man," said Amleth softly. "That was the first thing Yorick taught me: if you're quiet, then no one can see you."

NINETEEN

"She is importunate, indeed distract.
Her mood will needs be pitied."

—*HAMLET*, ACT IV, SCENE V

Slesvig—1175 A.D.

Fengi looked at the body of his drost, laid out in the center of the four barracks at the front of the island.

"Where is Amleth?" he asked.

"In chains," said a captain. "Damn lucky he wasn't torn apart by the guards when they found him. He was trying to feed Gorm's body to the pigs."

"What stopped the guards?" asked Fengi.

"Fear of incurring a madman's dying curse," said the captain. "Or fear of his living mother's wrath. But blood demands a debt."

"Spoken like a true Dane," said Fengi. "Have his body prepared and brought to the cathedral."

He walked back to his quarters where his wife sat looking out the window.

"How are you, lady?" he asked.

"How should I be?" she said, not bothering to look at him. "I saw my son kill my friend. I don't know how to grieve for them both."

"Grieve for the one who deserves it," said Fengi.

"That is myself," she said.

"We'll bury Gorm tomorrow," said Fengi. "I am going to the convent to bring back Alfhild. I thought that I should be the one to tell her."

"How very good of you," she said. "And Lother?"

"I will send a letter by messenger," he said. "If he is half the man his father was, he will seek Amleth's blood."

"Is that why you are sending him the letter?" she asked. "To set him on Amleth?"

"Of course not," said Fengi. "But he will have the voice of the people. We must acknowledge it."

"The people," she said bitterly. "I have never heard you mention them as a force before. Will that be what you invoke when you hang my son?"

He was silent. She turned toward him for the first time.

"Please don't hang him," she begged him tearfully. "Don't put Amleth to death. He is all that I have."

"That was by your choice," said Fengi. He looked at her. She seemed to have aged overnight, but he knew that it had been happening all along. He wondered what he looked like to her. He hadn't thought about that in a long time.

"The captain of the guard said that blood demanded a debt," he said. "Old ways. The old ways keep pushing through this modern Christian veneer of ours, passed from father to son. That's why the Danes are the cripples begging at the Emperor's table. That's why I hire mercenaries. The only Danish soldiers worth a damn leave Denmark when they are young. The rest will fall when we rise against them. But I need my strategos by my side. Gorm was a terrible loss."

"But I am here," she said. "You still need me. You need my wealth. You need my family to support you. You need my blood, whether as debtor or creditor. Without my power, you fail. But I have my price."

"Your son's life," said Fengi.

"Yes," she said.

"Very well," he said. "I spare his life. But he must be exiled, for the appeasement of the people, and for his own safety."

"Banishment?" she screamed. "He might as well be dead."

"Then mourn him," he said, leaving her.

Amleth stood in chains, Rolf and Gudmund at his sides.

"Here is your commission," said Fengi, handing Rolf a sealed scroll. "Once he is on board, remove his shackles. I would not have England receive him in that disgraceful manner."

"Yes, milord," said Rolf.

Fengi walked up to Amleth and put his mouth next to the prisoner's ear.

"It is because of my love for your mother that I am sparing your life," he muttered. "Remember that."

"It is because of your love for my mother that I will not spare yours," Amleth whispered back. "Remember that."

Fengi stepped back.

"Take him," he commanded. "Return as soon as you deliver him. God speed you on your journey."

Rolf and Gudmund bowed, then took Amleth to the waiting carriage.

"England," grumbled Gudmund as they climbed in. "I know why he's being punished. But why are we?"

"Sooner started, sooner returned," said Rolf. "Let's go."

Fengi rode to the convent unescorted, a second horse tethered to his saddle. The abbess herself came to meet him. He explained to her briefly about Gorm. She expressed some suitable sentiments, then went to fetch Alfhild.

He was surprised at how nervous he felt waiting for her. He removed his helm and held it awkwardly against his side, fumbling with his hair, wondering if she would find his armored appearance reassuring or merely off-putting. He mentally rehearsed how he would break the news to her, how he would console her, how, if necessary, he should hold her, a comforting, fatherly embrace, not one that would inspire any suspicion, any thought that he might have designs upon her. He was so caught up in his fantasy that he was completely unaware that she had come into the room and was staring at him in surprise.

"What are you doing here?" she asked.

He turned toward her and caught his breath. She was wearing a white linen gown, unadorned, and her pale skin was set off by the tangle of auburn tresses that resisted staying tied back despite the combined efforts of three nuns. Like her mother's hair, he remembered, only Alfhild's was at war with itself, not the natural living force that permeated every aspect of Signe's being. The daughter was beautiful but untamable, even in captivity.

"I've come to take you out of here," he said.

She shook her head violently.

"No, you can't take me away," she protested. "Only he can. He said I wasn't to leave with anyone but him."

"There is no easy way for me to tell you this," said Fengi. "He is dead."

She was still for a moment, then very slowly sank to her knees, plunging her fists into her stomach and howling.

Fengi cursed himself inwardly for his maladroit method and knelt by her, clumsily taking her in his arms.

"I cannot tell you how sorry I am," he said. "He was as dear to me as he was to you. All I can offer in solace is that I will be to you what he was. You shall be as my own ..."

But she writhed out of his grasp, scuttling backward on the floor until she bumped up against the corner of the room.

"You filth!" she cried. "Telling of his death with one breath, trying to seduce me with the next. How dare you!"

"Seducing?" he said, horrified that she had divined the thoughts that he was certain he had suppressed. "Nay, I only mean the natural role of a father to you."

"A father?" she repeated.

"What else could I have meant?" he asked.

"A father," she said slowly. "Father is dead."

"I am sorry for it, more than you can know," he said.

"How did he die?" she asked.

"Amleth, in a fit of madness, slew him," said Fengi.

"Father is dead. Amleth killed him," she said dully. "Father is dead. Amleth killed him. And what is to become of Amleth?"

"He is banished," he replied.

"Banished?" she cried.

He mistook her tone for outrage at the lenient sentence and seized her hands in this.

"Know this," he whispered. "Your father's blood will not go unavenged. Amleth was indeed banished to the court of the English king, only an executioner's ax awaits him there."

"When will this happen?" she asked.

"He left this morning with Rolf and Gudmund," he said. "They will sail from Ribe."

"Very well," she said. "I will get my belongings and come with you. Tarry here for a while. I will not be long."

In her cell, she quickly scratched a note on a small piece of paper, then folded it and placed it inside her purse.

There was a kitchen garden beyond the door at the end of the living quarters. She ran quickly outside and looked around. There was a young man, the son of a local miller who brought in outside supplies, she had often seen eyeing her when she was working in the garden. He was just leaving the kitchen, having delivered a sack of flour to the cook, when he caught sight of her and tipped his cap respectfully.

She put a finger to her lips and beckoned to him. He looked around, then smiled lewdly and came toward her.

"Can I help you, lady?" he said, hooking his thumbs in his belt.

"Would you do something for me?" she asked, smiling at him.

"I think I might be able to accommodate your needs," he said.

She produced the paper from her purse. "There is a friend of mine, a prisoner named Amleth," she said. He looked surprised, but she rushed on ahead. "He is being transported to England, and I have had no chance to bid him farewell. I want you to take him this letter. He only left for Ribe this morning. Find some way of getting it to him unobserved. Here." She slipped a ring from her finger and gave it to him. "That should be payment enough."

"Payment enough?" he laughed. "For sneaking a note to a prisoner? If I am caught, this won't even be enough to bribe my way out."

"Bring me his reply, and I will double it," she said. Then she gave him a sidelong glance and fluttered her lashes slightly. "Or bestow upon you such favor as a maid may bestow upon a man."

He grinned.

"For a taste of that, lady, I would deliver this letter into Hell itself," he said.

"You are very brave," she said, kissing him quickly on the cheek. She handed him the note, then went back inside to her cell, where she gathered her possessions into a small bag. Then she rejoined Fengi.

"I will be allowed out of the stockade now that you are my father," she said.

"Of course," he said.

She nodded and handed him her bag, then wrapped a cloak around her shoulders and walked out of the convent. On the ride home, whenever Fengi turned to look at her, she had her eyes closed and was inhaling deeply.

Gerutha was waiting for their return. As soon as Alfhild dismounted, the older woman pulled her into a tight embrace.

"Welcome home, my dear," said Gerutha, kissing her on the forehead. "Would that it had been under happier circumstances."

"When do they bury my father?" asked Alfhild.

"Tomorrow," said Gerutha. "He will rejoin your sweet mother at last." They walked together back to the drost's quarters.

"I have prepared your room for you," said Gerutha as they entered. Alfhild looked around.

"I have never slept alone here," she said.

She climbed the steps, then stopped when she saw the bar across the outside of her door.

"May I have that removed?" she asked. "I am no longer my father's prisoner."

"I'll have it done in the morning," said Gerutha. "We'll cast it into the fjord together if you like."

"Actually, I just want them to remount it on the inside of the door," said Alfhild. "If I am to be by myself, I would prefer the extra protection."

"Very wise," said Gerutha. "I know too well the dangers of being an attractive woman surrounded by soldiers."

"I am certain you do," said Alfhild politely.

"She seems to be taking it well enough," said Fengi. "I thought that she would be in tears for the entire journey, but there was nothing once we left the convent."

"The shock may be too much for her," said Gerutha. "The tears may still come. Don't worry. I will be with her. You've done all that you can. Did you send Lother that letter?"

"Yes. Before I left to fetch his sister."

"Did you tell him that Amleth was banished?" she asked.

"I did," he said. "I told him that there was no need for him to avenge his father's murder."

"Will he return home? There will be nothing left for him to do by the time he arrives."

"I believe so. He and Alfhild are so close, I would expect him to come back and see her."

At the funeral, Alfhild had one outburst of sobbing when she first approached her father's corpse, but it subsided quickly. Gorm was buried next to Signe. After the last shovelful of dirt was thrown on and patted down by the gravedigger, Alfhild asked for a moment alone. Fengi and

Gerutha stood a respectful distance away and watched her kneel down by the grave, holding a bouquet of wildflowers, picked from the late autumn blooms of the meadow on which she had played as a child.

"She takes it well," observed Fengi admiringly. "She is a soldier's daughter."

"There may still be some change in her," said Gerutha. "I will spend as much time with her as I can."

"Do you really think that's necessary?" asked Fengi. "She's a grown woman now."

"Even grown women need comforting," said Gerutha.

Out of their earshot, Alfhild carefully placed the wildflowers on Signe's grave.

"Hello, mother," she said softly. "I hope that you are in Heaven and he is in Hell. At least Lother and I managed to survive him. Everything will be all right now."

Then she stood and walked to where Fengi and Gerutha awaited her.

Gerutha's fears proved prophetic. Within a week of the funeral, Alfhild became moody and sullen. Despite the older woman's attempts to draw her out, she kept to her old room, using the inside bar to keep away visitors. She began missing meals. Gerutha prepared baskets of food and left them outside her door. Sometimes they were eaten; sometimes they were not.

"I am starting to worry about the girl," said Gerutha one night. "She gets thinner and paler by the day. I wonder if there is some illness beyond the natural grief she would feel for her loss."

"She needs to be out in the fresh air more," said Fengi. "After saying how much she looked forward to her freedom, she has become her own jailer. It's odd. Perhaps I should take her for her daily exercise."

"She is not a horse, and you are no stablehand," scolded his wife. "You have your army to drill. This is no time to waste your energy on household matters. Leave that to me. I will take her for her walks. It will do us both good."

"Very well," he said, hiding his disappointment.

Lother returned from Paris a month after Gorm's death, spurring his exhausted horse straight to the graveyard north of the town. He stood by his parents' graves for a long while, his expression difficult to read. Then he took his horse's reins and walked it slowly to the island.

He raised his hand in greeting as he passed over the drawbridge, but did not tarry to speak with anyone. He went straight back to his quarters to see his sister before paying his respects to Gerutha and Fengi. His face now was a mask of concern.

"What's wrong with her?" he asked them. "How long has she been like this?"

"Ever since your father's death," said Gerutha, patting his cheek sympathetically.

"Actually, since a little after," corrected Fengi. "She seemed fine, at least physically, at the time of the funeral. But these things will out in time. You have to be patient."

"Has she seen the physician?" he asked.

"Of course," said Gerutha. "But he does not know the source of the illness. We had the priest pray for her as well, but that did nothing whatsoever."

"I'm sure that having you here will cheer her up immensely," said Fengi. "Come, walk with me. There are matters that we need to discuss."

"There are?" said Lother.

"Now that I am your guardian, we need to discuss your future," said Fengi.

They walked outside together.

"I had not even thought about my future," said Lother. "When I heard that he died . . . when I heard how, my only thoughts . . ." He stopped.

"Were for revenge," finished Fengi. "Is that what you were going to say?"

"I cannot believe he did it," said Lother. "Amleth was like a brother to me. He taught me how to fight, how to read . . ."

"You were taught by a madman, unfortunately," said Fengi. "You were too young to know that he was so strange in his ways."

"And yet his madness protects him," said Lother. "Because of it, he is banished instead of hanged, and because he is banished, he is beyond the reach of my sword. The right of the blood feud is mine, but I am powerless."

"Your words do you honor, and do your father proud," said Fengi. "If it be your will, stay with us instead of returning for the next term. It will do your sister some good, I think, and I could always use a strong right arm now that your father's gone."

"My arm?" said Lother in surprise. "What good can a boy's arm do you?"

"More than a boy," said Fengi. "And we've heard good report of your skill with a sword."

"By whom?"

"Lamord of Normandy. You know him, I believe."

"Lamord was here?" exclaimed Lother. "What did he tell you?"

"Of your exploits defending the honor of the Danes against some inferior Parisian blades," said Fengi. "Your father was quite proud to learn of it."

"Lamord overpraises me," said Lother. "I was lucky that day."

"Not according to him," said Fengi.

"And even if I was that accomplished a swordsman, what use will I be to you here?" asked Lother. "There's not been war in Slesvig since before I was born."

"Oh, you never know what might come up," said Fengi.

Alfhild allowed herself to be taken to market with Gerutha, though she paid little heed to the raucous bustle around her. So it wasn't until she had returned to the island that she noticed the small folded piece of paper that someone had slipped into her basket. She ran upstairs to her room, barred the door, and took it to the window.

"I have word from your friend at Ribe," she read. "Meet me tomorrow morning at the clearing in the woods. Remember your payment."

Payment, she thought. She and Lother now had money of their own, but it was under the control of Fengi. She rummaged through her father's old chest until, near the bottom, she found a small pouch. There were some coins in it.

She thought about expenses. Travel to Ribe and back, inns, food. What had she promised the man? To double the value of the ring, or to . . .

She remembered what, in her haste and desperation, she had offered him. Surely he would not hold her to that. He was a miller's son, not a rich man. She should have enough money to compensate him adequately without having to . . .

She reached into the chest and pulled out a small dagger in a scabbard.

The next morning she dressed hurriedly, securing the dagger on her left forearm under the sleeve. Then she threw on her cloak and picked up her basket.

Lother was up and doing stretches on the lower floor when she came down.

"I'm going to pick some flowers from the meadow," she told him.

"Do you want some company?" he asked.

"No, thank you," she said. "I'll be back before noon."

She walked around the outside of the great hall, seeking to avoid any questions from Gerutha or Fengi. She made it to the entrance and across the drawbridge without any interference, then took the bridge that led south.

Of all places to meet, she thought. The last time she was in that clearing was one of the worst days of her life. And it was so isolated. If the miller's son intended to act dishonorably, there would be no one near to help her. But there was no one she could trust with the knowledge that she had betrayed Slesvig to help save Amleth. Maybe her brother, but she wanted to shield him more than anyone.

She came to the path leading into the woods. She patted the dagger under her sleeve, took a deep breath, and went in.

It was still early morning, and the clearing was mostly in shadow. As

[269]

she came to it, she saw the man waiting at the other side, ready to fade into the trees in case there was any trap. She stopped.

"I have your money," she said. "What is the message?"

He started walking toward her.

"Stand where you are," she commanded. "I can hear you just fine from here. What is the message?"

"The message is that despite your best efforts, Amleth has been put on a boat to England," said Fengi, emerging into the light.

She took a step toward the path, and he was on her in an instant, his hand clamped around her wrist.

"The miller's son can neither read nor write, did you know that?" he said conversationally. "True of most men like that, but you've been too sheltered to be aware of it."

"Please let me go," she said.

"A patrol caught him returning from his holy mission," he continued. "They knew he had no business to be traveling to and from that direction. They began asking him questions. Then they turned him over to me for further interrogation. I could have used your father's help on that. He was always so good at guessing just the right amount of pain to elicit the truth from someone. But, alas, Gorm was not there because one of your lovers killed him."

"Lovers?" she said in shock.

"That innocent virgin act quite took me in," said Fengi. "But your messenger told us what you had promised him. In fact, that was the easiest part to get out of him. He was bragging about having you at the convent even as the blood was running from him."

"It's a lie!" she cried, struggling with him.

"I can only thank God that your father did not live to see you like this," said Fengi. He twisted her arm behind her back so that she cried out. "And I thank God that I did."

He clapped his free hand over her mouth and pulled her toward him.

"Come, Alfhild," he said. "I have delivered the message. I think that I am entitled to the payment. Don't you?"

. . .

She was running.

She did not know which way she ran. The trees attacked her on all sides, tearing at the remnants of her gown, clawing at her face, their voices howling on all sides. Her father's voice leading the pack.

Everything her father had ever said about her was true. She knew that at long last. She had been a stupid little girl to think that she could ever be anything else. Now, she had finally become what she had been meant to become all of those years.

A whore. Defiled. Like her mother.

She had to cleanse herself somewhere. She had to get rid of him, his stench, her blood.

And his blood.

She had finally freed her hands enough to get at the dagger under her sleeve and swipe at him. He howled and rolled away, clutching his side, and she was off, bolting into the trees that offered no protection, but the path would be worse, much worse, and it was already too late, she had betrayed him, she had betrayed everyone, she had betrayed herself and the Holy Mother, and there would be no place to hide in all of the world.

All she wanted was to be clean again.

She burst out of the forest, the sun blinding her. She was crying as she ran, pathetic mewing sounds that disgusted her even as she made them. Water, she thought. I have to find water.

She was in a meadow. It looked familiar. But how could it be familiar? she thought. I haven't been in a meadow like this since mother died.

Her mother. She remembered it all in a flash. Was it this meadow? A summer day, and she was chasing a butterfly. Her mother was reclining on a rise, great with child. With Lother. Alfhild was chasing butterflies through a field of wildflowers, and her mother was watching and smiling. And Yorick was with her. She remembered seeing them together, and they were sad and happy at the same time.

Was it the same meadow? She stopped and looked around. There were no flowers in bloom. No, there were some late fall blossoms, something she couldn't identify, near a tree. No butterflies, of course. It was far too late in the autumn to find them. Practically winter in the air. She wondered where they went in the winter, whether they migrated like the birds or simply died off. And a pond! There was a pond there.

She ran to it, shedding her shameful garments, the ones that had turned her into the horrible creature that she was. She couldn't think straight. She had been having trouble thinking straight for weeks, ever since she had come home from the convent. The water would help clear her mind. She peeled off what was left of her linens and jumped in.

It was colder than she expected, much colder, but she welcomed it. It numbed her, and she wanted more than anything to stop the pain. To stop feeling anything at all. She wondered if he had put a baby into her. There were girls at the convent when she was there, bad, sinful girls, who had told her what had happened to them, and how the babies got there. Some of the babies were born in the convent, and then smuggled away in the night. She didn't know where they went. Just like the butterflies.

There was nothing left, she thought dreamily, letting her hair drift in the water. I could just drift here until all the feeling stops. That would be a kindness.

Amleth, she thought suddenly. At least he got the message. He was still alive, even if he was on the boat that was carrying him to his doom. But she had warned him. He was smart. He would think of something.

Would he take her back, defiled as she was? She laughed abruptly, then coughed as she swallowed some pond water. Why should she worry about whether he would take her back, when he had killed her father? Was not his sin the greater? If she could forgive him that, then he could forgive her.

Amleth still lived, and that meant there was still some hope, even if it was small. She could hide, summon Lother, and run somewhere. Maybe Paris. Amleth had friends there, and Lother knew the city now. Lother and I could protect each other, even if Amleth doesn't find us.

She kicked her way back to the edge of the pond and pulled herself out, fallen leaves from the overhanging trees tangled in her hair. She started shivering fiercely, her energy drained. She mopped feebly at her body with her gown. Her feet had been cut during her dash through the woods, and she leaned forward and washed them, thinking she could bandage them when they dried.

A pair of hands rested on her shoulders.

"Well, here you are," said a voice behind her. "I have been looking for you. You'll catch your death like this."

She looked up at the other's face, and felt her small bit of hope flutter away and die somewhere, far beyond her reach.

"It doesn't matter anymore," said Alfhild.

"No," said the other. "It doesn't."

She struggled as she went under the surface, but the hands were strong, and the cold was stronger.

TWENTY

"Come, the croaking raven doth bellow for revenge."
—*HAMLET,* ACT III, SCENE II

Slesvig—1175 A.D.

Gerutha returned in the late morning, her market basket over her arm. She was met by a worried Lother asking if she had seen his sister. Her negative response sent him scurrying up the platforms for the fifth time that day. He looked around quickly, then returned to her.

"I thought she would be back by now," he said.

"She can take care of herself, you know," she said, smiling at him.

"I am supposed to keep her safe," said Lother. "I should have gone with her."

"She's probably just picking flowers somewhere, and lost in thought," Gerutha reassured him. "She gets distracted so easily. She'll come back when she's hungry."

"You make her sound like a pet," said Lother miserably. "Oh, well. I worry too much about her."

"It's only natural," said Gerutha sympathetically. "She's all the family you have."

He sighed.

"Let me carry your basket to the kitchen," he offered, reaching for it.

"No need," she said. "It's light. See?"

She held it up to demonstrate, then walked away. He stood there, feeling useless.

Fengi was in a foul mood at luncheon, picking at his food and wincing occasionally.

"I have no appetite," he said finally, pushing his bowl away. "I am going to visit the southern earthenworks."

"I thought that's what you were doing this morning," said Gerutha.

"I was at the northern walls this morning," said Fengi irritably.

"But surely you rode south..."

"I rode north," barked Fengi. "I ride south now. I will return before sunset."

He stormed out, and she looked after him in concern.

"What is the matter with him?" she wondered aloud.

"Indigestion, from the looks of it," said Lother.

"He's never had a problem eating anything in his life," she said.

As the sun began its descent toward the west, Lother paced the entire length of the island repeatedly, occasionally climbing different guard towers to scan the area, waiting for a glimpse of her white gown in the distance. His nervousness was contagious, and the guards were soon straining their eyes in their search of the horizons. Yet for all of their vigilance, Alfhild's return to the island near sunset went unremarked. It wasn't until the two farmers turned their cart onto the drawbridge that the guards at the gate realized that the lump under the blanket was a body.

If the captain of the watch had any hope of keeping Lother from seeing her corpse, it was shattered as the boy dashed through the men surrounding the cart, scattering them like skittles. He threw back the blanket and froze, taking it all in at once, the unnatural pallor, the hair still wet and stringy, the bruises on her shoulders, the broken fingernails and the cuts on her feet. None of the veteran soldiers present would have thought any less of the boy had he screamed or cried at the sight, but he merely stood there, then leaned forward and kissed her brow.

"Where is her clothing?" he asked quietly.

"Wasn't none," said one of the farmers. "How we found her."

"Where?" he asked.

"Meadow near the south forest," said the farmer. "Pond there. The horse was thirsty. She was floating, face down. We pulled her out right away, but she was gone."

Lother looked at her one last time, then pulled the blanket back over her.

"Thank you for bringing her here," he said. "I was worried."

"It must have been her madness that did this," said Fengi, coming up behind him. "She must have lost her senses, threw off her clothing, and ran until she found the pond."

"She didn't kill herself!" yelled Lother.

"No, no, it was an accident," said Fengi hurriedly. "Anyone can see that. No one will ever think it a suicide." He put an arm around the boy's shoulders and squeezed gently. "I'm sorry, lad. She was a troubled soul, but she's in a better place now. Go and pray for her. I'll take her to the church."

"I should have gone with her," muttered Lother.

"There was nothing you could have done," said Fengi. "If it hadn't happened now, it would have happened some other time."

"I could have saved her," said Lother.

"You could not be with her every minute of the day," said Fengi. "I blame myself. I should have returned her to the convent after we buried your father. I thought that she would benefit from her freedom here. But she was beyond help. I see that now. I am sorry, Lother."

Lother turned and walked back to his quarters. As he came to the door, Gerutha came running up.

"Oh, my poor boy," she cried, hugging him to her breast.

And it was in that maternal embrace, the first he could remember in his life, that he finally started crying. She held him for a while, then released him, wiping his face with her kerchief.

The Bishop was quickly persuaded that the death was accidental, and consented to have her buried by her parents. Privately he thought it a suicide, but it was not the first favor he had ever done for Fengi, and it was a small one at that.

He did not go so far as to preside at the funeral mass, leaving that task to one of his subordinate priests. Lother went to confession briefly before it began, but emerged looking angry and unconsoled.

The priest led the procession to the cemetery north of the town, the simple coffin on a cart drawn by a donkey. Lother walked behind it, his hand resting on his sister's final enclosure. When they reached the cemetery, the grave was already prepared, and the two gravediggers stood a respectful distance away, their caps in their hands.

An honor guard took the coffin on a pair of ropes and lowered it gently into the ground. The priest droned the final prayers over it, and Lother stepped forward and tossed a handful of dried wildflowers into the grave.

"You died because of Amleth," he said. "As did our father. I only wish that he could be here so that..."

Gerutha screamed, and Lother looked up into the eyes of Amleth.

"Did she die because of me?" said Amleth softly. "Then let my life be forfeit. You have a sword. I will not resist. But know that I never knew anything but love for her."

Lother's hand went slowly to the hilt of his sword.

"Lother, stay your hand," begged Gerutha. "There has been too much loss of late."

"Then what's one more?" snapped Lother, drawing his sword. "You say you loved her. Then join her."

Amleth knelt by the grave.

"I want nothing less," he said. "Promise me that you will bury me by her side."

"Excuse me, sir," called one of the gravediggers. "There isn't enough room for that. We'd have to widen it another three feet, and that's going to take at least another hour."

Lother turned and stared at the man in disbelief, then looked back down at Amleth.

"This is consecrated ground," he said, sheathing his sword. "I will not spill blood upon it. And if you think I would let a murderer's body rest for eternity by my poor sister, then you are mad."

"That's what they tell me," said Amleth. "May I stand up now?"

Lother nodded, and Amleth rose and walked over to Gerutha and Fengi.

"Hello, mother," he said. "I'm back."

"You were banished," said Fengi. "What are you doing here?"

"Long story," said Amleth. "I will tell you all about it. But not now."

Lother picked up a handful of dirt and threw it on top of the coffin, then stormed off. The rest of the assembly filed out of the graveyard. As Amleth stepped through the gate, two of Fengi's guards seized him.

"What will you do with him?" asked Gerutha.

"We'll lock him up for now," said Fengi as they carried him off. "I have to think."

He stopped. Horace was standing by the graveyard, crossing himself as he looked at Alfhild's grave.

"So, you're here as well," said Fengi.

"He's my friend," said Horace. "He needed my help."

"Are all of your friends madmen?" asked Fengi.

"A lot of them," said Horace.

"Come with us," Fengi ordered. "Turn your weapons over to the captain."

Horace unbuckled his sword and removed a knife from his belt, then surrendered them to a guard.

"I am at your service," he said, bowing to Fengi and Gerutha.

They left. Behind them, the two gravediggers, relieved that they didn't have to expand the grave, finished burying Alfhild.

. . .

Amleth sat calmly against the wall of the small storage room that doubled as a cell on the island, his eyes closed. Hanging from the ceiling around him were strings of garlic and onions, bundles of herbs, and dried fruit, their smells mingling pleasantly. Alfhild would have liked this room, he thought sadly.

The door opened, and he squinted in the sudden light to see Fengi standing before him.

"A long story, you say," Fengi said as he sat against the wall opposite Amleth.

"Depending on how I tell it," said Amleth.

"Summarize, if you please," said Fengi.

"Pirates," said Amleth. "Hostage. Ransom. I knew Horace would be good for it, so I sent for him. Redemption, at least in a strictly monetary sense. Came home."

"The last is what I find remarkable," said Fengi.

"Really? I would have thought the pirates were the strangest aspect of the story," said Amleth.

"That you would consider your life valuable enough to ransom, yet you would throw it away so easily by coming here."

Amleth closed his eyes.

"I came back for Alfhild," he said.

"Alfhild? Why?"

"I had made a promise," said Amleth. "I should have kept it long ago. And now it's too late to do anything about it."

"You were going to run away with her," said Fengi. "Perfect. A mad man marries a mad maid. You would have produced an entire litter of lunatics."

"Alfhild was not mad," said Amleth. "She suffered from her isolation, from the cruel practices of her father, but she was not mad. I knew her, I daresay, better than anyone. I carried her as a baby. I comforted her when her mother died bearing Lother, and I wore her favor when I left for Paris the first time. I wear it still."

"She was mad, and she drowned herself," said Fengi.

"She was sane, and someone killed her," said Amleth. "Was it you?"

"Why would I do that?" asked Fengi softly.

"Because she warned me of your plans," said Amleth. "The longer version of my story includes my pilfering your commission from my close friends Rolf and Gudmund. An interesting request under your official seal."

"Where is that scroll now?" asked Fengi.

"With a man that I trust," said Amleth. "Along with my own account of your secret army. If I die at your hands, he delivers it to Valdemar. If he doesn't hear from me by a certain date, the same."

"How do I know that he hasn't taken it to Valdemar already?" asked Fengi.

"Because you are still alive and in power," said Amleth.

"And what is to prevent me from keeping you prisoner until I launch my attack?"

"Nothing," replied Amleth. "Oh. There's always mother."

Fengi winced.

"You have the freedom of the grounds," he said, unchaining Amleth. "You come within ten feet of the drawbridge, and you will be cut down on the spot."

"Understood," said Amleth. "May I at least go to church on Sundays? I would like to get my spiritual affairs in order."

"I think that would be wise," said Fengi.

Fengi stood with Reynaldo on the topmost archers' platform, looking west. The Tuscan was swathed in furs, huddling as far inside them as he could possibly get.

"Feels like it will be a cold winter this year," Fengi commented as the wind whipped into his face.

"Wonderful," sighed Reynaldo. "I still cannot get used to your winters. Far too cold, in my opinion. When you become king, do something about that, won't you?"

"When the winters are bad, the Danes huddle inside closed doors," mused Fengi. "They sleep by the fires, practically piling on top of each other for the warmth."

"Pile me high with Danish maidens, and I will survive this winter," said Reynaldo.

"The Danes feel safe in the winter," continued Fengi. "Do you know why?"

"Why?"

"Because they know that the winter is their shield," said Fengi. "Because they know that no one would dare risk an attack during the winter. So, the Danish soldier sits by the fire, comfortable and sleepy. Unarmored, of course."

"Of course," said Reynaldo, smiling.

"And if there is an alarum, he loses valuable time getting his armor on," said Fengi. "They don't make them sleep in their armor anymore. They've grown soft, fat, and complacent. So, there's an attack, and it takes him five minutes to turn into a real soldier, which will be five minutes too late. And he will burst through the door and immediately be assaulted by an angry foe."

"You?" guessed Reynaldo.

"The Danish winter," said Fengi. "The surprised soldier will go from a hot fire to frozen gales in a matter of seconds, and the shock will take away his will to fight before he takes a second step toward the battle."

"But will not that same weather fall upon the attackers?" asked Reynaldo.

"Of course," said Fengi. "But the attackers will have been out in it long before, and will be cutting through the frigid winds like a longboat through choppy waves. Our men will not feel the cold settle into their bones until the last defender is run through."

"And then you will be king," said Reynaldo.

"And then I will be king," said Fengi. "Your spies say that Valdemar will have all of his allies and advisers at the Feast of the Epiphany?"

"Yes," said Reynaldo.

"We shall leave on New Year's Day," said Fengi.

"Good," said Reynaldo. "It's about time. Of course, some of your men will think it sacrilege to launch a war during the Christmas season."

"Fortunately, others worship a wooden, seven-headed monstrosity and would like nothing better than to take one more shot at the man who destroyed their people," said Fengi. "I just worry."

"About what, milord?"

"About Amleth. Does he really have a man ready to warn Valdemar? And until when must we keep Amleth alive to keep that from happening?"

"Amleth knew about the letter," said Reynaldo. "He knows about the mercenaries. I think that he made sure there would be someone ready before he came back here."

"My thinking as well," said Fengi. "And I still need his mother's family fortunes and blood ties to back me in this little venture. Therefore, I must not harm him. And that irks me."

"I could kill him," suggested Reynaldo.

"No," said Fengi. "His death cannot come from anyone under my command."

"Is there no one else who would have cause to kill him?" asked Reynaldo. "One who could do it without suggestion of an outside motive?"

Fengi smiled.

"There is one," he said.

"Come with me, Lother," said Fengi. "I need to talk to you."

They walked across the drawbridge, side by side, and headed toward the fjord. Fengi sat heavily down on a bench, rubbing his side, and motioned to Lother to sit by him.

"There is something you should know about your sister," said Fengi. "You know how devoted she was to Amleth."

"Of course," said Lother.

"Amleth took advantage of her," said Fengi. "It's as simple as that.

He took advantage of her, as young men will of susceptible maids. That's why your father put her in the convent."

"I don't believe it," said Lother.

"You are young," said Fengi gently. "There is much about humanity that is wicked and sordid. It all happens as we leave childhood for the adult world. Some demon takes hold of us, and those of us not strong enough to conquer it succumb to all manner of sin. Your sister was a victim of her desires. And his."

"How do you know this?" asked Lother.

"Your father and I talked of it many times," said Fengi. "And as Duke of Slesvig, I have sources of intelligence that encompass many different areas. Sometimes I hear things that I would prefer not to know. Your sister was seduced by Amleth, and it was her sin that drove her mad. Do you think that it was chance that brought him back on the very day of her funeral?"

"What do you mean?" said Lother hoarsely.

"How did he know to find us there?" asked Fengi. "How did he know she was dead? She left on the day of her death to meet her lover, and this happened. At least she had the courage to flee him, naked and beaten as she was."

Lother was shaking, balling his hands into fists.

"I shall kill him," he said.

"Now, now, hold on for a moment," said Fengi, taking the boy's arm. "Your honor does you proud, but you cannot just cut him down in cold blood."

"I cannot let him live knowing what you told me," said Lother.

"Agreed, but there are more subtle ways," said Fengi. "I am having a feast on New Year's Eve for my captains. I am suggesting for entertainment that you give a demonstration of your prowess with a sword."

"I'm listening," said Lother.

"I will suggest to Amleth that he be your opponent in this demonstration," said Fengi. "Then, an accident will occur."

"One problem," said Lother. "I am good, but he is still older and stronger. I cannot guarantee that the accident will suffice."

"But I can," said Fengi. "I have a syrup that I obtained on my travels long ago. Apply it to the edge of your blade, and even the smallest scratch on your adversary will be enough to send him to his death."

"Have you ever tested it?" asked Lother curiously.

"How do you think I managed to defeat my brother?" replied Fengi, smiling at Lother.

Lother smiled back.

"There is to be a feast on New Year's Eve," Amleth said.

"Oh, good," said Horace. "I love a good meal to end the year. Am I invited?"

"I doubt that you will be allowed to eat anywhere else," said Amleth.

"I wonder if there is anyone I could hire to taste my food first," said Horace. "Or would that be bad manners?"

"You could probably get out of here before then," said Amleth. "There are some sympathetic guards. And some bribable ones."

"What, and miss a good meal?" laughed Horace. "That would violate my most sacred code."

"Have I thanked you enough?" asked Amleth.

"No," said Horace. "And if we survive, there will not be enough thanks in the world. And if we don't, then that will still be true."

The Danish guards overlooking the drawbridge watched with foreboding as the mercenary captains filed through the gate, speaking six different languages.

"Sixty of them," said one of the guards. "That means there has to be at least three thousand men under them."

"There were Wends in there, did you see that?" said the other. "Holsteiners, Switzers, God knows what else. He's been keeping them hidden away for years. Now, he has them out in the open. That can only mean we're going to war."

"But against whom?" asked the first man.

"I don't know," said the other. "But I have a bad feeling about all of this."

Fengi looked across the mass of warriors who sat on long benches by the tables surrounding the central fires. He thought back to that fateful feast in Roskilde, when he had fought his way to safety along with Valdemar. The trick to a feast, he thought, is to be the man throwing it. He stood, and the room became silent.

"My friends," he said. "We come to celebrate the end of an old year, and the dawning of a new age. We shall eat and drink until it is 1176!"

There was cheering as thralls swarmed in, carrying bowl after bowl of stews and puddings, platters of roasted hogs and chickens, and pitchers of spiced mead.

Lother sat at the end of the table, picking at his food with no appetite. Occasionally, he glanced across the room to where Amleth was sitting quietly, looking at the foreign faces in his father's hall. Horace sat to his left, chattering merrily with Gerutha.

Fengi stood again.

"Gentlemen, we have some extraordinary entertainment for you tonight," he said. "Although you have come from many lands, tonight you have become my brothers." Cheers at this. "Which means that you are now all Danes." Laughter and hooting followed this pronouncement, and Fengi changed his expression to one of mock sternness. "Are you saying that this isn't the culmination of your hopes and dreams?"

"You have purchased our loyalty and our arms," said one of the Wend captains. "But why should we choose the nationality of the very people we seek to conquer?"

"I stand by the prowess and might of the Danish soldier," said Fengi. "As fierce a warrior as you are, I would match even that stripling at the end of my table in skill with a sword with anyone."

"Him?" scoffed the Wend. "He's still a boy."

"But a prodigy with a sword nonetheless," said Fengi. "Shall I call upon him to demonstrate?"

"Is this our entertainment?" asked the Wend.

"Well, the beginning," said Fengi. "Lother, step forward."

Lother strode to the center of the tables, turned smartly, drew his sword, and saluted all sides to the mocking applause of the assembled mercenaries.

"Now, we need to find him a worthy opponent," said Fengi.

"I will be happy to teach him a lesson," said the Wend.

"No, my friend, I cannot spare you," said Fengi. "I will not risk harm to any of my captains. At least, not here. But there is one present who has boasted that he taught Lother everything he knows. Perhaps a match between master and pupil would be a good one."

"Are you referring to me, milord?" asked Amleth, drumming his fingers on the table.

"A friendly contest," said Fengi. "Striking only with the flat of the blade. Most hits out of ten bouts. Let's see you put your brag to the test."

Amleth stood reluctantly.

"I have no sword," he said as he walked into the center of the hall.

"Here is one for you," shouted the Wend, tossing his to him.

Amleth caught it, then swung it a few times experimentally.

"You must have a strong arm to wield such a mighty weapon, good captain," he said, saluting him. "I will try and do you honor."

"Well spoken, my son," said Fengi. "And for my part, I will drink to the first man who lands a blow."

He snapped his fingers, and an ornate golden goblet was placed before him and filled with wine. He held it aloft so that it gleamed in the firelight.

"This was passed down from my ancestors," he said. "According to family lore, it was taken from the hoard of a dragon whom the founder of our line slew in single combat. Let us see who earns the first toast."

Amleth turned to face Lother.

"I must confess that I have not been practicing," he said.

"I have," said Lother.

They began circling each other slowly. Amleth feinted toward Lother, but the younger man refused to acknowledge it. He kept his eyes on

Amleth's sword hand. Amleth's eyes seemed to be looking into the distance, almost as if he were dreaming.

"Strange," he said. "This almost . . ." Then he lunged forward in midsentence. Lother knocked the thrust aside, but Amleth's momentum took him inside his sword arm. He reached around him and swatted him playfully on the rear with the flat of his blade.

"One to me," he said as the mercenaries started laughing.

Fengi raised the goblet toward Amleth.

"May God grant you a long life," he said, and drank.

"Amen," said Gerutha.

"Fill the cup again," Fengi commanded, and a thrall rushed up with a pitcher. "Again, gentlemen."

Lother and Amleth faced each other.

"Well," said Amleth. "Maybe I'm not as rusty . . ."

"Shut up," said Lother. "There are no conversations on a battlefield."

"Nor are there children," said Amleth, and the mercenaries roared as Lother chased him around the fires.

"Nor are there madmen!" shouted Lother.

"As for that," began Amleth, then he tripped over a table leg. Lother dashed in, sword raised, and Amleth rolled at the last second, his sword snaking through the air to swat Lother on the calf as the latter's sword banged off the floor.

"Second hit to the madman," grinned Amleth as he got to his feet.

"Here, son," said Fengi, holding up the goblet. "Now, you must drink to your ancestors."

"I will when I have won this match," said Amleth. "Until then, I must keep my wits about me."

"Then I shall drink to my son," said Gerutha, taking the goblet from her husband and downing it in one motion as the mercenaries sounded their approval.

"I am surprised at you, Lother," said Amleth. "I thought you knew that trick. I guess it is one thing to fight in the classroom, and another when something is actually at stake."

"There is nothing at stake here," growled Lother, and he swept his sword up and across.

Amleth lurched back, grabbing his wrist.

"What is wrong with you?" he protested. "We hadn't begun again, and this was to be the flat of the blade only. This was to be a friendly bout."

Lother said nothing, but held his sword up, crouching slightly.

"You killed my father and drove my sister to her death," he said. "There is nothing friendly about it."

He attacked, and Amleth sidestepped and seized Lother's wrist and twisted it. The younger man grimaced and dropped his sword. Amleth planted his foot in the other's side and sent him spinning away.

"I see," said Amleth softly. He looked at Lother, who was braced against the edge of a table. "You need a sword."

He threw the Wend's sword to Lother and ducked down to grab the fallen blade. Lother caught the tossed weapon by the hilt and charged just in time to take the point of his own sword in his stomach. Blood poured through his tunic and dripped onto the floor as he collapsed.

"Get him a surgeon!" shouted Amleth.

"Too late," gasped Lother.

"Come on, boy, it isn't that deep," said Amleth.

"Gerutha!" shouted Horace.

She was clutching her throat, her eyes turning with terror toward Fengi.

"What ails her?" said Fengi as she fell into his arms.

"Poison!" Lother managed to shout. "The poison you intended for Amleth."

"What?" cried Amleth.

"It was a trap," Lother choked out. "You die by the poison from my blade, as do I." He began to cough, then looked up at Amleth with a weak smile. "As did your father by the same treachery." He sagged back to the floor.

Amleth grabbed Lother's sword with his free hand and took a step toward Fengi, staggering as he did. Fengi stood and backed away, drawing his own sword.

"I don't fear you," he said. "You have less than a minute to live. You will die just as your father did."

Amleth smiled at him.

"I had two fathers," he said, and began juggling the two swords with his right hand. "They both taught me well."

Fengi watched the blades flip through the air, bouncing the firelight around the room. Suddenly, Amleth threw the Wend's blade at the roof above Fengi's head. It stuck in a rafter, quivering, and as Fengi's eyes momentarily followed it, Amleth hurled Lother's sword into his chest. The Duke of Slesvig fell through the doorway into the kitchen.

For a second the only sound heard in the great hall was the crackling of the logs on the fires. Then Amleth fell to his knees.

"My mother?" he gasped.

Horace felt for a pulse.

"Dead," he said.

Amleth looked down for a moment, then around the room at the stunned expressions on the faces of the mercenaries.

"Gentlemen," he said. "I apologize for my bad manners. The entertainment has ended for the evening."

Then he pitched forward onto the floor.

Horace leapt over the table and ran to him. An old priest came into the center of the room and knelt by Lother.

"He's dead," said Horace, looking up at the mercenaries with tears streaking his face. "My friend is dead."

The priest crossed himself.

"This one as well," he said. "God have mercy on their souls."

The captains looked around at each other.

"What are we supposed to do?" said one. "Who is going to pay us?"

"I don't know, and I don't care," said Horace. "There is food, there is drink. Let some soldiers from the barracks carry them to the cathedral. I will maintain the vigil myself. You captains decide what you want to do in the morning."

Eight of the barracks guards came in as Horace covered the faces of Amleth and Lother with their cloaks. They placed the bodies across spears carried lengthwise, and slowly trudged out of the great hall, the priest preceding them, intoning prayers in a quavering voice. Horace followed them.

The captains sat there looking at each other. Then one of them turned to a terrified thrall.

"Well?" shouted the captain. "What are waiting for? Get us more to drink!"

Father Gerald stopped, leaning wearily on his staff. Around him, the fools, troubadours, and children sat in silence.

"I have often wondered if Gerutha knew that there was poison in the goblet that Fengi offered to Amleth," he said. "I like to think so. I like to think that at the end, she sacrificed her life to save her son."

"But he died anyway!" shouted Thomas. We all turned to look at the boy who was on his feet, outraged. "What kind of story is that?"

"What do you mean, Thomas?" asked the priest gently.

"That's not a proper story," shouted the boy, near tears. "They're all dead. What good is a story where everyone dies?"

"Death lies at the end of all of our lives," said Father Gerald.

"I know that," said Thomas impatiently. "But this is supposed to be a story."

"Very true," said Father Gerald, smiling. "But I never said it was over."

The honor guard carried the bodies to a room inside the cathedral where they could be prepared for burial. They lowered them gently onto several tables, then looked up at Horace.

"You are men of honor," he said quietly. "But there is no need for you to be here. Your late commander would wish you to be at your posts. I will remain here with this good priest and pray for them."

"Then God be with you, sir," said one of the guards, and they filed somberly out of the room. The priest blessed them as they left, then watched for a moment. Then he closed the door and turned to Horace.

"Quickly," said Father Gerald, handing him a stoppered flask and pulling another one from his pouch.

Horace pulled the cloak back from Amleth's face and shook him roughly, then hauled him to a sitting position and slapped him several times. Father Gerald did the same with Lother. Suddenly the two Danes started coughing heavily.

"Drink up, lad," urged Father Gerald, shoving the flask in Lother's mouth.

"Come on, old man," said Horace, grinning as Amleth's eyes fluttered open.

Amleth clutched the flask weakly and forced some of the liquid down.

"Dear God, that was awful," he muttered.

"The effects of the drug should wear off in a while," said Father Gerald. "Well played, boys. Both of you."

Lother looked blearily around the room.

"My head hurts," he said, then he caught sight of Fengi's and Gerutha's bodies, lying under blankets.

"Are they . . . ?" he began.

"Yes," said Father Gerald. "Unfortunately the poison she took was real. I'm sorry, Amleth. I didn't see that coming."

Amleth tried to get to his feet, and nearly fell.

"My legs are still wobbly," he said.

"You walk all right for a dead man," observed Horace. "All right, so we need to weight down your coffins and seal them before—"

The door crashed open. Reynaldo stood there, a crossbow in one hand and a sword in the other. He looked at Amleth, a sick smile on his face.

"I thought as much," he said. "The blood gushing out of the boy. There was too much for that wound. Pig's blood in a pig's bladder under the tunic. You think you could fool me? My ancestors invented that trick."

Father Gerald leaned upon his staff, looking every bit the old man.

"Repent, my son," he quavered. "For your eternal soul is in jeopardy."

"I fear no priest," laughed Reynaldo, pointing the crossbow at Amleth.

"No one does," said Father Gerald. "That's the trouble with the world today."

He struck up at the crossbow with his staff. The bolt flew harmlessly over Amleth's head. The priest hit Reynaldo once in the throat, and the Tuscan fell, grabbing his neck.

"Pity," said Father Gerald, squatting down to watch him die. "I had some questions I wanted to ask you."

He administered extreme unction, then straightened and looked at Amleth.

"I have longed believed him responsible for the death of a man we both loved," he said. "I swear that I do not seek revenge in life, but the opportunities do keep presenting themselves."

"Well, that's one coffin weight taken care of," said Horace, dragging Reynaldo's body away.

Father Gerald turned back to Amleth and Lother, who looked at him dumbfounded. He reached down and pulled two bags from under the table.

"Here's your jester gear," he said. "Get into your motley. Full makeup, but cloaks and hoods over everything."

The two changed, then applied the whiteface and stared at each other.

"I wouldn't recognize you in daylight this way," said Lother.

"You wouldn't recognize yourself," replied Amleth.

"All right," said Father Gerald. "Get going. You know how to avoid the patrols. You should make Gustav's Stone before daybreak." He handed each of them a small purse with coins. "Then Lother to the Guildhall, and Amleth to England. You have the passwords. Every Guild member on the way will help you."

"And what happens to you?" asked Amleth.

"I leave for Roskilde," said Father Gerald. "I have to convince Valdemar to send an army here to reclaim Slesvig."

"He won't be happy to see you," said Amleth.

"No, he won't," grinned the priest. "Now, let me embrace you both. It may be the last time we see each other."

Amleth flew into his arms and hugged him hard. Lother, who had known him for much less time, did so hesitantly.

Horace came in.

"Well, this is it," he said, clasping each by the hand. "I'll hold the fort. Metaphorically, that is. Don't start thanking me, I'll get all weepy, and that isn't me, is it? Now, get out of here."

Amleth and Lother shouldered their packs. Amleth touched his mother's face briefly, then the two fools vanished through the door.

"Need help weighting the other coffin?" asked Father Gerald.

"You don't have time," said Horace. "Go. I'll be fine."

Father Gerald sighed.

"Valdemar was not happy to see me," he said. "When he heard my news, he threw me into a dungeon. I sat there for six months, not knowing what had happened. Then, one day . . ."

The King and the priest looked at each other.

"You look old," said Father Gerald.

"So do you," said Valdemar.

"I am old, I think," said Father Gerald. "What's your excuse?"

"Do you want to hear what I have to tell you, or shall I come back in another six months?" asked Valdemar.

"I am listening," said Father Gerald.

"You were a good fool," said Valdemar. "I should have listened to you. I am sorry."

"I have the power to forgive," said Father Gerald.

"Of course, I cannot admit this to the outside world," continued Valdemar. "The King cannot be wrong."

"Of course not," said Father Gerald.

"Which is why you were imprisoned for your insolence," said Valdemar. "And why you will now be banished forever from Denmark."

"But not put to death," said Father Gerald.

"No," said Valdemar. "Not that."

"Very well," said Father Gerald. "What happened to Slesvig?"

"Slesvig is still mine," said Valdemar. "I have placed a man that I trust there."

"You trusted Fengi, once," the priest reminded him.

"When I was less experienced," said Valdemar. "I think that I have gotten better at this by now."

"We'll see," said Father Gerald.

"I have a son, you know," said Valdemar.

"I know," said the priest.

"We made him co-king," said Valdemar. "He's still young, though. I was thinking that he might benefit from some entertainment. Maybe a jester. I thought that you might be able to recommend one."

Father Gerald smiled.

"I think that I can help you there," he said.

$\mathcal{T}$WENTY-ONE

"And you, the judges, bear a wary eye."
—*HAMLET*, ACT V, SCENE II

Swabia—1204 A.D.

Another Valdemar now sits on the Danish throne," said Father Gerald. "The grandson of the first. He looks like a good one. And he has a fool by his side. Is that ending more satisfactory, Thomas?"

"Yes, Father," replied the boy. "But what became of Amleth and Lother?"

"They both went on to have careers in the Guild," said Father Gerald. "But that is a different story. Many different stories, in fact."

"And the moral of this one?" asked Sister Agatha.

"Moral?" said Father Gerald in puzzlement. "I am no Aesop. Draw what morals you wish. No, that isn't right. One lesson I could teach from this is that both Terence and Amleth had chances to run from Slesvig and live long lives far from responsibility. Both chose to honor their commitments to the Guild instead, and it ended up costing Terence his own life and Amleth the lives of his mother and the woman he loved. But a war was averted and thousands of lives saved because they did not run from their appointed tasks. Now, I have talked too far into the night. Those who have regular morning chores must still perform them, but tomorrow, the rest shall sleep late."

There were cheers at this, and the gathering broke up.

"Every time you tell that story, you kill more people," Sister Agatha teased Father Gerald as she joined him.

"I do not," protested Father Gerald. "That's exactly how it happened."

"You personally killed Sveyn?" she laughed as she escorted him to his room.

Claudia and I walked to our tent in silence. Helga followed us carrying a blessedly sleeping Portia. She placed the baby gently in her cradle, then yawned, waved, and staggered off to the novitiates' quarters. We sat by the cradle watching our daughter as the moonlight shone into the tent.

"Well?" said Claudia.

"Well, what?" I replied.

"You were part of that story, weren't you?"

"Was I? I didn't hear my name anywhere."

"Father Gerald always changes the names when they involve Guild members," she said.

"All right, who do you think I was?"

"You were Amleth," she said triumphantly. "That's why you were so tense about hearing it again."

I sighed.

"Truly, wife, you usually do better than that," I said. "How old a man do you think I am?"

She looked at me carefully, then shook her head.

"You're right, that was stupid of me," she said. "Amleth, if he lives, would be on the verge of fifty. You're younger than that."

"My next birthday will be my forty-second," I said. "But you're right about one thing. I was part of that story. I was the one called Lother."

"It must have been terrible, living through all of that," she said.

"It was."

"But to affect you so powerfully even now . . ."

"It was much worse than what you heard," I said.

"But didn't Father Gerald . . ."

"He told a story," I said harshly. "An old man with fading memories told it to us from his viewpoint and gave it the fool's version of a happy ending. You only think you know this story."

She took my hand in hers.

"Tell me," she said.

The two earliest memories I have are of Amleth juggling silks in front of me and of my father beating me for the first time. The two came so close together that they are forever linked in my mind, the defiance of nature and the shock of reality. Magic and pain. Illusion and disillusionment.

I was four years old. I did not know why he started beating me, or why it happened so frequently. I assumed that I had done something meriting punishment, but I could not figure out what it was, and my father refused to enlighten me. Sometimes, all it took was my appearance in his presence to set him off.

My only comforts were my sister and Amleth. She would hold me and press cool wet cloths to the bruises, and he would make me laugh, which would ease the pain. The healing power of laughter, that was another early discovery.

I have no memory of Ørvendil, of course. Fengi and Gerutha were husband and wife since I first became aware of such matters, so it was a surprise when Amleth first told me that he had had another father. Having had only one parent, and a cruel one at that, I said that it was unfair that he had so many parents and I so few. He actually laughed at that, which seemed to make him feel better, confirming what I was learning about humor.

Of the fool, Yorick, I only have the vaguest of images. A tall man in whiteface smiling at me. I think that I remember him carrying me on his shoulders, but whether that is an actual recollection, or merely something that was told to me later so that it took root in my imagination, I cannot tell. For all I know, it may even have been something Amleth told me that happened to him.

I don't remember my mother.

Once when I was older, Amleth at my request tried to draw me a picture of her, but after several attempts were crumpled and thrown into the fire, he gave up and dragged me to a nearby stand of trees whose leaves were turning. He picked up one reddish one that had fallen and handed it to me. Her hair was that color, he said. Only shiny.

I cannot see the change of the trees in autumn without thinking of her.

My father never spoke of her, and Alfhild tended to look distant and cry when I brought her up. Amleth was the one who ended up telling me stories about her, often while teaching me the rudiments of juggling and tumbling that he had absorbed from Yorick. I would become so enraptured in the sound of his voice as he repeated these tales that the juggling became automatic to me. I could negotiate the most treacherous landscape with the clubs keeping pace over me as if they were a band of trained birds.

My father, when he was not punishing me, did pay attention to my spiritual upbringing and my education. I was at the school at the Slesvig cathedral at an early age, and when I wasn't fooling around and making the other boys laugh, or being punished by the priests for doing it, I found that I had a knack for languages and literature. My father encouraged this. He taught me those tongues that he knew, and recruited resident foreigners to teach me theirs. Reynaldo taught me Tuscan dialect, which I liked, and kept calling me the little spy, which I didn't like. I still remember the first time I said something funny to him in his own language. He looked at me in astonishment, then roared with laughter, clapping me on the back. When he reported this triumph back to my father, I was taken into our rooms and whipped, despite Alfhild flinging herself on father's arm to try and stop him.

When I stumbled out later, Amleth was sitting in his little fort, whittling a stake. He beckoned me over to him, his face solemn.

"You may have noticed that Gorm does not possess a sense of humor," he said.

"So what?" I said, wiping my nose on my sleeve, sitting painfully by him.

"Yorick once told me that people without humor are the mortal enemies of people with it," he said. "That's why Gorm beats you."

"I don't understand why that's so," I said.

"Neither do I," he said. "But I have seen it, so it must be true."

"How did I get a sense of humor if he has none?" I asked.

"From your mother," he said, smiling. "She had the most marvelous laugh. Yorick and I loved to hear it."

"Was she funny?"

"Oh, yes. I remember a time . . ." he began, and was off into a new reminiscence about her, one that made me laugh and tolerate the welts on my back a little better.

It never occurred to me that Amleth's behavior was anything unusual, but then he was behaving like that ever since I knew him, and my knowledge of how normal children played in the town was limited, thanks to my restrictive father. Amleth was my playmate, teacher, inspiration, and idol. He was my brother, and he was going to marry my sister when she was old enough and adopt me and take us all to a better place.

That was my plan.

When I turned eight, I was given more freedom, and began to explore the town, sometimes with Amleth, sometimes on my own. Whenever I returned, my father would sit down with me and ask me in great detail about who I saw and what they did or said. I was so happy that he took an interest in anything I was doing that I would rattle on, occasionally inventing incidents to make up for a slow day. The inventions, when discovered, would bring on more chastisement, and I learned to confine my observations to the real.

He demanded more and more as these conversations continued, wanting specifics on certain people that he found of interest. I gradually realized that he was training me to become a spy. I remember thinking, oh, well, most boys follow in their father's footsteps, and I tried to become better at it. I learned how to hide using any cover available, and how to climb buildings and eavesdrop without actually dropping from the eaves.

When I told Amleth about this new occupation of mine, he became concerned.

"It's not the spying, mind you," he said as we juggled near the ruins of the Viking tower. "It's who you're doing it for, and why. I know that he's your father, but . . ."

He stopped.

"But what?" I asked.

"You won't like what I am going to say," he said.

"Say it anyway," I said.

"He is not a good man," he said.

"I know," I said. "But he is my father, and I have no other choice."

"You will," he said. "I will make sure of it. Will you promise me something?"

"Yes."

"Never tell him anything that could end up hurting anyone."

"But if he catches me, I will be the one who gets hurt."

He squatted in front of me and put his hands on my shoulders.

"Then don't let him catch you," he whispered.

I still remember our last day together before he left for Paris, both for how forlorn I felt and because we juggled nine clubs together for the first time. I took his request to amuse my sister seriously, and since my father forbade her the world, I devoted myself to bringing the world to her. Strange, looking back, but I essentially did for her what I had done for my father: I sat and described in great detail everyone and everything I saw, and she would practically inhale the words from my mouth, so starved was she for anything that wasn't a stockade wall.

She would devise games in which I would follow a person of her choosing for a week, giving her a slice of an individual life over time rather than the confusing profusion of many lives swimming by a moment. I would shadow that person for as long as I could stay unobserved, which was a great amusement to me. At night, when I would finish my daily account as we lay in bed, clinging to each other, she would sigh at the simple pleasures of living in the world, then kiss my cheek.

At some point, she crossed over into womanhood, and it was then that my father shut her in the upper room by herself at night while he and I slept downstairs. Needless to say, I did not consider this a fair trade.

When Amleth came back from Paris to visit the first time, I could tell that something had changed in him. He was to the rest of Slesvig still a brooder with a tinge of madness, but when I finally got him alone, he seemed both more guarded and more purposeful than I had known him to be.

"Do you like the cathedral school?" I asked as we walked to our old juggling spot.

"More or less," he said. "I like the city itself very much."

"Do you think I will manage well enough there?" I asked as we began our warm-ups and stretches.

"I am sure you will do fine," he said. "When do you think Gorm will allow you to go?"

"I don't know," I said. "He's disappointed that his old school has declined so much. He went to Ste. Geneviève, and thought the cathedral students were licentious drunkards."

"He was right, for the most part," laughed Amleth. "I now room with two of them. Of course, Rolf and Gudmund were like that in Slesvig, too."

He had six clubs going effortlessly over his head, his hands a blur.

"If I didn't know any better, I'd say that you've been studying juggling with someone," I said. "You never did six that well here."

He looked at me in surprise, then grinned.

"Don't tell anyone," he said. "I have found a juggling master who gives lessons. It is my version of vice."

"Fine, so long as you teach me what you've learned," I said.

"All right, try doing this," he said, and the lesson began.

When we had finished, he looked at me for a moment.

"How are you with a sword?" he asked.

"My father has taught me how to use one," I replied. "And I practice with the guards some of the time."

"Not good enough," he said, pulling a pair of wooden practice swords from his bag. "It's about time you learned how to fight properly."

And every day he would teach me what his father had taught him. Of course, he had begun at an earlier age, and with daily instruction from the source, but he passed on all that he could when he was home, and I added swordplay to my routines when I would sneak out to practice.

When he returned to Paris, my sister, who had brightened considerably for the course of his visit, became more and more moody, despite my best efforts to cheer her up. I begged my father to be gentler with his methods, but that only produced the opposite effect. Oh, and I earned another beating for my pains.

I tried to dissuade Alfhild from entering the convent that last year, but she had convinced herself of Amleth's betrayal. It was wholly out of character with the Amleth I knew. I suspected that it had something to do with his juggling lessons, but he had sworn me to secrecy about them, and to my everlasting regret, I honored that oath rather than tell my sister. When father drove off with her inside a closed carriage, I felt that the last vestige of my childhood was gone. I had turned thirteen two days before she left. She was the only one who remembered my birthday, and gave me an embroidered kerchief.

That last summer Amleth came back with his friend Horace, who lightened the mood at the evening table and flirted shamelessly with Gerutha. I was old enough to notice how starved she was for this kind of attention. Fengi was so busy with his plans that he barely noticed her, and despite her grand airs, she was so familiar to the stockade guards that her parading by no longer merited a glance, even with my sister no longer there to distract them.

Amleth on his arrival heard of Alfhild's predicament, and dashed off. Upon his return, he retreated to his stockade and would speak only to Horace. He would let me sit with him, but I could never get more than the occasional monosyllable out of him. I had placed so much hope in his return that this quite devastated me.

One morning I dragged myself out of bed and walked down to the promontory to do my daily exercises. To my surprise, I found Horace there, sitting on a rock, watching the fishing boats in the distance.

"Good morning, young warrior," he said. "I hope that I am not disturbing you."

"I was going to . . ." I began, then stopped, suddenly shy.

"Going to juggle," he said. "I know. Amleth has told me about you for years. He says you are a better juggler than he was at your age, which would be astonishing if true."

"Did he really say that?" I said, pleased beyond all imagining.

"I always speak the truth," he said with a solemn expression that made me laugh for some reason. "Show me what you can do."

I started with the basics, then added a fourth club, then a fifth. Then Horace reached into a bag and pulled out some clubs of his own.

"You juggle?" I exclaimed.

"I dabble," he said, immediately giving that statement the lie with his obvious skill. "Amleth says the two of you could get up to nine clubs passing between you. Let's see."

We practiced together for a while, and he nodded, satisfied.

"Very impressive," said Horace. "I am told, Lother, that you will be joining us in Paris this term."

"Yes, sir," I replied. "I was hoping to live with Amleth there."

"You speak langue d'oïl well enough?" he asked.

"Fluently," I said. "Plus Latin, Greek, Tuscan, German, Slavic—"

"And what will you do with your education when you are done?" he interrupted me. "Be a spy for Gorm? A soldier in Fengi's revolt?"

"His what?" I exclaimed.

"Didn't you know?" he asked. "Fengi and Gorm have raised an army to seize the crown of Denmark. I would have thought an observant lad like yourself would have known about that by now."

"What army?" I said. "There are guards at the earthenworks and here, but they aren't enough for an army."

"Stow your gear and come with me," he said.

We walked south, a direction I rarely traveled, preferring the busier human entertainment in the town. Horace was no longer the convivial dilettante of the dinner table, but an alert prowler on the hunt, his hand never straying far from his sword hilt. When we reached a stand of trees near a road I had never been down, he turned to me.

"From now on, not a sound," he whispered. "Not a gasp, not a cough, not a broken twig nor a rustling of leaves. If you see me stop, you stop. If you see me drop, you drop. And if you see me run, then you better damn well keep up with me if you want to live to see the sun set tonight."

We crept through the woods for another mile until they began to thin. Horace suddenly hit the ground, and I immediately dropped beside him. A second later a patrol passed by the edge of the tree line, speaking Slavic. When they had passed out of sight, Horace tapped me on the shoulder and pointed to an oak that overlooked the area in front of us. Without a word, I climbed it just as I had climbed so many rooftops at the behest of my father. I soon was forty feet up, looking through a space in the leaves.

There was an army there, drilling in the field before me. Beyond them was an encampment, with emblems from different lands. There were hundreds of soldiers there, and I had never seen any of them before.

I climbed down, and nodded to Horace. Then the two of us made our way back to the road.

"I hereby proclaim that the ban on noise is lifted," said Horace, back in his jovial persona. "You did well back there. What do you make of it?"

"It looks like treason on a grand scale," I said. "And Fengi is behind it."

"So, what do you intend to do?" he asked.

"Me?" I said. "What can I do?"

"What would you be willing to do?" he asked.

"Who are you?" I asked.

"The best question yet," he said. "But answer mine first. What would

[304]

you be willing to do to stop a war? Would you risk your life?"

"Yes," I said without hesitation.

"Would you kill someone?"

I didn't answer.

"Good," he said. "If you had answered in the affirmative right away, you would have failed the test. No one should take killing lightly."

"How many tests have there been this morning?" I asked.

"Many, and you have passed all of them," he said. "Would you be willing to give up the life that you lead if it meant saving others?"

"This life?" I said. "There is nothing for me here except for my sister."

"What if we could get her to safety?"

"Who is 'we'?" I asked. "You still haven't told me who you are."

"You might call me a recruiter," he said. "An advance scout seeking a very peculiar combination of talents."

"A spy," I said.

"Sometimes," he said.

"A killer?"

"When necessary."

"For which king? Or do you work for the Church?"

"No king, and Heaven forbid," he said, crossing himself impishly.

"Then for whom?"

He shook his head.

"You haven't passed that test yet," he said.

"What must I do?" I asked.

"Betray your lord," he said. "And your father."

We walked on for a while in silence while I considered everything that I had seen and heard that day.

"My father is a traitor to Denmark," I said.

"Traitor is a strong word," he said. "He supports a rival claimant to the throne. If that makes him a traitor, then Valdemar was a traitor before him."

"If Fengi succeeds, then many will die," I said.

"Yes, both in the heat of battle and the cold darkness of dungeons," he said. "And if Fengi fails, Valdemar will descend upon Slesvig and lay waste to this treacherous countryside. The best solution is to stop him before he makes the attempt."

"And I can stop him?"

"You can try. Along with the rest of us."

"And then we get my sister out."

He smiled. "That is part of the plan."

I did not learn the details of whatever plan he and Amleth had concocted. It didn't matter, as things changed when Fengi and my father used Alfhild as bait for their trap. It was Horace who informed me of what had happened when he returned, and a cold rage possessed me and sent me charging at my father before anyone could stop me.

It was then that I realized that I could beat him. I was finally big enough to take him on. I was tall, even at thirteen, and my frame was beginning to fill out. The daily regimen that Amleth had imparted to me, which was a fool's routine unbeknownst to me, had given me a strength and speed that I had finally mastered.

And so I was sent to Paris, fuming all the way there. Fortunately, my journey was with Horace, who was riding Amleth's old horse. He spent the entire time chattering to distract me. I gradually realized that every one of his stories contained a subtle lesson, one that I was eager to learn. He also taught me a number of bawdy drinking songs, which would endear him to any thirteen year old.

I also noticed that every large town that we passed through had a jester in it, and every one of them seemed to know Horace. He had a long, whispered conversation with one in Bremen whose expression became serious underneath his whiteface.

When we came to the outskirts of Paris, we paused to look at the city.

"That's the biggest place yet," I said excitedly. "I cannot wait until . . ." Then I stopped. "I'm not going to the cathedral school."

He looked at me, expressionless.

"Am I?"

He shrugged and we rode on.

"There's something I want you to do, now," he said as we came to his quarters.

"What?"

"This is a personal favor," he said. "Since you are a stranger here, I propose using you for a little scheme of my own."

"What kind of a scheme?" I asked.

"Well, this will seem petty," he said, laughing ruefully. "There is a poor excuse for a fool who juggles in the market at les Halles. He is a miserable juggler, and when I took the time and trouble to point that out to him, he became quite rude."

"Imagine that," I said.

"I thought it would be amusing if he were to be humiliated a little more," continued Horace. "I want you to go heckle him for me."

"But I have no quarrel with this stranger."

"Whose side are you on?" he asked indignantly. "Here I am, prepared to risk life and limb to save your sister, and you won't do me this little favor?"

"All right, I surrender," I said hastily. "One question."

"Yes?"

"Where is les Halles?"

When I got there, the market was bustling. I think there were more people in it on that morning than in all of Slesvig. I wandered around, keeping an eye out for pickpockets. Then I saw Horace's target.

He was clearly drunk, even though it was only midmorning, and he lurched about, bellowing some old song while heaving three clubs into the air in an ungainly manner. He watched each one with trepidation as it spun over him, and snatched it almost desperately from the air. The sparse audience watching him was more interested in when he was going to miss one, and when he finally did, there were cheers. He gave an ironic bow, and went to pick it up. I took a deep breath.

"What's wrong, old man?" I called. "Are they too heavy for you?"

There were raucous laughs from some young clerks standing nearby, and the fool turned toward me with an appraising air.

"Well, my fine young cock," he said. "I suppose you think this is easy."

"I do, as it happens," I replied.

"As it happens," he echoed me, looking up at the heavens in supplication. "Here I am, eking out my meager living by bringing a moment of joy to these good, hardworking people, and I am harassed by a pipsqueak who thinks he knows something about juggling. Well, young cock, let's see how you do with those two scrawny wings of yours."

He tossed me the clubs. I caught them and weighed them in my hands for a moment.

"Two wings for three clubs," I said. "Too easy."

I held all three clubs in my right hand, put my left behind my back, and began a one-handed routine. There were respectful cheers from the crowd, and the fool raised an eyebrow in mock irritation.

"He has bested you, La Vache!" cried a merchant from one of the stalls.

"Not in the least," declared the fool. "He has skill, no question. But I am still La Vache, the greatest fool in Paris."

"Not from what I've seen," I said, tossing him back his clubs.

"Brave words, little boy," said the fool. "Do they bespeak a brave heart, or are you just a large bladder full of wind?"

"Try me," I said as boldly as one whose voice had broken only a few months before could.

"Very well," said the fool. He picked up a sack from the ground and raised his voice. "Ladies and gentlemen! I shall now perform the trick that brought me fame and fortune. The one that I performed before crowned heads and mitered, and at the very Hippodrome of Constantinople in front of one hundred thousand astonished spectators."

He reached into the sack and pulled out two short logs. Each was about a foot in length, and as wide around as a blacksmith's forearm.

"Log juggling?" I said. "Is that the trick?"

He smiled at me. It was an evil smile, and I felt a pang of fear in my breast.

"In this trick, the log will not move," he said. "I need a volunteer to hold it for me. Will you be so kind, my young master?"

I nodded. He walked up to me, handed me the log, and positioned my hands so that it was directly in front of my chest.

"Hold it tight, strong, and steady," he said.

"Why?" I asked as he walked back to his sack. "Is this trick dangerous?"

"Not at all," he said. "At least for me. For you, quite a lot."

Then he reached into his sack and pulled out an ax.

"You must be wondering if this is a sharp instrument or not," he said, holding it before the crowd and turning it so that it gleamed. "Behold!"

With a swift, strong motion, he split the second log neatly in two.

"Looks sharp enough to me," he said as the crowd chattered and grew. "Now, what I propose to do is to throw this ax from where I stand into the center of the log that my new assistant is now holding thirty paces away. If I err by the slightest amount, or if he moves the least distance, then he will suffer the same grisly fate as my last assistant, and I will once again be carted off to prison to repent of my foolish ways. Are you ready to face your destiny, young one?"

"How much did you have to drink this morning?" I asked, trying not to shake.

"Almost enough," he said. He lifted the ax over his head with his right hand, then licked his left thumb and held it in front of him, squinting at me in concentration. Then, to my vast relief, he lowered the ax.

"No," he said. "Not like this." He paused as the crowd groaned in disappointment, then leered maliciously at me. "Too easy."

He took a large kerchief from his belt with a flourish and tied it around his face, then again held the ax aloft.

"Boy?" he cried. "Are you still there?"

"Yes," I replied, my voice definitely breaking at this point.

"Do you still hold the log in the same position? Straight and strong?"
"I do."

"Then pray!" he shouted, and there was a blur of steel and a thud as the ax buried itself in the exact center of the log, the blade stopping just short of coming out the other side. I held on for a moment as women screamed on all sides, then the two halves gave way in my hands and the ax clattered to the ground. The crowd roared and coins flew through the air toward the old fool, who caught most of them, his hands no longer the clumsy helpers from the earlier part of his act.

I picked up the ax and the pieces of the log and walked up to him. "Yours, I believe," I said.

"Well?" said Horace from behind me. "Does he pass?"

La Vache flipped me a coin and looked me over.

"I have a riddle for you, boy," he said. "What do you call someone who will willingly let an insane old drunk throw an ax at him?"

I looked at him and realized that he was completely sober, although I had my doubts as to his sanity.

"A fool," I replied.

"He passes," said La Vache. "Come with us, Lother. I want you to meet some friends of ours."

La Vache led us to a shed, threw open the door, and motioned us inside. When I crossed the threshold, I saw a gathering of fools, male and female, doing a stretching routine that was very familiar. One of them looked at me and whistled.

"He's so pale he won't need whiteface," he said.

"This is Lother, the new novitiate," announced La Vache. He turned to me. "You have skills, boy. Can you juggle three clubs in the other hand?"

"Yes, sir," I said, provoking some hoots from the rest of the fools.

"Don't call me 'sir,'" growled La Vache. "Three in one hand is a good trick for thirteen. Can you do four?"

"Not yet," I said.

He took four clubs, put a hand behind his back, started juggling them, then switched hands and kept them going.

My jaw dropped.

"You must be Amleth's juggling master," I said.

"Among others, yes," he replied. "Go do your stretches."

"Master La Vache?" I said.

"What?"

"May I see your kerchief?"

He tossed it to me. I examined it thoroughly and found no eyeholes.

"Satisfied?" he asked, holding out his hand.

"No," I said. "Let me see the one you actually used."

He beamed. "Now, that would be the one with the holes in it, wouldn't it? I wondered if you spotted the switch."

"It didn't make it much less terrifying," I said.

I spent the rest of the summer in intensive training. When the school term arrived, I did not register, although Horace continued with his classes.

"I already know how to be a fool," he said. "Now I strive to become an educated one."

"You know, if there is no revolt by Fengi soon, then I am going to be in serious trouble for not going to school," I said.

He handed me a stack of books and scrolls.

"My work from my first year," he said. "You can read it in your spare time. The most important part of education is being able to repeat precisely what everyone else has already said."

One day in early October, I came to the shed to find Horace, La Vache, and some of the older fools deep in conversation. La Vache saw me and motioned me over to the table.

"This concerns you," he said. "There's a new plan. You're a decent swordsman by now, are you not?"

"I have studied it, most recently with Amleth," I replied.

"Good," he said. "There are several goals involved. First and most important, we have to stop the revolt. That means stopping Fengi."

"You mean killing him," I said.

"Valdemar will not listen to us," said La Vache. "There may be no other way. But we have to manage it so that no attention is drawn to the Fools' Guild. That's our other main goal. The lesser goals involve getting Amleth and Alfhild out of Slesvig alive."

"And Lother," added Horace. "And me, I hope."

"I'm going back to Slesvig?" I said, my face falling.

"Not until Christmas," said La Vache. "You will come in with a reputation as a swordsman who has made his mark dueling in Paris."

"How will I do that?" I asked.

"Because your fencing master, Lamord, will inform them," said La Vache.

"But I've never studied under Lamord," I said.

"Lamord will say that you have," he said. He pulled over a bowl of water and a glass and started washing off his whiteface.

"Why will he do that for us?" I asked.

He dried off his face, looked sadly at his reflection, then began shaving off his beard.

"He won't," he said. "No one in Slesvig knows Lamord by sight. He and I are of an age, and I am proficient enough with a sword to pass. I am going there to puff you up, and to contact Amleth. Now, when you get back, you must make your peace with your father and insinuate yourself into Fengi's confidences. Show some ambition to follow your father's path. Make yourself known as a useful tool, and I am certain that Fengi will find a use for you."

"Am I to be the one to kill Fengi?" I asked.

"Unlikely," he said. "But you may be instrumental in helping Amleth get away."

"He's going to do it?"

"If Amleth does it, then it will be attributed to vengeance for his father," said Horace. "No one will think otherwise."

"But Fengi's guards will cut him down on the spot," I said.

"We're working on that," said La Vache. "Your contact when you go home will be a priest at the cathedral named Gerald. You're a good boy, Lother, so go to church and confess your sins as often as you can."

"I don't have that many to confess," I said.

"You will," said Horace.

La Vache opened a chest and removed a set of Norman armor. Two of the others helped him on with it.

"Too much weight for an old man," he said. "Where are the birds?"

"Here," said Horace, handing him a cage with some carrier pigeons in it. "Try not to eat them."

La Vache thumbed his nose at us and left.

At the dawning of the first of November, I was shaken awake by Horace. My first impulse was irritation, but something in his expression stifled my protest before it could be uttered.

"Change in plans," he said. "I am afraid that I have some bad news."

"What is it?" I said.

"Your father is dead. I am sorry, Lother."

Almost without thinking, I started rubbing my jaw, the site of many a parental bruising.

"How did he die?" I asked.

Horace swallowed. "Amleth killed him."

Whatever sleep was left in me fled on the instant.

"Tell me that this wasn't part of the plan," I said. "The great plan to save Denmark."

"It wasn't," he started, then he sighed and began pacing the room. "It was always a possibility, depending on how much of the command we needed to disrupt. Fengi might not have been enough. But it wasn't supposed to happen like this."

"When did this happen?" I asked.

"Four days ago," he said. "We just got word by carrier pigeon from Father Gerald."

"Where is La Vache?"

"On his way home," he said. "He won't know anything about it yet. And I have to leave Paris."

"Why?"

"Amleth has been banished officially, but we think that is just a cover. His life may be at stake now."

"His life," I said.

"Are you still with us, Lother?" asked Horace, his face a mask. I suddenly feared him.

"Yes," I said. "They'll be sending for me."

"Then act as though you are hearing about it for the first time," he said. "See Father Gerald as soon as you can. If all goes well, you will see me in Slesvig before the year ends."

He left. I was alone with my thoughts.

I had been brought up by my father to respect the blood that bound us. Of course, the man who brought me up spent much of my childhood beating me. And my sister. And he did not shrink from betraying Ørvendil, who he was tied to both by blood and by honor.

Honor and blood demanded that I avenge him. But everything about my life now screamed against it. It wasn't the love I owed Amleth, the fables I heard from Horace, or the immersion in the lore of the Fools' Guild that dissuaded me.

It was the realization that I hated my father and was relieved that he was dead. And if his death suited Guild policy or Amleth's own vengeance, so much the better. I felt as if I had been living with an iron clamp around my lungs, and for the first time I could breathe freely, knowing that my father would never again be able to harm Alfhild or me.

I was glad that someone else killed him before I did.

I took the official news of his death with quiet dignity, which impressed the messenger no end. I packed my belongings, leaving Horace's books and notes where he could find them, saddled my horse, and galloped back to Slesvig. I made the obligatory visit to my father's grave, noting that what flowers there were lay on my mother's side, then announced to the escort that I wished to pray at the cathedral. I went inside, knelt before the altar, crossed myself, then glanced quickly around. A priest was watching me solemnly. He walked to the confessional, and I entered the other compartment.

"Forgive me, Father, for I have sinned," I began.

"*Stultorum numerus* . . ." he whispered.

"*Infinitus est,*" I whispered back.

"We'll save your soul later, Lother," he said. "I am Father Gerald. My condolences on the loss of your father. Now listen."

He filled me in on what had taken place since he had sent his message, and gave me mercifully few instructions. Then I rode my horse home.

I went straight up to Alfhild's room without speaking to anyone on the island. I hesitated before knocking on her door. It looked different, somehow. Then I realized that she had had the outside bar removed. Good for her, I thought, and knocked.

"Who is it?" she asked, her voice sounding strained and weary.

"It's Lother," I said.

There was the sound of a bar being removed, then the door opened and she stood before me. She was beyond pale, and her hair was wild and loose about her. There was something lackluster in her eyes, but then she brightened for a moment and embraced me.

"Father is dead," she said. "Amleth killed him."

"I know," I said.

"Can I tell you something?" she asked. "Something you must never tell anyone?"

"Yes."

"I'm glad of it," she whispered.

"So am I."

She sat on a bench and looked out the window.

"Have you ever looked at Amleth's fort from here?" she asked.

"Not in a long time," I said, joining her.

From one flight up, the design of the miniature stockade seemed even more impressive, the fanciful patterns of the stakes curling away from the main circle, the solitary brick anchoring the center.

"Sometimes I pretend that I can fly," she said. "Then I look down

[315]

at the fort and see all of the people from up high and wonder about their tiny lives behind their tiny walls."

Her hands hung limply at her sides, and she sagged a bit against the window frame.

"Are you ill?" I said with concern. "You don't look well. Have you been eating anything?"

"Gerutha brings me food," she said. "Of late, I have no appetite. I so longed for a chance to escape this prison, but now that I am free, I find that I cannot leave."

"He'll come back and save us," I said. "I know it."

She smiled, put her arm around my shoulders, and squeezed.

"It's good to have you back home, little brother," she said.

I paid my respects to Gerutha and Fengi. It was odd speaking to people whom I had known all of my life, yet now saw in a new light. I felt awkward, knowing that I was playing a scene with every new conversation. I was outside of my body, watching the actor Lother listening for his cues, then feeding him his lines. Father had raised me to be a spy. Now, at long last, I was one, and it was in my own home.

The day that Alfhild died was the worst day of my life. I still replay the last time I saw her alive in my mind. I should have gone with her. I should have spotted something in her manner that would have served as an alarm, or just accompanied her as a matter of course, but I didn't. I was still only thirteen, and she was still my big sister, and there was no danger to her in Slesvig now that my father was dead, was there? She presented no threat to Fengi or his plans. If Father Gerald had known at that point that she had sent the messenger to warn Amleth—but he didn't.

I'll be back before noon. Those were the last words Alfhild ever said to me. She was back long after noon, thanks to the kindness of the farmers who delivered her to me. I looked at her, knowing that I had nothing left to lose. I looked at the bruises on her shoulders, the other cuts on her body, and knew that she had died at someone else's hands. She might just as well have taken me with her.

I remembered Fengi's strange behavior at lunch, his denial of having been south that morning, the way he kept wincing. When Gerutha came up and held me, I decided then and there that Alfhild's murderer would die at my hands.

I rode to the pond where she had met her fate. The farmers were right—there was no trace of her clothing. I saw some late blooms by the water side, many of them crushed. That was where she sat. Where she struggled for her life. I looked around the open meadow, then rode toward the nearby forest.

There it was, a small piece of her gown, the broken branches showing me a way back into the darkness. I tied up my horse and began following the trail she had left behind, occasionally finding other scraps. I emerged in a small clearing. A glint of steel caught my eye, and I picked up a small dagger from under some leaves that had fallen. I recognized it. It was my father's. And there was blood on it.

Was it hers? I saw no wound on her body that looked as if it had been from a blade. And where was her clothing? If she had torn it off and run through the woods, then she wouldn't have left pieces of it on her path. But if she took her clothes off after, then they would have been found.

Unless someone else had taken them. Either a scavenging passerby, or someone wanting to make it look like she had finally succumbed to her madness. But I did not think that she was mad. And nothing I had seen dissuaded me from my original suspicion.

When I returned, a thrall informed me that there was no dinner. Gerutha's basket lay by the glimmering coals of the fire, and I kicked it in a fit of frustration. I poked around the kitchen, then grabbed what scraps of food I could find. Then I slept alone in my family's quarters.

. . .

At the funeral mass Father Gerald signaled that he wanted to speak to me. I was ill inclined to hear him, but I dutifully followed him to the confessional.

"Forgive me, Lother, but we have little time left," he said.

"And some of us have none at all," I said.

"I can pray for the dead," he said. "My principal concern is for those still alive. I want to keep them that way."

"Not all of them," I said.

"There's one in particular I need kept alive," he said. "Amleth is back."

"What?" I exclaimed. "He escaped transport to England?"

"Your sister sent a warning to him in Ribe," he said. "He got word to Kanard, the local fool. Kanard arranged with a group of mercenaries to take him off the ship after it left port."

"But if he's in Slesvig, then Fengi might have him killed."

"The blood debt is to you as Gorm's son, not to Fengi," said Father Gerald. "If you assert the right to collect it, then Amleth stays alive at your will. His mother will still try and protect him, and he has one other trick up his sleeve, but in order for him to stay alive, we need you to play a scene of forbearance."

"When?"

"When you go to the cemetery. He's waiting there with Horace."

I wanted to put my fist through the lattice separating us.

"This is my sister's funeral," I said. "How can you ask me to do this?"

"The time may come when I will ask you to do something far worse," he said. "Are you with us or not?"

"God have mercy on my soul," I said.

"I'll take care of that as well," he said wryly.

Playing that scene at my sister's grave site was the hardest thing I have ever done. Looking back, I wonder now if it was yet another test on the part of the Guild. I wouldn't put it past Father Gerald.

In any event, we convinced Fengi, and that was my way in. When I reported back to Father Gerald about Fengi's plans, he was practically gleeful.

"But that's perfect," he said. "He's given us the means of his own death and your escape. All you have to do is cut Amleth with your sword, then let him get it from you and return the favor. He can kill Fengi, and you will both die in front of a room full of drunken witnesses."

"Excuse me," I said. "I thought we were escaping Slesvig, not the burdens of existence. If we are cut with a poisoned blade, then don't we sort of die?"

"You won't be using his poison," said Father Gerald impatiently. "There is a potent brew known to the Guild as the Sleep of Death. Very powerful. One drop will have you splayed out on the floor inside a minute."

"But won't I only look like I'm asleep?"

"Not from a distance, and not if a priest gets to you first and pronounces you dead."

"Know any priests?" I asked him.

Amleth and I worked out the details of our duel by messages passed through Horace and Father Gerald. On the day of the feast, Horace slipped me a stoppered flask no bigger than my pinkie.

"Don't take it until you are down and ready to die," he said. "I recommend sewing it into your collar just below your chin."

"Have you ever used this?" I asked.

"No," he said. "But Gerald tested it on himself after he made it. He woke up eventually."

And so it was that I found myself on the clay floor, pig's blood oozing from under my tunic, sucking an unknown potion from a flask and hoping as I fell into the blackness that I would emerge from the other side.

I woke on a stone slab with Father Gerald hovering over me, shoving something from another flask into my mouth. I coughed, and resolved to give up flasks of any kind. I sat up, saw Amleth looking at me, and then the bodies of Fengi and Gerutha. The next few minutes were like a fever dream—unlike the others, I had no idea that Father Gerald could wield a staff like that. I had never seen a man killed before. It wasn't pretty.

Before I knew it, I found myself standing outside the cathedral in cloak, makeup, and motley, ready to run through the night. Then Amleth plucked at my sleeve.

"I want to go to the cemetery," he said. "I want to say good-bye."

"Me, too," I replied, and we ran silently north, vaulting the fence and locating our families in the faint moonlight.

Alfhild's grave was by that of my parents. I sat at its foot. With no scene to play, no Lother to act, I was suddenly at a loss for words, and could only offer her my silence.

Amleth came back from visiting his father's unmarked grave and sat by me.

"I would have given my life to save her," he said.

"I know," I said. "Yet she is dead, and you live on."

He said nothing.

"There was a moment in our duel when I thought you might really kill me," I said.

"Why would I do that?" he asked.

"Because I let your mother die," I said. "I saw Fengi poison the cup after it was refilled."

"Ah," he said. "I wondered about that. Why did you let her die?"

"Because she killed my sister," I said.

He leaned forward and rested his body on her grave.

"How do you know this?" he asked.

"I saw the bruises on Alfhild's shoulders when they brought her back," I said. "They were made by the hands of whoever drowned her. They were not large hands from the spacing. When Gerutha came back to the stockade, supposedly from the market, I noticed that her sleeves were damp, and her basket was light. I searched the meadow near the pond that day."

"What did you find?" he asked.

"Alfhild's clothing had vanished, but she still had it on when she escaped from the forest—there were scraps of it caught on the brush. I found our father's dagger in the clearing . . ."

"The clearing," he echoed, rolling onto his back and covering his face. "That accursed clearing."

"I came back and went into the kitchen," I continued. "I learned from a thrall that Gerutha had brought nothing back from the market to contribute to that day's meals. Her basket lay empty by the fire. There was a crushed flower stuck to it, one that had come from by the pond where Alfhild had died. And there was a charred scrap from Alfhild's gown in the fireplace.

"I think that Gerutha suspected that Fengi had cast his eye on Alfhild, and could not let her live. She killed my sister, Amleth. I did not take vengeance upon Gerutha, but when I saw the cup rise to her lips, I said nothing. I let her die."

"You had just cause," he said. "More than you know. But I have no quarrel with you for it. I had reason to want my mother dead as well."

"Because she married your father's murderer," I said.

"Because she helped my father's murderer," he said. He sat up and looked at the moon. "It's going to snow tonight."

"You said I had more cause than I know," I said. "Tell me."

"You see things as a child that you don't understand, that have no meaning until you look at them from the vantage that the passage of time can give you," he said. "My mother was a wildly ambitious woman. She wanted to rise, and rise, and rise until she was mistress of all. My father was no match for her ambition. I saw things, heard things, learned more from Yorick and Gerald. When my father refused to kill Valdemar, she knew that he was not the one who would take her where she wanted to go. She needed an ambition worthy of hers. She needed Fengi. And he needed her. It's hard to say who seduced who.

"But Fengi was no equal of my father when it came to swordplay. On the day my father rode to the Sacred Hill for the Slesvig *thing*, my mother gave him a libation of mead that she prepared herself. She drank from it as well, and soon after felt the need to retire to her room to sleep. So early, I thought, but it gave me the chance to slip out to watch, so I paid it no more mind. Then I saw my father fight like a man weighed down by chains. She had drugged him, and that allowed Fengi's poisoned blade to do its work."

"And my cause?" I asked.

"You said she was jealous of Alfhild," he said. "You were right, but it was not just of Alfhild. She despised any woman who she thought might supplant her, who would deny her supremacy within her tiny realm. I think if you live too much of your life inside walls, you go mad. I think she did. I think that I get some of my madness from her. I saw you born, did you know that?"

"I know that you were here . . ."

"You misunderstand," he said impatiently. "I was actually in the room when you came out of that mysterious place between your mother's legs. And before the midwife came, my mother attended your mother. My mother, who knew how she was hated on our island, and how Signe was loved and praised. Every word was wormwood to her. Even their gardens mocked her. She attended your mother at your birth, and gave her something to drink. For the pain, she said. Then your mother died, and when I brought flowers to place by Signe, my mother threw them away and I saw the mask drop for a moment. She hated her from the depths of her soul. And then the midwife was murdered, and it was never discovered by whom. I think that she must have noticed something, and my mother killed her to prevent it from coming out."

"Alfhild was behaving so oddly this last month," I said. "She told me that Gerutha fed her special meals and took her personally in hand. Gerutha must have been giving her something that was slowly sapping her life. But something must have happened to make her want to kill her quickly."

"My mother was quite the connoisseuse of poisons, it seems," he said. "Did she recognize the one that killed her as it passed her tongue? I hope so. You see, Lother, you had ample cause to want her dead."

I struggled to my feet and looked down at him.

"It ends here," I said. "We are the last. The blood feud between us ends now."

"Why should there be one?" he asked.

"You did kill my father," I reminded him.

"Actually, I didn't," he replied.

"Do you deny killing him?" I said in amazement. "All of Slesvig knows that Amleth is Gorm's killer."

"Oh, I killed Gorm," he said easily, getting to his feet. "I admit it, and I am glad of it. But Gorm was not your father."

"What?" I shouted. I felt as if the earth itself were moving under me, preparing to split asunder and pull me down to join Alfhild.

"You have to know this," he said urgently. "We may never see each other again after tonight, and I am the only one who can tell you this. I saw it happen, the love between them grow, the attraction pulling them together in spite of all sense and logic. I saw how they looked at each other, how they talked to each other, how they talked of each other when they were apart."

"Who?" I begged him. "My mother and who?"

"Yorick," he said, taking me gently by the shoulders. "You are his image on earth, Lother. No one knew him better than I. No one saw him without his whiteface on except me. Look at you, you're thirteen and already nearly my height. You'll be tall and slender like he was, not the tree stump that was Gorm. Alfhild was Signe reborn, but you are your father's son."

"But I didn't know him," I whispered. "I thought I still had a parent, and now you've taken him away and given me this phantom."

"And when I killed Gorm, I killed your father's murderer," he said.

"No, no more," I said. "I cannot take it all in. Father Gerald said that Reynaldo . . ."

"Father Gerald thinks Yorick was killed because he discovered Fengi's plans," said Amleth. "But the memory that kept coming back when I was older was the day before Yorick disappeared forever."

"What happened?"

"We were swimming," he said, almost dreamily. "When we came out of the water, Gorm approached us. He was looking at Yorick so oddly. 'I have never seen you without your whiteface on, Fool,' he said. 'I understand now why you wear it. Your face is quite hideous without it.' And that night, Yorick vanished."

"I don't understand," I said.

"You were four," he said. "Your features had settled into your face. And Gorm saw them for the first time on Yorick's face, cleansed of its mask by the waters of the fjord. In that instant, Gorm knew Signe had betrayed him, and Yorick's very existence would mock his every waking moment.

"It took me so long to understand all of this, but I've had plenty of time to sit and think behind my wall of stakes. There was a time when Yorick could have run from Slesvig. I begged him to go, to take me with him, but he said he had to return, even if it meant his life. 'I have my reasons,' he told me. I thought then that it had something to do with his Guild mission, but later on I realized that there was something more powerful binding him here. Something worth dying for."

"What?" I asked.

"You," he said. "He stayed because you were here, and even though he had fallen out of favor and was rarely allowed in your presence, those few times were enough. You were his son, even if he couldn't be your father."

"Did you ever find him?" I asked.

"Yes," he said. "In the last place any of us thought of looking."

"Where?" I asked.

"Here," he said, leading me over to a patch of ground strewn with dead weeds. "I was chatting with the gravedigger once a few years ago while visiting my father's grave. He's a simple man who asks few questions about anything. The subject of Yorick came up, I cannot say why, and he mentioned burying him. I asked him when, and he scratched his head, and said he had been roused from his sleep by none other than the Duke's drost, who ordered him to prepare a grave posthaste. He had Yorick covered in a cart, and did not want to distress young Amleth, meaning me, begging your pardon, good sir, over the news, for we all know how sensitive and prone to fits the boy has been since his poor father's death, alas."

I looked down at the spot, which had no stone or marker of any kind.

"It ends here," I said. "Here and now."

"It ends tonight," he agreed. "But not quite yet."

"What do you mean?" I asked.

"I have told you all of this because I may not live out the night," he said. "There is one more task I need to accomplish. As the heir to Slesvig, it will be my first and last official act."

"What is it?"

"Father Gerald is optimistic if he thinks that Valdemar will come here straightaway," he said. "And even if he does send the army, it will be two weeks before it arrives. A band of mercenaries this large and this organized can do quite a lot of harm in two weeks."

"What do you propose to do?"

"Kill their leaders," he said. "That should send the rest of them packing."

"There are sixty of them," I said.

"I know," he replied. "But this is still my home. I have to try. I have no right to ask you this, but would you like to help?"

I plucked a weed from Yorick's grave and stuck it in my belt.

"All right," I said.

The drawbridge was still down when we arrived at the island. Our cloaks were folded inside our packs, and our caps and bells were on our heads.

"What ho, guard?" cried Amleth in a voice not his own. "We are here for the feast. I hope we are not too late."

"Too late for some," replied the guard. "But the rest still make merry. Go on in, I care not."

We entered the great hall to find the feast a near riot. A Wend had challenged a Holsteiner to a wrestling match, and the two of them were rolling around the center of the room, banging against the tables while the rest of the men gobbled down the available food and wagered heavily.

The Wend won, and one of the captains yelled for more wine. Then Amleth leapt into the center of the room.

"Greetings, brave soldiers!" he cried. "I am Aloysius the Fool, and yonder is my young colleague, Leander. We have come to amuse you."

I took a running start and did a handspring between two startled Slavs into the area where Amleth and I had so recently killed each other.

"Tonight, Leander and I shall perform feats of merriment and mayhem for you," continued Amleth. He looked around and grinned. "It will be a night that you shall never forget, no matter how long you live."

And we began to perform, improvising routines on the spot. Amleth was the experienced fool, while I had only my short period of training, so I followed his lead. But then he pulled out his juggling clubs, and all the days by the Viking tower came flooding back. Soon we had six clubs going between us, then seven, eight, nine . . .

"Now, gentlemen," said Amleth as the mercenaries thumped the tables in approval. "Leander and I shall attempt something that not even we have ever done before." He turned and winked at me. "Ten clubs!"

"Are you mad?" I cried.

"Absolutely," he said, holding up five clubs.

I gulped, then added another to my current four. We looked at each other, breathed, then began juggling five each. I counted down, then tossed one across with my right, catching his a moment after. I felt a strange calm settle into my being, and we made it through five rounds before a club was dropped. And he was the one who dropped it.

I think if we had been discovered and killed then and there, I still would have died a happy fool.

"You look parched after watching us with your mouths hanging open," said Amleth as the room applauded. "Allow me to refill your cups."

The thralls had fled long before, so this offer was met with approval. Amleth dashed to the kitchen and returned with two massive pitchers of wine. He jumped up on the table and dashed around the room, filling the cup of every man before him.

"To warm beds and Danish maidens in them!" he shouted, and the mercenaries guffawed and drank.

And in a minute, they were, to a man, slumped over the tables, snoring.

"So, that's what we looked like," said Amleth, looking around the room.

"What did you put in the wine?" I asked.

"The Sleep of Death, of course," he said. "Now, we must hurry. I will kill no more Danes tonight. Take those two over there and drag them into your quarters."

As I did so, Amleth threw on his cloak and scurried out the rear of the great hall. By the time I had returned, so had he, the cloak bulging and rattling. He upended it, and onto the main table fell the brick his father had given him, along with some five dozen stakes plucked from his stockade.

With each mercenary he removed the man's cloak, then tied it around him so that the knot hung just off the clay floor. Then he took a stake, put it through the knot, and pounded it into the floor with the brick, pinioning the soldier where he slept.

When he was done, he tossed me my pack.

"Get your cloak on," he ordered me. Then he grabbed one of the barrels of pitch kept in the corner for waterproofing the stockade walls and tilted it on its side. He took an ax from one of the soldiers and hacked several holes in the barrel. Then he gave it a shove, and it rolled the length of the hall, spilling its contents everywhere. He repeated the process on the other side with a second barrel, then surveyed the scene before him.

"They'll be waking soon," I said, horror creeping into me.

"They won't be waking at all," he replied. He took three torches from sconces in the wall, then turned toward me.

"Ever juggled torches?" he said, sending them into the air over his head. "Trickier than clubs, because the balance is uneven and there's only one safe end to ... oops! Clumsy of me."

One of the torches went sailing across the room and landed in a pool of pitch on the left. The flames shot up immediately.

"Well, since I've only got two left," he said, and he put his left hand behind his back while keeping them going with his right. "Damn, there goes another."

The right side of the room was burning now. He caught the last torch, then looked about the room critically.

"You know, I never did like these tapestries," he said, and he touched the torch to the cloths hanging on both sides. The flames encircled the room like a noose.

Smoke was everywhere, and through it, I saw soldiers gasping in their sleep. Some were even moving feebly, trying to shake off the effects of the drug, but the stakes held them fast.

"How long have you been planning this?" I asked.

"Since I was nine," said Amleth.

I turned and started to leave the room, but he clamped his hand down on my arm.

"Wait," he said. "The secret to comedy is timing."

We stood there, the sweat pouring through our whiteface as the heat intensified. Then he pulled me out and shouted, "Fire!"

I took up the cry, and we fled through the stockade, screaming for the guards to come down, our cloaks concealing our motley and white-face.

"We'll alert the town!" shouted Amleth as we raced across the draw-bridge, but once we passed the first building we cut left and ran from Slesvig. Behind us, there was a thundering crash as the roof of the great hall collapsed and the flames soared higher than the stockade walls. We stopped to look at it for a moment.

"Listen," said Amleth. "I drugged them. I killed them. Take no part of this burden upon yourself."

"I helped you," I said. "The sin lies with me as well."

"Then I owe you my thanks," he said.

"I have a price," I said, turning to him.

"Name it," he said.

"Tell me about my father," I said.

"We have to run," he protested.

"Then tell me while we run," I insisted. "Everything that you can remember about him until we reach Gustav's Stone."

"Agreed," he said. "Let's go. We can still make it there before dawn."

And we ran into the night, never setting foot in Slesvig again.

Claudia leaned into me, holding me tight.

"Why did you never tell me this?" she asked.

"I've never told anyone," I said. "What could I tell you, Duchess? That you married a bastard born of an adulterous affair? That the man you married once helped burn sixty men to death in their sleep?"

"Do you really think that matters to me?" she asked. "I gave up nobility and prosperity to follow you into poverty and danger. Why do you think I did that? Because I was worried about rank or social niceties? I married you because I loved you. I followed you because I believed in you, and in the Guild. And I am here with you now, and will still be here in the morning, and the next day, and every day after that."

We held on to each other for a while.

"Whatever happened to Amleth?" she asked.

"He went to England," I said. "Worked his way into the English court and attached himself to a lady there. He became known as a melancholy fool, a most paradoxical and ironic creature. Had his share of adventures, from what I heard, then ended up fleeing with her into the country where he met a shepherdess and fell in love. He quit the Guild, married her, and now keeps a farm and carters as far away from courts as he could possibly get. I never saw him after we split up."

"And Horace?"

"He's the Chief Fool in Paris, now. La Vache died a few years ago."

"Did Amleth tell you about your father?"

"What he could. I still don't know anything about Yorick before he came to Slesvig. The sparrow-hawk he had meant that he must have won the fools' contest at Fécamp, but I have never met a fool who knew much about him. All I have of my father are stories from Amleth and Father Gerald."

"And this absurd, tall, skinny body," she said. "What strikes me is that both you and he were fools who fell in love with ladies who ended up marrying other men. His lady ended up loving him, but they died unhappily. You, on the other hand, ended up winning your lady. For all the horrors that you have been through, you were still judged worthy of that."

"Judged by whom?"

"By the world, by fate, by God, and by the First Fool, Our Savior," she said. "Let's set about the task of raising our daughter, and we'll call it a happy ending. Shall we?"

I held her to me, and we eventually went to sleep. And when I woke up in the morning, she was still there.

CODA

"... what would you undertake
To show yourself your father's son in deed
More than in words?"

—*HAMLET*, ACT IV, SCENE VII

It ends like this.

Two fools stood at a crossroads in southern Jutland. They had run through the night, the older one gasping out story after story while they dodged patrols and clambered over windbreaks. They passed Magnus's farm not long before dawn. The old farmer, who slept little these days, saw them run by, and thought he recognized someone he had long thought dead. But then they were gone, and he thought he had dreamt it.

The faint glow of the flames behind them had vanished, but the first glimmerings of the sun tried to pierce the thick clouds coming in right as they crossed the tiny bridge over the stream east of Gustav's Stone.

"Sunrise," said the younger fool. "We made it."

"May I stop talking now?" pleaded the older one hoarsely. "I have no voice left. We should eat before we go on."

They sat with their backs to the stone as they ate, looking at the bridge.

"Good old Gustav," said the older one.

"Good old Gustav," echoed the younger one. He hesitated. "Will you ever come back?"

"No," said the other one. "There's nothing left for me there. Best to make a clean break with the past." He looked at the ancient burial mounds to the north. "There's too much past here, anyway."

They finished eating, then stood and stretched.

"I guess this is it," said the younger one reluctantly.

"I guess so," said the older. Then he fumbled inside his pouch. "Look, I want to give you something."

"What?" said the other.

"When I found Yorick's grave, I buried his bundles with him," said the older fool. "But there's one thing of his that I still carry."

He pulled out a small wooden flute and handed it to the younger fool.

"But this was his birthday present to you," protested the younger fool. "I can't take this."

"Please," said the older. "I want you to have it."

"All right," said the younger. "Thanks."

They stood awkwardly for a moment.

"Well, touch stone for luck," said the younger, rapping his knuckles on the standing stone.

"What?"

"I've always heard that if you pass Gustav's Stone on a pilgrimage, you touch it for luck," he explained.

"We're certainly due for some," said the older fool.

He rapped his knuckles on the stone.

"Touch stone for luck," he said. "Touch stone, turn and leave. Touchstone. I like it."

"Like what?" asked the younger.

"I need a new name," said the older.

"Oh," said the younger. He turned to look at the runes. Then something caught his eye. He leaned over and picked up a small stone that sat by the larger.

"Look at this," he said, and the older fool peered over his shoulder.

There were faint words scratched onto the face of the stone.

"Terence was here," read the older fool.

"Wonder who he was," said the younger.

"No idea," said the older. "At least he has a stone."

"I suppose so," said the younger, setting it carefully back where he had found it.

They looked at each other.

"I guess this is it," said the older fool, holding out his hand. "*Stultorum numerus...*"

"*Infinitus est,*" said the younger, clasping it.

It began to snow as they let each other go.

"I told you it was going to snow," said the older fool. "Good thing. It will cover our tracks."

"See?" said the younger. "Our luck's changing already."

They thumbed their noses at each other, then the older fool took the west road across the bog, and the younger fool headed south into the forest. The wind scattered the snow about, covering the bog, the bridge, the burial mounds, the large stone and the small. Around them the forgiving snow fell, until the face of the world itself was white.

HISTORICAL NOTE

"Good my lord, will you see the players well bestowed? Do you hear?
Let them be well used, for they are the abstract and brief chronicles of
the time. After your death you were better have a bad epitaph than their
ill report while you live."

—*HAMLET*, ACT II, SCENE II

The Danish town of Slesvig is now the German town of Schleswig, the border between the two countries having moved north in the nineteenth century. It was of this long-standing dispute that Lord Palmerston famously observed, "Only three people understood the Schleswig-Holstein question. The first was Albert, the Prince consort, and he is dead; the second is a German professor, and he is in an asylum: and the third was myself—and I have forgotten it." The St. Petri Dom, or cathedral, has been somewhat modified from its twelfth-century origins, but with its tower and striking red roof preserved. Another survivor of the time, the church of St. Andreas, still stands south of the Schlei inlet, not far from the Wikinger Museum Haithabu.

There is no record of the palace started by Ørvendil ever being completed, but the foundation of the Gray Monastery is believed to be originally from a palace built in town. There is no trace of the stockade on the island at the mouth of the river, although a very fine fifteenth-century castle, the Schloss Gottorf, now stands on the site. Its status as a museum and landmark prevents any further excavation on the island.

The success of Valdemar the First in unifying the Danish throne in 1157, combined with the rise of Absalon to the Bishropic of Roskilde, and later the See of Lund, marked the beginning of a Golden Age in Danish history, often referred to as the Age of the Valdemars for the three kings of that name. Perhaps their most lasting achievement was the founding of a merchants' haven, or Kjoebenhavn, on the eastern coast of the island of Sjælland. It would eventually become Copenhagen, the present capital.

The story of Amleth was first found in written form in the *Gesta Danorum*, or *History of the Danes*, by Saxo Grammaticus around the beginning of the thirteenth century. Saxo was a clerk to Archbishop Absalon, and probably wrote it at his behest. It remains our principal source for Danish history of this period, which is unfortunate, as it is also widely considered to be unreliable. Saxo uncritically mixed in Norse mythology, folklore, gossip, rumor, and religious moralizing in unequal measure. (English translations are difficult to find, but a nineteenth-century one of the first nine chapters is at http://www.sunsite.berkeley.edu/OMACL/DanishHistory/.)

His account of the fatal dinner of the three kings in Roskilde differs significantly from that of the Fools' Guild. He places his patron Absalon squarely and heroically at the side of Valdemar, and fails to mention anything of the crucial contributions of the jesters Gerald and Larfner. Father Gerald's version, as recorded by Theophilos, makes it clear that Absalon, or Axel as he was known then, was absent from this key event in the life of Valdemar, although his brother Esbern Hvide ("The Swift") is given prominence. Considering the long, mutual antipathy between the Guild and the Church, it is not surprising that each favored itself at the expense of the other. As to which version is more likely to be true— there may not be enough grains of salt in the Lübeck mines with which to take in reading either one. It is worth noting, however, that while Saxo wrote to publicly flatter the Archbishop, the Fools' Guild account was a private history, meant only for Guild archives. That alone might tip the balance toward the Guild's version, but we can never be certain.

Yet while the *Gesta Danorum* makes an inadequate history, it has unquestionably provided us with the source of one of the greatest plays in the history of Western civilization. Or was it just one of the sources?

Scholars generally believe that the history passed to Shakespeare first through a 1570 French version, *Histoires tragiques*, by François de Belleforest, then possibly through an earlier staged version in English known now as the *Ur-Hamlet*, possibly by Thomas Kyd. (A good discussion of this transmutation may be found in *Saxo Grammaticus and the Life of Hamlet* by William F. Hansen, University of Nebraska Press, 1983.)

However, as has been proposed in earlier historical notes for this series of translations, it is possible that Shakespeare received Fools' Guild records that included this story, either pilfered from their repository at an abbey in western Ireland by William Kempe, as believed by this author, or through the poet Edmund Spenser, the theory of the historian and author Peter Tremayne. A close analysis of Shakespeare's play will find numerous instances of plot never mentioned in Saxo's history, but found in that of Theophilos.

I am sorry to report that with this translation I have finished the store of surviving manuscripts at the abbey. I would like to take this opportunity to thank the good souls there for their generosity of spirit, and for their discretion. Also, for bearing with my disastrous efforts in the kitchen—Brother Liam, you remain in my prayers, and I am glad to hear that you are back on your feet.

However, as this translation goes to press, I am the recipient of some exciting news. A recent earthquake in northern Italy has dislodged a pile of rubble that had blocked a previously unknown tunnel entrance at a ruined monastery in the Dolomites. The archaeologists who had been excavating the site were stunned to find a group of sealed casks containing scroll after scroll of records marked with the seal and motto of the Fools' Guild! I have been invited to assist in the examination of these documents, and will report back to you any new discoveries contained therein. Until then, fellow fools.

ACKNOWLEDGMENTS

Thanks go first and foremost to Professor Anthony Perron of Northwestern University, for pointing me in the right direction. The author gratefully acknowledges the scholarship of Birgit and Peter Sawyer, Tobias Faber, William F. Hansen, Hastings Rashdall, F. M. Powicke, A. B. Emden, Palle Lauring, Robert Bartlett, and the many contributors to *Medieval Scandinavia: An Encyclopedia*, Phillip Pulsiano, editor.

Thanks to Jim Huang, Sue Feder, and Jo Ellyn Clarey for guiding me through the convention thickets; to Keith Kahla, my editor, and Mitchell Waters, my agent, without whom this book would not exist, and you would be standing there with empty hands, perhaps being mistaken for a mime.

Above all, to my wife, Judy, and son, Robert, for sharing their time, their space, and their lives.